Half-Moon
and Empty Stars

A Novel

Gerry Spence

A LISA DREW BOOK

SCRIBNER

New York   London   Toronto   Sydney   Singapore

SCRIBNER
1230 Avenue of the Americas
New York, NY 10020

DESIGNED BY ERICH HOBBING

Set in Adobe Caslon

Manufactured in the United States of America

1   3   5   7   9   10   8   6   4   2

Library of Congress Cataloging-in-Publication Data

Spence, Gerry
Half-moon and empty stars: a novel/Gerry Spence
p.   cm.
"A Lisa Drew book."
1. Indians of North America—Fiction. 2. Executions and executioners—Fiction. 3. Brothers—Fiction. 4. Wyoming—Fiction. 5. Murder—Fiction. I. Title
PS3569.P448 H3 2001
813'.54—dc21   00-054738

ISBN 0-7432-0276-7

To the countless, nameless lawyers who, despite the infamy cast against them, give deeply and generously of themselves to the lost, the poor, the powerless, the voiceless, and the damned. Through their brave and untiring commitment to justice they preserve the sacred rights of all of us.

Part I

1

For more than half a century the Redtail shack, distinguished only by its fine dilapidation, had stood mute and patient, waiting for the first human regard over its blistered siding and crumbling foundation. Inside the family shivered like ground squirrels hiding from the coyote.

The shingles on the roof were grayed and curling, some blown from the underlying boards. The roof leaked. When it rained the two Redtail boys, twins, put out gallon coffee cans to catch the dripping, and in the winter when the thaws came, they hauled the cans out once more to catch the melting snow. Mary Hamilton, their mother, had tried to keep the wind out with cardboard nailed up against the holes and with rags stuffed into the cracks.

A '58 Ford pickup came coughing in a blue cloud of exhaust and died in front of the house. The fender on the driver's side of the nearly ten-year-old truck had been ripped off, the tailgate missing. The windshield on the passenger side was cracked, and dried reservation mud coated the truck like ugly frosting.

Mary Hamilton had seen the truck pull up, the man get out, and with urgency in her voice she whispered, "Billy, you get in the closet. Charlie, go hide behind the couch." She stood up against the wall watching the tall man slam the truck door which refused to latch. The man walked quickly, smoothly, with a plentiful stride to the front door of the house, jumped the two rotted steps at the porch, and knocked at the door. The woman held herself up against the wall out of sight, and did not breathe.

The man knocked again, and waited, thumbs caught in the front pockets of his denim pants. Then he looked up and down the street. The houses on both sides were small single-story bungalows built in the twenties. Over the years most of the original shiplap siding had been replaced, some with colored stucco and some with new aluminum siding sold to the householders by itinerant peddlers. The neighborhood was a menagerie of multicolored houses, some sided yellow, some pink, a blue house guarding one corner, a bright avocado green another. The citizens of Twin Buttes were Americans. They had the right to paint their houses any damn color they pleased. But since the day it was built no one had painted the Redtail shack.

The man on the porch hollered, "Hey, anybody home?" The sound of his voice came from in front of his teeth, the man standing alert as if waiting, watching for the first sign, big hands now loosened from the pockets. He walked to the window. The missing pane in the bottom half had been replaced with the side of an Oxydol carton, the blue and yellow stripes. The man walked around the side of the house and looked in the south window as he passed. The kitchen. A pot of geraniums sat in the window without blooms. He stopped at the back door and knocked by slamming the screen door hard against the jamb half a dozen times.

Then he walked to the driveway and saw it was empty, the other driveways in the neighborhood crowded with an assortment of old campers used in the fall by the man of the house for his mobile hunting camp; outboard motor boats of every description on trailers used by the man of the house a couple of times a year for his fishing excursions to Bull Frog Lake; motorcycles used by the man of the house, occasionally, in furtherance of his masculine image, and pickup trucks driven at all times by the man of the house who would not be caught dead in a Chevy station wagon. Two lots down a couple of women were hanging out their wash on galvanized clotheslines, talking across the fence to each other. They paid no attention to the man at the back of the Redtail house.

The houses were built on fifty-foot-wide lots, an anomaly peculiar to those small western towns surrounded as they were by hundreds of miles of vacant prairie. But within the city limits the lots were huddled together as if grasping one another in fear of being alone in such a desolate place. The original builders, eager for anything green, had planted saplings robbed from the banks of Twin Buttes River, which in the ensuing decades had grown to magnificent old trees that shaded the neighborhood and created a charming archway over the graveled streets, the corduroy surfaces shaking the occupants in automobiles until their teeth rattled. But no trees grew on the lot occupied by the Redtail residence.

The man walked around to the far side of the house and attempted to look in the bedroom window. The shades were drawn. He started once more for the front of the house. Thinking better of it, he returned to the back door and again hollered, "Hey, you in there. Anybody home?"

Then the back door opened a crack, small eyes peering out. From inside the man heard Mary Hamilton holler, "Charlie, get back." But when Charlie Redtail saw his father he flung the door wide open, ran through the screenless screen door, and grabbed the leg of his father as if hugging a tree in a hurricane. The mother followed the boy to the door.

"What do you want, Joe," she said. The weary face emphasized her otherwise young good looks. She stood in the doorway, bare feet, the faded cotton housedress.

"I come to see the kids," Joseph said. He put his hands in his back pockets.

"You shoulda called first." She grabbed at Charlie and started to close the door.

"I couldn't call," the man said, his voice as flat as planks. "You ain't got no phone."

"I'd have a phone if you'd pay your support."

"Hard times," he said. He took a hesitant step toward the door but she stood in the way.

"Not hard times, Joe," she said. "Hard booze."

"I ain't been drunk for a long time," he said.

"You were drunk last week."

"Them waitresses don't know nothin'," he said.

Twice Joseph Redtail had gone to the priest at Hiram Falls to "take the pledge," his vow to Jesus not to take the first drink, a vow that if broken would bring on the manifold terrors of hell. Twice he had stayed sober for more than three months. But Mary knew: Promises are for today. One cannot live on yesterday's promises. Yet Mary Hamilton had continued to cling to thin strands of hope.

The man stood looking at her. Finally he said, "I could come home." Home was not the shack. Home was not even where the boys were. Home was where the woman was.

"No, Joseph," she said. "This is not your home. You live out there. I live here. Have you forgotten?"

"I don't forget," he said. The words like the sound of slow water. "I don't drink no more."

"I've heard that a thousand times."

"Not a thousand times," he said. He bowed his head so that the broad bridge of his nose was in her eyes. She pulled at the boy and tried to shut the door, but the man put his hand up against the door, easy like. "Can I see the boys?"

"The judge told you you can't see the boys if you don't pay your support."

"They get their allotment checks."

"I know," she said. "But the checks aren't much these days. Don't even pay the rent. You should get a job."

"They don' hire no Indians."

"Your drinking buddy, Jacob Yellow Dog, has a job working for Jensen Brothers."

"Don' work for Jensens no more."

"I 'spose he got drunk."

Joseph Redtail put his hands partway back in his pockets and waited. He wore an old T-shirt where you could make out AMERICAN INDIAN DAYS in faded red letters across the back, and his face was long and flat across the cheeks. As she looked at him, the eyes without pleading, without pride, she wondered how she could have loved the man.

"The boys need shirts," she said.

"I'm gonna go get me a job at the Middle Fork." He referred to the ranch run by the Arapahoe tribe. "I bought me a pair of work gloves. See?" He pulled a pair of orange cotton work gloves out of his back pocket. "I can go to work."

"Like I haven't heard that before," she said.

He forced a hand into the front pocket of his pants and pulled out a five-dollar bill. "Here," he said, "buy the boys a shirt."

"Right," she said. "You can buy two shirts for five dollars 'bout anywhere today." She tucked the bill in the pocket of her dress.

"Then buy Charlie a shirt," he said.

"The boys need shoes."

"I'll get 'em shoes next month. Can I take the boys? I got me a new truck." The boy, Charlie, standing there still holding on to his father's leg, his twin, Billy, looking out at his father from behind his mother's skirt.

Mary's hands were on her hips, looking up at the tall man. "Why are you buyin' a truck when the kids need clothes?"

"Didn't cost much. Cost a hun'ert. Pay for it by the month."

"You should pay for your kids by the month," she said.

"Gonna."

"Don't make me any promises, Joseph," she said. "You only break 'em."

He looked at Billy hanging on to his mother. "Okay," he said. "Can I take Charlie? I'll bring him back tonight. Take him up to the mountain." The way the man said it, "the mountain," the hint of life in his voice, the faint suggestion of hope. She and this man had gone to the foot of the mountain together for the Sun Dances in the late summer, the Arapahoe people gathered, their tepees in a wide circle. The willow-thatched roofs lashed to new cottonwood poles saved the old people and the children from the sun while the dancers joined with the spirits and made their sacrifices of sweat and pain to coax a blessing out of the firmament, to heal the sick, and to accept retribution for past wrongs. And they danced that good times might come again.

"If you get drunk it'll be the last time," she said.

"I don't drink no more."

She stared at him for a long moment. Together in the night they had walked up Spirit Mountain, the drummers below beating the rhythms of their blood, the beat of their young bodies, the coolness of the August night on the mountain. And behind the dancing, back from its rhythm, they had found their own on the ground, the clean smell of sage around them, his body, fresh and strong, and he, not able to say that he loved her.

"Can't you tell me now?" she had asked when it was over and they had looked up at the full moon and pregnant stars. In the distance, the drums, and in the distance they could also hear the laughter of the children running.

"There is no word for it in the Arapahoe language," Joseph Redtail said, sitting up and looking at her with eyes she could see in the moonlight.

"There's a word for it in English," she said. "You speak English." Then she laughed and threw him back down and sat on his chest, and she bounced up and down on his chest like a girl on a trotting horse. "Tell me you love me or I won't stop."

He let out small groans.

"Tell me," she said.

"Can't speak with you jumpin'."

"You just did," she said.

"It is not our way," he said, and then he pulled her off of him and, once more, showed her in his way that he loved her.

At the back door of the Redtail residence the woman stood with the face that men liked. Her large mouth. The face looking naked into the face of Joseph Redtail. She bit her lower lip, stared, the eyes still tired.

Finally she said, "You take Charlie and you be careful, Joe, and you have him back for supper." Then the boy let loose of his father's leg and ran into the house. Back again, he pushed past his mother, the boy holding a small leather pouch his father had given him on his last birthday. It contained the power of the mountain, a stone and leaves of sage from it. At ten the child was deemed weaned from the mother like the fawn from the doe. At ten the child became an entity separate from the mother, and at ten the child could go with the father.

Then the two of them had walked out to the truck, the father and the son walking beside each other, the son walking tall and smoothly like the father. Mary Hamilton followed them around the side of the house, and as the truck drove away the boy did not wave to his mother watching after them for a long time.

The other boy, the twin with the same face, also looked after them. "Go back in the house, Billy," Mary said.

"I woulda gone," Billy said.

The mother didn't answer.

"I woulda gone," he said again. He looked up at his mother as if she knew the rest.

"You've always been good to your mother," Mary said. Then she closed the door behind them.

2

The old Chevy pickup bounced over the road, the father, both hands on the wheel, the windows open, the spring wind through the small boy's hair. No braid like the father's, the hair standing on end like fine black quills on a frightened porcupine's back. Where the boy sat the seat had worn away and over the protruding springs Joseph Redtail had placed a two-foot plank.

The boy, Charlie, held tight to the pouch in his hand. He slipped the pouch strings over his head and tucked the pouch under his shirt. He looked up at his father, intent on the road. They passed the tar-papered shacks on the reservation, no trees, the long, skinny dogs lying in the yards, the tattered army tents for summertime sleeping, the half-naked children buzzing like brown flies.

Joseph Redtail nodded at the paper sack between them. "Got us some bread and a can of Spam. Got us some Coca-Cola. Make us a good lunch."

The boy didn't answer. Sometimes they hit a washboard stretch and the truck jumped, and the boy's head bobbed up and down, the father's head, too, and they looked at each other, nodding at each other involuntarily and the boy laughed and the father laughed.

The boy glanced at his father with quick looks so as not to stare, the father intent on the road, both hands fighting the old truck, the brown hands, and big. He saw his father's braid extending half down the length of his back, the braid black and glistening. Then the boy turned away again before his father saw him looking.

"How come Billy don' wanna come with us?" the father asked. The boy shrugged his shoulders and the father, respecting the child, did not press it.

At the foot of Spirit Mountain Joseph Redtail turned off the ignition to stop the motor, but the old truck kept on spurting and coughing, the truck jerking along with the spasms of the motor. Then the boy stepped out of the truck on the passenger's side and, saying nothing, started up the mountain after his father.

They climbed slowly, the father in the lead. At times he stopped to let the boy catch up, but when the boy was abreast, the father, already rested, began climbing again before the boy could catch his breath. Still the boy climbed on without complaint.

After more than an hour the father and son had reached the top of the mountain, where they stood looking over the valley below. The boy could see for eighty miles. He wondered what was beyond the Twin Buttes range. He'd never been beyond the boundaries of the reservation, never beyond the far greening prairies. He heard the prairie larks and saw them fly low to the sagebrush, their white tail feathers spread. And in the warm afternoon sun he saw the great golden eagles soaring overhead keeping watch, not for mice or prairie dogs or small singing birds, but for trespassers who might come to this holy place with wrong intent. The boy and his father stood gazing silently over the land that folded and unfolded and rose again, as if the mountains were making great speeches to the endless, listening plains. When at last the father put his hand on the boy's shoulder, his hand covered the whole of it.

"The spirits like it here," Joseph Redtail said.

The boy, saying nothing, looked up at his father and in his presence felt a reverence he could not speak. With quick glances he saw again his father's dark eyes squinting into the sun, and he knew that his father's eyes were better than his, that they saw farther, and deeper. He knew they saw the spirits and that his own eyes could not see the spirits. He looked where his father was looking, and he squinted his eyes like his father until they were almost closed. He looked hard, looked until his eyes hurt and his eyes watered. But still he could not see the spirits.

The father stood there straight as the lodge pole pine, his hands hanging easy at his side, the big fingers at the level of the boy's face, and the boy had wanted to grab the big fingers and hold on to his father, but a boy did not hold on to such a man.

"The spirits of our ancestors come here," Joseph Redtail said to Charlie. "This is a holy place," and Charlie Redtail felt the holiness, and although he could not see the spirits, he felt them.

"Can you see the spirits?" Charlie asked his father. He wished he had not broken the silence, that he had not trespassed into those holy spaces.

"No," his father had finally said. But Charlie thought his father did not wish to make fun of his son's weak eyes, and he loved his father for saying no, that the father could not see the spirits. Then they let the holy spaces of their silence set in again. And into the silence they heard the prairie lark singing, but the song of birds did not break the silence. The song of birds only put borders around the silence, like frames around great pictures.

Joseph Redtail sat down on a large boulder as high as his waist, and lifted his son up on the boulder. He took out the brown paper sack he had carried tucked in his shirt front and from it he lifted the small can of Spam, broke the key loose from the top, and twisted open the can. Then he took out his pocketknife and sliced four slices of Spam and made the sandwiches.

The boy bit into the sandwich and chewed like his father chewed his, and he washed the bite down with the warm Coca-Cola.

"Good lunch," the father said. The boy nodded.

"See the hawk? Over there." Charlie looked where his father pointed, the hawk peering, peering, perched on the top of the dead cedar tree to the east of them. "That is the red-tail hawk. That is the sacred bird for us. The red-tail hawk knows the spirits of our ancestors. We are red-tail hawks." The long silence. "The red-tail watches over us." The boy waited until the father broke the silence again.

"Hawks fly high. They can fly with the spirits," the father said.

Then Charlie spoke to his father. And the father listened because the boy did not often speak. "I wish I could fly like the hawk."

"You can fly," the father said. "We fly in the spirit. That is the Arapahoe way." Then the father said something more. "You are Arapahoe." The father looked at his son. "You are Arapahoe," the father said once more. And the boy could feel the words take hold as if they had great power. And he knew that when he looked in the mirror again his eyes would be as black as his father's, for he was Arapahoe and Arapahoes have black eyes. The boy felt very powerful and when the father touched him on the top of the head lightly, the boy felt tall like his father and he felt as if he could fly. After that they started down the mountain together. Even then the boy did not grab the father's hand, not even when the father held it out where the trail fell steeply over the high sandstone outcroppings.

When they had finally descended the full length of the mountain they crawled into the old truck and drove across the prairie on the long peninsula of sagebrush and rock that jutted out into Bull Frog Lake. Where they walked the cattails rose in jungles on the water's edge, the redwing blackbirds wild in song, laughing, cackling across the rushes, carrying on in bucolic reverie. Then Joseph Redtail stopped on a small grassy inlet, the clover fresh in bloom and smelling sweet, and they sat in it, father and son, looking into the soft, silent water.

After a long time Joseph Redtail picked up a stone and cast it into the water, the rude splash breaking the silence. The concentric rings expanded outward, larger and larger, leaving their wake, their circles, one ring after the other, moving in all directions toward distant shores. And when each small wave had finally blurred into the others, Joseph Redtail handed a stone to his son, and the boy threw the stone as far as his small arm could hurl it. And once more they heard the splash and saw the expanding circles and watched them at last fade away.

When the water was smooth again Joseph Redtail said, "We are the stones and we make the rings." He said nothing more as if the boy understood. It was not a time for Charlie Redtail to ask questions.

Then Joseph Redtail got up from where they sat and took the boy's hand, but only for a moment. The father and son, remembering promises, hastened their pace, but when they arrived at the truck and begged it to start it refused and balked like an intransigent old mule. And when the battery had died, the two of them began to walk up the road, the truck, abused by many a former master having at last taken its revenge.

No one drove by and there were no phones in the shacks along the road. After five miles they came to the Big Chief bar. The father stopped in front of the bar and stood there a long time looking in. He started to walk on but then turned and came back.

"I go in and use the phone," he said without looking at his son. "Long ways home. You wait here."

The boy could hear the nickelodeon hollering inside, the noise of it in his ears like dust in the eyes. The boy felt afraid watching his father walk to the door. This was the place. He had heard his mother speak of it often. "The place where men get crazy," she had said. And the boy knew that was true for he had seen the crazy father who was not his father, who did not have the spirit of his father, whose eyes were bloody and the lips, the drool, and the sound of his voice sunken like wet wood at the bottom of the creek.

The crazy man had pounded at the front door of their house wanting in and his mother hollering at him, "You get the hell out, Joe. I told you not to come here when you been drinkin'."

"I come to see the kids."

The door locked. His mother shooing the boys into the closet. "Your father is drunk again," Mary had said.

"He is not my father," Billy said.

Then they heard the pounding at the door again and Charlie had heard his mother screaming, "Joe, you go away or I'll call the cops," but the pounding went on, and the boys and their mother were frightened.

"You get to the closet, Billy," she said. "You go, too, Charlie."

Her face was tight and her eyes wide and the sight of his frightened mother through the crack in the closet door had frightened Charlie. Then the door burst open against the lock and Joseph Redtail stood there swaying back and forth, bumping against the jambs, the man filling the whole doorway.

"I come home to see the kids," he said. "I got a right ta see my kids."

"This isn't your home!" Mary was screaming. "You live in that damn bar and you are *drunk!* Get out of here." The boy, Charlie, had seen it and Billy hiding had been behind him.

"I am gonna call the police," his mother screamed. She ran to the neighbors, but before the police had come, Joseph Redtail got up and staggered out the front door. "I come to see you boys," he hollered.

And in the closet the boys held on to each other.

"I need to use the phone," Joseph Redtail said to the bartender at the Big Chief bar. He looked out the window above the blue neon Coors sign and saw Charlie standing in the road.

"Phone is for private use," the bartender said.

"I could pay somebody a dollar to take me and my boy ta town," he said out loud to the room. Then he saw his friend Jacob Yellow Dog at the end of the bar.

"You got yer car, Jake?" Joseph Redtail asked.

"Ain't got no car."

"Where's yer car?"

He pointed at Ronnie Cotler. "Give it ta him fer credit."

"You ain't supposed ta be drinkin'," Joseph said. "You took the pledge."

"Why don't you mind yer own fuckin' business," the bartender said. He poured Jake another shot. "Ya got all the credit ya need, Jake," the bartender said. "Ya get an honest deal here." The bartender looked over at Ronnie Cotler.

Joseph Redtail didn't raise his voice, because he was not one to raise his voice. "This ain't right." He walked over and put his arm around Jake and said, "Let's get out of here, Jake."

"They owe me," Jake said. "I got credit comin'." He was drunk. Joseph Redtail could see it in the eyes that were nearly closed, the wet mouth hanging open.

"You can take yer credit some other time," Joseph said. "Come on, Jake." Then he looked at the man's eyes, and he saw that the eyes would not focus. "You come on, Jake," Joseph said.

"You get the fuck outta here," the bartender said.

"I am gettin' out. An' I'm taking Jake with me."

"He don't need to go. He's got credit comin'," the bartender said. "So you get the fuck offa his case."

"It's up to Jake," Joe said. "You wanna come or not, Jake?"

Jake didn't answer and it was when Joseph Redtail pulled his friend off of the stool that the bartender hit him across the temple with a beer bottle and knocked the man to the floor. "I tol' ya ta mind yer own fuckin' business," the bartender said.

When Joseph Redtail didn't move, Cotler called the sheriff's office. Then the bartender and Ronnie Cotler had hauled Joseph Redtail out of the saloon, the bartender with his arms under the man's shoulders, Cotler carrying the feet. They dumped him on the ground beside the boy at the edge of the road.

"Is he dead?" Cotler asked.

"Don' know," the bartender said. He got down on his hands and knees, his big belly hanging over the body of the unconscious man. The bartender put his ear to the man's chest and listened. "Nah, he ain't dead. Not yet, anyways." He laughed and went back into the saloon.

After that Charlie Redtail ran to his father and the boy tried to awaken his father, but Joseph Redtail wouldn't wake up. The boy looked down at his father and he couldn't think of what to do. Maybe he was drunk, he thought. He stooped down to his father and touched him. His eyes were open, but he did not speak, and the boy knew his father did not see him.

"Papa," he said. "I'm sorry." He shook his father. He was crying. "It was my fault, Papa. I shouldn't a let you go in there." But his father, bleeding from the mouth, did not answer. The boy shook the father, but the man's eyes did not blink. Then the boy grabbed the large hand with both of his hands and he pulled as hard as he could, and when he let loose of the hand, the hand fell to the dirt.

"Come on, Papa, get up. Get up, Papa." The boy pulled at the hand again, and again, and finally when the boy could do nothing he stood there sobbing looking down at his father. He grabbed the pouch that hung from his neck and held onto it with both hands.

After a while, Joseph Redtail stirred and blinked his eyes slowly, and once more the boy began to pull at his father's hand. At last the man got to a sitting position.

"Are you okay now, Papa?" Charlie asked. "Please, Papa." But the man didn't answer his son.

Then the man staggered to his feet and stood there, not knowing where he was, the boy holding on to his leg. And Charlie Redtail knew that if he held on to his father's leg long enough and hard enough his father would be all right. And he did not let loose.

At about five o'clock in the same afternoon Deputy Dean Miller and Deputy Lynn Maxfield arrived at the Big Chief bar situated on State Highway 236 , eleven miles east of Twin Buttes. Deputy Maxfield had answered a call placed half an hour earlier by Ronnie Cotler, owner of the saloon. Miller was off duty, but had accompanied his friend. Their plan was to handle the problem at the bar after which Maxfield would be off duty as well, and the two, unmarried and horny as young goats, would take in the dance at the Elk's Club in Twin Buttes.

When the two deputies walked into the bar they saw nothing out of the ordinary. A drunk Indian lay on the shoulder of the road, which was not unusual, a kid standing beside him. The juke box was playing country & western and Ronnie Cotler was sitting at the bar. There were three Indians in the corner of the saloon on the floor sleeping it off—two men and a woman.

"Couple of beers for the officers," Cotler said. Cotler could be seen in his eyes. When eyes have seen too much, the eyes lose their softness. But Cotler did not know he possessed such eyes, for men never see their own naked eyes.

"Buy these boys another round," Colter hollered to the bartender, their last beer still half full. "When I came in little while ago this Indian was causing trouble. Big son of a bitch. Joe Redtail. You know him."

"Right," Miller said.

"Had a breed kid with him."

Miller nodded.

"Didn't want my bartender to get his hands dirty, if ya know what I mean. This Redtail is too fucking big anyway. But we got it handled before you boys got here. Sorry to cause you the trouble. He's layin' out there on the road."

3

Abner Hill had known Joseph Redtail as a tall man, but lying facedown on the concrete in the north cell of the Fetterman County Jail the Indian seemed strangely diminished. His long braid was covered with blood from the head wounds, the many cuts in the back of the head puddled and drying.

When Miller, the deputy left, Hill hollered down at the body. "Hey, Joe, I'm here. Mary bailed you out again." The Indian didn't answer. "You been in another fight, Joe?" He reached down to shake the man, the hand limp, the skin the color of a catfish after it had lain in the dust. Then Hill yelled for the jailer and up and down the cells on each side of the walkway the inmates began rattling the bars, screaming, raising hell. After a while Miller came, his keys jingling as he walked, the boots stomping on concrete.

"Didn't move anything," Hill said. "I suppose he had all those cuts when he came in here."

"Yeah," Miller said.

"Why didn't you take him to the hospital?"

"We don't take no war-whoops to the hospital less there's an emergency."

"How long has he been dead?"

The deputy looked at the body. "He dead?" He put his boot on the man's rump and jiggled the body back and forth.

"He was alive when he came in here, wasn't he?"

"Who the fuck knows," the deputy said. "You able to tell a live war-whoop from a dead one once he's dead drunk?"

"Better call the coroner," Hill said.

After that Hill crawled in his pickup and headed for the old part of town. He drove north on Main, turned east at the Skelly station toward the Redtail residence. Then he drove slowly down Kendrick Street under its arbor of cottonwoods, the young leaves green and waxy, the kids in the street playing baseball, the kids yelling at his truck as he drove by.

Earlier in the day Mary Hamilton had come to his office still in her white waitress uniform. "Could you go get Joseph out of jail again," she said. She looked down at her red hands. "I don't know why I do it. I've left him there for a week already. I keep thinkin' he could learn somethin' but he never does," her voice tired. Then she dropped the Folgers coffee can with her tip money on his desk. He counted it. Ninety dollars and a few cents. The justice of the peace set his bail at the usual hundred.

Abner Hill had bailed Joseph Redtail out of jail a dozen times. More. Drunk. In fights. Mary Hamilton, too, had often trudged to the jail looking in at the man, the pity of it at first, the anger later, and after the years, the eyes no longer angry, no longer sad. The eyes like the voice, seeing, speaking out of duty. "Hope," Mary Hamilton sometimes said, "was for fools." Yet she had hoped for the man, and even after their divorce, she had been there for him—too often, she thought.

"Father of my boys," she said as if that were reason enough.

Hill parked his pickup in front of the Redtail residence, climbed the rotted steps, and knocked on the door. The messenger, he thought. Always the messenger.

In the depth of Joseph Redtail's pain Hill had sometimes seen glimpses of the man. Shallow men cannot have deep pain. Once the man had suffered in the Sun Dance, danced for four days and four nights without food or water, danced nearly naked in the sun of August, the white war paint on his body, the body caked with the mud of sweat and dust, the skewers piercing the hide on his chest, the skewers secured to long thongs tied to the top of the center pole. Around the pole he and the other warriors had danced. Through the pain of it he had danced to drive out his accursed infirmity. He had danced to regain his pride. He had danced on after the others had fallen, and he had danced also for his past with Mary Hamilton, a place lost in broken promises. And as he danced, hesitant dribbles of joy had seeped in through the pain, from the knowing—that he, Joseph August Redtail, was at that moment a warrior and a man.

For Hill the pain of his clients beat at his shell like the turtle feels the beating of the stick on his. And although the shell protects the turtle, still the turtle feels the beating stick.

He stood at the door waiting for it to open. Mary Hamilton's old pain was done. It would slide over to make room for the new pain when he announced that Joseph was dead. He knocked again. He hoped she wouldn't answer.

He'd seen it all before. Two years earlier he'd found Abraham Ghost Bear dead in the drunk tank, and he'd wondered then why he was standing there looking down at that pile of human flesh in a pool of blood and spew in about equal proportions. Now, Joseph Redtail. He'd felt sick. The profession smelled. His clients were poor. The American Indians he represented didn't pay. They paid him with promises that they intended to keep. But they got drunk instead. They got drunk to escape the pain, the humiliation of being prisoners in their own land. They escaped the pain by dying in the prisons and lying on the street corners too drunk to stand and at last freezing to death in the alleys. Drunkenness proved to be the lesser misery. Drunk, they got thrown in jail to molder until their government allotment checks came in. Then the checks went to the county to pay their fines. And if there was money left over they bought another quart of Thunderbird and got drunk again.

Hill knocked on the door once more and waited.

Fees had never been important to Hill if he could meet the office rent and buy a few groceries. A man had to do something with his life and at the moment, he didn't know anything better to do with his. He was like the people of Twin Buttes. They did what they did because it was what they did. Their tolerance included the whores on Front Street facing the railroad tracks and the preachers who preached against the whores, three streets up. The people tolerated the preacher who got caught in the whorehouse when the sheriff made a raid to collect his payoff. The people tolerated the sheriff and the people also tolerated Abner Hill, "that Indian lawyer," they called him.

Other notions prevailed. Equal rights for Indians? How could savages have equal rights? Best you could do with Indians was keep the drunks and their old jalopies off the highways. The more Indians the sheriff jailed the better a citizen's chances one wouldn't run into you head-on and kill your whole family. Ask Mimi Heatherington whose husband and three kids were killed on their way home from church in a head-on with a drunk Arapahoe. The Lord had spared Mimi, the people said. She'd stayed in bed that Sunday morning with a migraine that she never recovered from.

Yet some Native Americans had been honored as upstanding citizens, war heroes especially. Some ran a few head of cattle on reservation lands.

Some tried to maintain their Native American customs. Some sent their children to the white man's schools. A few worked at the agency office in Hiram Falls. Some rode rodeo horses, and others worked as ranch hands for white men. But those who "had made it" were usually exterminated by their assimilation. They murdered the Indian in themselves by taking on the white man's ways.

Yet the townspeople accepted the Native Americans as an immutable part of the environment, like winter storms and the hot winds of summer. Not many thought of the old men sitting in front of the JC Penney store wearing their black stovepipe hats and cheap cotton blankets as the remnant of a once great Indian Nation. Few felt guilt for the white man's original crimes against the aboriginal people, for these were not the crimes of the townspeople of Twin Buttes.

Abner Hill's representation of the Arapahoes in Fetterman County had nothing to do with "do-gooderism," as he called it. What he did he did out of deep respect for the law, out of his need to prove that the law and justice, even though distant relatives, were occasionally united. He thought that if the law could bring justice to the American Indian there was hope for the law. If there wasn't any hope for the law, then the country was in a shit-pot full of trouble.

He admitted that early on he'd been smitten with the Don Quixote disease, believing, as he had, that the search for justice was the first and final goal of an honorable profession. But the actual practice of law soon cured him of it. No one could define justice. He discovered that justice, a human invention, was another paradox, so that what was just for one was unjust for another, and only the lawyers won, all except Abner Hill. Yet he kept at it, and sometimes he knew he was still searching for justice even though he couldn't define it.

Once more Abner Hill knocked on the door at the Redtail residence and as he turned and started down the steps the door opened. Mary Hamilton stood there in her white waitress uniform, her face as if it did not recognize him. He thought he knew how to say most things but he'd never learned how to tell a person someone they'd loved was dead. In Mary Hamilton's case, he didn't know whether the news would be good or bad. He gave her the benefit of the doubt.

"I got bad news for you, Mary," Hill said. He was holding his black Stetson in his hand. "I found Joseph dead in the county jail."

She stood at the door staring at Hill.

"You want me to tell the boys?" Hill asked.

"No," she said.

"You want me to make any arrangements?"

"No," she said.

"Well, then," Hill said politely, "I'll be going."

It was then that the woman said after him, "What about the bail money? I gave you 'bout a hundred dollars."

"I gave it to the sheriff to get him out."

"I'd appreciate it if you got my bail money back," Mary Hamilton had said. "It came outta my grocery can. I need the money."

The man had wanted to comfort the woman standing at the door of the shack. In his rearview mirror he could see her still standing there, looking small and helpless. Alone. When Joseph was alive he provided something to hang on to, the anger which she held against the man, the hope she held for him, the places she had continued to feel for him through the bitterness and frustration. Now she would find the loneliness, a loneliness Hill understood. As he turned the corner he saw her walk back into the house.

He headed to his office. His practice was made the more painful by his isolation in that no place called Twin Buttes, a town of less than five thousand souls where those who locked their doors at night were considered hopelessly paranoid. Casper, the closest city, was over two hundred miles to the south. In the year 1969, the year of Joseph Redtail's death, Casper was the largest town in the state, a budding metropolis of more than twenty thousand oil field hands, oil field land men, oil field promoters, oil field equipment dealers, oil field company men, and a score or more of oil field lawyers and their spouses and girlfriends who were shuffled back and forth among those rugged, rednecked individualists as fate, exacerbated by an endless stream of booze and a scarcity of women in the town dictated.

Across the two hundred miles between Twin Buttes and Casper lay the long, empty prairies marred by only an occasional lonely ranch where could be heard the lonely wail of the coyote, the lonely howl of the irrepressible wind, and the lonely cry of the rancher's wife. Whenever one ventured out of doors the wind, ready and rude, lay waiting to slap one squarely in the face like some shrieking inmate from the mental hospital in Evanston, where the perpetual wind blew even harder.

Abner Hill was lonely. He had no mentor in Twin Buttes to offer him advice. He had no friends of the bar, the other four lawyers in town being engaged in the pious art of making a living. They gave little heed to the more illusive art of practicing law, Hill thought. Of the other four, none but Richard James Everhart had ever tried a contested case from beginning to end before a jury, and Everhart had lost that case so miserably to Harold Yancey of Casper, the state's premier trial lawyer, that Everhart vowed privately he would never again enter the courtroom. Yet the lawyers of Twin Buttes would posture and bark and make all measure of abominable noise about suing one another's clients, the racket, most thought, for the benefit of those who paid them. But when it came down to the trial, everyone knew that in the courtroom they would be as impotent as plucked capons. And none, of course, would represent those redskins. No money in it.

All except Hill were married and had secretaries. Three of the lawyers had wives for secretaries who year after year typed up the same forms, two carbon copies each. In order to eke out an existence all the lawyers in Twin Buttes engaged in a general practice that covered such a wide range of specialties that none had become expert in any. All but Hill enjoyed monthly retainers—usually no more than $100 a month from their institutional clients—the bank, the city, the irrigation district, the school district. All except Abner Hill wore gray suits without vests, with the exception of Gerald P. Sackman, who wore a black dinner jacket to work as if the formality might somehow reflect on the superiority of his work. Sackman was a stern, bald-headed man with a large beak and beaver teeth who, despite his black dinner jacket, refused to carpet his office floor because he thought the farmers would be uncomfortable coming into his quarters with their manure-covered boots. He represented the bank on a $100-a-month retainer.

Hill's dress lent little to his image—his worn black leather jacket, a blue denim shirt open at the collar, Levi's faded from honest wear, the Justin boots of high polish, the black Stetson with the dusty sweat marks around the band. Yet several of the Twin Buttes lawyers secretly, grudgingly admired Hill, for his causes were usually hopeless, his clients usually poor. Despite the odds against him and to the dismay of the other members of the Twin Buttes bar, he charged on in his quixotic elegance and sometimes he won his case, if not out of brilliance, out of a stubborn persistence.

Once Gerald Sackman, representing the bank, had invited Hill to meet with him after office hours at the Elk's Club to discuss the settlement of a case Hill had brought on behalf of Emily White Antelope for the remainder due the woman when the bank had repossessed her Chevy pickup truck worth an easy $300 and only $25 principal, $53 interest, and a $117 attorney's fee and costs were due on the note and mortgage against it. As Hill figured it, the bank owed the woman $105, and when the bank ignored Hill's demand, he filed suit for it—for exactly $105.

After the two lawyers had had a beer or two Sackman finally came out with it.

"I just don't understand you, Abner," he said raising his right eyebrow to emphasize his point. "Your client Emily promised me every month for over a year to pay the bank. Why, once on Indian payday I even drove out to her place up by Hiram Falls to see if I couldn't collect it. She promised on her mother's grave to pay me when her next allotment check came in. Never even called. I say your client has proven herself to be, should we call it, a contemptible fraud." He raised his right eyebrow again and gave Abner Hill a long look.

Hill had known Gerald Sackman for many years, but he addressed his elders properly. "Mr. Sackman," he said with undisguised umbrage, "you can call me whatever you wish. But don't you ever refer to one of my clients in such a manner." With that Abner Hill got up from the table at the Elk's Club and left Gerald Sackman sitting there, his right eyebrow still cocked at Hill's empty chair. But on the next motion day when the matter was to be taken up by Judge Henry Hankins, Sackman agreed to pay Emily White Antelope the full $105. He agreed to pay it, he said, to get rid of what he called another of Abner Hill's nuisance suits.

Abner Hill sat at his desk looking down on the Main Street of Twin Buttes. The people passed each other on the sidewalk, tipped their hats, and smiled. Pickup trucks covered with dust and dried mud passed one another slowly, the dogs and the kids in the rear, the kids sitting on the spare tire. Abner Hill saw none of this. He saw the body of Joseph August Redtail on the concrete, the blood, the cuts, the long braid soaked in blood, the stale smell of old blood still in his nose. And he saw the woman standing in the doorway in her white waitress dress, and it was then that, in the way of men, Abner Hill made his decision.

4

Strictly in accordance with the law Elmer Johnson, Fetterman County coroner, had called the coroner's jury to determine the cause of death of one Joseph August Redtail whose body lay before them. The members of the jury were drinking friends of Elmer Johnson who owned the only mortuary in town, the Johnson Funeral Home. The Johnson family lived in the apartment above the funeral parlor. Elmer Johnson and his wife kept their business respectful and quiet.

Belloise Johnson, her name a contraction of Belle and Louise as invented by her father, was Elmer Johnson's wife, a large barrel-shaped woman with hair died jet black, her sharp eyes under heavy graying brows. Folks said she ran the funeral home. She gathered the data on the dead and gave the information to the *Twin Buttes Times* for its obituaries. She saw that the programs were printed for the funerals, got Rosy Moriarity to sing "The Old Rugged Cross," arranged with the sexton for the burial plot and for the sheriff's escort to the graveyard. Coordination was a major issue for every funeral cavalcade through the streets of Twin Buttes. Then after a full day's work, she cooked supper for Elmer and their three kids, and after supper and the dishes, she made up the corpses, did their hair, their fingernails, and finally dressed them. You could tell her touch. Even the male corpses were helpless against Belloise Johnson's clear polish on their nails. If you didn't want the dead to have polish on his nails you had to specify it. Otherwise Belloise would be at them as soon as Elmer had withdrawn the trocar needle from the corpse's abdomen.

The coroner's office was also Elmer Johnson's business office, which adjoined what Elmer called his "slumber room." As he worked on his accounts with his office door open, on a good day, Johnson could see as many as three open coffins with their smiling, somnolent occupants. For among the other talents of the artful mortician, Elmer Johnson knew the trick of sculpturing smiles on the faces of his guests, smiles that looked like his own, a small, permanent tuck on the right corner of the mouth secured by a single stitch that raised the right cheek muscle a fraction— enough to convince the living of the promised peace of the dead.

But for certain skillful manipulations of Joseph Redtail's legs, the full length of the latest resident of Elmer Johnson's slumber room could not have been stuffed into the standard pine box. The coffin, draped in black flannel to hide its crude construction, sat closest to Elmer Johnson's office. The coffin's split lid was affixed to the box with ordinary strap hinges of the sort farmers used on their barn doors, and the top half of the lid was laid back so that the upper part of the corpse was fully exposed.

That June afternoon Hardy Jacobson, a longtime member of the coroner's jury, had picked up the other two perennial members of the jury in his new '69 Jeep station wagon. The jury always convened for an inquest in the afternoon at four o'clock sharp, and, unless one of the jurors was sick or out of town, which was rare, the jurors were on hand and on time.

Unlike the inexperienced riffraff who might be gathered in the district court to hear the cases on Judge Hankins's calendar, Elmer Johnson argued that his three jurors were experts. This same jury had sat on more than a hundred fifty cases, for by law, in every unattended death, the coroner was required to assemble a jury of three citizens to determine "how, when, where, and by what means the deceased came to his end."

Dr. Edwin Billingsley, the town's general practitioner, a small marmot of a man with dark sunken eyes and a bristly mustache, had performed the autopsy on Joseph Redtail and in the most perfunctory manner. As always Billingsley began his work at the head. He made an unsteady cut around the back of the scalp and up and around the back of the ears, skinned the scalp upward and toward the front. Then he pulled the whole of the scalp down over the forehead so that the scalp hung easily over the rest of the face. At last he took an electric bone saw, a device that cut not by rotation but by vibration, and sawed off the top of the skull as if he were removing the top of a boiled egg.

At times he got too close to his work and the bone dust would cloud his thick glasses and cake his lips. Then he would stop, pull off his glasses, and wipe them on the tail of his surgeon's smock and look around to see if anyone was watching.

"Jesus H. Christ," he would say, spitting and wiping his mouth with his sleeve, "bone dust!" and then he'd smile like a man of good humor, as he was, and add, "A little bone dust won't hurt ya at all."

Billingsley performed his autopsies with a butcher knife equipped with an eight-inch blade and a wooden handle. He took some joy in emphasizing that no moral or practical difference existed between cutting up a side of beef and cutting up a cadaver. From the standpoint of science, meat was meat. Accordingly, he pushed the brain aside with one hand so that he could reach in with the butcher knife with the other. With a couple of slices at the base of the skull, he pulled the entire brain out in one piece. After conducting a cursory inspection of the wormy glob in the manner of a pitcher examining a new ball before he throws it, he placed the brain on an old chopping block provided him by Belloise Johnson from her kitchen. Then Billingsley proceeded to slice the brain into sections about the thickness of fried potatoes, held the pieces up close to his face for careful examination, and, seeing nothing of interest, dumped the slices back into the cranium, fit the skull cap back in place as one replaces the lid on a jack-o'-lantern, pulled the scalp back over the skull, and left the mess for Elmer Johnson to sew up. In the case of Joseph August Redtail, Dr. Billingsley attacked the remainder of his vital organs in the standard way, a canon of the medical profession holding that if one does what one does in the standard way, even if it is wrong, one does it right.

Accordingly, Billingsley made one long slice from Joseph Redtail's pubic bone to his sternum, pulled out a stomach that looked like an empty pink bladder from a smallish football, sliced it from its biological moorings with the butcher knife, laid it on the chopping block, and cut it in half with a single efficient slice. Then he picked up one of the halves, held it close to his thick glasses, turned it inside out, and dropped it back into the stomach cavity, after which he picked up the other half and examined it.

In this perfunctory but proficient manner Dr. Edwin Billingsley completed the autopsy of Joseph August Redtail, whose body lay before him awaiting the last clean stroke of his butcher knife and the doctor's final discernments that in Twin Buttes, Wyoming, were deemed as infallible as the pronouncements of the pope himself.

Elmer Johnson was about to swear in the coroner's jurors, the statute providing that "the said jurors shall, at said time and place, be sworn over the body of the deceased." To Elmer Johnson, that did not mean that the swearing should be made in the vicinity of the remains, but *exactly* over the corpse. The casket bearing the remains of Joseph August Redtail was open, the hands of the corpse neatly crossed so that all ten of its fingernails glistened like wet stones at the creek's edge. Despite the efforts of Belloise Johnson to lighten the skin of the deceased in order to make him look as white as possible, it being her belief that Indians should at least be given such benefit in death, the corpse looked nearly as dark and gray as when Abner Hill had found Joseph Redtail lying on the floor of the jail, but the long black hair of the deceased which, thoroughly washed and oiled with Fitch's hair oil and freshly combed, shown brightly in the diminished light of the slumber room.

The corpse was dressed in a blue flannel shirt and a new pair of dark blue JC Penney jeans. He wore an old pair of moccasins bearing the geometric designs of the tribe, the beaded top of the moccasins of red, white, blue, and yellow. The pant legs were too short to cover the bare stockingless ankles although the Arapahoe tribe guaranteed stockings and a standard suit of long underwear, a shirt, and pants, the cost of such clothing not to exceed twenty-five dollars, which items of clothing the deceased had often been without during his lifetime, even in the dead of winter.

"Come on over here, boys, and raise your right hands," Elmer Johnson said to the jurors assembled. Obediently the three men gathered around the coffin; Bill Sellinger, owner of the local Gamble's hardware, and Faye Bosworth, manager of the Twin Buttes Hotel and its coffee shop and bar, on one side of the pine box; and Hardy Jacobson, owner of the Rexall drugs on the other. They raised their hands and, looking at one another rather than the corpse below them, listened to the coroner inquire in a weary voice, "Do each of you swear to return a true verdict, finding when, where, and by what means this deceased come to his end?"

The three nodded, but adding to the solemnity of the proceeding, Hardy Jacobson spoke in loud affirmation, "I do."

"Well, then let's get started," Johnson said. He pulled up a green folding steel chair in front of a green folding steel card table, sat down, and motioned to the jurors to take their seats in the green folding chairs he'd arranged alongside the coffin. Next to the far wall lay two other corpses in their coffins lately pulled from a wreck on U.S. 26, who thus laid out were, for the first time in recent memory, sober and the only other observers in attendance at Elmer Johnson's coroner's inquest.

"I call Deputy Dean Miller as my first witness," Elmer Johnson announced. Miller, who had been sitting in Johnson's office, hearing his name, swaggered up to the folding chair at the head of Joseph Redtail's remains. The deputy raised his hand, took the oath administered by the coroner, and told his story without direction. He had gotten to the part where Abner Hill had found the deceased on the floor of his cell, when at that precise moment Abner Hill, himself, entered the slumber room.

Hill nodded to the coroner and the three jurors, but there being no extra chairs, he leaned up against the doorway. Elmer Johnson stared at the man without saying anything. Johnson knew Hill as a bachelor who allegedly led a secret, profligate life, although not a soul could rightly say they had ever witnessed Abner Hill have one drink too many or show any disrespect for another man's wife. He attended the Methodist church on Christmas and Easter, bought a case of Girl Scout cookies once a year whether he could afford it or not, and drove an old red Ford pickup, all of which was well within the local standards of good citizenship. But to the same extent that a man is judged by the company he keeps, so a lawyer is judged by the clients he represents. And Abner Hill's clients, the Indians, the petty thieves, the drunks, and the county's other poor miscreants lent little to his standing in the community.

Elmer Johnson paid the lawyer no heed. Instead, as if his appearance had not been discovered, he began his crux question. "So Deputy Miller, in your expert opinion when, where, and by what means did this Indian, this . . ." he stopped for a moment to glance at the papers before him in order to get the name exact, "this Joseph August Redtail, come to his death?"

"I figure he got beat up when he was drunk and that he died of the injuries."

"Right, Dean," Elmer Johnson said in confirmation of the deputy's findings. "I got Dr. Billingsley's autopsy report right here, and it says he died of internal bleeding. Says he figured he got kicked to death. His kidneys was both jarred loose and he had a broken jaw and all of his front teeth was kicked out. Belloise had one hell of a time trying to get him put back into any shape whatsoever. Worked half the night on him and even when the priest from the chapel come ta see him, he tol' me he wouldn't a knowed him 'cept I told him who he was. But I'll tell ya one thing for sure: That wasn't no fault of Belloise's. She done a pretty damn good job on him, if I do say so myself." He smiled proudly at the deputy.

"Right, Elmer," Deputy Miller said. "She sure did."

"So when, where, and by what means did he come to his death?"

"The time—that there is the sixty-four-dollar question," Miller said. "I couldn't say without guessing some."

"Well, I notice here the doc says four in the afternoon, give or take an hour. Doc sorta lays his hand on the liver, ya know, and feels it, and if it's still a little warm he figures he ain't been dead too long. One thing I know: it is cold down there in that jail. I guess we can just find that he come to his death about June twenty-third in the Twin Buttes County Jail by assault and battery at the hands of an assailant or assailants unknown. You don't know who beat this Indian up, do ya, Dean?"

"Well, no, I don't," Miller said, getting up from his chair. "I ain't got the first idea, Elmer." He was reaching for his hat when Abner Hill stepped in front of Miller and said, "I was wondering, Elmer, if I could ask the deputy here a question or two?"

"On account of what?" Elmer said. "This is a coroner's inquest, and I'm the coroner, and I'm the only one who's supposed to be askin' the questions."

"Well, that's so," Hill said, blocking Miller's exit at the doorway.

"So what's your interest in the case?" Johnson asked, Miller starting for the door again.

"I represent the Redtail family," Hill said.

"The family's got no right at the coroner's inquest," Johnson said. "This is official business of Fetterman County, Wyoming."

"It seems a little strange that a man can't ask the deputy a question or two," Hill said. The deputy had stopped in front of Hill not knowing whether to arrest him, push on by him, or wait. "What's it hurt?" Hill asked. "The facts are the facts. The truth is the truth." Perhaps it was the lawyer's cowboy boots that created the illusion of his uncommon height as he peered down on Elmer Johnson. "Mary Hamilton is a citizen and a voter, you know, and so am I."

"Well, I don't know," Elmer said, scratching his head and looking at his feet for a long time. He had great respect for the townspeople of Twin Buttes, whom he considered not only potential customers, but also voters. Elmer was the friend of all, spoke to every person the same, nodded to every passerby on the street, graced them all with the same sad smile, and gave them the same friendly wave with his forefinger from the steering wheel of his car when he met them driving down the town streets. Although Abner Hill and his client were voters they were not entitled to special privileges. Hill was not a member of the Kiwanis

Club or the Lions Club, nor was he even a member of the Chamber of Commerce. Nor was his client. And anyone who gave a damn for the growth and prosperity of Twin Buttes, and considering the small price of its dues, should at least join the Chamber of Commerce.

At the higher echelon of Twin Buttes society Hill's presence was also lacking. He was not a member of the Twin Buttes Country Club, a member of the Twin Buttes Drama Society, and more than all else, the Twin Buttes Volunteer Fire Department. He was never known to socialize with any of the town's leading citizens, not even for an occasional cup of coffee at ten in the morning and three in the afternoon at the Twin Buttes Hotel coffee shop where the town fathers met. Moreover, during the Christmas season when the community's elite held their holiday parties and when many were invited who were socially ignored the rest of the year, Abner Hill was not known to have ever made his appearance at one such function, nor to anyone's knowledge had he ever been invited to any.

Hill, still standing in the doorway, then added to his argument. "The Redtail family needs to be satisfied that everything's on the up and up, Elmer. I can do you a service here if everything checks out. You want the family satisfied, don't you, Elmer?"

"Well, yeah," Johnson said. "But I don't want to set no precedent by lettin' a lawyer come into my inquest and ask a buncha irrelevant questions." Then he quickly added, "No offense, Abner. I know you wouldn't ask no foolish questions. But, after all, you ain't the coroner. Ya gotta admit that."

"So, Elmer, you want me to whisper the questions in your ear that I want you to ask the deputy?" Hill asked. It was then that Hill felt the presence of someone behind him and, turning, saw Mary Hamilton standing there with her two young boys, holding one by each hand. Hill stepped aside and after some hesitation, the woman entered the slumber room, the two boys still in tow.

"This is Mary Hamilton," Hill said, nodding in the direction of Elmer Johnson.

"I know her," Elmer Johnson said. "See her at the hotel coffee shop all the time. Good waitress. Let me tell you how sorry I am about your husban'."

"He *was* my husband," she said, emphasizing the past. "I took back my maiden name after the divorce."

Elmer Johnson said, kindly, "We all make mistakes."

"I think you know my father," Mary said.

"I know your father well," Elmer said, smiling. "Fine man. Good businessman."

"No," Mary said. "He went broke while I was in high school. He took up carpentry after that."

"Hard times then."

"No," Mary said. "He drank it up."

"Sorry to hear that," Elmer said.

Mary's father had once owned the grocery store in Harvard, a wide spot in the road twenty miles west of Twin Buttes. In addition to the Hamilton grocery store, Harvard boasted one run-down motel with seven cabins, a Conoco filling station that was sometimes open and sometimes not, and the Harvard Saloon. Yale, another wide spot in the road ten miles farther west, had only the one business, its infamous saloon, the county residents finding it nearly too funny for words to claim that in a single night of revelry they had attended both Harvard and Yale.

"I came to let the kids see their father one last time. Kids entitled to see him at his best."

"Well, I would say so," Elmer said. By this time the coroner's jurors had gotten up from their seats and were standing off in the shadows by one of the corpses where Deputy Miller also stood. Abner Hill followed his client to the casket.

"I want the boys to remember their father when he wasn't causing trouble."

"Well, I think that is a wise thing to do," Elmer said. "A good last memory can have an effect on a child."

Mary Hamilton walked over to the casket and looked down, the pine box standing above the eye level of the children.

After a long silence Mary Hamilton said, "This isn't Joseph Redtail."

"It sure is," Elmer Johnson said. "I can prove it by his fingerprints if ya wish."

"It doesn't look like him."

"We did the best we could," Elmer said. "Belloise worked practically all night on him. He was in pretty bad shape when he come in. Ask Abner here."

"I agree with Mary. It doesn't look like Joseph," Hill replied.

"A person can only do so much, you know. A person can only work on what they bring him."

"His nose isn't the same and his chin is wrong," Mary said. "He had a good chin."

"He was all kicked in," Elmer said. "You shoulda seen him."

"I don't think so," Hill said. "And I don't think we should be talking about this in front of Billy and Charlie here."

"I plum forgot about the kids, " Elmer admitted. "I beg yer pardon." He shot his sad smile at the mother. The two boys stood looking up at their mother and at the coroner, their eyes as wide as new quarters.

"It's him, all right," Mary Hamilton finally said. "I can tell by the hands. But he never had his fingernails polished like that. That isn't like him at all."

"I want to go home," Charlie, said, a horror emerging on the child's face.

"Don't you want to take a last look at your father?" Mary asked. She started to lift the boy up.

"I want to go home." The boy stiffened.

"He saw them beat Joe up," she said pointing to Charlie. "Can't get him to talk about it, but he saw it. I should never have let him go with Joe."

"Terrible thing," Johnson said.

"He was with his father when they killed him," she said. "It was my fault. Should never have let him go."

"Nice-looking boy," Elmer said.

"The boys look like their father," she said again. "'Course, not how he looks now."

"I can see that," Elmer said. He had his thumbs tucked into his vest pockets, his belly pushing out against the vest.

"I didn't go," Billy said. He hung to his mother's right forearm, his head hidden behind her.

"I want to go home," Charlie said, sobbing softly from the other side of his mother.

"Well, you take a look at your father first," Mary Hamilton said, struggling to lift Charlie above the level of the casket. "This is your father," she said breathing hard as she spoke, "and this is the way you'll end up if you go the way of those Indians."

"Maybe that's enough, Mary," Hill said.

"You look at him good," Mary Hamilton said, still struggling to hold her son above his father's corpse.

The child was stiff, his eyes shut tight, his head shaking *no*. "I want to go home," he sobbed.

"You look, now, Charlie," his mother said. "Just one look."

"I think we ought to let the boy go," Hill said. He came over and took Charlie from his mother, sat down on one of the steel chairs by the corpse, and put the boy on his lap. Then he pulled the child to him, but he was too stiff with terror for comforting.

Then Mary Hamilton picked up Billy. "Take a look at your father, Billy. This is what happens to Indians in America."

"Now that ain't exactly true," Elmer Johnson said. "We try to treat everybody the same here."

"You only bury 'em," Mary said. "If it wasn't for all the drunk Indians in the county you'd go broke."

"That ain't exactly true, Mrs. Hamilton," Elmer said. "We charge the same for everybody. You can chose the casket and—"

"This is what your father came to," she said to the child, Billy. "You go the Indian way, this is how you'll end up, too."

Billy looked into the casket. Then he said, "Don't worry, Momma. I'll take care of you."

And with that Mary Hamilton put the boy down. She walked over to where Charlie was still sitting on Abner Hill's lap, Hill slowly stroking the boy's hair, the boy's head now up against the man's chest. The mother stood watching, the child's eyes closed, Hill looking down on the top of the boy's head. Hill nodded to Mary Hamilton but kept on stroking the boy. The child's hands were limp and his mouth was pushed askew against Hill's shirt, a wet spot where the boy had slobbered, the room silent while she waited. Finally Mary Hamilton reached out her hand for Charlie, pulled him gently from Abner Hill's lap, took her two sons, one by each of her hands, and led them out of the slumber room of the Johnson Funeral Home. As she left she turned back to Abner Hill.

"Did you get my hundred dollars bail money, Abner? I need the money."

"I'll drop it by," Hill said.

Then after Mary Hamilton left the room, Abner Hill turned to Elmer Johnson. "Would you ask Deputy Miller to take the stand again, Elmer? I have a few questions for him."

5

They had not known each before they met in that curious way after a basketball game. Joseph Redtail was the tallest boy on his All-Native American team from the reservation. They had just beaten Twin Buttes High. Laced with the euphoria of victory, the Indians had decided that as the spoils of war they should also capture the Twin Buttes cheerleaders. Joseph Redtail, along with Jacob Yellow Dog, another member of the team, had captured both Mary Hamilton and Mary's best friend, Sherry Wickstrom, another cheerleader. Neither of the girls had struggled much.

"Ya wanna go to the movie?" the kidnapper, Joseph Redtail, had asked.

"What's on at the drive-in?" Mary asked.

"Don' know," Joseph Redtail said. Sherry giggled.

Then Mary said, "We could go and see," and after that the two cars, the Indian boys driving down the road rattling in clouds of exhaust, entered the Twin Buttes drive-in theater.

It had been in the middle of an old Errol Flynn movie, the sword fighting, the hordes storming the walls of the castle, the hot oil pouring over the parapets, when a mob of boys from Twin Buttes High invaded the theater. You could hear them coming even over the music and the slashing of steel on steel on the screen. Somebody hollered, "They're over here!" Then someone yelled, "Let's get the fuckin' dog-eaters," and more than twenty boys from Twin Buttes High, most wearing their blue-and-gold letter sweaters and tight, peg-legged jeans, swarmed over the two cars.

When they pulled the doors open, Mary Hamilton got out and ran. No one chased her. What happened to Joseph Redtail she didn't know until the next day when she heard that he and Jacob Yellow Dog were both in the Twin Buttes Memorial Hospital. It was her fault that

Joseph Redtail was beaten up, the promontory of guilt already projecting into her psychic landscape. She should have fought them off. She shouldn't have gone with Joseph in the first place. The next day she went to the hospital to see him.

The boy's face was still caked with old blood and she couldn't see his eyes behind the swollen brows, the cheekbones buried behind the puffy hide, his brown skin blue, his hair dirty and filled with small pieces of gravel where they had dragged him in the road by his feet.

"Why haven't they cleaned you up?" she cried.

The boy didn't answer.

"It was my fault, Joe," she said. "I shouldn't have gone with you in the first place."

His lips said something but she couldn't make out the words. Then several weeks later he telephoned her, and when her father asked who it was she told him it was Dwayne Thompson, the banker's son.

"Didn't sound like Dwayne. Sounded like some Injun," Arnold Hamilton said.

She met Joseph Redtail down by the river because they couldn't be seen together. "My father would kill me," she said.

"I know," was all he said.

After her father had gone bankrupt at the Hamilton store he'd gone back to his carpenter trade, a solemn, quiet man who worked six, sometimes eight months in a good year.

"The old devil," as Mary's mother, Sarah, spoke of him, had never abused them, never even yelled at either of them. When contention arose in the family he popped another Coors. Behind his back Sarah claimed her husband was "one of those alcoholics," but he argued Coors was made from pure Rocky Mountain spring water. "Never get ta be a drunk drinkin' Coors, I'll guarantee ya that much," he said.

Sarah was a women burdened with a massive, unidentified fear. She was small of bone, but in her later years a fleshy woman. She had never finished high school, married Arnold Hamilton in her junior year and promptly dropped out. She was seventeen and had the child the next year. They wanted more children, but after Mary, for reasons that were not part of the family chronicle, there had been no others. The mother took care of the home—an old-fashioned girl, Arnold Hamilton called her. Her father said he was an old-fashioned husband as well. He "ruled the roost," he liked to say. He was "the cock on the walk," another of his clichés. He was a man full of sayings, and when he put them all together with his rules, the structure of his life was formed and the family lived within the structure, a kind of cage, as Mary thought of it.

It was springtime in Twin Buttes and the willows along the river were in full and furry bud. Mary Hamilton walked with the young Arapahoe, Joseph Redtail. They walked slowly without holding hands, ambling though the forest of cottonwoods at the river bottom, the young leaves of the trees tender, the yellow of bud still on them. They did not talk because Joseph Redtail did not talk much and Mary did not know what to say to a boy who did not talk much. After the rain of the night before their feet got wet in the spring grass and the mud clung to their soles.

They met like that all during that spring, he driving to Twin Buttes in the same old Plymouth with its sun-blistered skin, the windshield still broken where the mob had beaten it in. Early in the month of June she got pregnant and when she told him he said, "You can move to the reservation with me."

Joseph's father was dead. Big man like Joseph, his mother once told him. He was killed in a fight with the Indian police at Hiram Falls. Shot six times, his mother said. She showed Joseph the place where it happened. More than once Joseph had gone alone to the place to meet his father, to see the mist of his spirit pass through the sagebrush, to speak to his spirit if the spirit would come. And when the spirit did not come the boy rejected his father in the same way that the spirit of the father had rejected him. After that he had tried to put his father out of his mind.

"You can live with me and my mother," Joseph had said. "We got a good house. Got a good roof." And that was all he had said.

They were married in the Indian chapel by the Catholic priest because a child could not be born without a father, and a woman must have a husband even if the husband was Arapahoe. Mary heard of another white girl who had married an Indian, the woman still living at Hiram Falls. Her name was Juney White Plum. She was a potter and sold her pots for big money. She had three kids and the people respected her because they said she was a true artist. But Mary Hamilton was not an artist.

After Mary married Joseph Redtail she had to drop out of high school. When Arnold Hamilton found out that she had run off and married an Indian he got drunk and stayed drunk for three weeks. After he sobered up he never spoke to the girl again.

Joseph Redtail's mother had three other children, all of whom lived in the same two-room shack on the reservation. There was Naomi, who should have been in the eighth grade but who refused to go to school. The mother, who was drunk most of the time, could not make the girl do anything. Naomi slept on the army cot in the sleeping tent in the summer and in the winter she moved the cot into the house. There were two other boys, Harvey and Moses, seven and four, who slept together in the corner on a pile of rags under an old army blanket. Joseph slept in the one bedroom and when his mother was home—and many nights she did not come home—she slept in the same room on the other small bed.

Mary Hamilton, now Mary Redtail, sat beside her new husband in the front seat of the battered Plymouth, the seat covered with new gunnysacks so as not to get her wedding dress dirty. They drove directly from the chapel where they had been married to the Redtail shack. The wind through the broken windshield was in her face. What was in her belly she understood, but what was in her mind she could not understand, and she was crying softly.

"Don' cry," was all Joseph had said. He didn't reach over with his large hand to touch her. He looked straight ahead down the gravel road past the other shacks on the reservation, the tar paper on the outside, some sided with slabs. Some of the Indian people lived in old house trailers, the aluminum paint on the roofs peeling. He pulled up in front of the Redtail place and kicked at an empty wine bottle on the hard-packed earth in front of the shack. He didn't open the door of the car for her. When he headed for the shack she got out of the car and followed him over the threshold, she in that white JC Penney dress with the blue ruffle at the bottom, she with no flowers, carrying a small tin suitcase with her clothes.

It was dark inside, the room lit only from the open doorway. Then he hollered: "Hey, you kids com'ere. This here is my new wife." He had a proud look. "Put yer stuff over there," he said to Mary. He pointed at the bed. It was unmade. No sheets. Couple of old army blankets. "Good house," he said. He didn't look at her. "The roof don't leak."

She put her suitcase on the bed. In the dark against the other wall she saw the woman in the other bed. The woman looked dead.

"She ain't usually home," Joseph said as if his mother couldn't hear him. The woman lay still, her back to the door.

Finally Mary spoke. "Did you tell your mother I was coming?"

"She won't care," he said.

After a week Mary, in heavy tears without sobbing, said she would die if they didn't move from his mother's house. She had not eaten for a week. She had been sick and had vomited often, but nothing came up. She dreamed in the night of going home, but in the day she knew she could not go home. She thought of running out on the road and begging for a ride to any place, but the cars went nowhere. She had watched them, the long trails of dust behind, the drivers like flies beating at the window not knowing how to escape or where to go because there was no place to go on the reservation except places from which there was no place to go.

Naomi begged her not to leave, but Mary said she had to leave. "I cannot live in such a place," she said without anger, and after that Naomi said nothing more and was, herself, gone for two days.

The next morning Joseph took Mary for a walk out on the prairie. They walked thought the sage, the ground between the plants nearly barren except for small marbles of black dung left by the cottontails. The soil where they walked was red, the small pieces of red granite like coarse red sand. When he saw her face in the sunlight, he said to her, "I don' want you to die. I been lookin.' I know another place." He said he knew of a place down by the Twin Buttes River where he and some other boys had gone to drink, but it was not as good a place as his mother's house, he said. The roof leaked.

Later that day he took her to an abandoned twelve-foot-long house trailer. The windows were broken out, but nearby she could hear the soft sound of the river over smooth rocks and there were no crying children and no woman who had not spoken to her except to grunt as she pushed past her to fall onto the bed. The trailer had no lights, no water. The plywood floors were curling up from the rain that had leaked in and the snow that had melted. The place smelled of mildew. Nothing to sit on except a couple old sections of cottonwood logs that had been sawed for firewood and were yet to be split. There was no bed and no broom to sweep out the mouse nests and their droppings.

They slept in the car the first night. Then Joseph took her to town and she and her girlfriend, Sherry, found an old table in Sherry's garage and they bought a mattress at the Twin Buttes secondhand store for a dollar and a half. Joseph brought a lantern from his mother's place and two tin plates and a cup. When they drank they passed the cup between them. And they bought a broom.

She had worked hard to fix up the place. Sometimes she felt a nascent joy in it, as if she were living in native times, her man often gone, hunting perhaps, at war perhaps. Although he was of warrior age he was not hunting and he was not at war. Warriors did not work. And warriors did not stay with the women. They stayed with one another and Joseph was with the others at the Big Chief bar, then operated by Ronnie Cotler's father. When they left drunk they slept it off on the prairies and shot sage hens and roasted them over a fire of sagebrush and old cedar fence posts.

She patched the floors, used old rags to fill in the cracks in the roof, and put new cardboard in the broken windows. Three weeks later Mary's mother found her and brought blankets and an old wood stove, so that the place was finally their place. But once when Joseph came to the trailer he found her crying. He said nothing.

Then finally he asked, "Why you cryin' this time? This is a good place."

But she could not answer him. She didn't know why she was crying.

Once when she talked to Sherry she admitted she didn't know much about love. Perhaps, she thought, she had really been in love with Ronnie Cotler. When she was with him she felt a certain excitement she had never felt before. He was a tall boy, handsome and a smooth dancer, but he never said he loved her. He tried to put his hands on her and even then he didn't say he loved her. He kissed her. And he was rough in ways that made her feel hungry in places and at first she thought the feeling was love.

But Sherry said no. "Ronnie just wants to get in your pants. He doesn't love you. He's in love with his dick."

True, Ronnie was always after her, his hands always on her, his hands pinching her breasts, his hands on her butt, and sometimes he tried to put his hands at that place. She had to fight the hands. And sometimes Ronnie Cotler would say, "Don't you love me?"

"Do you love me?" she would ask back.

"You know," he said, kissing her hard and trying to get his hand there, her legs held tightly together like a vise in her father's wood shop. "Keep yer legs together like that," her father said once, "and you won't get into trouble, if ya know what I mean." And then she had made Ronnie Cotler take her home because she had to be in by 11:30.

Still after Twin Buttes had played Greybull and Twin Buttes had won, Mary had felt proud to be with Ronnie Cotler. And after she and

Ronnie had become "an item" as the girls said, the other girls treated her differently. Treated her with respect. Listened to her and wanted to be with her. Once Ronnie had said, "If you don't give it to me I'm going to drop you," and that had scared her.

That night at the drive-in theater she let him put his hand at that place. Then he pulled it out of his pants and he had a wild look in his eyes and he was breathing very hard and looked crazy. She fought him off, got out the car door, and ran for the concession booth. He followed after her and found her standing in front of the counter.

"What's the matter with ya?" Ronnie Cotler asked. He was mad.

"Nothin'," she said.

"What's the matter with you?" he asked again.

"I want a Coke," she said. He bought her a Coke and then he wouldn't speak to her and took her home.

The next weekend she was kidnapped by Joseph and after that she had felt love. And although she knew that Joseph was not one to say many words, still he could not say the word either. When she was with him she felt something deeper—that's how she said it to Sherry. Something she could feel, that she had never felt before and she could not understand.

"We walked and we picked mushrooms down by the river," she told Sherry.

"Mushrooms will kill you."

"He knows the ones," Mary said. "And he never talks much but he smells good." And then they laughed.

"What does he smell like?"

"You know how a dog smells good? He smells like a dog smells good but not like a dog."

"That's 'cause they eat dogs, those Arapahoes," Sherry said.

"That is a lie," Mary said. "That is a white man's lie."

Then they had laughed some more. "His skin is soft like . . ." and she could not think of a word.

"Like silk?" Sherry said.

"Yes, like silk. And he never says loud things. He is very quiet and shy, Sherry," she said. "He never says much because he's so shy."

"Does he say he loves you? He could at least say that."

"No. But I can tell the way he touches me, and the way he looks at me, and I look back at him in the same way, and we talk that way. We talk that way a lot, with our eyes."

"That is soo neat," Sherry said.

"Yes," Mary said. "I am very lucky."

"What does your father say?"

But Mary did not answer and they did not talk anymore that day about love.

The babies were born in their place. Joseph's mother was mostly sober on that day. Joseph had taken his mother from her bed to their place and he had kept her there when Mary began her labor, and although the mother's hands were dirty and unsteady and the nails long and filthy, she had delivered many a child, and she delivered the twins, born in the trailer.

Mary named the firstborn Billy, after her grandfather Billy Hamilton, who had fought in the Second World War with great valor and who was a hero at the Twin Buttes post of the Veterans of Foreign Wars. And she named the second boy Charlie. She liked the name. Happy name, she thought. People named Charlie must be happy. Maybe names can change people, she thought. Names have power.

After that Mary Redtail spent another year in the trailer. Often, when Joseph Redtail came home, he was drunk. He had not finished high school and after they were married he didn't work. They lived on his allotment check, which was small. Enough to buy a few groceries when he didn't drink it up. She couldn't get him to work. When she asked him why he didn't work like her father he was silent. And once when she pressed him and had ended up crying because they needed many things, he finally said, "White men work." When he spoke to her he looked away.

Sometimes he hunted and brought home a deer and one time during the summer he killed an elk, and always they used up all of the animal. Not to use up all of the animal was against the Great Spirit. Once Mary had called Joseph Redtail lazy and when he said nothing back she felt she had wounded him. He left the trailer and was gone for three days. Mostly she was alone except when Sherry came. Sometimes her mother would bring her fresh eggs from her chickens and in the summer, corn and peas from her garden. But when Mary asked about her father her mother had little to say.

"Does he even miss me?" Mary asked. She held back the tears.

"He never mentions your name," her mother said.

"Does he know I love him?"

"He does not understand things like that," her mother said.

But when the boys began to crawl around, her mother insisted that she leave the trailer. The trailer was too small, and it was cold, and even with the stove the children could die when the temperature got to twenty below—one night in February to twenty-seven below. And when Joseph was not there she couldn't chop firewood and keep the fire going all night and still watch the boys. When the fire went out, the trailer soon fell below freezing. The babies' milk froze. The food was frozen. The snow, sometimes two feet deep, made gathering firewood difficult and when she went out for wood there was no one to watch them and to keep them from being burned by the stove.

She had no running water. She'd carried the water from the river and Joseph thought that was good because the water was good. And even when the snow was deep, the trail to the river was kept open because she walked over it once in the morning and once before sundown.

"Why doesn't your husband stay home and help you?" her mother asked.

"He's an Indian, Mother. Indians don't stay at home all the time. They go out and hunt and they do Indian things. And when the hunt is over or they get tired they come back. It has always been that way. The women help one another. That is what the tribe is for." But Mary Hamilton was not part of the tribe.

One Sunday during the summer, without saying anything, Joseph dug a shallow pit for an outhouse. He built a small shed over it, but in the winter the wind blew through it and sometimes the snow blew through it. It was before the third winter that her mother had rented a place, a small old house with a leaking roof in the old part of town. Her mother said Mary should apply for welfare. She applied, but she did not qualify because of Joseph's allotment check. Out of desperation she went to the Indian lawyer, Abner Hill.

"Why do you want a divorce," Hill had asked.

"I gotta have a divorce because I can't get welfare."

"I know your father," Hill said. "Can't he help you?"

"Sometimes the kids are hungry."

"Can't your father help you?"

"He is a poor man," she said.

"He could help you a little."

"Sometimes the kids are sick and need to see the doctor. Billy almost died."

"I'll talk to your father. I know your father."

Then she started to get up and leave. And Hill, seeing that he had touched a tender place in the girl said, "Well, let us see what we can do here."

"I can't pay you," she said.

"Well, someday maybe you can," he said. "I'd be rich if all the people who owed me paid me." He laughed. The girl looked tired. She was wearing the same white cotton dress with the blue ruffle she'd been married in. She held the child, Billy, on her lap. Charlie was with her mother and when Billy became restless and began to cry she got up from where she was sitting and turned her back to the lawyer and let the child nurse. But her breasts were mostly empty.

"It's none of my business," Hill said, "but do you love this man?"

"I don't know," she said.

"You are hardly old enough to get a divorce."

She began to cry quietly, her thin back to the lawyer, but she could not hide the way her body spasmed in the sobbing.

Joseph Redtail was not present when, with Abner Hill as her lawyer, Mary went before Judge Henry P. Hankins. Joseph had, as Hill explained, defaulted, and the law would therefore take her allegations against her husband as true. At the hearing she'd been sworn by the judge himself. Except for the judge the courtroom was empty as usual. When the time came, Abner Hill put Mary in the witness chair. A cold blankness seeped into her body and she began to shake. The judge paid no attention to her suffering. But he liked to interrogate the complaining witness in such cases.

"Did he ever hit you?" Judge Hankins asked.

"No," she said, still shaking.

"Well, did he ever yell at you?" the judge asked.

"No."

"Did he ever run around with other woman?"

"Not that I know of."

"Did he beat the kids?"

"No."

"Sounds like a pretty damn good man," the judge said.

She tried to explain it to the judge. She could not enter into Joseph's private place. It was as if it were a temple or something, a holy place in which he treaded quietly, alone. He came to see the children. Often he was drunk. Sometimes he was beaten up and more than once she had a hard time recognizing him.

"You are Arnold Hamilton's daughter, aren't you?"

"Yes, sir," she said.

"Well, I know your father. Knew him when we went to Harvard and Yale together." He showed his teeth but no smile. "What does your father think of this marriage?"

"He won't talk to me."

"Well, you shouldn't be married to that Indian anyway. We both know that. As a matter of fact there's a law against it. Did you know you broke the law when you married an Indian?"

"No, sir," she said.

"Miscegenation it's called, in case you'd like to know. Well, I'll fix that," he said. "Your divorce is hereby granted."

Then she got a job at the coffee shop at the Twin Buttes Hotel.

There were times when she let Joseph take the boys. She thought it would surely keep him sober, the boys with him, the responsibility. Sometimes he was sober when he brought them back. Once the Twin Buttes Police came to the house and the officer at the door told her that Joseph was in jail, that the police had the boys at the jail and that she should come get them. For over a year after that she didn't let him have the boys. But the man made promises and at times he kept them. When the boys came home they had stories to tell about having met the holy man. He was the Old Man of Much Medicine. His name was Henry Old Deer. He showed them magic things about the Great Mother that they did not know how to explain to their own mother.

One time when the boys were eight and Joseph came for them, Billy didn't want to go. "Why don't you want to go with your father?" she asked.

Billy didn't say at first. He said, "I jus' don' wanna go." But after his father left with Charlie, Billy told his mother that they'd gone hunting and that his father shot an antelope. "The animal was hurt," Billy said. "When we got up to it, its eyes were sticking out because it was so scared and it couldn't run. It was shot in the back and it was dragging its hind legs and then Papa walked up to it and grabbed it by the horns and he took out his knife and cut its throat. And there was blood all over everything and it made me sick."

"He was only putting the animal out of its misery," Mary said. Many times she'd heard her father tell how he'd cut the throat of a wounded elk.

"He could have shot it."

"He was saving bullets," Mary said. "Bullets cost money."

"Then he wanted us to take out its guts."

"He was teaching you the way of a hunter. He was getting the meat to make jerky. When you were a small boy and we lived in the trailer we used to make jerky."

"But his hands were all bloody and he took out the guts. It made me sick," Billy said. "It didn't make Charlie sick. He put his hands inside the antelope and got 'em all bloody, too. He liked the blood."

After that only Charlie would go with his father to the reservation. Often they went to visit the Old Man of Much Medicine. Already the old man had taught the boy to sing the Indian chants, his high voice like the loon. The chants were not words. They did not exist on the page. They were carved into the hide of the universe. They were sounds that flew up to the sun and beyond. The sounds touched the spirits of their ancestors whose sounds were in the same place, whose sounds also came from the lips of the Old Man of Much Medicine, and whose sounds, clean as the prairie primrose, as innocent as the white sago lily, also came from the throat of the boy, Charlie Redtail.

6

As they waited to hear the mortuary door close behind Mary Hamilton, Elmer Johnson smiled at everyone in attendance, including the three corpses. "Well, I guess we better get back to the business at hand. It's way past time to adjourn, if ya know what I mean." He gave a look at Hardy Jacobson.

"Right," Hardy Jacobson said. "It's gettin' a little thirsty in here."

Abner Hill repeated his request. "I just have a few questions to ask Deputy Miller. You don't mind if I ask you a few questions, do you, deputy?"

"Be my guest," the deputy said. He walked over and sat down in the green folding steel chair.

"Well, I don't know," Elmer said to Abner Hill. "You gonna cause us some trouble or somethin'?"

"Didn't figure on it," Hill said. "Just trying to get my file closed."

"Well, like I say, I am the coroner."

It was then that Hardy Jacobson chimed in. "Why you could swear Hill in as the deputy Fetterman County coroner, Elmer. Then he could ask the questions under your control and supervision."

"Good idea," Faye Bosworth said.

"I could do that, I guess," Elmer said. "But a man's gotta be careful ta do everythin' accordin' to the book."

Then before anyone could stop him, Abner Hill began with an easy question. "What time did you discover the body, Deputy Miller?"

"You already know. You was the one who discovered it," Miller said.

"What time was it for the record?"

"There ain't no record here."

"Glad you mentioned that," Hill said. "I almost forgot." He reached into his briefcase and extracted a black tape recorder about the size and color of the Bible. Turning to Elmer Johnson he said, "As deputy coroner I recommend that we record this proceeding to satisfy everybody, the voters and all, that this proceeding has been conducted in strict accordance with the law."

"Well, there ain't nothin' in the law says this proceedin' should be recorded," Elmer said. "I have read the law from top to bottom and bottom to top, an' there's nothin' in there about recordin', I'll guarantee ya that, and furthermore, for the record, I never have recorded any of my inquests."

"For the record, Elmer, you never have been asked before," Hill said. "And if you had you wouldn't have any record to prove it." He strung out an extension cord and plugged in the recording machine behind Elmer's desk.

"I will say one thing, Elmer," Hardy Johnson said, "An' I will say it for the record. It would not look good if somebody asked you to record this inquest and you refused."

"Well, Abner here can't be making any official requests on the record because he is only my deputy," Elmer said, smiling at Hill as if he had finally cornered the man.

Then Hill said, "As a public servant, I must request that this proceeding be recorded because I happen to know that certain people, who are citizens of this county, want it recorded."

"Like who wants it recorded?" the coroner asked, suddenly alarmed.

"Like a certain lawyer named Abner Hill."

"All right, then," Johnson said. "But let me say for the record you are in conflict of interest." He pointed a long, white finger at Abner Hill. "You can't be the deputy coroner and the lawyer for them Redtails at the same time."

"How can there be a conflict?" Hill asked. "How could a search for the cause of death of the deceased create a conflict?"

After a long pause, during which he stared at his shoes again, Elmer Johnson finally said, "Ya got me there, Abner. Let's get on with 'er. Ask your questions."

"Not yet," Hill said. "You have to swear me in."

"So raise yer right hand. Do you swear by the Almighty God, who is the maker of us all, that you will faithfully perform the duties of the deputy coroner of Fetterman County, Wyoming?"

"I have a little trouble with that oath," Hill said. "There is nothing in the statute about swearing to an 'Almighty God, who is the maker of us all.'"

"Okay, okay, okay. So let's get on with it," Elmer cried, his voice in a plaintive quaver.

"What time did you find the body?" Abner Hill asked.

"'Bout quarter 'til five in the afternoon. I was jus' goin' off shift. You come in ta bail the guy out, 'member?"

"Well, it says here in Dr. Billingsley's report that the autopsy was completed at seven the same night."

"That's right," Elmer Johnson interposed from the doorway where Hill had been standing before. "I want the record ta show that I was there when Doc done it. Doc left a hell of a mess, like he always does. I had to close the body up and everythin'. An' I done it before supper."

Hill continued. "And Doc Billingsley's report says that the time of death was four in the afternoon, give or take an hour either way. When did you arrest him?"

"Well, I don't rightly remember," Miller said, scratching his red hair. "I brought him in. He was drunk. Raisin' hell at the Big Chief bar. Ronnie Cotler called in. We had a little set-to with him, nothin' much."

"What do you mean, 'a little set-to'?" Hill asked.

He was causin' trouble out there. You can ask Ronnie Cotler. And he had that kid with him. Kids ain't supposed ta be there, ya know."

"Which kid?"

"One of 'em. Can't tell them breed kids apart."

"I see," Hill said. "Well then, I haven't any more questions of the deputy. I call Jacob Yellow Dog as my next witness. He's out in my pickup truck. I have to go get him."

"Well, wait just a little goddamned minute," Elmer Johnson said. "I never authorized no other witnesses."

"Well, Jake is a witness. A man's gotta call all the witnesses, doesn't he?" Hill turned to go before anyone tried to answer.

Deputy Miller, who was still sitting in the folding witness chair, turned to Elmer Johnson, and when he was sure the man was listening he said, "Ol' Jake was drunk as a skunk that night. He never saw nothin', don't know nothin', and can't say nothin' a man can rely on. You know how them Indians lie."

Elmer Johnson nodded.

Shortly Hill returned with Jacob Yellow Dog following at his heels. Hill checked the recorder and pointed to the folding steel chair beside the casket. The Indian glanced at the coffin, saw the body, hesitated, but at Hill's urging finally sat down. The man was emaciated as if starved, his chest sunken, his cheekbones the most prominent feature, his hair matted and unbraided under a black woolen cap that he pulled down over his ears as if he were cold. He peered around the room and when he saw the other corpses he jumped up from his chair to leave.

"Hold on, Jake," Hill said. "You told me you knew something about this."

"Yeah," Yellow Dog said. "I gotta go."

"Let him go," Miller said.

"Well, I don't think he should go 'til he testifies," Hardy Jacobson said. Then Hardy Jacobson said to the witness, "You take it easy now, boy. You take it easy, son, you understand? Nobody here's gonna hurt ya. We are all yer friends. You know that. Why, Jake, I've knowed you for twenty years more or less. Ain't that right?"

The man didn't answer, his eyes darting from casket to casket.

Hill broke in. "Jake, you were at the Big Chief bar last Friday?"

The man didn't answer.

"I told ya, he don't know nothin'," Miller said, his fingers drumming on the long, black baton he carried at his waist.

"And did you see your friend, Joseph Redtail, there?"

"Yeah," the witness said suddenly, his voice as flat as floors.

"He don't remember nothin'," Miller said.

"I seen him," Yellow Dog said. He cut his words short as if to save the breath. "They was beatin' him up."

"Who?"

"Him." He pointed to the deputy. "Him and that other deputy."

"That is a fuckin' lie," Miller shouted. "You lyin' fuckin' dog-eatin' Arapahoe. I never touched the big bastard."

"Now, Dean, you gotta stop that," Elmer said. "This here is a coroner's inquest and we are on the record. Don't ferget that. Besides, that is no way to speak in the presence of the deceased."

"Well, you gotta stop this shyster from putting on false testimony. That dog-eater is a lyin' bastard, and he knows it. Wait 'til I get him outta here."

"Are you threatening my witness?" Hill asked.

"I ain't threatenin' nobody. But I will tell you one thing: When I get him outta here I will teach that son of a bitch ta lie."

"I think you should ask the deputy to leave," Hill said.

"Maybe so," Elmer said, looking at Miller. "We don't want no trouble here, Dean."

"I ain't leavin'. This is a public hearin' an' I got a right ta be here."

"Well, then, you have ta stop interrupting the proceeding, if you please, Dean," Elmer said.

"I will if that shyster quits putting these fuckin' dog-eaters on the stand to tell their fuckin' lies. I never touched the man other than to just get him into the police car. He was causin' trouble. You ask Ronnie Cotler. An' he had the kid there, too."

"They was drinkin'," Yellow Dog said. He didn't look at the deputy, his eyes still roaming from casket to casket. "They was drinkin' them free drinks from ol' Cotler. An' they was havin' fun beatin' up Joe."

"I was off duty," Miller said. "You can put that on the record. I come along with Deputy Maxfield ta help him. Ronnie Cotler called. You can put that on the record, too."

"Seems like you have somethin' more to say," Hill said to the deputy. "You want to take the stand again?"

"I said all I'm gonna say."

"Well, I hope so," Hill said. Then in a soft voice he began to speak to Jacob Yellow Dog again.

"You forgot to swear the witness," Elmer said. "We gotta follow the procedure here." Then Elmer looked ashamed for having criticized his deputy and said, "You ain't had as much experience at bein' coroner as me. Even I ferget to swear a witness once in a while."

Elmer turned to the frightened Yellow Dog. He was sitting on the edge of his chair as if to leap at any moment. "Raise yer right hand," he said. "Do you swear by the Almighty God, who is the maker of us all, to tell the truth, the whole truth, and nothing but the truth."

Yellow Dog looked confused. He looked over to Abner Hill.

"He can affirm if he wants to," Hill said.

"Well, then, do you affirm?" Elmer asked, not wanting any further trouble at that late hour. Hill nodded his head at Yellow Dog who nodded in return.

"Let the record show the witness has affirmed," Hill said.

"All right, now what happened?" Hill asked.

"You better be sure and tell the truth," Miller said. Then as an aside he added, "Those A-raps don't know what's true and what ain't."

"I know," Yellow Dog said. He looked sick. "I seen it."

"What do you know?" Hill asked.

"I know them deputies was havin' fun beatin' him up. He was jus' standin' there and his boy was holdin' on ta him and they come outta the bar ag'in, and that Cotler pulled the kid offa his ol' man and they started beatin' Joe ag'in. Said he shoulda knowed better than ta get up."

"I never touched the son of a bitch," the deputy said.

"And they was laughin' seein' who could hit him the hardest and the kid was tryin' ta stop 'em. The kid was hittin' 'em with his fists. And they was laughin', sayin' he was sure a little devil. An' when Joe couldn't stand up no more, they took turns holdin' him up and hittin' him."

"Why were they hitting him?" Hill asked.

"Hittin' him because they said he was causin' trouble and they was gonna teach him a lesson. I come outta the bar and I tried ta stop 'em but I couldn't stop 'em." Yellow Dog began to cry.

"That's a fuckin' lie if I ever heard one," Miller said. "An' I've heard plenty." He started toward the witness, but Hill stood in the way and ordered him back with a wave of his hand.

"And where was the boy?" Hill asked.

"I come out there . . . but there wasn't nothin' I could do by then." Yellow Dog finally got the words out.

"Jake, I didn't ask you that," Hill said in a kind voice. "I asked you, Where was the boy?"

"The kid was trying to pertec' his father. Like I say, he was running at the deputies and hitting at 'em, but they just pushed him off of 'em. After while that Cotler threw the kid down and put his foot on his chest so he couldn't get up while the deputies done his old man in."

"You yella lying son of a bitch. How come you makin' that shit up like that?" Miller hollered. "I oughta kick the shit outta ya right here and now."

"Just hold off," Elmer said.

"An' then when they got tired a beatin' on him," Yellow Dog stopped to catch his breath, "an' he was layin' on the ground, they pulled off his pants and they was laughin' real loud an' makin' a lot a noise and ever'-body was watchin'."

"And then what?"

"An' that white man, Cotler, was watchin'. The guy that owns the place."

"And then what?"

"An' the bartender was watchin', too."

"Jacob, what happened next," Hill asked again.

"Them two deputies pulled his pants off."

"You said that."

"And that Mildred Looking Horse was watchin', too. Ever'body was watchin'."

"What did they do then?"

"They drug him up inta the bar with his pants off an' he didn't have no underwear on."

"And then?"

"An' then they threw him in on the floor without no pants on, and ever'body was laughin' and pointin' at him."

"What did they say?"

"Well, that bartender he says, 'That Injun is hung real good. No wonder he can get all them white womens.'"

"Say anything else?"

"The bartender says he was hung like a fuckin' nigger."

"And then what?"

"Well, then that Cotler, he goes up to him an' says right into his face, 'You took my woman, dog-eater.' And he kicks him. An' he is already done in. Ain't talkin'. Ain't even hardly breathin'."

"How many times did Cotler kick Joe?"

"Once. An' when Joe don't say nothin' because he is out, well, he kicks him again, an' says, 'You pay attention to yer superiors. When I speak to you, you answer.' But he was already out."

"And where was the child. The boy?"

"That kid, I seen him. I seen him standin' in the door screamin'."

"And then what happened?"

"I seen them deputies pick Joe up an' they was still laughin' an' they set him up on the bar, an' when they done that a lot a blood come out of his mouth, an' the deputy there"—he pointed to Dean Miller—"that deputy he says, 'You are not being very polite, bleedin' all over the bar like that,' an' so he jus' lets him fall on the floor. Fell on his face. An' pretty soon that fella Cotler, the one that owns the place, he says, 'You guys better get him outta here.' An' the deputies drug him out by his braid. Called it his tail. An' they dumped him in the police car and hauled him out."

"What happened to the boy," Abner Hill asked.

"I don't know. After that I got real drunk."

7

After the coroner's jury rendered its verdict Abner Hill went to the Hamilton shack to deliver Mary Hamilton the bail money he had retrieved from the sheriff. When he sat down at the table for the cup of coffee she offered, he saw the boy watching from the adjoining room, only part of his head visible, one large brown eye on him.

He called to Charlie to come to him and to his surprise the child walked out from behind the door and crawled up on his lap. The man felt the child breathing close to him, felt the small heart pounding, and as he stroked the boy's hair something changed in him, perhaps only came alive from buried places. He had never seen himself as a man with a purpose, a destiny. He had no agenda. He took each day as it came. He took his impoverished clients, their hopelessness, and their pain along with his own reflected pain as if both were part of the landscape.

For a moment they were silent in the room. As he stroked the child's hair with one hand and sipped his coffee with the other he was aware of the new feeling. He had never been a father, never wanted to be one. Something in the configuration of boy to man, the heart of the boy beating against him, the good smell of the boy and his sudden need to protect the child had called up the instinct like pine sprouts make their appearance deep in the forest when sun and seed and earth and water join at some precise moment to bring on the magic of new life. And he saw the woman, Mary Hamilton, different from before, saw her good face. But he did not wish to think of it.

As he stroked the boy's head he looked across the kitchen and saw the other child, Billy, sitting at the kitchen table, watching.

"Come over here, Billy—I guess you're Billy." He turned to Mary. "Have a hard time telling these boys apart."

"That's Billy," she said. "His left foot is a little bit crooked, turned in, like. But it doesn't bother him any. And his face is a little fuller. Can't you see it? 'Specially in the cheeks."

Hill looked. "No, I can't see it," he said.

"Mothers see things like that," she said. "I could tell 'em apart the minute they were born. But nobody else could. Don't you want to go sit on Abner's lap?" his mother asked the child.

The boy shook his head.

"He's shy about things like that," she said. The boy stared at Hill. "But he's very good at numbers and he's way ahead of his class in reading. He was in the school play. But he got scared and ran off of the stage." She laughed, walked over to the child, and patted him on the head. "That's okay, honey," she said. "I 'member one time I was up on the stage. Same stage. I forgot my poem and I just stood there too scared to run off the stage like Billy did. And I wet my pants." She laughed again, and patted the boy again. "Stage fright comes natural in our family."

The coroner's jury had returned their verdict with the finding that "Joseph August Redtail came to his death on or about the twenty-third day of June, 1969, at the hands of unknown assailants." Elmer Johnson suggested the wording.

"Somebody kicked the shit out of that Indian," Hardy Jacobson said.

"Yeah, but I say we should leave this to the county attorney," Elmer said. "We don't have no business stirrin' up trouble by accusing folks. Just make us look bad when some smart lawyer gets his hands on the case and proves that Yellow Dog made it up. You can't never believe an Indian. You know that an' I know that."

"Well, who in hell done it, then, Elmer?" Jacobson asked.

"I ain't got no idea. That's for somebody else ta figger out."

"We shoulda gone along with Hill," Jacobson said. Before the jury had adjourned, Abner Hill had moved that they call Ronald Cotler to testify and that they subpoena his bartender.

"This hearing has gone far enough," Elmer said to Hill when he made his motion. "We are plum out of our jurisdiction. Besides, it's time to get out of here. Have a heart, Abner," the coroner said as if jesting. "A man's entitled to his evening libation." But Hill demanded that the coroner also call Mildred Looking Horse. It was then that Elmer Johnson lost his patience.

"Now damnit all to hell, Abner. Like they say, 'Enough is enough and too much is a plenty.' We ain't gonna do no such thing. I am still the coroner and yer term as deputy has just expired." He squinted his eyes at Abner. "Do you catch my meanin'?" Then he quickly shot Abner Hill that small smile to make it all right again.

After the coroner's jury returned its verdict, Hill took his tape recorder along with the tape of Yellow Dog's testimony and called on Ava Mueller. She'd been elected the preceding fall as the county and prosecuting attorney of Fetterman County, the first woman to hold such an office in the state's history. She'd come from an old-line family in the community, her father a small rancher who ran the family spread that his father had run before him. She'd been a well-known horsewoman, the county barrel racing champion, a champion debater in high school, and an honor student at the University of Wyoming. After she passed the bar, and with no available jobs for lawyers in Fetterman County, she ran on the Republican ticket for the office of county and prosecuting attorney. The people liked the girl. Seemed like she belonged to them. And when it came to making a choice between William H. Haas, the fat, pipe-smoking lawyer and transplanted Missourian who ran on the Democratic ticket and their own Republican Ava Mueller, the choice had been easy and her victory a runaway.

From the beginning Ava Mueller was an astute politician. She knew how to talk to people, to make them feel comfortable in her presence, to make them feel as if they were her protectorates and somehow had a duty to see that her best interests were served. They were not her constituents. Instead, she was their girl as she had always been her father's, and no one could lure her into a position that threatened that safe port.

Hill sat down, plunked his recorder on the desk, loaded it, and gave Ava Mueller his best smile. "We been friends a long time, Ava. Now as friends, pull up a chair and listen to this."

After the tape had played, Hill sat back in his chair and waited for her response. She took the man in for a long moment. She liked Abner Hill although she did not understand him. Finally she said, "I'll have a good talk with Dean Miller. Abner, he shouldn't have conducted himself at the inquest in that manner." She smiled over at Hill and got up as if to say good-bye.

"I'm not interested in your having a good talk with Dean Miller, Ava. I want him prosecuted for murder, him along with Maxfield and Cotler."

"You can't be serious, Abner. A person doesn't prosecute two deputies and a businessman based on the testimony of a drunken Indian. Let's be a little practical about this."

"The boy can testify. He saw it all." But as soon as he said it he wished he hadn't.

"The boy's too young," she said. "His testimony would never stand up against the denials of those three. Besides, Abner, I don't believe Jake Yellow Dog. You can get an Indian to testify to anything you want if it serves his purpose. Weren't Jake Yellow Dog and this Redtail fellow friends?"

"Yes," Hill said. "And you can get a white man to testify to anything if it serves his purpose, too. I want those men prosecuted for murder. Let the jury decide who's lying."

"I'll give it some thought," she said. Then she asked how Mary Hamilton was faring and said she would look in on her boys the first chance. "Always good to see you, Abner," and with that she walked him to the door and shook his hand vigorously as her father had taught her.

Hill was still holding her small hand in his when he said, "Listen, Ava, you tell Dean Miller that if he so much as looks cross-eyed at Jake Yellow Dog he's got me to contend with. Jake's in my care. If anything happens to him I'm personally going to go looking for Miller."

"Sounds like a threat, Abner."

"Threats are in style around here," he said, dropping her hand. He walked down the stairs of the courthouse and out into the clean June air. He walked past the old cannon in the front yard and on up the street to his office, his steps hard, his boots pounding. As he met the people on the street he failed to smile and nod to those who smiled and nodded at him, a major crime in Twin Buttes, Wyoming.

The *Twin Buttes Times* reported on page three that Joseph A. Redtail, a member of the Arapahoe tribe, had died in the county jail, and related the findings of the coroner's jury. Roger Alred, the owner of the paper, its publisher and editor in chief, its social editor, its sportswriter, and its photographer was, at the time, covering the high school baseball game between Twin Buttes and East Casper High. He did, however, make due inquiry of the sheriff's office, and Sheriff William Marsden, then in his second term, said his office had no further information.

The funeral was sparsely attended. Mary Hamilton stood next to the grave, her two small boys, one on each side, looking down into the abyss, the casket sitting on the straps of one of those lowering devices, the lid closed, a bouquet of pink carnations on the top, standard in the $300 service. Mary Hamilton was wearing her white dress with the blue trim. She held Charlie's hand with her left hand and Billy's with her right, both boys in freshly pressed overalls and in their long-sleeved winter shirts.

Elmer Johnson stood by looking sad in his mortician's uniform, his black suit and black tie. Jacob Yellow Dog with his freshly braided hair stood behind Mary Hamilton. He was wearing the same dirty jeans held up with a belt, the end of which hung down like the ten-inch black tongue of a panting dog. Abner Hill leaned up against a cotton-wood tree some distance from the grave site. He held his black Stetson in his hand and his old black leather jacket seemed strangely appropri-ate. He kept back from the grave. Something about funerals that might be catching.

The priest from Hiram Falls mumbled words that few heard and no one understood, and when he finished the priest announced that anyone who wished to say a few words was welcome to do so. Two of Joseph's cousins stood behind Jacob Yellow Dog looking solemn but remained mute, as did Joseph's older sister, Helen Redtail. But Joseph Redtail's coach, Jimmy Lockhart, walked up to the grave and said that Joseph Redtail was the best natural athlete he had ever coached in his twenty years on the reservation and that he was a damn good kid when he knew him. Then Elmer Johnson went over to Mary Hamilton and told her it was time to go and she pulled the boys along with her, Billy looking back at the grave without tears and Charlie staring straight ahead.

After Mary and the boys had been driven away in the black funeral limo, Hill stayed on. He watched the casket being lowered into the hole by the sextant with a couple of skinny Indian laborers standing by, shovels in hands. He'd noticed them during the service. They stood next to the others and he thought them family members. He tried to gather his thoughts, to make some sense of it, to learn something from it, but his head felt empty and nothing came to him except that he felt a deep sense of sadness, not as much over the death of Joseph Redtail as over the waste.

He stood watching the two Indians slowly shovel the dirt into the hole. The one law that seemed to govern the human race more than any other was that misery begets misery. Then the anger began to replace his sadness and suddenly he was glad to be alive, glad to be a man, even glad to be a lawyer. Suddenly he felt as if he were the new paladin of justice. He slapped his hat against his leg, slapped it again, put the hat on, and pulled it down low over his eyes and headed for his pickup.

Abner Hill parked his red Ford pickup next to a dozen other dilapidated derelicts along the north side of the Big Chief bar. Inside the usual assortment of Indians was gathered, drinking and in various stages of inebriation, the nickelodeon blaring western music, the ex-bulldogger tending the bar.

"Where's Cotler?" Hill hollered from the doorway. The bartender didn't answer. Hill walked on up to the bar. "Where's Cotler?" he said into the face of the bartender.

"Ain't seen him all day," the bartender said.

Then Cotler came out of the men's room zipping up his pants. He looked at Hill with surprise, walked over to him, and said to the bartender, "Pour Mr. Hill a drink. What'll it be, counselor?" He offered no smile.

"Shot of Jack Daniel's," Hill said, standing at the bar. "Bud chaser."

"Outta Jack Daniel's," the bartender said.

"Never stock it, to be honest with ya," Cotler said. "My customers aren't the Jack Daniel's kind." The man laughed a tinny laugh.

"I'll just take the beer then," Hill said.

The bartender poured Seagram's 7 into a shot glass and shoved it over to Cotler.

"Here's to you," Cotler said. He lifted his glass.

At that moment Hill said, "Well, this Bud's for you" and smashed the man hard across the side of the head with the full bottle. Cotler fell to the floor.

"What the fuck!" the bartender hollered, stunned, his mouth open.

"I don't drink with scum who kick an innocent man to death," Hill said quietly. He looked down and saw Cotler blinking at the ceiling and emptied the bottle of beer on the man's head. He turned to the bartender. "You want a little of me?" The bartender measured Hill for a moment. Then he reached under the bar and pulled out a .357 Magnum Smith & Wesson with a six-inch barrel.

Hill looked at the bartender and the gun, then he turned and walked away. "You never will be able to explain a bullet hole in my back," he said, and with that he walked on out the door of the Big Chief bar.

*   *   *

That same afternoon Cotler, held steady by his bartender, staggered past Ava Mueller's secretary, and burst into her office. "I want to file charges against Abner Hill, " he hollered. Still wobbly he slumped down into the chair in front of her desk.

"What for?" Ava Mueller asked, surprised. The left side of his face was swollen and blue.

"For this," Cotler said. He pointed to his face. "I want to charge the son of a bitch with assault with a deadly weapon. He hit me with a beer bottle. Goddamn near killed me."

"Really," Mueller said. "Abner never struck me as the aggressive sort."

"The son of a bitch was crazy."

"I seen it all," the bartender said. He still had his bulldogger's hat on. "Attacked him without no cause at all. Jus' come up with a beer bottle and slugged him across the side of the head with it. I thought I'd never get Ronnie to come to."

"I'll have the sheriff investigate," she said.

Cotler said, "You do that. I'm not standing by for that sort of shit." Then the bartender helped him out of his chair and he wobbled out of the room.

"I tol' him to wait 'til tomorrow to come see ya when he'd be feelin' better," the bartender said as he left the office. "But he wouldn't wait. This man is plum mad. And if you don't take care of it he will."

The following week after Mueller read Dean Miller's report she said to him, "There were no disinterested witnesses except seven Indians. They were likely drunk and would testify to anything in exchange for another drink. And the bartender is hardly credible. He's the one who saw absolutely nothing when that Redtail fellow was beaten to death. He sees what he wants to see," she said.

Miller said, "We can't have jack-leg lawyers coming into a public bar and hitting people over the head with a beer bottle in the middle of the day and just forget it. Maybe I better take care of it myself."

"I wouldn't," Ava Mueller said. "And I was supposed to deliver a message to you from Abner Hill. He says you got him to contend with if you lay a hand on Jake Yellow Dog. Just thought I ought to tell you."

"I say there's trouble ahead," Miller said, tipping his hat and walking out. "More trouble than a girl like you might want to handle."

*　　　　*　　　　*

Abner Hill had taken Charlie and Billy Redtail with him on several excursions, places he wouldn't ordinarily go. He argued to himself that these were his friends, these boys. No pretenses with boys. The boys dragged him into the moment, held him there, and the moment was filled with curiosity and the childish astonishment of discovery. Once at the county fair they laughed at the chickens kids from 4-H had on display, the roosters with funny floppy red combs and some white speckled cocks with feathers growing from their feet. They saw the lambs, their wool fluffed and white, the 4-H kids kneeling by their projects holding the lambs' heads up high by their collars when the judges came by. Once, just as the judge reached down to feel the ribs on one of the lambs, the lamb let loose with a rain of black pellets, and the boy quickly threw his hat over them and everybody but the boy laughed.

The following night Hill took the boys to the county fair rodeo. Charlie held on to Hill's left hand and wouldn't let loose, not even when Hill needed to free his hand to get in his pocket for change to buy them each a Coca-Cola. Charlie liked the bucking horses, but not the calf roping. Some of the calves let out pitiful bawls while they were being choked down with the rope that was pulled tight by the horse backing against it.

"They're bawling for their mothers," Charlie said. Once he looked up into Hill's face and said, "They hurt those calves. They're going to jerk their heads off."

"Maybe when you're a man you can stop that sort of cruelty," Hill said.

"Why can't you?" Billy asked. "Mom says you can do anything."

"Lot of cruelty in the world," Hill said to Billy. "It's kinda like the books in the library. You only have time to read so many of them."

"If I was that calf I won't run straight so they couldn't throw the rope on me," Billy said. "I'd zig and zag quick like a fly and the horse couldn't keep up with me."

"Yeah," Charlie said. "If I was the calf I'd just lay down real peaceful right out there in the middle of the arena and then what would they do? Can't rope a calf that doesn't run." And when a cowboy missed a calf with his rope the boys cheered.

"What about the cowboy who won't get any of the prize money?" Abner asked.

"He should pick on somebody his own size," Charlie said.

"He should be a better roper," Billy said.

*　　　　*　　　　*

Mary Hamilton waited for Hill to retrieve his file, his rummaging through boxes stacked in the corner of the single room that served as his office. She pulled her chair to the front of his desk, his old typewriter there, the papers stacked on both sides. Out the window she saw the people nodding to one another at the crossings, the people, even in the rain, not too hurried to stop and exchange a word or two. She told Abner Hill plain out that she had no interest in a lawsuit. "Don't like people who sue all the time," she said. But after Hill's urging she decided to consider it for the boys' sake. Then she added, "We could use the money." And as if to justify the idea, she said, "I couldn't even recognize Joe when I saw him at the mortuary."

Hill looked across the desk at the woman. Had she been born into some other family in some other circumstance she could have been whatever the circumstances offered, a teacher, a socialite, the mother of kids going off to private schools, even a lawyer. He imagined what she would look like in a long, black low-cut evening dress, one with simple lines and a small string of pearls around her neck. He'd seen his mother dressed that way once when he was a small boy, and that night when she was about to leave for the high school prom where she was a chaperon he thought his mother the most beautiful woman in the world.

But a person gets used to seeing people in the same way. He had never seen Mary Hamilton in anything but white—her white waitress uniform and her cheap, white wedding dress. What if her hair were done up with small, soft curls at the temples and the rest fluffed up like the women in the magazines instead of the way she wore her long hair hanging almost straight down her back? But even with the straight black hair and the blue eyes she was beautiful. It was the blue eyes, he thought.

Looking across at her in the privacy of his office Hill felt a certain discomfort—an inability to think clearly, unemotionally as the profession charged. To be alone in his office with her—he had not anticipated such feelings. It had been different in her shack as he sat across from her drinking coffee, the children there, the reminders of her poverty all around. His feelings of sympathy were acceptable under the law. But in his office a different set of feelings emerged and surprised him. The law made no room for such sensations. Man was equipped with a cerebrum charged with the duty of overriding the cells of the primitive mammalian brain. The brain was the problem.

The brain demanded too much of itself, ran wild with itself, fought its own civil wars, hated itself and loved itself, then judged itself. And after the judgment the brain punished. Guilt. The inexorable pain of guilt. Man's brain concocted cold laws and unbending rules of ethics printed in black letters on the white page. This woman was his client and the law made no room for such feelings. He opened the Redtail file.

"Jake Yellow Dog—he may be a drunk, but he isn't a liar," Mary suddenly blurted out. "He was Joe's best friend. An' last night Jake came by to see me," she said. "He waited 'til the boys were in bed. And he was sober. That meant a lot to me. An' he told it all to me." She didn't cry. She turned to watch out the window again. The people, unaccustomed to rain, had no umbrellas. Some of the women held newspapers over their heads to keep their hair from sagging and the rain made small muddy streams in the gutters that carried the gum wrappers and crumpled cigarette packages and the cigarette butts that floated down the gutters like small, soggy logs. Then Mary Hamilton turned back to Hill. He leafed through the pages slowly, his lips moving slightly, his drugstore reading glasses low on his nose.

"We got a case here," he said. "But we have to get past the defendant's motion for summary judgment." The words meant nothing to her.

"I think Ronnie Cotler killed Joe on purpose," she said.

Hill looked up, surprised. "What do you mean?"

"He was jealous of Joe. We were in high school. I was datin' Ronnie when I met Joe. He told me once when I was waitin' on him over at the coffee shop, 'Someday you'll be sorry you married that war-whoop. He'll end up drowned in whiskey and planted in the graveyard along with all rest of 'em.' An' he laughed in my face. That's what he told me, Abner."

8

Of late Ronnie Cotler had been hanging with a baby-faced, cold-eyed man named Emmett. The blond man had no other name in the community. He had drifted in from nowhere. Liked to shoot. Nothing like cans or road signs. His targets were live—cats, dogs, owls, prairie dogs. In the small town, rumor had it that he liked to shoot people. Some said he'd shot Betty Yellow Calf. They'd found her lying out on the prairie where she'd gone to pick fresh sage for the half-moon ceremony. The right side of her face had been blown off, "perhaps by a bullet" Dr. Billingsley had written in his autopsy report. He could come up with no other explanation. He reported that he'd never seen such devastation in his entire career.

Emmett shot a .222-caliber Super Swift Magnum with a ten power scope. He liked to see the bullet explode when it hit its target. He was a man who laughed more than he spoke, a strangely irrelevant laugh, as when he shot the head off a kitten at two hundred yards.

Late in August Abner Hill drove out to the Big Chief bar to interview Mildred Looking Horse. The man, Emmett, was there. Hill's best friend, Ace Yokum, had accompanied him. Yokum, a long, skinny sort, ran the Skelly station at the corner of Main and Washington. As he often did in the evening, Hill stopped by to have a drink with Ace in the back room of Ace's station. He told Ace he planned to go out to the Big Chief bar to interview Mildred Looking Horse where you could usually find her. Yokum said he was going along. Just for the ride, he claimed.

"I don't need any protection, Ace," Abner said. "I can handle it."

"Why sure you can," Ace said. "I declare I have no doubt," the scoff barely hidden. "But I'm going—just for the ride," he said again. He gave Hill the look he'd seen many times that meant the matter was settled.

Hokum was self-educated, read Tolstoy, Hemingway, and Dostoyevsky and knew a little about the art of Braque and Chagall. He'd been in the Special Forces in the Korean War, left a lot of North Korean kids fatherless he said, and had an unexplained soft spot for Indian kids. Sent twelve or fifteen of them to college over the years— his hobby was all he would say about it. Did it quietly. Hill liked Ace not only because he was loyal to a fault, but because without any self-consciousness he displayed a large range of sensibilities. Given cause, the man could cut your throat to the bone with his hunting knife, sleep like a baby afterward, and the next morning cry over a poem that Abner Hill might write, Ace being the sole soul in Twin Buttes Abner Hill ever trusted with his poetry.

Yokum was known as one who was best entertained in a good fight, justified or not. Never known to have lost one. Fighting was an art. No karate, nothing fancy. Simple things, like a sudden first blow to the trachea or a stab with the long neck of a beer bottle in the solar plexus. He was also good with a knife.

Before that evening Hill told Ace Yokum about the incident with Cotler at the Big Chief bar. They both had laughed about it.

"This Bud's for you," Ace said, and he laughed again. "Well, my friend, your ass is grass." He walked to the closet in his office, extracted a loaded snub-nosed .38, and handed it to Hill. "Stick this in your pocket," he said. "And keep your eyes open. He's a snaky coward with a memory. Worst kind. Never kill you himself. Probably pay some drunk fifty bucks to blow your head off. Makes it worse. You never know where it's coming from." Then he stopped and thought a minute, took a long draw from a bottle of Cabin Still, and handed it to Hill. "On second thought, I could just slip out there some night and take care of the bastard for you. Be my pleasure."

Hill laid the pistol back on Ace's desk.

They'd talked at times about justice, Hill insisting that a good lawyer could make the system produce justice. Justice was the product of a scrap pile of tools. The tools were rusty, corroded, and mostly in the hands of the enemies of justice, the big insurance companies, the corporations, government. But the tools were there and a lawyer had to use them and create justice with them.

"I always figured justice was something you took for yourself or you didn't get any," Ace said. "Kinda like the spuds on the platter. If ya want it ya gotta grab it. Now take that Cotler, for instance. Why don't we just shortcut this whole fuckin' process and pay him a little visit?"

"You were trained to do justice in one way. I been trained another," Hill said.

When the bartender at the Big Chief bar saw the two men enter, he pulled out his .357 Magnum and laid it in front of him. "I don't want no trouble," he said. "I'll buy you boys a drink and then you leave, peaceful." Mildred Looking Horse was sitting at the far end of the bar, three young Indian men were gathered around her like dogs after a bitch in heat. She was already drunk but still young and pretty.

"Why, we didn't come for trouble," Ace said. "We have come in peace. On a mission of justice." His voice was high and biting with sarcasm.

It was then that the blond man with the cold, blue eyes, the man they called Emmett, walked over to where they were standing at the bar.

"Did I hear you say something about justice?" Emmett said. When he spoke his lips moved only as necessary to form the words and his eyes did not match the words.

"Why, I do declare, if this man doesn't have good hearing," Ace said, turning to face the blond man.

"And what is justice?" Emmett asked, his light blue eyes like cold glass.

"And who, may I ask, would be inquiring?" Ace asked.

"Justice is when I'm allowed to do whatever I like. Injustice is whatever prevents my doing so," Emmett said.

"That so?" Ace said. "I live a pretty just life then."

"As do I," the blond man said back. He laughed. Then he reached in his pocket, flipped open a five-inch switchblade, and began to pare his fingernails that were already closely trimmed. His hands were small and clean, his fingers delicate. He had never taken his eyes off of Ace even as he manipulated the knife. Now he smiled, but the smile was as cold as the eyes. "The saying was not original with me. Those were the words of Samuel Butler. Of all crimes, plagiarism is the worst."

"Well, do tell," Ace said. "Worse than murder?"

"Murder is not a crime," Emmett said and laughed, "unless you consider the universe as criminal. The universe kills as the whim may please it, viciously, without mercy, without logic. The universe is a mass serial murderer. Twelve hundred innocent people died in a hurricane yesterday in Haiti. I trust you read of it?"

"Don't have time to read the paper," Ace said.

"No one charges the universe with a crime when innocent people die. Murder is part of the natural law. But plagiarism—that is the worst of crimes, for nothing is identical in the universe, not even identical twins born of a splitting egg. Everything, every leaf, every fingerprint is unique and different. The energy of the universe is creativity. Murder is in harmony with the universe. It creates change." Emmett's eyes were still locked on Ace, the knife working easily, gently by feel at his fingernails.

"Well, I declare if you are not a philosopher," Ace said. "One does not often come across a philosopher in these parts, wouldn't you say, Abner?"

"Right," Hill said.

"And what pray tell do you do?" Ace asked.

"I entertain myself as does the universe. I create change. I cut jugulars, carotid arteries, and blow out the gray matter contained within the cranium known as the brain, all in harmony with the universal law of murder. I am an artist," Emmett said. He laughed again, his laugh thin and icy.

The bartender watched, fascinated, his mouth open, the man having forgotten the gun in front of him.

"I think ultimate justice is freedom," Hill ventured.

"No doubt you think that," Emmett said. "But you are a criminal in your own right, an ignorant one at that, I might say. You hold yourself out as the defender of the rights of the accused. By what right do you impose yourself into the game of the universe? By whom were you invited? When an innocent man is executed you protest to the heavens, but when two hundred twenty-seven were killed yesterday in that earthquake in Yugoslavia, you say it was an act of God."

"I suppose you believe doctors who attempt to save lives are equally ignorant," Hill said back.

"You are not as ignorant as I thought," Emmett said. "Absolute justice is achieved by the suppression of all contradiction: therefore it destroys freedom."

"Come again," Ace said.

"That, too, was not original with me. That wisdom emanated from the lips of Albert Camus."

"Anything original with you?" Ace asked in his high, accusing voice.

"Yes, of course," Emmett said. He laughed. "I am the first to isolate the primary laws of the universe and to extrapolate them as they apply to the human condition and to thereafter put them into action."

"Do tell," Ace said.

"Action is the first law of a dynamic universe. Action brings change. Nothing stands still in the universe. Whole worlds are being created and destroyed as we speak. Even the mountains are in constant change. Nothing is static."

"I do declare," Ace said, "I think the man has something there. In accordance with the law of the universe we should change the scene in here."

Hill saw the look . He had seen it before, the slight widening of the eyes, the teeth coming together, the small smile. He stepped in between Ace Yokum and Emmett, his front toward Emmett.

"It makes no difference to me which one of you I cut first," Emmett said. "Your entrails on the floor will be as pretty as your friend's." He laughed, the knife in his palm, the small hand closed, ready.

It was then that the bartender pulled out his .357 Magnum with the six inch-barrel. "Ace," he hollered, pointing his gun at him. "You walk out that door. Hill, you go with him. Emmett, give me that knife. I ain't havin' no murders on my shift. We could lose our license."

Abner grabbed Ace by the arm and pulled him out the door with him.

"Farewell," Ace hollered. "I shall live to fight another day. I don't know who the fuck said that. But I'll take credit for it." Then he laughed as Hill shut the door behind them.

On the morning the clerk called the court to order it was snowing again, the flakes small and without much moisture, the January freeze deep and unrelenting. The temperature had hung near ten below for more than two weeks, the countryside in cold storage, the willows bent in snow and leafless, the cottonwoods barren and stark like frozen corpses protruding from the ground, the snow like drifting sand in the wind, the sky thick and gray.

The Redtail boys, by then eleven, sat in the Fetterman County courthouse, a boy on each side of his mother. Each wore new flannel shirts, Charlie's blue like his father was buried in and Billy's red. Billy liked bright things. Both boys had new home haircuts, the uneven, ragged edges left by home clippers wielded in the hands of Mary. Abner Hill sat them in the front row. Perhaps the judge would see them, this clean-cut family, this wearied mother, see that she was as white as his own woman, this woman whose children were the children of the dead. Maybe the judge would refuse to throw the case out like he'd thrown out so many others. Perhaps this once he'd let the jury decide.

Abner Hill at counsel table and the Redtail family in the front row waited for the judge to take the bench.

Harold Yancey, the lawyer on the other side who represented the sheriff's insurance company, was seated at the other table in the courtroom. Yancey had a strategy, a litigator famous for his strategies. He was also Wyoming's representative to the House of Delegates of the American Bar Association and a past president of the Wyoming Bar Association. For twenty years he had been rated A-1, the top rating any lawyer could be awarded by *Martindale and Hubbell,* that imperious publication that judged the skills of the nation's lawyers. Lawyers with the highest ratings usually represented the insurance companies, the banks, and big business against the people or at least that's what Abner Hill said, he who hung so low on the rating totem pole that in the eyes of *Martindale and Hubbell* he deserved no rating whatsoever.

The trial judges of the state, mostly from smaller towns, were in deep awe of Harold Yancey. They looked to him for the last word on the law and were reluctant to contradict him. He knew the law, all right, particularly the law that favored his corporate clients that included the oil companies and the railroads. Should a judge rule against Yancey he always appealed. The clients paid for the endless hours of his appeals, Yancey quoting Abraham Lincoln in defense of his billing: "A lawyer's time and advice are his stock in trade."

But Yancey's appeals paid off. He had influence on the Wyoming Supreme Court. He had dutifully made his contributions to the campaigns of the various governors, Democrat or Republican, but mostly Republican. He argued to his partners at their budget meetings that if you were going to contribute to a campaign, contribute enough so it creates an obligation. "One thing a politician remembers and that's where the money comes from. Dry up the money and the politician withers like a flower in a piss pot." Yancey was famous for his picturesque metaphors. "And you never give with the thought of getting back. My mother always said, 'Giving is blessed.' But when the chips are down, and the nomination of your man for the judgeship is lying on the governor's desk, that's when you call the governor up and you talk to him like a friend. You never remind him what you gave him. You just tell the bastard what a good son of a bitch your man is and how he will serve the state and make the governor proud of his appointment—things like that.

"Then one day you look up and there's your man sitting on the supreme court, all robed up, looking judicial as hell and staring down at you like he never met you, like you are a complete fucking stranger to him. And you look up at him sitting there acting like he knows everything there is to know about the law, his nose up, and you think, last week that son of a bitch couldn't find his ass with both hands or a precedent in the law books if you led him to it. Last week that son of a bitch was three months in arrears on his office rent and now he's a supreme court judge looking down at me and I am looking up at him until my neck gets sore, and I am calling him 'Your Honor' and kissing his ass. That's when you have to be careful not to get too cynical. That's when you hope the son of a bitch has a memory. Most do."

Harold Yancey believed in the system. Said it worked. And he pointed to the Wyoming Supreme Court as proof of that fact. "Why," he said, "we have the best judges in the country sitting up there. Friends of mine. Good men, guys I worked with in the bar association who don't go around making decisions out of fucking bleeding hearts."

Yancey had been hired by the sheriff's insurance carrier, Hartford Mutual, to defend the suit Abner Hill had brought against the sheriff and his deputies for the wrongful death of Joseph August Redtail. He'd read the file the company's adjuster handed him along with a transcript of Elmer Johnson's coroner's inquest that included the testimony of Deputy Miller, Jacob Yellow Dog, as well as the autopsy report of Dr. Billingsley.

Hartford Mutual's adjuster had interviewed Ronnie Cotler at his home on Twin Buttes Road in late August. The adjuster and Cotler were sitting on Cotler's verandah overlooking the Twin Buttes River. Cotler offered the adjuster an Old Gold cigarette, which the adjuster took, and a shot of White Horse, which he refused, it being 4:30 in the afternoon and according to company policy too early by half an hour for any alcoholic beverage.

"That Redtail was a big bastard," Cotler said. "Troublemaker. Before he died my old man had trouble with him. Used to come in an' threaten to tear up his pawn shop if he didn't give him some drinkin' money. Already pawned everything he had. It'd be two, three days before his allotment check was due and Redtail would be in there claiming the old man had cheated him an' that he was going to kick in the showcases if the old man didn't lend him ten bucks. I don't know how many times he had to call the sheriff on the big bastard."

"I got his record from the sheriff," the adjuster said. "Not much on it but drunk."

"An' the bastard was out there at my bar that day raisin' hell. Had his kid along with him, too."

The adjuster wrote on a pad with wide blue lines. He looked more like a Safeway stocking clerk than a representative of one of the world's largest insurance companies.

"He was tryin' to bully the bartender into givin' him a drink. Said he'd pay him when his allotment came in. That's like sayin' the check's in the mail."

"What happened?"

"I saw it all," Cotler said. "I saw the big bastard pick up a beer bottle and start for my bartender and I hollered at the bartender just in time."

"Then what?"

"I called the sheriff. But before the sheriff got there my bartender— I mean he's been around—well, he grabs him and dumps him on the floor like a sack of spuds and he didn't get up for a while. Then the deputies came and they hauled him off. Good men, those deputies."

"See anybody kick him?"

"No. Nobody kicked him while he was at my place."

"What about Yellow Dog's testimony?"

"Can't believe nothing those Indians say. I remember one time Yellow Dog told the sheriff he seen one of those flyin' saucers come down on the reservation and suck up his mother and his two uncles. They'd been dead for twenty years."

The adjuster put it all down with a ballpoint pen, including the part about the flying saucers, and Ronald Cotler signed it, his statement engraved for all time in the official records of Hartford Mutual. Then the adjuster tucked the statement in the file, which was the last report that Harold Yancey reviewed as he prepared his strategy in the case.

In the first place, Yancey reasoned, even if the deputies had killed the Indian in a cruel assault in pursuit of some sadistic amusement, Hill couldn't prove it. Even if his witness, Yellow Dog, were sober enough by the time of the trial, no one would believe him. But Yancey had seen plenty of white people lie as well. People lie, he said. Lying is not race specific, but in Twin Buttes people thought that Indians lied as was convenient.

Maybe Mary Hamilton's ex-boyfriend, Cotler, administered the fatal kick to the Indian. Who could prove which blow, which kick, whose assault caused the death? Yancey could raise such questions on a motion for summary judgment and if Hill couldn't produce affidavits or deposition testimony to prove who did what, the judge could throw Hill's case out and Yancey would have saved his clients a trial and a lot of money in attorney's fees.

On the other hand, maybe the Indian died of injuries inflicted when he resisted arrest. In that case Hill had no cause of action unless he could prove that the force applied was excessive. It was Dr. Billingsley's autopsy report that caused the trouble. Billingsley's inventory of injuries created a mental image of what happened almost as if the jury were watching the whole thing take place. You could see the man being beaten and kicked while he was down. The liver was damaged, the kidneys both kicked loose, the lungs bruised, and there were numerous other internal injuries listed in the technical jargon of the medical examiner, including a ruptured spleen. After that there was the fractured jaw and a hairline fracture over the left orbit of the skull. Which injury caused his death and who inflicted it posed the question and created the peg upon which Yancey could hang his defense. But such a defense was too predictable for Harold Yancey.

Moreover, when all the evidence was in, even if his clients were as pure as puppies, it looked bad. Sheriff looked bad and so did his deputies. Pretty soon the jury could begin feeling sorry for the dead man and the two "quivering-lipped kids," as he called them. As the evidence came in Hill could argue about "reasonable inferences" so that the jury might find all three, the two deputies and Cotler, had joined in some kind of a macabre conspiracy to kill the Indian. Nobody claimed that jurors in Fetterman County were Indian lovers. But they usually exhibited a sort of raw, frontier sense of fair play. And it wasn't fair for three men to kick the life out of an Indian, even if he'd been a troublemaker. The Indian had been in jail for a week and the sheriff had never called a doctor. Besides, this Cotler character made his living off drunk Indians and some of "the petunia-souled," as Yancey called them, might look askance at his ignominious enterprise.

Yancey had checked out Abner Hill. He wasn't known as any Clarence Darrow, and he had no rating in *Martindale and Hubbell*. Yet he could make the obvious arguments. And although some might see him as a parasite living off an Indian clientele there'd likely be a parasite or two on the jury. In Twin Buttes it was hard to determine who was or wasn't a parasite. Safeway's sales jumped 40 percent on the day the Indian allotment checks came out and the owner of the Chevy garage viewed the Indians as a ready market for the worn-out pickups the ranchers traded in. If a tally were taken, nearly everyone in Twin Buttes, directly or indi-rectly, was a beneficiary of Indian money. If it was dirty money most of people in the county were dirty.

Even though Hill was likely no match for Yancey, Yancey knew that before the case was over Hill would portray him as a hot-shot, out-of-county-lawyer who came to town to pull the wool over the locals' eyes. That, along with Billingsley's report and those two kids sitting there, could deliver Hill the edge.

Cotler wasn't covered by Hartford's policy and had no insurance of his own and therefore had to hire his own lawyer. Yancey recommended a kid fresh out of law school, a tall, blond kid named Gerald Hersey from Casper who thought Yancey was hovering up there close to Oliver Wendell Holmes. By getting the Hersey kid for Cotler, Yancey could call the shots and keep everybody in line. He'd keep the case simple. If you made the defense too complicated you left the jurors little choice but to follow their instincts and that usually led to a plaintiff's verdict. Then Yancey would have to appeal and if the facts surrounding Redtail's death were too blatant, and got too much publicity, even the state supreme court might let the verdict stand.

In a pinch Yancey knew the sheriff could get some desperate snitch to testify that another inmate had been in the cell with Redtail, that they got into a fight, and that the injuries Redtail suffered were inflicted by the other prisoner. But that required an alteration of the records to show who exactly was in the cell with Redtail and when. The prosecu-tor might get into it and by the time all the facts got sorted out, who could predict what new ugly genies might escape from such a bottle of calumnies. "When you countenance a false defense," Yancey told the kid, Gerald Hersey, "one way or another it will come around to bite you in the ass, big-time."

So Harold Yancey's strategy was one that Abner Hill could never have anticipated. Yancey would admit it all—admit the beating, the excessive force, the negligent treatment of the prisoner and the pris-oner's death as a result. Admit it all! That way none of the bloody details from Billingsley's report would ever come in. "Once we admit the wrongful death they can't offer any evidence to prove what we've admit-ted," Yancey told Gerald Hersey. "Now, what's a fucking drunk worth to a couple of breed kids? So the kids were deprived of his 'care, comfort, advice, and society'? What did the kids lose? I'll tell you what they lost.

They lost a drunk as a role model. They lost the shame and degradation of a father staggering onto the front porch for the whole neighborhood to see. They lost a father and gained a little peace, a little dignity." Yancey was already making his argument.

"How much money is a drunk worth? Give them respect. Give them ten grand. That's a lot of money. More money than those kids would ever see from their father." Then he laughed and said to the Hersey kid, "The company will love it if I can get this case off their asses for ten grand which is half what it would cost them if I defended it—even if I won. And we'll get your client off on the coattails of my clients."

Judge Henry Hankins came sauntering onto the bench in his crimson robe like Moses ascending on high. He dropped into his oak swivel chair as if his legs had suddenly given way. The padding on the seat had worn through, but His Honor refused to have it repaired. Said the big hole was the one thing he could visualize that stood for his life's work and they weren't going to cover the evidence of it with a new upholstery job.

He struck his gavel, a present from the local Lion's Club commemorating his twenty years of service on the bench, and called the District Court of Fetterman County to order. He ran the fingers of both hands through his thinning hair, looked over his glasses at the mostly empty courtroom, and with a face that put one in mind of a brooding parson, announced the case.

Then from his high perch the judge looked down, first at Harold Yancey and then, out of deference to his reputation of impartiality, at Abner Hill. He spoke as if he were dropping off to sleep while reading from the Scriptures.

"Mr. Yancey, tell me the issues here. You know how I feel about these motions for summary judgment. They are dumped on us judges as a matter of course with or without good cause ."

"But Your Honor—" Yancey began.

"Approach the bench, Mr. Yancey," the judge interrupted. At the bench the judge spoke in a stage whisper, "My dear sir, as you well know, our time on this earth is limited. Yet our lives are wasted, our temperaments made inordinately worse, and our hemorrhoids irritated beyond endurance by these frivolous motions. And why? I'll tell you why. You file these endless motions so you can charge your clients at some inordinate rate while we of the judiciary are called upon to listen to your ghastly arguments. I remind you, Mr. Yancey, you make more in one day than I do in a month. Therefore, could you spare me the usual, empty, inane polemics?"

Yancey regretted more than ever that Judge Hankins had taken the bench before Yancey's time. But he would deal with the judge. He had dealt with his kind before. Yancey put on his famous intimidating scowl and aimed it at the judge. "The scowl doesn't show on the record," Yancey once told his partners.

"Now, Mr. Yancey," the judge prompted again, "what are the honest issues here?" Then Judge Hankins stretched his mouth as if to smile, which exercise revealed a mouth plentiful of teeth but a paucity of mirth.

"Your Honor," Yancey began. He spoke into the judge's face so that the judge leaned back from the edge of the bench. "Indeed, I will not belabor any but the most irrefutable arguments that any court would require of me, short of malpractice. Should I remain silent and permit this dissimulation to go to trial without having first filed and argued this motion, your inquiry would then be, 'Why, oh, why, Mr. Yancey did you not save this court and jury the trouble, the time, our lives, and the irritation of our respective hemorrhoids by having long ago filed such a dispositive motion as the one before Your Honor?'"

"Very well, Mr. Yancey," the judge said. "Then dump it on me. Let's see what it grows."

In the front row of the courtroom the boy, Billy Redtail, was intensely focused on first the judge and then Yancey. Charlie was staring at the ceiling. He tried to see the face of his father. He knew that the case was supposed to be about his father. But he could not see the face of his father, nor hear the sound of his father's words. The boy tried to listen to the arguments of the attorneys and he could not understand how words had taken the place of his father. A father was not words. He wished the lawyers would stop talking. He thought that if the lawyers would stop talking the spirit of his father might enter the room.

At three in the afternoon on the same day and while the court was still in session Ace Yokum parked his pickup on the north side of the Big Chief bar. He took the front steps three at a time, ducked to miss the top of the door frame as he entered, and took a stool next to Sammy White Eagle. He nodded to the Indian. The bartender, his back to the door, was carrying on a conversation in high holler with Jimmy Hungry Horse and hadn't noticed Yokum come in.

"We don't owe you redskins nothin'," the bartender said. "You give up this portion of the reservation back in 1887."

"No," Hungry Horse said, "we never give up nothin.' You stole it. An' we are gonna take it back. Town a Twin Buttes, too." The Indian stopped as if dreaming, his eyes fixed on the blinking Bud sign. "And when we do I am gonna own this bar and I am gonna throw yer ass out." He laughed so the bartender wouldn't take him seriously.

"You be lucky I don't throw *your* ass out," the bartender said. "I been lookin' for somebody to throw out all day."

"How 'bout tryin' me?" Ace Yokum said.

The bartender looked over at the bean pole and for the first time saw Ace sitting at the bar.

"Why yeah," he said. "You'll do." He started over to where Yokum sat. And as he reached over to grab the bean pole by the collar he saw the knife flash and felt the blade at his throat.

"Why don't you buy the house a drink?" Yokum said.

The bartender backed off. "Good idea," he said. "Never thought of it 'til now."

Yokum stuck the knife into the bar, the pearl handle quivering. Then the Indians crowded up like bees on fresh honey and the bartender started pouring the drinks. They wanted whiskey, about fourteen of them that could still get to the bar. When he had poured drinks all around, the bartender turned to Yokum. "What'll it be?"

"Double shot a Cabin Still," Yokum said. As the bartender was pouring, Yokum said, "You tell Cotler that if something happens to my friend, Abner Hill, I will personally look him up. I mean, if he gets run over or somebody accidentally shoots him or if he wakes up in the morning with a heart attack—I mean if my friend so much as gets a bellyache, I will be over here to see Cotler. Understand?"

The bartender nodded.

"You tell Cotler that he is personally guaranteeing Abner Hill's safety." Yokum pulled his knife out of the bar. "Hand me that revolver you got laying there under the bar—by the barrel." The bartender reached under the bar and handed the revolver to Yokum. Then Yokum downed his double shot, thanked the bartender, walked out the door, and as he walked out, he emptied the gun of its bullets and threw it far into the weeds.

9

Besides the lawyers and the judge the only other officials in the court-room were the court reporter and the old bailiff in the back who dropped off from time to time and awakened himself with his own loud snorts. Mary Hamilton watched the judge. Over time he had slid even farther down into his chair so that his head was barely visible above the level of the bench. She thought the law was not about human beings. The law was about old cases, and names attached to the long dead. The law was dead and neither the judge who himself looked nearly dead, nor the lawyers, were interested in the two small boys she had to support, two small boys whose father had been murdered.

How could the judge throw out their case before a jury had heard it? Surely, marrying an Indian did not deprive her children of their rights as citizens. She had said as much to Abner Hill. Surely murder meant something. Surely justice meant something. Surely her need to feed hungry mouths and put shirts on the backs of skinny boys meant something. But what the lawyers talked about meant nothing to Mary Hamilton.

Billy was becoming restless. She had warned the child before they had gotten to court that morning, he on one chair and she on another polishing his boots. "Billy, you be a good boy. If you're not good the judge can throw our case out."

"Yeah, Mom," he said. "Don't worry. Charlie says the white man's court is bullshit."

"Charlie, did you say that?" she asked as she moved to Charlie's boots, an old black sock as a polish rag.

The boy didn't answer.

"Did you say that, Charlie?" she asked again.

"The old man told him that," Billy said. "He's always talkin' about what the old man says. He's just an old Indian."

"He's not an old Indian," Charlie said. "He knows everything."

She shouldn't let Charlie go with Henry Old Deer so often, she thought. Since his father's death the old man had often come for Charlie, sometimes every week. Charlie begged to go. And she had let him go thinking that the old man brought comfort to the child. But Billy was right. He was an old man. Perhaps he was poisoning the boy's mind.

Charlie, had not spoken much since *the time,* as his mother called the day of his father's murder, and when she dared look into the child's eyes she felt as if she were invading his private world. In that way the boy was like his father. But with Billy it was different. His mind was always open, always spilling over with the wonderment of a child. She could read Billy like a book, she said. But if the boys were books, since *the time* she could rarely break open the cover of Charlie's mind.

She thought it better to let the memory of *the time* fade rather than freshen it with talk. Let it die. In fact, she had not once talked about *the time* with the boy so that exactly what he saw she didn't know. Abner Hill told her Charlie had seen it all. The boy could be called as a witness, he'd said. All Hill had to establish was that Charlie knew the meaning of an oath. Any lawyer could prove that with a few preliminary questions before the judge. But no, she said, she was not going to let Hill call Charlie as a witness and put this child through the horror of *the time* again, not for any money.

Hill had agreed. "We can lose the lawsuit and all we've lost is the money. But we don't want to lose Charlie." He spoke as if he were the father and Mary had felt warm toward the man, although she had not allowed herself to see him in any other light than "Lawyer Hill" as she often called him, both to his face and to others as well.

She had not had a man since Joseph, nor one before. She had come to think of love as a dirty trick that Mother Nature played on the human race. The lovers were smitten. People called it "falling in love." The child in the womb was the price, the disease of motherhood, a lifelong ailment from which no mother recovered. Her mother had lived the tragedy before her, the drunken brooding father, and after that Mary had fallen in love with Joseph. Even if a love were perfect, which none were, all love affairs ended in tragedy—even the perfect ones. One died before the other. And the pain of it and the loneliness was what lingered, that and faded memories that made the pain worse. Joseph had been dead to her long before he had been murdered. And she knew the pain.

She had asked herself if given the chance would she pay the price again? No, she thought. Not again. Once in a lifetime is enough. One is born once, loves once, and dies once. Each is sufficient in itself.

She had had plenty of opportunities. The men had been after her at the café, "that doll with the high-ridin' ass" some called her when she was out of earshot. She joked with them and was often quick and funny with an almost golden laugh. But over the years the townspeople, especially the ten o'clock crowd, learned that the flower was not available for the picking. Look at it, yes. But do not touch it if you don't want a cup of hot coffee spilled down your front.

She made no effort to be pretty, didn't fuss with her hair. Let it grow as it willed and it willed to flow naturally over her shoulders. She put nothing on her lips, the large mouth left bare for men to stare at as if an intimate part of her body were naked. She laid no makeup on her eyes. But the men often spoke to each other about them in her presence. "Look at the eyes on that baby," they would say and they'd look at her and smile. "Make you think of Elizabeth Taylor?"

"Makes me think of something else, if ya know what I mean," somebody else would say and the men would laugh. But Abner Hill had never spoken in that way to her.

No, they would not put Charlie on the stand, Hill said, but he knew that Yancey would chop Yellow Dog into small, piteous pieces. "And Yellow Dog is all we have, he and Billingsley's report," he said.

"Weren't there others there?" Mary asked.

"Most were lying around on the floor passed out," Hill said. "And you know how they're afraid to testify in the white man's court. They're deathly afraid of the deputies and especially of Cotler." The Arapahoe people called him *Ho-mon-a-ro-ho* which meant "the rattler." They had seen it many times before, the nod from Cotler and the big bartender coming over the bar to smash the skinny bodies.

And although Hill had finally found Mildred Looking Horse sober and at home she wouldn't talk to him. She was Shoshone. She said this wasn't her business. It was the business of the Arapahoe people. Hill thought she would have talked to him but her father was on the joint business council, and didn't want his family mixed up in any intertribal politics.

"I don't understand why we have to prove anything," Mary said to Abner Hill. "They killed the boys' father. Then when we go to court and ask for justice they want to throw the case out without giving us a jury. You can kill kids, too, in certain ways like that." Hill didn't answer. "I never knew they hurt Joe," she said. "If I'da known he was hurt I would have called you sooner," and then for the first time he saw her cry, but she quickly pulled herself up straight, turned away from him, and when she turned back she looked as if she had fully recovered.

After *the time,* the child, Charlie, had retreated into himself. Before then he and Billy had played together, but Charlie no longer wanted to play the game—cowboys and Indians—a game in which Charlie had always insisted on being the Indian, which was all right with Billy. "The cowboys always win," Billy said. "They got the money. They got the guns. And the Indians are too dumb."

"They are not dumb," Charlie shot back. "I am an Arapahoe."

"Indians are not dumb," Mary had tried to explain. "They're different."

"I'll say!" Billy said.

"Indians have not been civilized as long as white people," Mary said. "In some ways that's better. But we do not live in the time of the Indian. This is the time of white people. The days of the Indian are over. It is not a matter of blood. It is a matter of time," she had said. "And so you boys are not Indians. Their time has gone."

"I am Arapahoe," Charlie said.

"No, you are *not* Arapahoe," she said. Then she went to the boy and put her arms around him and held him to her. "You can grow up to be a white man and have good things or you can grow up to be an Indian and have nothin', like your father." She had said such things many times before the murder of Joseph Redtail, but she had never spoken of Joseph Redtail in that way after *the time.*

To the blond man, Emmett, order and precision were among the most important human virtues. At night when he emptied his pockets of change he lined up the coins on the dresser, the fifty-cent pieces first, followed by the quarters, the nickels, but when he came to the question of the dimes and pennies he hesitated. The dimes were more valuable than the pennies but they were the smallest. The dimes, to be precise, should come after the quarters, but since they were smaller than the pennies, they should follow the pennies, and, for that matter, the dimes should be ahead of the nickels following the quarters. Since he took the visual to be more important than the abstract he resolved the conflict by putting the pennies after the nickels, the dimes bringing up the rear.

The blond man got out of the vehicle and carefully rearranged his freshly pressed khaki trousers, shifted his shoulders back and forth so that the cloth of his shirt lay evenly and without wrinkles. With precision he tucked in his shirt all around and then withdrew from its case his rifle with the ten power scope. He laid the case on the hood of the Jeep and rested his elbow on it as he surveyed the town below through the rifle's sight. The small log cabin nearest the river was but three hundred yards away. The cabin was tucked in between some towering narrow-leafed cottonwoods, their limbs spreading from their trunks as if in exultation and without design except as was necessary to keep the tree in balance.

He checked the rifle carefully, pulled the bolt back, and injected a cartridge. Then he waited, and to pass the time he counted his breaths, one count on the inhale and another count on the next inhale. Often he counted as high as three thousand breaths before he tired of the exercise. Still counting he viewed both sides of the cabin though the telescope. He could see where the owner parked his pickup, the grass nearest the river being bent where the vehicle occasionally overran the drive. The cabin below, its deck extended over the river, the river moving slowly underneath, the sound of the river always the same and, upon closer listening, never the same. The cabin, as the blond man knew, belonged to Abner Hill.

10

To the boy, Charlie, the lawyers' voices were the tuneless notes of the flicker that pecks on green wood, the noise dull and lifeless, for even the flicker did not work for long at green wood.

The lawyers in the courtroom made no good sounds. And without good sounds one would think the lawyers would have tired of their own noise, but they did not grow tired. They cherished the words without life, the dress of the lawyers like the dress of men at the funeral. Even Abner Hill wore his old gray suit in the courtroom because it was a rule of His Honor that lawyers must "attend the court in appropriate attire" and "appropriate" meant a suit and a tie. But the rule said nothing against boots and Abner Hill wore his boots and a string tie, because the rule did not specify what kind of tie was appropriate. Then as if they were dead and in caskets the lawyers buried each other with their words.

After some hours the heat of the hard oak pews made the boys' bottoms wet and itchy. Charlie squirmed, but his mother pinched him again on the arm. "Hold still," she whispered, "the judge might see you." Charlie sat looking down at his feet. It was better to look at one's feet than at the lawyers and the sleeping judge.

Yancey's knuckles shown white as he grasped the lectern and his fingers were long and curled up at the ends, his voice as dreary as the mumbling of moles. "I have admitted for the purpose of this motion that my clients killed this man. I admit it *arguendo*. You understand, of course, Your Honor, that for the purpose of this motion, and this motion only, we admit that the death of Joseph Redtail was wrongfully imposed by my clients. But we both know in order for the plaintiffs to prevail they must show the wrong *caused damage*. Damage, Your Honor! Lest I have not been heard, I wish to repeat myself—"

"You need not repeat yourself," the judge said, coming suddenly alive. "Every first-year law student knows there must be both a wrong and damage resulting from the wrong. Do you think you are talking to a stump?"

"Quite to the contrary, Your Honor. But as you can see, Mr. Hill has failed to show in any of his supporting affidavits that the heirs of the deceased suffered any loss. No damage, Your Honor! None! I admit the burial expense, of course. I admit even the cost of a decent tombstone. These are available for less than two hundred dollars which includes the name, the date of birth and the date of death, all nicely engraved, and I also admit the cost of one hundred and four dollars to install the stone on the grave. But what other damage?"

Yancey waited in silence for someone to speak. "This is no rhetorical question. It asks: Was there any income provided from the deceased father to these boys? None. Did he provide them with anything of monetary value whatsoever? No. Did he so much as take them to a movie? Never. Did he buy them a pair of shoes? I have not heard of it. Did he feed them a sliver of food? I have not heard of it. Did he provide any medical care for them? They would have died. The mother waits tables at a local restaurant. The father during all of those years provided *nothing*. Think of it, Your Honor: nothing!"

Then Yancey turned a page in his notebook. "But was there loss of care, comfort, advice, and society? Those are precious words meaning—"

The judge interrupted him. "Don't you think I know by now what those words mean, Mr. Yancey? Do you take me for a four-wheeled idiot?"

"Of course not, Your Honor."

"Do you think you know what they mean?"

"Yes, Your Honor, I do."

"Well, then tell me."

"I do not wish to offend the court."

"How can you offend the court when you comply with my order? I order you to tell me the meaning of those words."

"Well, they mean, Your Honor, that there was some relationship between the father and the children."

"Don't fiddle with me, counsel. I know there was a relationship. They were a father and two sons. That's already been established."

"The words ask if the father and the sons were close."

"How close?" the judge asked.

"Not close at all, Your Honor, not in any way."

Yancey, pale as blisters, was left standing there when the judge turned to Abner Hill. His Honor puckered his lips and wrinkled his nose and his glasses rose up with his nose and down again before he began to speak. "Mr. Hill, what damage have your clients suffered as a result of their father's murder?"

"Please! Please! I did not admit to a murder, Your Honor," Yancey cried.

"Aren't you as dead from murder as from any other cause?" the judge asked.

"Well, yes. But my clients did not murder Mr. Redtail."

"How do I know?" the judge asked.

"Because I have not admitted murder. I have admitted only a wrongful death."

"Isn't murder wrongful?" the judge asked.

"Yes, Your Honor. But so can an accidental death be wrongful."

"How does one accidentally beat another human being to death?"

"That is not the point. The point is we admit the wrongful death, but we do not admit murder."

"I have always admired logic whenever possible in the law, which is rare, and I see I shall not be favored with it today. And so, Mr. Hill, how were your clients damaged when their father was beaten to death accidentally?"

"They were deprived of the company of their father," Hill said.

"I take it that if you had the power you would provide all boys with the company of a drunken father, Mr. Hill?" the judge asked.

"No, sir. But a drunken father is not drunk all of the time. It is better to have a drunken father part of the time than no father all of the time."

Abner Hill himself had grown up fatherless, his father a mystery in the house of his mother, the daughter of a Baptist minister in Rapid City, South Dakota. She taught history in the high school there. Hill had asked about his father many times, but all his mother would say was that they would talk about it someday, but not then.

"What was he like?" he asked once, but again his mother had said she did not wish to talk about it. "What did my father do?" Hill asked when he was twelve, and, going into the Boy Scouts, the application form asking for the occupation of the father.

"You have no father so you don't need to write it in there."

"Was he killed?"

"Do we have to discuss it?" his mother had replied. "Have you done your homework?"

"Was he a bank robber?" Hill had asked his mother on his thirteenth birthday.

"Don't be silly," she said. But the idea of it was not silly to the boy. He had read of bank robbers and if his mother had married one she was not the kind who would admit it, not his very proper mother. And bank robbers were not all bad men. They were brave men who robbed, like Jesse James and Pretty Boy Floyd, and they gave to the poor.

One time when Abner's best friend, Niles Johansen, asked about his father Abner made him promise not to tell and after Niles promised, Abner told him that his father was a bank robber, that he had escaped the penitentiary, and that his father had come to visit him at night when his mother was gone. He described his father to his friend. He was handsome, dark, and quick like Tyrone Power in the movies and because his father was one of the ten most wanted men in the nation he could never go with him to the school programs like other fathers, nor on camping trips like Niles's father did.

On his fifteenth birthday the boy confronted his mother once again. "Momma, tell me about my father."

"All right, I'll tell you," she said. "You're old enough to know." She took her hair down from its bun and it fell to her waist. Their supper over, the two of them sat at the kitchen table and she began brushing her hair with long, leisurely strokes. She looked very pretty, the boy thought. He had not seen her so, never thought of her as pretty, never saw her as a woman. Only a mother. Perhaps it was the reflected light from the single bulb over the stove that made her look younger than he had remembered, made her look like a woman for whom Tyrone Power might have fought a sword fight. Then she began.

Before Abner Hill could say more, Judge Hankins, gazing at the ceiling, pulled himself up a little and turned to Yancey. "Now Mr. Hill's curious assertion launches us into an interesting question. Mr. Yancey, is it better for a child to have a drunken father part of the time than no father all of the time?"

"I say, Your Honor, that Mr. Hill has no concept whatever concerning the heinous effect a drunk can have on innocent minds. How," Yancey asked in a high whine, "do we dare hope to overcome the depraved state of the American Indian if the court is to approve, as a matter of law, that drunken fathers are, on balance, better than no fathers at all?"

"Following your logic, Mr. Yancey, must we not see to the immediate execution of all drunken fathers in the land in order that we may save the youth of this nation from bad role models?" The judge slid back down in his chair as if he had made the irrefutable argument.

"Of course, the court is not serious," Yancey said, jumping up from his table.

"Have you ever known me to jest?" the judge asked. Turning to Abner Hill he said, "Mr. Hill, what do you say about drunken fathers? Shouldn't they be eliminated altogether?"

"We have left out an important consideration," Hill said.

"Pray tell, what would that be?"

"Whether or not the drunk father loved his children and the children loved him."

"*Love* is not a word cognizant in the law," Yancey said. "And if it were, what is it worth?"

"You tell us, Mr. Hill," the judge said. "You seem to be an expert on love. Do you sell love by the yard or by the pound?"

Hill offered no answer.

"If you could purchase love by any measure would we not spend all of our money for it?" the judge replied. "Is it not quite the Jim Dandy stuff, this thing called love?"

Neither lawyer answered, both standing there staring at the judge, the judge's eyes turned upward as if the answer lay within the scurrying noise of the rats on the tin ceiling above them.

When his mother, Symantha Ann Hill, had begun to speak, her voice was soft. "Your father and I were very young—and foolish," she said. We were not much older than you, Abner. I was seventeen. He was a year older. We were in high school together, although he was not a great student. He was very handsome. All of the girls were crazy about your father. He was dark and tall," and when his mother had said that, Abner Hill knew that his dreams of his father were true. "And I fell in love with him," she said.

"Did he love you?"

"Yes," she said in a whisper. "Very much." Then escaping her reverie she continued in the tone and language of the history teacher that she was. "Your father's father—your grandfather—was a horse trader. He rounded up wild horses on the Red Desert in Wyoming and sold them to the Indians on the reservation in South Dakota. The Sioux love wild horses. And your father was a very good horseman and a bronco rider. When he was only a boy he had already won several bareback championships at the rodeos and we girls used to go watch him ride. Oh, he was quite as beautiful on top of a bucking horse as he was standing there in the hallway of Rapid City High." She had stopped brushing her hair and had gone to fetch hot water for her tea. When she came back she pulled her robe tightly around her, dropped two lumps of sugar in her tea, poured in a little milk, and she stirred it for a long time.

Finally she said, "He is gone now."

"What do you mean?" the boy asked. "Is he dead?"

"I couldn't say," she said. "He left with his father before you were born. He never had a mother that I know of. Never finished high school. His father put him to work—made a regular slave of him. Then his father was killed in an automobile accident. Some said his father was drunk." She sipped at her tea.

"What was my father's name?"

"His name was the same as yours—Abner," she said very softly. "I gave you his name, which was all of your father that I could give to you." She was looking toward the light, the light on the best part of her face. Suddenly Abner Hill saw that his mother was beautiful and that the beauty was also in the pain, in the still-young face, and for the first time that he could remember he felt love for his mother.

"Well, are you two lawyers going to stand there as silent as fly crap on the wall?" the judge asked.

"Drunk or sober, the love of a father is incalculable," Hill finally said. "It was all these boys had from their father. It was worth everything to them." He could think of nothing more to say. He looked over at Mary Hamilton in the front row. Hill gave her a small nod, but she gave no sign back.

"Well, all right, then," the judge said. "Now we are getting someplace. What is the value of *everything*? Twenty-three cents?"

"No sir," Hill replied. "As you well know, Your Honor, money cannot buy love."

"Well, if money cannot buy love, and if the loss of the father's love to these boys is the only damage they have suffered, does it not follow that they have suffered no damage calculable by man and that I should therefore grant Mr. Yancey's motion for summary judgment?"

"Such damage is for the jury to decide," Hill said. "We all know that that is what juries are for."

"Juries are smarter than you are, Mr. Hill? Smarter than Mr. Yancey here? No juror is smarter than a lawyer from the big city of Casper." Then he asked with fleeting incredulity, "Juries are smarter than I?"

Yancey grabbed the lapel of his pinstriped suit. "I wish to say that this drunken father could not love anyone, else he would not be drunk all of the time. I say *drunken love* does not exist. Drunken love is an oxymoron, and therefore my answer to Your Honor is that there is no damage and this case must be dismissed. That has been my position from the beginning. We are, thank God, finally getting to it."

"I knew we couldn't get through this argument without injecting God into the case," the judge said, sliding down in his seat in despair. "Shall we consult Him before I make my decision? Shall we all join hands and pray? What do you say, Mr. Hill?"

Hill smiled sadly at the judge, but the judge did not smile back.

"Well, then, are you ready for my decision?" the judge asked from a place nearly beneath the bench.

11

Like a condemned man Abner Hill waited for Judge Hankins's decision, one he had anticipated from the beginning. The judge cleared his throat, looked down at the court reporter to make sure the reporter was ready, and when he saw that the reporter, pen in hand, was poised, he began speaking to the ceiling:

"I find that Mr. Yancey, from the big city of Casper, Wyoming, is making an argument that he has not fully articulated to this court. He is arguing that by wrongfully killing the father of these boys, his clients have, in fact, done a favor for these boys, that is, these boys are better off without their drunken father than with him. This being so, for having performed that service the boys owe Mr. Yancey's clients a sum of money, which Mr. Yancey has yet to specify." Suddenly the judge swiveled in his chair and aimed his words at Yancey: "So, counsel, how much money would you say that your clients are entitled to for the merciful but wrongful killing of Joseph August Redtail?"

"I don't understand, Your Honor," Yancey said. His eyes began to dart around the room.

"Well, it seems to me that either your clients owe these boys or the boys owe your clients. That's logical isn't it?"

"Not quite, with all due respect," Yancey said. "There could be a draw."

"You mean, that your clients could kill a man and everybody is even? Mr. Yancey, you admit that your clients *wrongfully* killed Mr. Redtail. And since the killing was such a splendid gift to these boys so that, as you argue, these boys are better off without their father, then do these boys not owe your clients some yet unspecified sum? No free lunch, you know."

"I ... I ..." Yancey began to sputter.

"Well then, Mr. Yancey, how much, in your opinion, do these boys owe your clients?"

Yancey began to answer. For the first time, the judge looked over at Mary and the boys. "Did you ask the boys if they felt any loss of their father?"

"If there were damage, Mr. Hill, representing the boys, can demonstrate it. He has filed nothing that would reveal the slightest damage of any nature whatsoever. As a consequence, this court has no alternative but to grant my motion," Yancey said.

"I am staggered," the judge replied, popping to a fully erect position. "I never realized I had no alternative but to grant your motion."

"That was a manner of speaking, Your Honor, with all due respect."

"I would hope," the judge replied. "I had previously thought I had the discretion, based on the law, the evidence, and the inferences arising therefrom, to decide this motion either for or against your clients. Is that true, Mr. Yancey?"

"Yes, sir."

"In a manner of speaking then, Mr. Yancey, with all due respect and having been given no substantial guidance from either of you, I swear I'm as confused as you. I shall leave the question of damages in this case, if any, for a jury to decide. Your motion is overruled, Mr. Yancey." With that, Judge Henry Hankins rose from the bench and departed into his chambers like a sudden itinerant wind.

Then Abner's face got very serious, and the boy leaned forward to his mother. "Momma, did they put my father in the penitentiary?"

"Whatever gave you that idea, son?" Symantha Ann Hill asked.

"Did they?"

"Well, yes, they did, as a matter of fact," she said. She looked at her son with dismay. "I heard he was sentenced to the penitentiary shortly after you were born."

"For what?"

"He was a thief," she said. "Some men love money and steal it. Some men love women and steal them. Some love horses and are horse thieves. Your father loved all three. He was always in trouble. And of course, he loved you."

"He never stole me," Abner said.

"He was always in trouble with the law. In one jail and out of another. I could never keep up with him."

"Did you marry him?"

"No," she said. "That is our secret, Abner."

Abner Hill waited for his mother to tell him more about their secret, but she added nothing. Finally the boy said, "What was he like?"

"He was very charming. And he had dancing black eyes and everybody loved your father. That was the problem."

"How dark was he?"

She didn't answer.

"As dark as me, Momma?" He with the dark hair and the olive skin had felt separated from his blond mother, her blue eyes and skin that burned in ten minutes of summer sun.

"Yes," his mother said. "Your father looked a good deal like you. You have his mouth. For sure, his mouth, and he was tall like you."

"Was he Italian?"

"No, of course not."

"What was he then?"

"I think he was Irish and Sioux. I think his mother was mostly Sioux." He did not think of it then, his mind not absorbing the words, his mind storing them only. But later he thought of how he was Indian. The thought made him feel powerful. Indians were more powerful than Italians.

"If he loved you, why didn't he come to you when he got out of the penitentiary?"

"I think he was afraid of my father."

"Grandpa was only a preacher. He never even owned a gun and he was fat."

"I know," she said. "But he couldn't come to South Dakota because it would violate his parole. Couldn't leave Wyoming. When he was released from Rawlins the last time, I heard he was running wild horses on the Red Desert like his father. That was ten years ago. I haven't heard of him since."

"He never called you?"

"No," she said. "I think he was ashamed."

"He never came to see me?"

"I'm sure it would have been too painful for him. He was a very kind person and he gave everything he had away."

"What was his last name, Momma?"

"He had many last names. He changed his name every time he got out of jail. The last I heard he was going by the name of Thomas."

"Did he rob banks, Momma?"

"No, he stole horses."

"Did he give the horses to the poor?"

"I wouldn't doubt it," she said. "He was like that."

"Do you still love him, Momma?" the boy's careless question.

Then for the first time in his life Abner Hill saw his mother weeping. She got up from the kitchen table and went to her bedroom and did not come out the rest of the night, but even behind the door she had not been able to muffle the sounds of her sobbing.

In the morning, she was dressed as usual in her severe way, the hair up in its bun, the ugly shoes. She prepared his breakfast of oatmeal and a bowl of prunes. But on this morning, as she was leaving for school, and as she walked by the table, she let drop a photograph in front of him and, saying nothing, she closed the door behind her. He could hear their old Studebaker finally start in the garage.

The photograph was of a young, smiling man with thick, dark hair, a western shirt, a neckerchief tied at the side of the throat. He was standing against a corral, his cowboy hat in one hand, his other arm leaning casually against a railing. At the bottom of the photo were words he recognized as his mother's careful handwriting: *Abner Driskell, Bareback Champion, August 29, 1930.* And Abner Hill saw that he did, indeed, have his father's mouth.

The old Ford pickup bounced up to the river's edge and came to an abrupt stop. The tall man in a black hat stepped from the pickup and stood for a moment gazing out over the river. Chunks of gray ice flowed by, the ice also forming brilliant crystal margins to the river.

The man, Abner Hill, walked to the river's edge and looked into the water as if to find answers there. There were no answers in the water. The universe asks no questions and answers none. And having recognized the futility of asking such questions, he asked them nevertheless. Why was he in this case? Why him? Why not a lawyer with more experience, better skills, a lawyer with a more powerful delivery, one who could persuade the judge and jury as a father convinces the child? Why had Joseph Redtail been murdered in the first place? What did his ugly, wasteful death serve? His hands cold, he put them in the pockets of his black overcoat and stared into the water as if he did not want to go into the cabin.

Precisely three hundred and four yards on the opposite side of the river the blond man, the one with the baby face called Emmett, held the crosshairs steadily on the right eye of Abner Hill. He once blew out the eye of a calf at four hundred and seven yards. The sheriff said it looked to him like the calf had been struck by lightning or something. Never saw a bullet make a hole like that. But there had been no storms for weeks and after that, the mystery not forgotten, had been accepted as a mystery.

The blond man watched the lawyer, the blond man nearly translucent in his ecstasy. His was destiny itself. Something orgasmic about their relationship, the lawyer standing there gazing into the river and Emmett with the crosshairs on his right eye. His rapture sublime, he put off the climax, for after the simplest action, the steady squeezing of the finger, the breath held, the three-thousandth breath perhaps, the exhilaration would pass instantly and the depressing sense of emptiness would take its place. He held back.

The universe had no conscience and in that way he saw himself in tune with it. Never did the universe weep. When it struck with helter-skelter abandon it did so without joy, without pity, without caring. And people died helter-skelter at the hands of the universe. His father, a farmer, was killed when a boar cornered him in the pigpen and ripped him to pieces. But the universe had not cared. It had only pointed its nonfinger and his father had been in front of it.

A man could get killed in an automobile accident, as had been the fate of Jimmy, his younger brother, who was the quintessential slob, his dirty clothes on the floor wherever he dropped them, his possessions strewn everywhere. Death brought a new order and Emmett had been pleased by it. He moved Jimmy's things out of the room and for the first time in his life he had been happy because there was order in the room. But the universe had not cared. It only pointed its finger.

A woman could die under the hand of a drunken surgeon as his mother had. He had not wept over her casket. She had three lovers. His father never knew. But Emmett knew. He remembered the first. They thought they had the shades pulled to the bottom. He had watched without emotion, saw her making love with his father's best friend from the neighboring farm, saw the man on his knees between his mother's legs. And then he saw them trade places, his mother's large, hanging breasts, and the next morning when she tried to kiss him he spit on her and she screamed at him, "You are a crazy little cocksucker. I'm going to call the sheriff and send you to the reform school." Then she had gotten drunk and told him how pretty he was and she got fresh with him and he had to slap her—slap his own mother—and after that she had screamed at him some more.

The boy had finished high school at fifteen, the school's prodigy who had graduated at the head of his class, could speak French and Spanish fluently, and had read and memorized the salient portions of many of the classics. He entered Yale on a scholarship to study philosophy. His professors saw him as odd, but made room for his long, empty stares and his cold demeanor as the not unexpected trappings of the rare genius. As Professor Howard Gillman, the head of the department had observed, "This young man may possess the seed to modern philosophy. We shall be most interested to see how the plant grows and what blossom it bears."

The abstract held little meaning for Emmett. Action was the essence of the universe. The universe did not ponder. It asked no questions, engaged in no meaningless, endless rhetoric, made no judgments. The universe did not love nor hate. The universe was beyond loving and hating. The universe was not definable in terms of good or evil, which were the idiotic constructs of the humanoid. The universe was action, explosion, destruction, and out of destruction birth, and out of birth death. The nuclear bomb was in harmony with the universe as was war, as were the black holes and the exploding stars and the teeming cosmos. Yet nothing was static in the universe. It was, as he sought to be, pure action and to be in tune with the universe one must emulate its action.

Emmett, the blond one, in tune with the universe, a part of the universe, was at its service. He pointed a rifle as the universe pointed its finger. The rifle made only a small noise but had explosive power, high speed and low trajectory. The whole right side of the man's face would be blown apart before he could even hear the gun explode. To emulate the universe's empty action, its mindless selection of its victims, its destruction without judgment, without caring, was divine. Such, Emmett thought, was beauty. Such, Emmett believed, was the ultimate art.

He was amused at the man across the river, amused that the man did not realize the pointer was leveled at him, that he, Emmett, fate itself, at that moment had chosen him and with little more reason than that which moved the universe. He watched Abner Hill standing as if he were stone, his eyes fixed on the water. At the precise moment of the explosion, the stone would give way as, indeed, even stone crumples to sand. The knees would buckle and the man would fall face forward into the river and float peacefully down along with the ice floe. They might never find his body unless it got caught in a downstream logjam. That would be days later, too late, he thought, he, Emmett, already long gone.

The idea of justice was a ridiculous concept, Emmett thought, fools arguing, crying about justice. That the man standing on the riverbank three hundred and four yards away had never harmed him, that he did not even know him, was a marvelous irrelevancy. That Cotler wanted him dead was an irrelevancy. That was Cotler's problem, his pathetic human disease. Nor was he, Emmett, Cotler's instrument. Emmett made the choice. He could have as easily cut Cotler's belly, let his intestines fall out in the parking lot, stopped at a drive-in for a Coke and a hamburger, and driven on to some small town in Idaho. But some, not Cotler, had said that Abner Hill was a just man and that had been the attraction.

Afterward he thought he would head out for a small town south of Yuma, but he was also amused by the fat Wyoming farm women with the big asses and full tits like bitches with pups. He liked the older ones, those struggling at that desperate precipice before they plunged into menopause, their looks of adoration with soft eyes into his young face, their caressing his cheeks with rough hands as if he were a child. He used women, he admitted that. But they used him as well. That was not justice. That was balance. And after it was over he left them. Had they known him they would have left him as quickly. The difference was he knew them first and better.

The farmwives loved his lean, hairless body unlike the hairy paunches on their husbands. They devoured him with their tongues and sometimes wept before he touched them, sometimes shivering in anticipation. Once in Kearney, Nebraska, after having climaxed on the sixty-eighth stroke by his actual count, he had promptly arisen from the conjugal bed. The woman, still lying there, asked him in a whisper why he had cried out, "Mother." He looked at the woman a long time and when he pulled the knife she began to shake like a small, cornered bird. She could not scream, lying there naked, her husband still snoring in the next room. Then Emmett stuck the knife into her neatly and there was no sound to it except the faint puff of air escaping from the lungs.

Emmett had driven all night following the murder. He thought that his act was as perfect an evil as man might achieve. Evil was an art form, like painting. He reasoned that if the act were evil enough, it approached ultimate virtue, and at the precise moment that good and evil met, the state of the universe, void of judgment, could be understood.

He had laughed as he drove along, exhilarated to the maximum over his achievement—the seduction and murder of the farmer's wife. He did not always kill his lovers, not even usually. It depended upon the messages he received from the universe, he, Emmett, being in exact accord with the ever-shifting language that sprang from the ultimate body that some called God but that to Emmett was so perfect that it transcended life, death, and all consciousness itself. About noon the following day, and still driving without the first sign of weariness, he had stopped at the Big Chief bar for a beer where he met Ronnie Cotler.

At the river's edge watching the ice flow by, Abner Hill realized he had the power of that small family's well-being in his hands. Without justice their lives would continue to be sparse and hard. With even a small amount of justice the boys could get an education and Mary a decent roof over their heads. Maybe she could stay home and take care of her boys. He felt powerless. Yet he possessed immutable power over their lives, this small and powerless family he had grown to care for.

He thought that his own life was in the hands of some chaotic force over which he also wielded no control. The cases he lost by accident or won for the same reason were the result of conditions over which he had little control. It was the way his clients came off, the jurors he picked, the temperament of the judge on any given day. The instruments of death, the cancerous cell, the clogged arteries, the diseased organs—they came as they chose whenever they chose and without caring. The invading virus chose its victims pell-mell. The universe that randomly brought on death and injury and pain and loss in their endless variations did not care, for the universe was above caring. Perhaps the universe at last presented the ultimate caring, he thought, the long, endless nothingness that, for want of better words and understanding, man called death.

Then he saw the black-and-white bufflehead duck fly low and fast over the water like a strafing fighter plane and he realized once more that the universe was alive; and if there was life, there was caring and that there was great power in caring.

Even though Emmett held the crosshairs on Hill's right eye he found his mind wandering. That was not a good sign. His mind ought not wander at such a time as this. He found himself thinking of the plump farm woman—Madeline Hennisey was her name. He had seen her at the saloon one night at Harvard and, before she left, he had wanted to stare at her with his long, flat stare that caused women to look down and when she looked down he would move in front of her and she would have to look up. And there he would be, the baby face nearly in her face, no smile, the eyes on her. No man would have ever looked at her that way. Then without saying anything he would nod his head toward the door and the woman would follow him out.

He wanted to take Madeline Hennisey on the couch in her own living room, her old man sleeping off his drunk in the next room, and if the old man came stumbling out he would drop his guts on the living room floor with one efficient sweep of his blade.

Emmett watched Abner Hill standing at the river's edge, the man motionless as if in deep thought. He laughed, patted the gun on the side as if it were a pointing dog, slipped the gun carefully into its case, and saw Abner Hill walk to the cabin door. It was not Emmett who had, for the moment, saved the man. It was the plump farmwife named Madeline, who unwittingly possessed the power of the universe.

12

It was early in February of 1970 that Judge Henry P. Hankins had over-ruled Harold Yancey's motion for summary judgment. Then the tops of old weeds protruded through empty fields of snow, the dead grasses bent under, the cars struggling, spinning in deep ruts, the sky some-times as blue as blue marbles, the air so cold it scorched the lungs, the people bundled in many layers, waddling in wool and fur and emitting small clouds of steam as they passed one another.

In the spring the mushrooms in the soggy mulch on the river bot-tom sprang up once more and the flickers drummed endlessly crying out their virility, their life, their readiness to enter into that inexorable cycle. Then in tune with the libidinous spirits of spring, Judge Henry Hankins had called a jury into session.

Time to burn the dead growth of the past. Time for new life, new cases, a new jury to try the same old sins, the same crimes, the same miserable conflicts of the species. And, the judge, perhaps with little empathy but with the amusement of one duly detached, felt it time for the circus of the law to once more begin its performance in his court-room. If he could not always prevent injustice, which he could not, he could at least endure it in tolerable good humor. The law was the law. He did not make the law. He only attended to it like the doctor who did not create the disease but only treated it. He jumped up to the bench with the vigor of a schoolboy taking the stage.

Harold Yancey was there looking quite fine, quite fit, smiling and conversing pleasantly with the court officers, his black, round-toed, high-laced shoes polished. He slipped the old bailiff a fresh cigar and told the court reporter, the last of the old boys who took it all down with pen and ink, that he considered the reporter "a true genius and a blessed anachronism from the old school."

Abner Hill was quiet, restive, and preoccupied beyond the contest that overhung the courtroom. His eyes were troubled. He walked slowly, aimlessly to one end of the courtroom and then, as if to catch someone in a furtive act behind his back, he whirled and walked slowly back again to his table. Yancey noticed. Hill had visited the men's room three times in fifteen minutes, a sure sign, Yancey thought. His opponent was in a state of deep and irretrievable anxiety. He smiled.

Mary Hamilton sat with her two boys in the front row, the boys, their growth stagnated during the long Wyoming winter, on each side of her, these boys who had been wrongfully deprived of a drunken father and who had brought this suit for his worth in money, whatever the sum might be.

Yancey had not wavered from his strategy. After the jury of twelve citizens of Fetterman County, Wyoming, had been selected and duly sworn, the judge, precisely following the law, had laconically and correctly instructed the jury as follows:

"Ladies and gentlemen. The defendants in this case admit that they are legally liable for the death of Joseph August Redtail. The only question remaining, therefore, are the damages, if any, suffered by the plaintiffs as a result of that wrongful death. The testimony in this case will be directed solely to that issue. You may call your first witness, Mr. Hill."

Hill called Mary Hamilton. She walked from counsel table in quick self-conscious steps.

She and Hill had gone over her testimony, but Hill had never thought about cautioning her to be pleasant. Although Mary Hamilton was a pleasant person, under fire, she fought back. She had been frightened up there on the stand, the jurors staring, judging, the questions hard. She struggled to tell the whole truth as she had been sworn to do. But telling the whole truth was nearly impossible in a court of law even when the witness knew the whole truth. And it was harder yet to be stared at and judged, especially in a public place.

"Tell the ladies and gentlemen of the jury who Joseph Redtail was, as you knew him," Hill had asked.

"He was an Arapahoe. He had his ways."

"What do you mean, Mary?"

Yancey objected. "Improper to call the witness by her given name, Your Honor."

"Sustained," the judge growled.

"What do you mean, Mrs. Hamilton, that Joseph 'had his ways'?"

"Well, he was hard to know."

"Did you know him?"

"Some of him."

"Did he love the boys?" Hill asked.

"Well, yes, I'm sure he did in his own way. He never said so."

The examination went on like that. She told how he took the boys to the mountain and how he took them hunting. She struggled to tell the truth yet not hurt the boys' case, that fine line she was not prepared to walk with any grace. Her father had said, "You always tell the truth, Mary, and remember, the truth is not all gussied up with a bunch a bullshit. The truth is the truth."

At recess, Hill took her aside. "Why did you tell them that he never said he loved the boys?" Hill looked tired. She had never seen the man sweat like that.

"Well, I never heard him say he loved them. Joe said there isn't any word for love in the Arapahoe language."

"Yes, but he was speaking English to the boys, not Arapahoe."

She felt like she couldn't explain it, even to her own lawyer, and she grew very quiet, as when she couldn't explain things to her father.

On cross-examination Yancey was kind to the woman. He smiled a lot and nodded, even bowed at times.

"I take it that you and Joseph and the boys were a regular family?"

"What do you mean?" The sound of her voice had changed when Yancey began his questioning. You could hear it, like a different person, an angry person taking on this wholly pleasant man.

"Why, I suppose you and your husband and the boys often went to your father's house and to his parents' house as well, and you were a regular family, you, the boys, the grandparents, and all."

"No."

"No?" Yancey feigned surprise.

"My father wouldn't speak to Joseph."

"Why was that?"

"You'll have to ask him."

"Well, your father would come to your house, then, and see the boys."

Hill objected. "This is all irrelevant, Your Honor."

Yancey argued back. "Your Honor, Joseph Redtail either was or was not an important and integral part of this family, which consisted of the boys in their relationship with their father and with the father in the context of the family as a whole."

"I don't understand what you are saying, Mr. Yancey," the judge said, still slumped down as if protecting himself from stray bullets. "It is all mostly Anglo-Saxon verbiage. From up here it sounds like gibberish. Proceed."

"Did your father come to see your boys at your house?"

"No."

"Why not?"

"Object." Hill was on his feet again.

"Overruled."

"Because," Mary Hamilton said, "he never spoke to me after I married Joseph."

"Why?"

"Because he didn't want me to marry an Indian." She thought she was going to cry but she didn't cry. Instead, the anger took hold to protect her, the anger that had always protected her. "You can't make it in the world, standin' out there bawlin'," her father used to say.

"So have you seen your father since Joseph's death?"

"I saw him once at Safeway. Ran into him shopping."

"What did he say?"

"Never said anything. Just walked by like I wasn't there."

"Do you hope to reestablish a relationship with your father now that Joseph is dead?"

It was then that she did begin to cry. She held it back, the sobs choking her. And at last Judge Henry Hankins called another recess.

Hill tried to comfort the woman, but she was huddled up in the corner behind their table. She was shaking. He put his hand on her shoulder while she let out the pain in long sobs. He didn't say anything and when she'd stopped sobbing, the woman felt ashamed. Finally she said, "I'm ruining the case."

"You're doing fine," Hill said. But she knew he didn't mean it.

Back on the stand Yancey was after her again, still in his nice way, but pressing, relentless. "So because of your husband, these boys were deprived of their grandparents?"

She didn't answer. She was staring at her hands.

"And don't you think that grandparents are, in their own way, as important as parents?"

"I suppose," she said.

"And what about Joseph's parents. I suppose the boys had a good relationship with his parents?"

"No."

"What do you mean?" Yancey knew what she meant.

"I mean Joseph's mother hardly ever came by," she said.

"Why?"

"Well, you know why." She was suddenly angry again.

"Could you tell us, please," Yancey said in a kind way.

"Because she is a hopeless alcoholic."

"Did the boys ever see her?"

A long silence. The silence made things uncomfortable in the court-room. Finally the judge said, "Answer the question."

"She came once when Joseph was at the house. She wanted money. She was drunk."

"Were the boys there?"

"Yes."

"Did the boys see her?"

"Irrelevant," Hill said, this time without getting up.

"I suppose so," she answered before the judge had ruled.

"And since his death, your little family has not been bothered fur-ther by this drunken Indian woman, isn't that true?"

There was no way out. She told the truth. No, she had not seen Joseph's mother since his death. She didn't know if the woman was dead or alive. She had never come to see the boys.

"And isn't it true, Mrs. Hamilton, that you are relieved that this drunken woman hasn't made her appearance at your house? That she hasn't humiliated the boys with her presence?" Yancey was parading now in front of the jury box, glancing at juror after juror to emphasize the points he was making.

Mary looked at her hands again, but she didn't see them, the veins close to the surface, the fingers clutching one another as if the fingers were panicked.

"Now, Billy: I take it he liked to go with his father."

"No."

"No?" Again the feigned surprise, the jury leaning forward, their eyes peeling back the hide of the wounded.

"Billy didn't like to go with his father."

Yancey didn't ask why. He left it where it was—the picture of a boy who didn't want to be with his father—such a picture in a trial in which the money claim was for the boys' loss of their father's *society*, that one big word that stood for how parents are with their children and children with their parents, that one big word in the law that stood for those sacred times when the parent and the child are bonded. Yancey had left it there. Then he took another tack.

"You divorced your husband?"

"Yes."

"You divorced him because he didn't support these boys, isn't that true?"

"That wasn't the only reason." Hill stared disbelieving at his client.

"What else, pray tell?"

"He was drunk a lot."

"You didn't want him near the boys when he was drunk, isn't that true?"

"Yes."

"That's *true,* isn't it, Ms. Hamilton?"

"Yes. Yes. It's true," she said, her voice rising to match Yancey's.

"And so, Mrs. Redtail—"

"My name is Mary Hamilton," she said, interrupting Yancey.

"Of course, my error," Yancey said, bowing again. "And so, Ms. Hamilton, it was a very sad day for you and your boys when Joseph Redtail was found dead in the county jail?'

"I suppose," she said.

"And your boys, they missed their father?"

"Yes," she said.

"You took them to the funeral parlor to see their father's remains?"

"Yes."

"And what happened?"

"They didn't want to see him."

"I have no further questions, Ms. Hamilton. My deepest condolences, Ms. Hamilton." He bowed once more, gave Mary Hamilton a sad smile, and retreated on tiptoes to his table.

It was then that Abner Hill knew he had to call Charlie to the stand or the case was lost; Charlie, the one who had seen his father mutilated, kicked until he would die, the one son who had mourned deeply, always silently, over his death and who had suffered the impenetrable loss of the child ripped by the roots from the father's soil. He had to prove damages. Mary's testimony had done the opposite.

"I ruined the case," she said.

"I gotta call Charlie to the stand," Hill said, "or we'll lose it."

"I'm not gonna allow it." She could hardly be heard.

"Good," he said. "I agree. Maybe I can talk the jury into some kind of settlement. Maybe I can do it in the argument, a few thousand maybe."

"It'll be better than what I got," she said. "We could pay some bills."

And with that, as abruptly as the case had begun, Abner Hill rose from counsel table and said, "We rest our case, Your Honor."

"You haven't got any other witnesses?" the judge asked in undisguised astonishment.

"No, Your Honor."

"Counsel will approach the bench," he said, and when the lawyers were standing side by side looking up at Judge Hankins, he peered down at Abner Hill, his glasses at the end of his nose. "Mr. Hill, do you understand what you are doing?"

"Yes, Your Honor."

"Do you understand that this jury has heard no testimony that suggests your clients, those two little boys over there, suffered any damage."

"Well, I think there's evidence of loss. Certainly the jury can make such inferences as they wish from the facts. I expect to argue it to the jury."

"You haven't got a case," Yancey said. "There is no evidence of loss— none whatever. I move the court for a directed verdict."

"Well, Mr. Yancey, you *should* move this court for a directed verdict. I would have felt neglected if you hadn't made such a motion. It is lonely up here." Awaiting his reply the judge stared at the defense counsel.

"I say there is no evidence of loss. There is only evidence that this family will actually be better off than it was before the decedent's demise," Yancey said.

"We have been over that before, Mr. Yancey," the judge said. "Would there be nominal damage?"

"Like six cents and costs?" Yancey said and laughed.

"Like maybe ten thousand dollars?"

"That's certainly not nominal. I would appeal any such verdict based on this vacuous record."

"Mr. Yancey, under the circumstance, I am unable to put this court's stamp of approval on the proposition that any child is better off with his father dead, no matter how worthless the father. Were I to so hold, hope for both father and child would be eternally lost." The judge turned then to Abner Hill. "I have just bestowed upon you the best argument you could possibly make to this jury for damages in this case, Mr. Hill." Then back to Yancey: "You may proceed with your evidence, Mr. Yancey."

After the attorneys had left the bench and had taken their seats at their respective tables, the Hersey kid leaned over to Harold Yancey and whispered, "Jesus! He didn't even call either of the kids. The jury would have eaten it up, bawling kids and everything."

"I'm not going to let him get away with it," Yancey said. "We got a chance to walk out of this case with a zero verdict."

"How do you figure?" the kid asked.

"Watch," Yancey said. He rose from counsel table. "I call the plaintiff, Charlie Redtail."

"You mean this child?" the judge asked.

"Yes, I mean that child."

13

Abner Hill rose up from counsel table and addressed His Honor, Judge Henry Hankins. "This boy will not be called to the witness stand."

"What are you saying, counselor?" It was Yancey. "I have a right to call him. He's the real party in interest in this case."

"This boy will not be called as a witness," Hill repeated.

"Well, Mr. Hill, Mr. Yancey is correct. All he need do is demonstrate that the boy knows the meaning of an oath. Indeed, he must, if requested, take the witness stand."

Hill turned to the boy sitting next to his mother in the front row. "Charlie, I want you to leave this room immediately." The boy got up and before anyone could stop him he walked out of the room. As he left they could see that the boy had begun to plait a single braid down his back, by then no longer than three or four inches, barely noticeable where his mother had tucked it neatly under his collar. He walked very straight. Then they heard the courtroom door close behind him.

"Mr. Hill, do you realize what you've just done? Don't you wish to reconsider? If you refuse to permit the child to testify, the court has no alternative, upon the appropriate motion of counsel, than to dismiss your case."

"So be it," Hill said. "This boy will not testify. It would be detrimental to his well-being."

"I have no evidence of that before me," the judge said. "Do you wish leave of court to produce competent forensic testimony to that effect?"

"You mean, do I want this boy examined by a psychiatrist?"

"Of course," the judge said, leaning over the bench toward Hill.

"No. I don't want this boy examined by a psychiatrist or by anybody else. He's been through enough."

"You refuse then?"

"Yes, I refuse."

"Ought you not consult his mother?"

"I have already consulted her."

"Madam," the judge was addressing Mary Hamilton, "do you understand that if Mr. Hill has his way here I have no choice but to grant a dismissal of the case."

"I understand," she said.

"Do you agree to that?"

"Yes, I do."

"Mr. Yancey, surely you will reconsider. Can't you see the corner you have forced the plaintiffs into? Is it just?"

Then Yancey went to the bench with Hill and answered the judge outside the hearing of the jury. "My duty is not to justice, whatever it is. I have but one duty and that's to my client."

"But you are an officer of this court and this court has a duty to render justice. Don't you feel you have a duty to aid in its rendition?"

"No, Your Honor. That's Mr. Hill's duty. He made his choice. I've made mine. I move for the dismissal of this case as a sanction for the plaintiff's refusal to present the plaintiff, Charlie Redtail, for questioning as ordered by the court."

"Very well," Judge Henry Hankins said. "I hereby grant your motion. The case is dismissed." He turned to the jury, thanked them for their service, and dismissed them as well. Then he fled the bench as if it were on fire.

Where the boy, Charlie, hid that night while they were searching for him, they never learned. He had walked down the highway in the dark and when the cars came by he laid flat in the barrow pit. Once he heard an old car rattling down the road and he knew it was an Indian car. The Indians saw the boy and hauled him to the shack of the Old Man of Much Medicine. By that time it was already dawn. When the boy found out that Henry Old Deer was not at his shack, he knew where the old man had gone and followed the trail from the old man's place up Spirit Mountain.

That same morning, on Buffalo Creek when the willows were blooming, their silver buds as fuzzy as young caterpillars, the meadowlarks crying out in the ineffable pain of their joy, in that early morning, the darkness having set, the Old Man of Much Medicine walked, his face in the long, early sun and the faces of the other old men also walking, their faces golden in the sun like the yellow light of glory on the faces of old angels.

On that morning the old men on the Twin Buttes Reservation walked silently and apart, alone with themselves in that war zone where the birds waged their battles with song. The old men came to Spirit Mountain and followed the trails of their ancestors upward as if they were following the spokes of a great wheel toward the hub where the spokes came together.

The old man with the single braid down his back, his name was Henry Old Deer. They called him the Old Man of Much Medicine. His legs were as thin as his arms and his ribs were like the ribs of a deer that had died in the winter, the ribs picked clean by the magpies. His belly was the belly of an old man, not flat and hard, the muscles having given way in the nearly eighty years of the beast standing upright, the sag of years, and yet the proud, silent walk. As he climbed the mountain Henry Old Deer made tiny gasping noises with each step, the heart beating too hard for an old man.

A small pouch on a leather thong hung from his neck and in the pouch were the pebbles and the leaves of sagebrush from his father's grave. By midmorning the sun was only as high as the heads of the old men, the men walking upward as fast as the sun rose in the sky. By the time he reached the top, Henry Old Deer was no longer tired. The numbness had gone from his feet. The legs had left him and that was good, because they had been heavy before and now, at the top, they were nothing and he felt he could fly. The sweat made small rivers down his sides so that his deer hide shirt was wet.

When he was certain that all of the old men had arrived, the Old Man of Much Medicine sat down and from the pouch around his waist he withdrew the flint and steel. The old man carefully unwrapped the folds of leather made waterproof with bear grease. The leather contained the charred cloth and tinder. He tucked the charred cloth into the shreds of the inner bark of the dead cottonwood tinder he had patiently dried in the sun. Then Henry Old Deer began to strike the steel against the flint for the sparks. When one caught on the charred cloth, he raised it gently in his cupped hands, a nest with a spark at its center like the nucleus at the center of the cell, like life in the nest, like the heat from the womb of the Great Mother. And his hands raised to the clear spring sky were in worship of the Mother. He blew on the spark and the tinder burst into flames. Then he made the fire of sagebrush.

At first the old men gathered around the fire, for the smoke from the sage purified the old men, the smell of it on their hides driving the bad spirits from their hearts, the hatred from old hearts, the smoke of sage purifying them, for bad spirits do not like the smell of fresh sagebrush burning.

Then the singers who were also the drummers, the ones with the old wild throats, gathered around Henry Old Deer and they pulled out their sticks from under their belts, willow branches as large around as a man's thumb with the soft leather pulled over the batting at their ends and tied with rawhide. Seven of the drummers, some with their backs to the fire, some with their faces to the sun, all warmed, all with their old eyes squinted like cracks, began to sing. They sang to their ancestors who could, like the coyote, like the wild goose, understand the sounds that were the sounds of the Mother.

Below them the prairies were mostly empty, the timorous antelope still there, the frightened deer at the foot of the mountains, the elk hiding high in the Twin Buttes range. But the buffalo were gone and in their place could be seen the red hides of Hereford cattle grazing on the prairies, the many small spots below. The tepees gone and the villages of the Arapahoe people also gone.

Then Henry Old Deer looked past the far waters known as Bull Frog Lake, past the terrible swamplands made by the white man to irrigate the barley they would sell to the breweries to make beer. The farmers, some poor as barnyard chickens, would sell the grain to the company, but not for big money, the land blistered by the farmers, the land cut and bruised, the sky brown from the dust of plows, the farm yards filled with rusted iron—old tractors, their tires flat, ancient threshing machines long dead and too large to be buried, battered trucks, twisted mowers and manure spreaders and old junked cars, dead and not buried. Dead machinery that stood for the farmers' profit: their junkyard their only profit. Beyond the farmer's junkyard the only living thing, the bankers' mortgages.

Henry Old Deer looked off to the Thunder Mountains to the north and he saw the great canyon scratched deep with the steel of the railroad and the blue veins of the highway that made the land look sick and bruised. He saw that it was all gone—the words of his ancestors gone, the buffalo of his ancestors, the great prairies gleaming in the high grass of his ancestors gone. Freedom to soar over the land like the golden eagles, to pull the travois behind old mares to wherever the buffalo wandered, the squaws walking, the children running and laughing, the old men slumping on top of old spotted horses, their heads bouncing to the time of the hoofs, the young warriors riding high and fast without saddles, with only their hard crotches stuck to the withers of their ponies, the young men in the wind. It was all gone. Freedom, Henry Old Deer said, was a bad word. It brought memories of pain.

The old men sang the songs that called in the summer. May there be much rain on the dry prairies. May the small animals be happy once more. May Coyote escape the traps. May Antelope have twins. May our ancestors bless us here on this blessed mountain, on Spirit Mountain. All the rest is gone. This mountain is all that is left, and that because the white man's plows cannot dig up the ribs of this mountain. The white man's roads cannot climb this mountain. It goes nowhere. It only rises up like the head of the Great Mother and then down again, as is her way, and from this holy mountain the Mother sees all and from this mountain one can see the Mother.

Then the men began to call out the names of their ancestors: "Little Owl, he is with us. And the Arapahoe who was taken as a boy and schooled by the whites but returned to his people and became a great warrior, his name, White Crow, is with us. And Yellow Thunder is with us. And also Sharp Nose.

"And when our ancestors drove the whites from the Powder River they were led by Black Coal, and the old chiefs who were sometimes our enemies—Crazy Horse and Red Cloud and Sitting Bull—these great warriors, they are with us, for now in these times of misery we are brothers," came the words of the singers. The singers called out their names and some sang the names in the native tongue. For as the Old Man of Much Medicine said, all of the native peoples will one day come together. For in this day the enemy is the same.

In the singing there was the sense of joining, man with mountain, man with man, man with the spirits of men, man with the bursting springtime that could not be held back, with the song of the meadowlarks that could not be held back. Then the old men walked down the mountain and for some it was pain, for going down the mountain was more difficult than the climb upward. The way down wore at the bones, stabbed at the bones and was the devil for old men.

It was then as Henry Old Deer was descending that the boy saw the old man and that the boy began to run to him. Sometimes he stumbled and fell and sometimes he was like a small, shot deer, but that did not stop the boy.

It was then that in the distance Henry Old Deer had seen the boy. The old man stopped and squinted his eyes. In the spring the boy left long shadows as he ran. The old man knew the boy. And the old man had known that in the spring when the meadowlark was mad in song the child would come.

"That is that Redtail kid," Arthur Antelope said. He was an old man with better eyes.

"I know who he is," Henry Old Deer said.

"That is that breed kid, that Joseph Redtail's kid. Kid name a Charlie."

"I know who he is," Henry Old Deer had said again and the Old Man of Much Medicine had walked down, in the hard way of old men going down, to meet the child coming up. And when they reached each other the boy grabbed hold of the old man and held on to him.

On the evening of the following day the Indian police stopped in front of the Hamilton residence, Charlie in the backseat, the boy weary, but straight like sticks. Mary Hamilton had been up all night. Abner Hill had stayed with her, trying in the best way he could to comfort her. When they saw the child they ran to the car and grabbed him and without thanking the officers, Mary led him quickly into the house.

"Where did you go, Charlie?" She shook him. Silent, his eyes far away. She shook him again. "I've been worried crazy, out of my mind crazy. We've been up and down the highways looking everywhere for you." Then she began to cry and she grabbed him and held him close. At last she pushed him back and looked into his eyes and he was staring back, his eyes still distant as if the light behind had gone.

"The judge threw our case out, Charlie." She couldn't help but say it and after she had said it she wished hadn't.

"It's all right," Abner Hill said quietly.

Then she took the boy again and held him to her. "It doesn't make any difference," she said, crying and holding on to him.

Then Billy came out of the bedroom.

"Yeah," he said. "Chief Chicken Shit couldn't even get up there and answer a few questions. Now we don't get nothin'. I coulda answered their questions," he said.

"Hush," Mary said.

Then Mary said, "Charlie, you can't be an Indian anymore. This has gone far enough." Suddenly she got up and grabbed her scissors. He stood his ground in front of her. "Come here, Charlie." She was crying. "We are going to get rid of that hair. You are a white boy, not an Indian."

"I don't think you should," Hill said.

"Yeah," Billy said. "Indians ain't worth nothin'. The judge threw our case out."

Still the boy stood his ground. Then Mary walked over to the child, her scissors in hand. "Do you want to grow up like your father?" The mother still crying.

"The kids at school don't have nothin' ta do with him, Mom. He is strange, Mom."

"Well, he's not going to be strange anymore." She tried to cut the braid all at once. Hacked at it.

"I don't think you should do that," Hill said. But he did not try to interfere.

"Scalp 'em, Ma," Billy hollered.

"Stop it, Billy!" She hacked again, sobbing.

"I beat up Jimmy Hollingsworth for calling Charlie a dog-eater."

She began to unbraid the hair, then she cut it one strand at a time, the hair falling to the floor.

Billy was talking very loud and fast. "The kids think they are better because we don't have good shoes. And we don't even have a car."

She was hacking at the strands.

"Cars don't make the man," Abner said.

"An' at the party, Harmon Blakely said that no injuns were allowed. An' I told him I wasn't an injun. An' he said I was half an injun and I was still an injun."

"You are what you are," his mother said, trimming up the sides of Charlie's hair. "You can be whatever you want to be."

"An' Harmon Blakely said that injuns and niggers were the same. Couldn't tell 'em apart. An' he said that only one of us could go to the party. He said me and Charlie made one nigger and one white. So we could choose and only one of us could go to the party."

"Who is this Harmon Blakely?" Mary asked, still cutting at the hair.

"He's a big kid in the sixth grade."

"Did you tell Miss Winkley?"

"No. He woulda beat us up. Me an' Charlie didn't go. We went out and shot some hoops."

As she cut at his hair the child, Charlie, stood without tears. The child stiff, without the light of the child in his eyes.

"Now tell me, where did you go when you ran out of the courtroom, Charlie?"

He did not answer. He went to the bedroom where the two boys slept and he lay down on his cot and covered his freshly shorn head, and after that he did not speak in the house for many days.

When Billy saw that his brother was injured in ways he did not understand he tried to comfort him. "You're okay," he said. "Ma, she's just scared. When I grow up I'll buy you good shoes. You look good with your hair that way." He walked over in front of his brother. "See, we look alike now." His brother didn't answer, staring like stone at the wall. "You can have my BB gun." He offered his prized Daisy air rifle, but Charlie did not take the gun. Then, as if he were the father, Billy picked up a book and began to read to him aloud. It was a story about a poor orphan boy who lived in an alley behind the opera house and who one day became very rich. And after that he took Charlie outside and they shot some hoops against the south wall of the Redtail shack.

That night Mary saw him coming through the front door of the bar, his black Stetson down low, the long steps of a man comfortable in cowboy boots. On that summer night she saw him look around the room for her. Finally he spotted her at the far end of the bar where she sat.

"Just tryin' to have a little fun," she said as he sat down. "Been through a lot, the trial and all." She was taking small sips of a margarita. After a time she said, "Maybe you could learn to relax."

"Look who's talking," Abner Hill said. "I never knew you to do anything but work."

"Mom came over and told me to leave. Said I was gettin' too old too quick. Kicked me out of my own house." She laughed a small laugh. "That's why I called you, the kids at home with Mom, an' all. I didn't want to be here alone."

It was too loud to talk much and finally she had shouted over the noise, "You want to dance, Abner?"

"I'm not much of a dancer," Hill hollered back.

"Lawyers are not good dancers," Ace Yokum said, stepping up to the bar. He acted as if he hadn't seen Hill. His way. Then suddenly he laughed and shook Hill by the shoulders. "I'll dance with the lady," Yokum said. He pulled Mary off of the bar stool to her feet. He smelled like oil and inner-tube patching cement, and she held on to him, her head against his coveralls as he took long steps to slow music, this praying mantis dancing with an ant. "I do declare," Ace said, "if we aren't the handsomest couple on the dance floor."

It was the first time she had laughed since the trial, her head still against his coveralls. They danced that dance and two more fast ones before they came back to the table where Hill was sitting.

"Now this woman is a woman," Ace said to Abner Hill with all confidence in his assessment.

"You got something right for a change," Hill said. Hill lifted his bottle of beer in Mary's direction.

"If you were to dance with her, the evening would be a success," Yokum said.

So that night they danced, Hill awkward and trying, the woman helping with the lead, the two like a team of young horses pulling the plow, but not yet in sync. She was his client, this Mary Hamilton, this woman with two boys, their father a dead Indian. "You can always drive the thoughts away," his mother had said, the man still the boy listening to his mother.

"You could be a real good dancer with a little practice," Mary said, showing him how to twirl her in a dance that was something like a cross between a jitterbug and a two-step.

After the music stopped they sat down at the bar again and what he saw he could not put out of his mind. There at the bar with Ace Yokum stomping his big foot to the music, Hill saw a transient happiness, perhaps only relief, steal on to the woman's face. And in that light and at that moment she was very beautiful.

"I gotta go home," she said. "The boys an' all. Mom wants to get up in the mornin' to go to church."

"I'll take you home, Mary," Hill said.

"I do declare," Ace Yokum said, "if once more I am not left alone by the telephone." He got up, bowed to the two of them, and sauntered over to another table, couple of farm women there with their men. Hill saw Yokum pull up a chair, and Yokum, without looking at the men, said something that made the women laugh, especially the blond one with large red lips you could see halfway across the smoky room. Yokum leaned over and kissed the woman with the large lips lightly, laughed, and slapped the man on the back. Then Yokum put his arm around the back of the woman's chair.

"I don't want to see this," Abner Hill said to Mary.

That night they drove Hill's pickup to her house, the old truck rattling its complaints over the corduroy road, she on her side of the seat looking straight ahead, and silent.

They drove down the street with its small, poor houses on both sides until they came to the Redtail shack on the corner.

Her mother had been waiting, her mother saying good night, not lingering, as if to stay a moment longer to put on her coat against the cool night air would be an intrusion.

"The boys are sleeping good now," her mother said as she walked out the door. She didn't look at Abner Hill, talking to Mary as if the man weren't there. "Charlie had a nightmare and was crying, but he's all right now. Billy's all right. Nothin' bothers Billy."

Hill opened the bedroom door and looked in, the boys sprawled over each other in the same small bed, the covers mussed, their hair mussed, their faces innocent in the light from the kitchen. He saw that Charlie was breathing heavily, that he wasn't crying. It had taken months after *the time* before Charlie could go a full day without his eyes growing wild against the scene that played out before him. It had been Hill who could best calm the boy.

"I can't seem to comfort him," Mary had said. "I think he blames me."

"He doesn't blame you, Mary. You blame yourself."

It was as if the child had been born into a prison of ghouls, she thought, and that when Hill was there the ghouls were frightened off. Abner Hill thought it was the way of the man to the child, different from the way of the nurturing mother, the man the protectorate.

At first Charlie had been wild-eyed with terror after his father's murder, the boy trembling but not yet crying, too traumatized to cry, to hear his own sobs. For many nights Hill had held the boy before he went to bed, held him until the boy drifted off to sleep. He held Charlie until the man's own peculiar smell that marks each person like a fingerprint became the smell of father to the child and the child's smell became the smell of the son to Abner Hill, like a man can bond himself to a colt by rubbing it dry with his hands right after it's born. He had not intended it, but the two of them had become grafted to each other not by name and not by blood, but by the power of the absorbing heart.

As for the boy's mother, well, Hill knew a lawyer ought not get involved with his client and Mary Hamilton had been his client for many years. But he couldn't remember the last time she had paid him any money. Paid him in coffee that they drank as they sat across from each other at her kitchen table. Paid him with her quiet presence, a silent bravery some women have who, without many weapons, fight alone to rear their children.

That night after they danced Mary shut the door behind her mother and asked Abner Hill if he wanted coffee.

"It isn't the coffee that keeps me awake," he said. He sat down at the old table, as usual, he at his end and she at the other and, as usual, when she brought him his coffee he poured in the condensed milk from the Carnation milk can and dumped in two spoons of sugar. As usual as they sat across from each other he stirred his coffee looking into the cup, and, as usual, she watched him.

"You're a good dancer," he'd finally said. Then he looked at her and her eyes were soft, but when he kept looking she looked down. Nothing more to say to each other, this attorney and this client in this relationship that brought them together but held them apart. Then suddenly he lifted his cup, emptied it, and stood up. "Gotta go," he said. "Got a trial comin' Monday. They got Horace Little Eagle up for robbery again."

"Probably a liquor store," she said.

"Yeah," he said. "How'd you know?"

Days later, the blond man, Emmett, observing from the bluff across the river, saw Abner Hill get out of his pickup and walk slowly toward the cabin. This evening he walked as if he were an old man. He appeared tired, beaten, his shoulders slumped, his hat askew. Emmett thought he would get no pleasure in putting the bastard out of his misery and if pleasure were evil, as the sweet sisters of Jesus insisted, he wished for pure pleasure.

He had shrugged his shoulders when he told Cotler he hadn't done the job. "Things weren't right at the moment," he said. He asked the bartender to pour him a touch of Old Jasmine brandy out of the bottle he'd furnished for his special use.

It was Indian payday. Cotler was at his ear, talking urgently, like a man in panic, sometimes hollering over the noise of the bar crowd.

"I want you to do the fuckin' job. I thought you were good, Emmett."

When Cotler showed the blond man that disrespect, Cotler had not known the closeness of the brink, as Emmett called it. Emmett's response would not be in anger, for the universe does not act in anger. The blond man began to pare his fingernails. Thankfully he had been spared the foppish sentimentality of the species. To Emmett, revenge was of human fruit and had no meaning in the meaningless cosmos.

Along the way and in every town Emmett had searched for the purely evil man as one searches for treasures. He thought he would also be a man of great virtue. Often he looked for him in the churches, for always the preachers laid a lashing tongue on evil and unless they were themselves evil they could know little of it. In each town he had done his work with pleasure and precision and then moved quietly on, leaving an unknown victim with his face blown off, sometimes the right side, sometimes the left depending on the phase of the moon. Occasionally he cut a woman if, afterward, she were not appreciative, if she did not keep her eyes soft, or if she laughed at him except with deep affection.

He had lingered longer in Twin Buttes than in most of the other small towns. At the Big Chief bar he had stumbled on to Cotler, who often spoke with a singular hatred concerning the man Abner Hill. Emmett found such hatred entertaining, Cotler's hate so intense, so focused, and the man so consumed by it that at first Emmett thought the hatred had traveled full circle so that hatred and love had become joined and the evil had become pure. But Cotler, like the others, had proved to be a disappointment.

Men, Emmett thought, were but animals engaged in a process. He could not speculate as to what the process was or where, if anywhere, it was going. Processes do not have a destination. Nor did he care. He only knew that if he killed, the universe would be irrevocably shaped by the killing. He had the power of the kaleidoscope in his hands. Its most imperceptible shaking would change the pattern and that was why he called himself "the pattern changer."

At Harvard on a Saturday night he had met Madeline Hennisey, the farmer's plump wife. She had been standing at the gate when he appeared out of the darkness and he had turned and kissed her and left her frightened because she had never felt out of control in that way before. He followed her into the living room and in the dark he had taken the woman on the couch, her husband asleep in the next room. He had counted the strokes in the copulative exercise to seventy-two, but when she whispered that she loved him, he stopped suddenly, withdrew, and left the woman lying on the couch still clutching in her right hand the panties he had earlier cut from her with a single stroke of his knife.

Now behind the cottonwoods and the river willows he had waited once more for Abner Hill, the rifle at his shoulder, his cold eye an extension of the cold scope. As Hill walked slowly toward the cabin he followed with the crosshairs fixed on Hill's temple. At this range and at the slow speed of the man's gait he would need to lead the man but an inch. He pushed the safety off with his thumb.

Then he began to slowly squeeze the trigger. Suddenly he stopped and backed away from the scope. Once more he was not in concentration. Nor did he feel the exhilaration. Why should he kill without delectable pleasure? And to kill this man called Abner Hill would put him in the service of Cotler, which was not a part of the design, for the universe is in service of nothing.

Something about the man, this Hill, perhaps he possessed a power he had yet to encounter, for twice the man had escaped the explosion of his rifle. The blond man dropped the rifle from his shoulder and replaced it in its case, his eyes without expression, his face without sadness, without anger, like a resplendent cipher. As he began to close the case he realized he had not served revenge and that was acceptable. But Hill, not he, had changed the pattern and that was not acceptable. He pulled the rifle out of its case again, but by this time Abner Hill had already entered his cabin, which had been the third time the man had avoided his destiny.

In the morning Emmett came to the realization that at that moment Twin Buttes was not a place in harmony. Something strange about this lost, two-bit town with its prissy people and its tight, thin-lipped morality. Except for the Indian girl, Betty Yellow Calf, whose head had merely been a convenient target, his work had been frustrated. The farm woman, Madeline, had escaped, as had her husband, and three times Abner Hill had evaded his power.

Then he realized he should leave Twin Buttes, leave Cotler untouched, leave Abner Hill to his own powers whatever they were, and that he should return one day when the stars were aligned in a different configuration, when the stars were not so empty and the moon perhaps full. It would take only a slight shaking of the cosmic kaleidoscope to change the course of eternity. That same night he drove out of Twin Buttes headed for whatever destination the universe directed, but yes, of course, he would return, if for nothing more, to absorb the power of the place.

Part II

14

By the time Charlie was fifteen he would have run off to any other place than Twin Buttes. He longed to be gone from that dreary, tight little town, dreamed of it at night, thought of it as the algebra teacher droned on and scratched his ugly formulas on the blackboard. What did formulas have to do with anything he had learned from the Old Man of Much Medicine? He had asked the old man. And the old man just laughed. "It is the way the white man plays with himself," the old man had said.

Billy was good with figures. He was good in school. And sometimes he helped Charlie, who seemed slower in the wearisome academic trek. Despite Billy's near precocious performance in the classroom and his excess energy that permitted him to drag Charlie along, Billy needed Charlie, each brother sheltered by a brother in a world that seemed hostile to both.

"Strange thing, those Redtail boys," Horace Oliver, their history teacher once said of them. "They look alike but that only goes to show that 'looks are only skin deep,' as my mother used to say. They are as different as two peas in a pod."

"Your metaphors are fucked," Paul Osterland, the school's lit and journalism teacher said.

"Well, anyway you know what I mean," Oliver said.

The boys rarely socialized with the other students, but not out of choice. Natural boundaries emerged like great rivers, the boys standing on one bank gazing at the distant shore. The boys were not white, not at all, the dark eyes, the olive skin, dusky under the eyes. They were handsome in their way, the prominent features of their father displayed, especially a handsome protuberance at their noses, the higher structure of the cheekbones and the jet black hair. And they were not Indian, not quite. Yet Charlie came the closest. His words, when he spoke them, had taken on the flat quality of the Arapahoe, the sound of the Old

Man of Much Medicine. Charlie spoke slowly as if in deep thought and he used a paucity of words as if they were precious. Billy on the other hand spoke with a quick Wyoming twang, a sort of midwestern full-in-your-face sound where the words seemed round enough, but impatient.

Yet on the basketball court they were the same. They were each other's shadow. Enriched by their father's genes and strengthened by their mother's they were powerful players at the game, coordinated, indefatigable, and possessed of a sixth sense in the strategy of the split second. And when the kids in school were at other play, the Redtail boys were shooting hoops in the backyard, the ball in their hands as if all misery, all degradation, all disappointment and all poverty were somehow dissolved in the rhythm and the release.

Both boys understood the burden their mother bore. From the time they were old enough they held jobs—lawn jobs in the summer, shoveling the walks of the neighbors in the winter. Charlie did odd jobs at the elevator, swept the granary floors, and choked in the dust while Billy sold magazines. Charlie had tried it once. That time the boys each took a side of the street. They were to knock on the doors and offer their specials to the householders—three subscriptions to magazines no one could do without and for the price of one. But after Billy had finished his side of the street Charlie was still standing in front of the first house. Billy crossed over.

"What's the matter?" he asked.

Charlie didn't answer. Just stood there staring at the door.

"Come on," Billy said. He grabbed him by the arm and led him up the steps. "Now knock."

Charlie tapped timidly.

"No, knock hard. Like this." Billy pounded on the door. Shortly the door opened. It was Jessie Haywood. Her husband owned the Jersey creamery.

"What do you boys want?" she asked. "I'm already late for a hair appointment."

Billy nudged Charlie. Charlie stood there, panic on his face.

"Well," the impatient sound of the woman, the door beginning to close.

"Ma'am," Billy said, "my brother, here, has to sell a magazine subscription before he goes home or our old man will beat him."

"Well, I declare. I think that's terrible. I'll call the police."

"Then we really will be in trouble. After the police leave he'll beat us both."

"Well," she said, "you boys come in here. And hurry. My hairdresser is waiting." And after that she chose three magazines including *Boy's Life*, which she said she would have sent to the boys' house since they "needed some support at home they surely were not getting."

Down on the street again Billy said, "We should do that everywhere. You just stand there dumblike. It comes natural for you. I'll do the talking. We can sell a shit pot full of magazines and make a lot of money and go to New York and see the Statue of Liberty and the Empire State Building."

The next day Billy dragged his brother to the house next to Jessie Haywood's. A big man with a belly answered the door.

"What do ya want?" he asked. He looked mean, his voice like a hack saw.

"My brother wants to sell you a magazine," Billy said.

"I 'spose your old man will kick the shit out of him if I don't buy, right?"

"How did you know?" Billy said with astonishment.

"Me and my brother used ta pull the same gag thirty years ago. Now get yer ass outa here, afor I turn ya in to the cops." And after that they both delivered papers for the *Twin Buttes Times*.

As the boys grew older they approached their responsibility to their mother in different ways. Billy got a summer job selling Kirby vacuum cleaners. Earned twice as much as Mary in the same three months of summer. Her salary, the minimum wage. Her tips, a dime. Big tip, a quarter. "I don't believe in tippin'," Ham Blumenshine, the mayor, said. "Them waitresses get paid for what they do like anybody else. Nobody ever tipped me."

"You ain't got an ass like hers," Fisher said. He was the new guy at the Bank of Twin Buttes. Came floating in from New York and nobody trusted him. He tipped Mary a dollar once. But she wouldn't take it. Thought he wanted something more than what she had to offer under the bright, florescent lights of the café.

That summer Billy made enough to pay off the family grocery bill at Harbor Grocery and to bring them current on their gas and electric bills. And he had enough left over to make a down payment on a '46 Chevy coupe.

Charlie, on the other hand, against his mother's admonitions and protestations, was spending more of his time with the Old Man of Much Medicine. Often the old man said, "Only white men work. They have the brains of a jackrabbit. They jump from job to job leaving their little black turds behind them, and when they take their last jump all they got to show for it is their pile a turds." He laughed. "What good are a pile of dollars? They are good for nothin'."

Charlie said, "They'll buy the Snickers bars you like."

"That is what you are for," the old man said. "You buy me a Snickers bar the next time you come. Don't forget. It's the only good thing the white man ever done."

Charlie lived with the old man during most of the summer. He slept on the floor wrapped in an old army blanket and he and the old man took long walks in the forest and over the prairies. He learned the Indian names of many flowers and herbs. He learned to catch fish with a snare and to kill the antelope cleanly, efficiently with one patient shot. He learned to live off of the land, off the wild game and young sage chickens that in the late summer he could kill with a rock. And he learned the language of the Arapahoe, the language of his father which held the stories of his people, their history and the words of which carried the spirit of his ancestors.

He argued to himself and once to his mother that she didn't have to feed him for those three months. In that way he contributed to the family. And when he came home he brought a mess of brook trout and some fresh venison he and the old man had taken on the reservation where there were no hunting seasons. In the late summer he brought home buckets of chokecherries and sometimes currants. Then on his mother's clothesline he dried the venison in long, thin strips and with the stone mortar and pestle the old man had given him he smashed the chokecherries into the dried venison, seeds and all, and made pemmican for their winter use. Even Billy acquired a taste for it and although Mary only nibbled at it politely from time to time, the boys ate it regularly, especially before a big game. Some claimed that their pemmican was the secret to their prowess on the basketball court.

Even during the school year Charlie was often on the reservation with the old man. Sometimes he would not come back until Evertte Langly, the coach, and Billy came for him in the coach's old Dodge pickup. Then Billy would help Charlie catch up on his schoolwork, write his essays for him, and tutor him for his tests. Billy would holler about it. Sometimes they would fight about it.

"You cause me a lotta fuckin' trouble," Billy said. "I'm always havin' to take care of you."

"You don't take care of me," Charlie would say with slow words. "I come back so you can play basketball."

Together they were magical on the court, one knowing where the other was even without seeing, as one hand knows where the other is in the dark.

Yes, Charlie thought, he and Billy were high school heroes. But for them being heroes was lonely. They were magicians with the ball, all right, and the school gave them credit for that. But they were still "breeds" and strange ones, especially Charlie with his long braid down the back. The moment after a game that they walked back out the locker room door a different magic took over, and they were suddenly transformed to "those breed twins" again.

Both boys called the locker room door the "Black Door." Once when Billy called it that in front of Greg Smith, the forward on their team, he wanted to know what Billy meant.

"It's black," Billy repeated.

"Jesus, Redtail, you color blind or somethin'? That door is light green," Smith said.

"It's black to me," Billy said.

"Yeah," Charlie said, "it's black. You wouldn't understand."

"You better go get yer eyes examined," Smith said.

"They see shit we don't see, if you know what I mean," Bobby Watson said. "Wished I had eyes like that. I'd get me a scholarship to the University of Wyoming and be a big shot. Get a lotta girls to suck my dick." He laughed. "I say the fuckin' door is black."

Early on some of the other boys had been jealous and had ganged up, but Charlie and Billy had stood back to back against them. Together they had been as invincible in the school brawls as on the court.

As for their dress, on the court the boys on the team looked alike in their blue-and-gold shirts and shorts. But after the game and at school the Redtail boys were different. They wore old clothes that were mostly out of style. Got them at some church rummage sale. And Charlie had that braid, a strange boy who came alive on the court in the presence of his brother Billy, but who otherwise was reclusive and shy.

Charlie Redtail's braid even became the subject of the town fathers who met every morning at the Twin Buttes coffee shop for breakfast.

They sat in the big round booth over by the window, the place reserved for them. They smoked their cigarettes and drank their coffee and talked about their championship basketball team. They also pronounced the fate of the community on issues ranging from whether there should be parking meters on Main Street to the acceptable length of hair for the high school boys.

"Damned kids," Rudy Andrews, councilman from Ward Two said, lighting up a Lucky and offering the pack around. "You can't tell the girls from the boys anymore."

Mary Hamilton topped his coffee cup. "Aren't you a little old, Rudy, to be caring what the difference is?"

"Right," Bill Morris, manager of the light company, chimed in. "There's other ways a tellin', ya know."

"I don't 'spose he'd know," Mary said, and everybody laughed, including Mary.

"Bring him his prune juice," Bill Morris said. "That'll help." And everybody laughed again.

And when Mary walked from the table toward the kitchen carrying her empty coffeepot and was out of earshot, Fisher said, "Look at the ass on that tomato."

Ham Blumenshine, the mayor, said. "One a them high-ridin' kind. Her mother had one just like it."

"Never could figger out how come nobody snatched her up after all these years," Bill Morris said. Then they talked about their basketball team and the Redtail boys and Charlie's braid.

"School made ever'body cut their hair above their ears, except Charlie Redtail," Ham Blumenshine said. "Woulda made Charlie cut his, too, 'cept Charlie said he'd quit. And Billy said he'd quit if his brother quit and there'd go our champion high school basketball team right out the fuckin' window. It all depends on a fuckin' hank a hair." He laughed.

"You don't fuck with a winner," Morris said. "That kid's one hell of a shot. 'Nother Jim Thorpe."

"He ain't no Jim Thorpe. He's a half-breed," Blumenshine said.

"Well, Billy Redtail never had a braid and he was just as good a shot as Charlie," Bill Morris, manager of the light company, said. "Shows you: Charlie's braid never helped any and it never hurt any."

"That's what I been arguin' from the beginning," Jake Motherswell, the city engineer, said. "Hair doesn't make a damn. I said all along, leave the kids' hair out of it."

"Kid's gotta show some respect," Rudy Andrews said. " 'Member that time when Billy and his brother Charlie was playing Three Forks an' that long braid of Charlie's was bouncing all over the place, an' that kid from Three Forks grabbed hold of his braid and slammed ol' Charlie to the floor. 'Member that?"

"I 'member that," Bill Morris said. "Before Charlie could do anything, Billy was all over that Three Forks kid like flies on shit. Took both refs and half the team to pull Billy off."

"Spooky. If it wasn't for that braid of Charlie's I challenge ya ta tell them kids apart. Can't be done," Ham Blumenshine said.

"I wished I was a twin like that. I'd slip in some night an' get me a little offa my brother's old lady," Fisher said.

"God ain't that cruel ta make two in the world like you," Bill Morris said, and everybody laughed again.

None of the girls had much to do the Redtail boys. The cheerleaders cheered for them during the games, but gave them only passing nods in the hall, as if they were strangers from another world. Occasionally Billy did better. He had that derelict car that was greatly better than no car at all. But the girls had nothing to do with Charlie. He had that awful braid, and some of the boys had whispered to the girls that maybe he was "a little you know what," because real men cut their hair short.

As the boys grew up Hill had always been there for them, been there when the cops hauled Charlie in for stealing milk off the neighbor's porch when his mother didn't have the money to buy it; been there when the game warden caught Charlie poaching deer off the reservation and out of season, venison to feed the family. And once he went with Charlie to the principal's office to get him reinstated in school after he was expelled. Charlie thought that Horace Oliver, his American history teacher, had belittled Native Americans when he claimed that the white man brought civilization to the West. Charlie stood up and said in his slow, flat voice, "All the white man brought to the West was syphilis and whiskey." The class had laughed and Horace Oliver had expelled him on the spot.

"You do not talk about syphilis in the classroom," Mr. Asay, the principal said. "That is an American history class."

"Syphilis is part of our American history," Hill said. "And what about the boy's First Amendment rights?" Then Hill looked at the man for a long time. "You know, Asay, you wouldn't dare expel him during basket-ball season. So is it syphilis or basketball we're interested in here?"

Hill had been there during all of the hard years that had dragged both him and Mary Hamilton through the boys' angry puberty, through their intransigent revolts against authority—their mother's, the school's, the law's. Billy Redtail had also been in trouble—got the Murphy girl pregnant.

"It was that car of his, Abner," she said. "I always say that boys' cars are baby-making machines."

The girl's father wouldn't let her marry a breed. He'd wanted Billy Hamilton prosecuted for statutory rape and Hill had gone to see Ava Mueller, the prosecutor.

"That rape law is silly," Hill argued to Ava Mueller. "It says that any boy of any age, even a twelve-year-old, can be guilty of statutory rape if he has sex with a girl sixteen or under."

"That's because the law says that a girl sixteen or under is legally incapable of giving her consent," Ava Mueller said. The prosecutor still looked too young to be taken seriously.

"That's a fiction. We both know that," Hill said. "Say the kids are in love. Say, the girl is begging for it, and—"

"Girls don't beg for it," Ava Mueller said. "Boys beg for it and girls give in. That's why the law protects girls. And love? Who knows any-thing about love at sixteen?"

Although Hill never thought he'd won the argument with Mueller she had refused to charge Billy. Later he discovered that Asay, the high school principal, had intervened. It was basketball season and Twin Buttes was looking for the state Class B championship again that year. Down the line the Murphy girl had a miscarriage and things were for-gotten as they were in Twin Buttes—not lost from the minds of the people, but edited from their tongues. The year after her graduation the girl married a rig hand from Hanna and those who knew her father said he was very proud.

In his junior year after the Twin Buttes homecoming football game Billy had been thrown in jail and charged with drunkenness and resist-ing arrest. Hill found him behind the bars looking pitiful and when his mother was unable to scrape up the money for his bail, Hill, contrary to the lawyer's code of ethics, put up the boy's bond himself. After that Hill pled Billy guilty to disturbing the peace and paid his fine of $100.

But Billy had to work it off. Cleaned Hill's office for three months, emptied the waste baskets, washed the windows, and whatever else Hill could muster up for the boy to do. It was during that time that Billy got interested in how the law worked. He said he wasn't going to be a lawyer. Lawyers like Hill worked too hard for too little.

"I'm gonna hire lawyers," he said to Hill one day. "Big shot lawyers. And I'm gonna be rich and come back and buy Twin Buttes, buy the damned hotel where my mom works, throw out all those bastards who make a slave of her. I'm gonna own the town and they can come beggin' to me for a change."

In his senior year at Twin Buttes High something else lent to the transformation of Billy Redtail. On his first day in her class, his English teacher, Miss Thelma Melbourne, had confronted the boy. He'd been causing a disturbance in the back of the room and she'd called him to the front of the class. He strutted up like a peacock in pinfeathers, his hands in his pockets, that derisive grin on his face, the others watching and giggling.

"What is your name, sir?" Miss Melbourne asked quietly.

"You know my name," Billy said.

"What is your name?" she repeated in the same quiet voice.

"Billy Redtail," still the smile.

Then she pointed at him with a quavering finger and said, "Class, behold the fool," and when everyone in the room laughed, Billy slouched back to his seat looking down at his feet, his face red.

After that he sat morbidly silent in her room until several weeks later when she took him aside after school and told him he was extremely bright, that he could be successful, more successful even than Fred Hobbs, who ran the grain elevator where Charlie had worked and who was the town's richest man.

Then before he left the room she said, "Billy, I want to be proud of you," which was something that no one had ever said to the boy. "It is important to me," she said, and her eyes were soft, even a little wet.

Some claimed that when Harvard University had offered a full scholarship to a Native American in the area it was Miss Melbourne who not only discovered the scholarship but nominated Billy for it. At the urging of his mother, Billy accepted it, and early in the following September, Billy Redtail left Twin Buttes for Harvard University where he excelled beyond the expectations of everyone, all except Miss Melbourne.

At Harvard Billy had taken his mother's maiden name so that there and thereafter he was known as William R. Hamilton. He took an MBA from Harvard Business School and was soon solidly in place as a partner in the Wall Street investment banking firm of Willis and Bentley.

At Christmastime in his third year at Willis and Bentley, William R. Hamilton bought Miss Melbourne a full-length mink coat. By then she was sixty-three years of age. Shortly after that he became a partner in the firm and Hamilton had tried to buy his mother a comfortable house in the new Twin Buttes addition. Mary had refused his offer. She said she hadn't taken charity from anyone up until then and she wasn't going to take any charity from him.

Hamilton had argued back, "It is a matter of some embarrassment to me, Mother, that I am this affluent investment banker, but I abandon my poor mother to a shack. How can you humiliate me so?"

"This is where you grew up," she said. "It was good enough for you then. It is good enough for me now." And that had ended it and he had not come home after that until, of course, Charlie Redtail was charged with murder.

15

That holy place to the Arapahoe people, Spirit Mountain, had been excluded from the treaty of 1867 by mistake, the title reserved to the United States government. In modern times it had fallen under the jurisdiction of the Bureau of Land Management, Department of Agriculture. The mountain had little commercial value. Its steep slopes with their sandstone outcroppings discouraged development. A single attempt at drilling a water well had been abandoned in the fall of 1963 after the hole was still dry at a thousand feet.

Seismograph crews thoroughly explored the mountain but discovered no oil structures beneath the surface, the underflesh of the mountain as barren and unproductive as its epidermis where nothing but sagebrush and the curling, hard fescue grasses clung to the sandy soil like desperate, sparse hair clinging to the head of a balding man. And there was no market for scenery. The BLM could not catalogue beauty. You cannot feed beauty to cattle. Cattle do not grow fat on sunsets.

In June of 1976, the BLM had welcomed the petition brought to its regional office in Casper, Wyoming, by Gerald P. Sackman, the bank's lawyer in Twin Buttes, who, representing Ronald Cotler, by then a member of the bank's board, offered to exchange his good two-hundred-acre irrigated, bottom farmland along the Twin Buttes River for the twenty-three thousand acres encompassed by what was generally referred to as Spirit Mountain. The farmlands along the river adjoined the prairies beyond and opened a welcome corridor for ranchers to water their cattle on otherwise chronically drought-stricken lands.

The Arapahoe tribe, advised of the proposed land exchange by public notice in the *Twin Buttes Times,* did not understand the concept of land exchange although the elders of the tribe had been told of the proposal in person by one George Beaty, regional manager for the BLM.

Beaty had met with the elders of the tribe and explained the procedures as best he could to "those uneducated aborigines," as he called them.

But how, the Indians reasoned, could the government exchange the mountain? The white man had no such magic. The mountain could no more be exchanged for other lands than a man could exchange his heart for the heart of a stranger.

"This mountain belongs to the Mother Earth," the Old Man of Much Medicine said. "These are the lands of our ancestors. This mountain does not belong to the gov'ment. White men do not walk on the ground anymore. And even we walk on the ground with rev'ert feet."

"I understand," George Beaty, the BLM's manager replied. He did not understand. "But, Chief, the legal title to this land is in the United States, not the tribe."

"I am not the chief," Henry Old Deer said. "I only speak for the people. I speak out of the heart of the people."

"I understand," Beaty said. He did not understand. "But we are considering a swap for some better land on the Twin Buttes River and we are advising you of this in order that you may file your response to this proposal in accordance with our regulations."

"We do not understand," the old man said. Two other Arapahoe elders nodded.

Hiram Cut Nose said, "I do not understand. The mountain was given to us in the treaty."

"Afraid not, Chief," Beaty said. He flipped through the pages of his black loose-leaf notebook, then stopped, looked at both sides of the page in front of him, and shoved the notebook to Hiram Cut Nose. "It's right here, Chief. Take a look."

But Hiram Cut Nose hadn't looked. He had been looking beyond the notebook to the mountain. "I am not the chief," he also said. "No one has ever said we do not own this mountain."

"Well, I hate to be the first," Beaty said.

"A man cannot own a mountain," Henry Old Deer said. "A man cannot own a mountain any more than the fingers can own the hand or the hand can own the arm. They belong to each other."

"That's all well and good, Chief. But unfortunately that isn't the way things work with the United States Government."

Beaty had tried to be patient. These were old men. The old man, Hiram Cut Nose, could not read. And Henry Old Deer's eyes were faded. "I could read you the description of the lands included in the treaty, if you wish," Beaty said. "It's right here. But it's mostly a meets and bounds description. Frankly, doesn't make much sense to me, but our engineers plotted it out." Beaty was trying to be friendly. He wore no uniform. Dressed like a local rancher in jeans and a shirt open at the neck. But his face was pale like a man from the sick house.

"We will talk," Henry Old Deer said at last, which was to say that the old men in the tribe would consider the matter.

Then in the spring the old men had climbed Spirit Mountain when hope was in bloom, the meadowlark delirious in joy, the clouds boiling up in great billowing smiles, the sky as pale cerulean as the lupine. But the old men came from their shacks on the reservation with heavy hearts.

"Our feet are in the quicksand," Henry Old Deer said when the old men had gathered at the top of the mountain. The others could hear the sinking in his voice.

"The white man takes. And leaves the leavings. Then the white man takes the leavings," Hiram Cut Nose said.

They called upon their ancestors for wisdom and they called upon the Great Spirit for its blessing and the drumming and their cries could be heard across the valley below.

At last Henry Old Deer stood up. It was not easy to get from the ground to his feet. The ground is asking for me, the old man thought. The ground is getting stronger. Then he said, "It is not possible for the gov'ment to trade this mountain. That is the talk of foolish men. You can trade hides for salt and horses for women."

"No more," said Horace Weasel Horn. "That was in them good days."

"The white man is loco," Henry Old Deer said. "The white man cannot trade this mountain," and the drums began again and the beating of the drums beat the white spots deep into the feathers of the loon. And the loon laughed long and wildly at the loco white man and the song settled onto the valley below along with the smoke from the old men's fire.

Then in the late summer, when the leaves of the arrowroot were dry and rattled in the hot wind and the grass was curled and brown, when the grasshoppers exploding in delight made those popping noises with wings in short flights, the creeks nearly dry, the trout hiding in cool places under deep rocks and the dust on the distant prairies rising in dense brown clouds, the Arapahoe people had gathered at the powwow to hear the wisdom of their elders concerning the holy place called Spirit Mountain. They met at the powwow under open roofs thatched with river willows, the roofs held up by crooked cottonwood poles.

They met with the sun going down, the women sitting in a large circle on the outside, the men of families sitting in the center, the dogs running among the people, yapping and skinny, the children with dirty faces from the dust of summer, the children chasing one another and chasing the dogs.

Then the old men gathered around the drum and they began the beating, seven old men beating. The sound came like the noise of the heart at the throat. The rhythms of the beating were of the earth, for as there is a beating in the heart of the man there is also one in the wolf, and the muskrat in the swamps, and in the hummingbird as well, and there is a beating in the heart of the earth. And when the beating of the drums is in sync with that of the earth, the magic of Mother Earth is opened and flows out like a fresh spring bursting from the mountainside.

Then came the high, anguished cries of the drummers, their singing like the coyote sings. That night the songs were to drive the pain of fear from the hearts of the people. The beating filled their ears and grabbed hold of their feet, and the young dancers began to dance, and the older family people tapped their feet, and the children danced on the edges, jumping high at the beating of the drum like the summer grasshoppers.

The dancers, some nearly naked, wore round harness bells on their brown ankles and beaded moccasins on their feet. They wore war bonnets of eagle feathers that fanned out like the tails of the strutting prairie chicken. The dancers danced, some with great abandon as if driven by bad spirits, and some danced easy with small steps and some turned in circles, around and around until they were surely dizzy but they did not fall. They danced to the songs of the old men, and the songs sought the guidance of the Great Spirit and the wisdom of their ancestors.

When at last the dancers were sweat and dust and their legs heavy, the dancers having woven themselves in and out of one another like the threads of the weaving women, the children sleeping, their heads on their mothers' laps and the dogs silent, then the people stilled.

Charlie Redtail had danced like a bucking, crazy horse on locoweed, his frame wet with sweat. After the dancing he and the others had wrapped themselves in blankets, he in an old khaki army blanket, and after the dancing he walked slowly among the people, his blanket over his naked shoulders. Some of the people nodded to him. And one woman, Lucy Sitting Eagle, whispered that she had known his father, Joseph Redtail, and that he was a great man and Charlie Redtail thanked her with his eyes. At last he sat on the ground with the other young men, the Arapahoe people gathered there, the earth against their bodies where they sat.

When at last there was silence, the Old Man of Much Medicine had risen from the people and walked as straight as a young aspen to the fire, his face aglow. There were many valleys across the old man's cheeks and marks of small rivulets across his forehead washed out by the waters of time. He stood bareheaded before the people, his silver-and-black hair glistening in the firelight, the one long braid down the back. He looked tall standing alone before the fire, but the years had cut height from his body so that when he stood among the young men of the tribe he was shorter than most.

At last the Old Man of Much Medicine began to speak in a quiet voice. "My people, I do not speak out of anger. My heart is at peace. And therefore my heart will speak the truth.

"Some say the white man will pay us for the mountain. We cannot sell this holy place of our ancestors. We cannot sell what we do not own for we cannot own a holy place.

"Some say the white man will give us money for the mountain. Money is not good. Money buys trouble. Money does not buy peaceful hearts.

"Some say the white man will give us better land. But the white man gives us only the pox. He gives us our dead and our prairies turned to dust." The old man did not speak to the people. He spoke to the fire and at last to the stars.

"The white man is born without memory, like the crippled child born without legs. And without memory, the white man forgets his promises at the moment he makes them. For that he must be pitied, not hated. But we, the Arapahoe people, are a people of memory." He waited for a long while and all that could be heard was the wailing of a child in the distance.

At last he said, "We remember the treaty of 1851. But the white men in Washington have no memory of that treaty and that is good for them. Men need not keep promises if they have no memory.

"At Horse Creek our people met with those who spoke for the Great White Father as we called the gov'ment in those days. We met with those white men along with the Cheyennes and the white men gave us back only a pitiful part of the land that had been ours from the beginning, like giving back a caged bird a shed feather. That land, the white man said, would be ours forever. It was in the treaty in the black-and-white writing of the white man. That land had always been ours and a hundred more.

"Then the white man went loco for gold. The white man killed many of our people and came charging over our land, killing our buffalo and frightening the game from the land. The white man does not remember he was loco, for the loco do not remember. I speak out of pity.

"Once there had been an endless sea of buffalo, but the loco left only their carcasses rotting in the sun." Following the old man's hand the people could see the horror on the long, rolling prairies.

"Our people starved in the winter. I remember well my own father weeping, his memory of our dead piled up in the winter and our children with bellies bloated like pregnant women. We are a people of memory."

The Old Man of Much Medicine waited. He heard the quiet coughing here and there, but no other sound from the people. The old man looked off into the dark as if he could see into the past.

"Then the railroads cut an ugly steel line though our land and what was left of the game was frightened away. And because our people starved, the white man divided us. Some, with promises of food from the white man, went south and some stayed in the north. But our people were no longer a people and many who did not die had to leave their land to keep from starving." He stopped. The fire was silent, the silent flames in the night. At last he said, "And we were too weak to fight."

The old man's voice was as clear as the brown forest thrush, but it was not an angry voice and it was not a voice of lamentations. It was a voice of memory. Then the Old Man of Much Medicine turned to the people behind him who had seen only his back and his face still glowed in the embers of the fire. He spoke again to the half-moon.

"Then the white man without memory said we must leave the land given us in the treaty of 1851 and that we must live with other tribes on their reservations. We did not wish to leave our land and live with the Cheyennes or the Sioux on reservations so small and the land so poor and the air so sick that the place was like prison to us.

"After that the white man came again," the old man said in a voice as flat as the prairies. "He brought his sheep and his cattle, and they ate all of the grass and they ate the roots of the grass and trampled the sage. And the white man tore up the ground with his plows. The buffalo were dead. The elk hid shivering in the high mountains. The deer were as wild as rabbits chased by the wolf. This reservation is small, like a stone clinging to the mountainside, and in this empty place our people were hungry. And our people became sick from the white man's whiskey and the disease that makes sores on our bodies and our children blind at their birth.

"We had no choice. We joined the white man like the starving wolf became the house dog. We did not join with the other tribes at the Little Big Horn where Custer's troops were killed in the summer of 1876 like fish trapped in a pool. We scouted for the white soldiers. We were loyal as we were taught by our ancestors. Then when the general asked us what land we wanted we told him: " 'Here, here at the Tongue River is where we want to be,' we told him. And the white man agreed. But the white man has no memory. In the winter he turned our people away from the agency and did not give the flour, the beans, and the bacon as he promised and once more our people starved."

Sometimes when the old man paused to let the silence set in, the people could hear the small explosions from the burning embers of the pine logs. Now the old man looked up to the sky again and for only a moment to the stars. Then he looked back at the fire.

"Spirit Mountain was the place of our ancestors. It was the place where they took counsel, the place where my father took counsel. It is the place where we take counsel, where we have taken counsel even during this moon to consider what the white man has told us. And we have come to the truth. And I speak it to you."

The smoke from the fire smelled of pine and at times a woman had come softly to the fire and laid a branch of sage on the fire. The smell of the sage was good, and the smell of the sage cleaned the air and drove away bad thoughts.

Then the old man spoke once more. "I say it is better we make no agreements with the white man, for agreements require memory. Better we let him be, like one does not disturb the sleeping bear. Better to speak no words to him and hold on to our words, for a man has only so many words to speak in a lifetime and they ought not be wasted.

"If, therefore, we speak no words and there are no agreements, nothing can be forgotten." He waited a long time. He looked down into the glowing embers and his face was at peace. At last he said, "I have spoken," and many nodded and many saw the wisdom in what the old man had said.

After the old people and the families had gone home, some of the young men rolled in a keg of beer. They were the irrepressible ones who drove their old cars fast on the highway like the white man. The young men were without authority and most were seen by the white man as renegades in the tribe, the young bucks who fought for the fun of fighting and who often were up against the law. To many of the renegades, being in trouble with the law was more or less their business, as warring and hunting and dancing was the business of their ancestors. Most did not work. Work was the way of the white man, the trading of life for money, for dirty paper. Only the loco man beats up his body, as if he hates the body. How could a sane man make the body sore and blistered, the muscles crying, and for dead money? Their ancestors hunted and fought great wars. Their ancestors were brave men who gathered in hunting parties, who scouted and fought the enemy. But they did not dig holes in Mother Earth and they did not rip up the soil and sweat like fools in the sun.

Many of the renegades hung out in the bar at Hiram Falls and many at the Big Chief bar. They drank until the money from their allotment checks was gone and their credit used up. Besides, there were no jobs, except in the deep summer in the hay fields, and most of those were taken by the soft sons of the white man. During the summer there were only twenty jobs at the Middle Fork Ranch, a ranch run by the tribe, and those jobs were only for men with good horses.

The renegades were too young to garner the respect of the tribe, but not too young to fight for the tribe. They were too wild, but no more wild than their elders had been. They drank too much, but no more than their elders had drunk, and they got into trouble with the law, but no more trouble than their elders when they had been of warrior age.

Charlie Redtail was of the warrior age. And after the Old Man of Much Medicine had spoken and the family people had left the pow-wow, the renegades drank the beer and sang their songs, many without words. Many danced and made noises like crazy men dancing on coals and some went looking for the girls who stood in the shadows on the edge of the firelight talking to one another and giggling. At the fire the smell was of beer, the smell of sage long gone into the night air. By then the half-moon was setting behind the Twin Buttes Mountains.

After the elders had gone and the family men had left for their homes with their wives and their sleeping children, Charlie Redtail stood to speak. Although he was of their age he spoke with the voice of the elder. He stood before the war shield that had been given to Sitting Eagle. The shield had much power and belonged to the tribe, the shield entrusted to Charlie Redtail by the keeper of the tribe's sacred objects, Harvey Crying Horse.

Simon Yellow Dog held up the shield to hush them, and those who had been dancing stopped. Some staggered to the fire where Charlie Redtail stood. The young renegades listened even though some called him a breed, but not to his face, because although he was known to be a peaceful man, he was also known to be very strong.

He spoke to the half-moon then setting. "The old man has spoken, and the old man is right," he said. "The gov'ment has no memory because the gov'ment does not breathe like we breathe. The gov'ment does not drink like we drink. The gov'ment is like this." He made a flick of his fingers through the air. "No one can see the gov'ment. If the gov'ment cannot be seen how can it have memory?"

Like the old man, he waited for an answer. His voice was the deep voice of a young man speaking, but the tones were flat like the old man's and the words came slowly.

"The gov'ment has already taken Spirit Mountain from us," Charlie Redtail said. "This I know. And it is for the warriors of the Arapahoe people to take it back, for the mountain is a sacred place and the spirit of our ancestors cannot rest if the mountain is in the hands of the white man."

Then he looked at the renegades around him and he spoke as the old man spoke. "How can our ancestors rest in the house of the enemy?" He waited, and when there was silence all around he finally said, "I have spoken."

That night after he had spoken at the powwow, Charlie Redtail drank the rest of the beer in his cup and walked to the edge of the fire. He looked into the fire and what he saw he did not say, not to the people nor even to Simon Yellow Dog, who stood by him. In the shadows the young white woman also stood quietly watching. And that was when she came from the shadows and stood in front of Charlie Redtail.

"You speak like a great chief," she said. Charlie looked at her, her in her old jeans and her black cotton shirt, the moccasins with the beaded Arapahoe design. He thought she was mocking him.

"Who are you?" Charlie had asked.

"My name's Willow," she said.

"Why are you here?"

"Why are *you* here?" she asked back.

"These are my people," he said.

"Yes," she said. "They are mine as well." She lifted her cup full of beer as if to toast him. And after that they got drunk together.

In the morning they awakened in the old man's house. Charlie was asleep on the floor, the skinny, black dog curled up next to him. She had come with a cup of coffee retrieved from the iron pot that boiled on the wood stove, the old man at sunup having gone off to the mountain alone. Charlie sat up, blinked hard, and looked around.

"Who are you?" he asked.

"Don't you remember?"

He didn't answer. Then he said, "How did we get here?"

"I don't know," she said. Then he laughed and she laughed after him.

That day they walked to the top of Spirit Mountain, "to catch the air," as Charlie said, and to find the old man. She had walked behind him but kept up with him. She did not breathe hard like the old men, nor like Simon Yellow Dog who panted like a sick cur when he climbed the mountain with Charlie. Charlie climbed the mountain often where, in the language of the spirits, he spoke to his father, Joseph. At the top of the mountain he stopped and wiped the sweat from his eyes with his sleeve. The woman was not sweating.

The thunderheads forming in the south billowed upward, creating great white mountain ranges that dwarfed the Twin Buttes range in the distance. And soon after that the lightning began its show, slashing across the darkened sky in the south. "Coyote is crazy," he said. "He was struck by the lightning once."

"Let's be struck, too," she said. She stood up, her hair trying to free itself to follow the wind, and she held her arms out like a mother to a child inviting the lightning to her.

"You are already crazy," he said. Then it began to rain and she stood there, the rain falling in great sheets as if the roof had caved in, the torrents stripping her blond hair straight and soaking her clothes so she looked as if she were emerging from the baptismal river. He saw her wet and naked in her clothing, her breasts, the nipples hard against the cold, wet cloth. She was laughing and shivering. And he was wet.

Without knowing why, as if it were the natural thing, he put his arms around her and she was shivering in his arms and their faces were as wet as their lips, their bodies as wet as their lips, their bodies wet and warming together. Then she stood up on the rock and she was even with him. She looked at his mouth as if to devour it. She looked at it with sadness as if she knew at that moment new, waterless rivers would flow, that the mountains would disintegrate into silly stones and that the oceans would collapse into fishless skies, and only the few who could breathe in the pain and exhale deep red sunsets, who could lull in the fires and wade through the neck-high ice could survive. And with such knowledge, she kissed the man.

Willow's name was Elizabeth Hodges. She had come to the reservation like the others—dragging behind her those fancy degrees from the eastern schools that qualified them to lay their judgments on a native people, a people they had never known except in textbooks written by others who had never known the people.

"How does one understand the smell of the wild rose when one's nose has always been tilted above the bloom?" Charlie had asked.

How could the white do-gooders understand the Native American? They knelt at the altar of Newton and Descartes, the white man's ancestors who taught that nothing is true until an established ground exists for believing it true. The white man called it science. But what did the white man know of the red man's ancestors who taught that man is of the spirit, that the spirit is of Mother Earth, and that the man and the spirit and Mother Earth are one? And how could these do-gooders understand the wounded spirit, *soul wound,* as Willow called it.

The white man judged those with tortured souls by the results of his epistemology, tested by such all-white scientific devices as the Minnesota Multiphasic Personality Inventory (MMPI) and intelligence testing that evaluated the linear thinking of the Native American according to the cosmology of the white man's mind.

"How do you measure pain with a ruler?" Elizabeth Hodges had asked such questions. But no one knew the answer, not even the Old Man of Much Medicine who did not understand the question.

The woman, Willow, was different. She had come to the Twin Buttes Reservation and refused the office provided her at the Indian Agency at Hiram Falls. She lived in the shacks with the people, drove to town with them in their old junkers, drank in the bars with them, got drunk with them, and because she was not like the "talking stumps," as the Arapahoes called the other government social workers, and because she bent easily to the way of the people, the people called her Willow.

Some of the other government workers called Willow a Jung junkie because she found Carl Jung's teachings of the collective unconscious important. But the white man could only believe the earth existed for his domination and exploitation. Such an idea was lost to the Native American and to Carl Jung, who saw the person as part of the earth, his mind, his spirit, and his body as engaged in the process, and joined in the whole. And on the night of the powwow when the Old Man of Much Medicine had spoken, and later when Charlie Redtail had also spoken, Willow had been with the other young women listening in the shadows.

The next morning they had awakened, naked, huddling together on the floor, the old man's buffalo robe beneath them, the same khaki army blanket thrown over them. Charlie woke up cold, his feet hanging out, the woman clinging to him for warmth, her breasts against his back. He lay there for a long moment feeling the softness, the heat. He turned his head slowly so as not to awaken her, so as to take in the shack. The old man was gone again. He saw their clothes hanging like scarecrows over by the stove. The stove held no fire. He pulled himself slowly away from the woman, leaving her asleep, walked naked and cold to the stove, opened the stove door, and built a fire, a stack of old newspapers in the corner, freshly split kindling in an old tin coal bucket, the matches sitting on the kitchen table. Then he hurried back to their bed. She was awake.

He crawled inside the womb of the bedding, put his arms around her, and brought her close to him and she pushed her nakedness into him as if to hurt him. She said nothing, the silence broken by her heavy breathing. Then she said, "Don't kiss me. I can't stand it if you kiss me." And he had not kissed her.

"God, don't kiss me," she said. "Not yet." And his hands were on her hard buttocks and then she pulled herself away from the man, rolled over on him, and she kissed him, and the kissing was hard and wet as if they were still in the rain.

When their clothes had dried—not all the way but dry so they could struggle into their dampness—they had walked out into the sun and it was as if they had been cleansed. She had braided her light-colored hair in two braids and he laughed and said there was nothing she could do to look like an Arapahoe.

"I don't have to look like an Arapahoe," she said. "An Arapahoe is in the spirit, not in the color of the hide."

"Looks help," he said and they laughed some more.

Then she walked up close to him and searched his eyes. "Do you want to trade eyes with me?" she said.

"What do you see with your eyes?" he asked.

"I see a great warrior."

She kissed him lightly on the mouth and when he pulled her to him and tried to kiss her in the sunshine she said, "Please don't kiss me. I can't stand it if you kiss me again." Then he kissed her again and they lay in the willows next to the ditch by the old man's house, and the mosquitoes attacked them, but in their wetness they did not know.

Sixty days later, the winter already threatening in the late fall winds, the sleet slapping against the tar paper walls of the shacks and melting on the tin roofs, and then covering the roofs again, George Beaty of the BLM made his report. He wrote that he had met with the chiefs of the Arapahoe people and had fully explained the proposed exchange under the appropriate title and sub-subsection of the Code of Federal Regulations, that the chiefs fully understood the proposed plan and had said they would report back to him. Having failed to respond within the time set by law for public input, the United States was entitled to conclude that the Arapahoe people had no objection to the proposed land swap.

Beaty further reported that the Twin Buttes Chamber of Commerce was in solid support of the proposal since the so-called Spirit Mountain area was an isolated tract belonging to the United States that was surrounded by the Twin Buttes Reservation and was therefore of no use whatever to the citizens of Fetterman County, Indian or white.

On February 14, 1977, the Bureau of Land Management in Washington, D.C., approved the proposed land exchange, and one hundred and twenty days later a patent was issued from the United States to Spirit Mountain transferring title to one Ronald G. Cotler of Twin Buttes, Wyoming. That was a year before the man was murdered.

16

In her last two years of college Willow had often gone to the streets to live with the homeless in their cardboard lean-tos by the pier. There she met Gertrude, a bag lady. Sometimes she slept with Gertrude next to 49 Piedmont Street in the alley by the streetlight. They slept in a basement entryway, Willow in her own sleeping bag and Gertrude in hers.

Sometimes when Willow visited Gertrude she bought her something from her mother's long closet where, when she pushed a button, a rack appeared out of the wall. Once Willow had counted over two hundred evening dresses on a single rack. That time Willow had chosen an evening dress with spangles that looked like pearl fish scales. She carefully wrapped it in scarlet paper and tied it with a gold ribbon and took it to Gertrude. When Gertrude opened the package she could not speak, her old eyes so large that the hanging skin over the lids gave way and her eyes looked like the eyes of a small girl.

The old woman stepped into the doorway of the warehouse and Willow stood in front of her while she changed into the dress, the woman's filthy rags dropped in a heap. She saw Gertrude pull the dress over her old skinny frame, the ribs showing against her white hide, her breasts like hanging flaps. Afterward, in her sockless tennis shoes she had paraded up and down the pier, her homeless friends in that exclusive society laughing and pointing and calling her "Lady Gerty," and the name had stuck. And she had been proud of her name.

But it was not the clothes that Willow brought that was the gift. Her gift was not the safe gift of most who kept an antiseptic distance, who slipped the woman a dollar and a sad smile and then pulled their hands back before the woman's dirty fingers could touch them. Willow had brought a different gift. It was a gift of the spirit, Lady Gerty said. Willow was her spirit child.

Lady Gerty had had children, but they had been kidnapped by her husband, a typesetter at the Eagle Print Shop in Bellingham. After the divorce, when she took her two children for his first visitation, he had never returned them. She had searched frantically for them, the girl, Tiny, six, and the boy, Rex, four. She got no help from the sheriff. He put out a bulletin, of course, as he did for all the others. Said he didn't have the manpower to put a bunch of detectives on the trail of every father whose crime was stealing his own kids. He had to find the ones who killed their kids.

She had been looking for her children for maybe twenty years. She was not sure how long. Once the cops took her to the city jail for loitering and after the county psychiatrist examined her they sent her to the state mental hospital and put her in a long ward with other women where she wandered the halls looking for her children. Then one day they let her walk out of the hospital.

Willow did not try to analyze the woman, as she had been taught in the school. The theories of psychology have no life. There is no power in their labels. There is no power, Willow had learned on the streets, except the power of caring.

After she had taken her master's in social psychology, a degree she did not respect but that she was required to brandish in order to get a government job on the reservation, she had been sent to the Twin Buttes Reservation in Wyoming. There she had lived with the Native American people as she had lived with Lady Gerty and the others. She argued that one cannot understand people from a comfortable bed in some apartment. Understanding does not arrive by parcel post in some book or magically come by the laying on of labels out of a psychiatric handbook. Understanding comes from a magical gift. The gift is the gift of self. But she had not intended to fall in love with Charlie Redtail. That had not been in her plans at all.

Then Willow sat with Charlie Redtail for many hours at Bull Frog Lake and they did not speak. Their silence was the way they spoke to each other in the profound way of silence and her quiet presence filled him. The white man calls such joy love. But there is no word for it in Arapahoe, because it is the one pure joy. It is at the root of the paradox so that the joy becomes pain. How can there be a word for such joy?

Once, after an hour of silence, he touched her hand lightly and looked at her with a glance. The sight of her brought pain from the joy of it. Then she said, "Do you love me?" And when he was silent for a long time she wished she had not said the words. She wished it the moment the words escaped, but she could not bring the words back.

Finally he said, "There is no word for love in the Arapahoe language. Love is not a word." He threw a stone into the silent water and watched the rings expand outward and he said nothing of it.

But he learned from her as well. He learned that falling in love was when she could show him his own beauty, could show him himself so that he could catch a glimpse of himself and love himself. There were no words for such joy in the English language. Perhaps his ancestors knew the words. Perhaps the words were in the language of the redwings and in the cry of the red-tail hawk overhead. But he had no words for the joy he felt with her. After that, she had gone with him everywhere, she his shadow, he hers, each the other's light and lighting each other's way.

Long ago a darkness had descended upon the people at the Twin Buttes Reservation. The darkness of the people was of poverty and subjugation. The darkness was a darkness of pain. The pain was in the ceaseless reminders of defeat. The pain was in the imprisonment by their captors on the reservation. The pain was in the broken promises. The pain was in the government policies against the Native Americans, forced against them as if in a pernicious, endless torture. The pain was in the white man's order that the American Indian give up his place on the Mother Earth, that he deliver the earth to the white man to rip and to spoil and to pollute. He must permit the rape, witness it, and join in it, and the pain of it was too great.

The pain of it was that he must give up his culture and take up the plow, give up his language and take up the language of the enemy, give up his children and send them to the government boarding schools where their hair was cut short and they were forbidden to speak the words of their ancestors and taught that their ancestors were savages without souls. The pain of it was too great. And the pain was without end, like the devil's torture is rooted in eternity.

The pain permeated the culture like an evil disease handed down through the generations. The pain invaded the family, for the pain destroyed the family, took the children from the parents, took the parents from the tribe, took the tribe from the Mother Earth, at last took the Mother Earth and from her, the soul of the Native American. Willow had called it *soul wound.* And soul wound was the most painful wound of all. It could not be endured without inflicting pain.

The pain brought on anger. And sometimes the anger was turned inward and was reborn like a noxious moth from the evil worm of self-hatred. Some put the gun to their mouths and sucked the blessed lead through the back of their heads. Sometimes in psychotic rages they killed those who were their fellow sufferers. Willow had studied the statistics. Native Americans suffered the highest rate of violent crimes of any cultural group in the United States. Dysfunction of family at last became the norm and was passed down from generation to generation.

In the early days whole tribes had been exterminated by the government, a government that preached from its holy lectern about freedom and equality. But the American Indian was not a person, not a citizen, not a fully enfranchised human being. Those who saw themselves as humanitarians, the weeping, pitying do-gooders in the government programs opted for the assimilation of the Indian. Willow opted to become one with the people.

She had brought focus to Charlie Redtail's role in the drama, as she called it. But it was a role Charlie Redtail did not wish to play, one he fought against, denied, buried, spurned, even mocked. His white blood had become darkened, she said. But his white blood gave him insights into the enemy that his brothers did not have. In this way she, too, was like him. But she had been transfused. She said she carried the blood of the Indian in her soul and that is where it counted. She was of the people and she would give her life to the people. It belonged to them, she said. But Charlie Redtail thought that her eyes were too young and too sad to have said such a thing.

She had gone with him to the powwows of the brothers. She had heard him speak to the renegades, and there was a swelling in her breast when she listened to his deep, flat voice speak of the holy place, of Spirit Mountain, and of their ancestors who would lose their place in the universe if Spirit Mountain were lost, this axle around which the spirits of the people, which were their souls, revolved like many moons around the earth.

When the meetings were over, the renegades went to the turnaround spot where Cotler stopped his Jeep to show his potential investors the lay of the land and to point out where the golf course would be, the pipeline from the river to provide the water, the tennis courts and swimming pool. The turnaround spot was at the base of Spirit Mountain. There Cotler pointed to his map that he laid out on the hood of his Jeep and from the map he would point to the sandstone outcroppings where the roads to the great homes would be cut into the mountainside and where the shopping mall would be built east of the equestrian complex.

But the renegades, in turn, had taken their places at the base of Spirit Mountain. They hid their old cars in the river bottom among the willows and the cottonwoods and walked to the turn-around place. Sometimes they crouched down in the sagebrush and came rushing out to surprise Cotler and his party of Eastern prospects, and although they did not attack the white man, they counted coup, which among Native Americans was a feat of greater bravery, since it required the touching of the enemy's body, but without injuring or killing the enemy.

Previously, Cotler had sold pieces of the project to half a dozen small local investors, including Elmer Johnson, the coroner, Hardy Jacobson, who owned the Rexall drugstore, and Ham Blumenshine, the mayor himself.

But that was before the Arapahoe people fully understood Cotler's plan and before an Eastern businessman named William R. Hamilton, known to the townsfolk as Billy, had secretly taken over the project.

When the renegades had discovered Cotler's plan to cut up the holy mountain they organized under the quiet direction of Charlie Redtail. Every day Arapahoe warriors were assigned to the turnaround place. The interference, well publicized in the *Twin Buttes Times,* was enough to halt any hope of further local investment. It was then that William R. Hamilton had secretly bought out Cotler's interests just ahead of the investors' petition to force Cotler into bankruptcy. Why tell his brother, Charlie, Hamilton thought. It would only cause problems in the family. His brother had no head for business and Spirit Mountain on the other hand was an investment opportunity of colossal potential. The renegades could be handled. Persistence, a little discouragement of a kind, and time—it would all work out. They didn't build the railroad through Indian country without persistence and an occasional heavy hand.

It wasn't that the child, Billy Redtail, had been excised from the core of the investment banker William R. Hamilton. It wasn't that he had no sensibilities, no caring for the Indian people whose blood he carried. He saw them as sadly curious and hopeless as his father, Joseph Redtail, had been hopeless. They were anachronisms, piteous vestiges of a time past. One had to make choices. One either became sentimentally attached to that which was hopeless and exacerbated the pain of it or one faced the truth, the times, and marched on. William R. Hamilton was a marching man. And Hamilton had another agenda not solely motivated by the vision of profit.

With Cotler continuing as the front man, Hamilton sent out new investors from the East, flying them to Twin Buttes in his private jet. Cotler picked them up at the airport, its long dirt strip, and entertained the excited easterners like royalty, took them on backcountry horseback rides into the pristine wilderness and on fishing trips down the Twin Buttes River laden with rainbows and browns. And some he took to the local brothel and some brought their own women along, who were introduced to square dancing and who thought the whole experience charming and picturesque.

But in time, showing the property at Spirit Mountain had become a problem. In nearly every instance Cotler and his investors were confronted by the renegades counting coup, often as many as ten at a time, their loud war whoops and hostile gestures causing the hide on the back of the investors' necks to tingle, their chins to tighten, and their checkbooks to disappear.

"Nothin' but a bunch a silly war-whoops," Cotler had tried to convince them. "Don't pay 'em the slightest attention. They only add a little color to the project. We should be paying them," he would laugh. But the renegades not only made threatening gestures with clubs and pitchforks, they also assaulted the investors with threats.

"We'll kill you white-faced gut bags if you come here" and "We'll skin you New York shit-eaters alive." And then the renegades would charge the investors and touch them, not in a hurtful way, but in the way of the Indian counting coup and when the renegades touched the investors, the war paint on angry faces, the shouting in the faces of these men from sedate and civilized places, most turned and ran. Those who did not stood frozen with fear and most never returned.

Once when the renegades charged, Cotler had pulled his gun and shot above them. But the investor in tow had said he wanted none of that. He hadn't come all the way from New York City to get involved in some "fucking twentieth-century Indian war." After that Hamilton had called Cotler.

"You get that goddamn bullshit shut down," Hamilton said. "You get this son of a bitching project under control or I'll send somebody out there who will."

Hamilton had been paying off Cotler's debts in small dribbles, enough to keep him out of bankruptcy—but only that much, Cotler beseeching Hamilton for every dime like a desperate street beggar.

Cotler had gone to the sheriff, William Marsden, and had laid pressure on him. It wasn't that the sheriff hadn't come whenever Cotler called, but as soon as the sheriff's car appeared, the renegades disappeared like ghosts into fog. And when the sheriff's car was gone, they reappeared, their presence too unpredictable to permit any consistent protection.

"I ain't got a big enough force to keep somebody posted there all of the time," Sheriff Marsden said. "You want to pay for six deputies, I'll hire 'em and put 'em on. I figure it'll take two deputies every eight hours for sixteen hours a day in the summertime. She's light at six and she ain't dark 'til near ten." But when Cotler approached Hamilton on the cost of additional deputies Hamilton had turned the request down flat.

"I'm not subsidizing the sheriff's office," Hamilton said. "You tell the sheriff I want protection. I got a lot of money invested in that project and there's going to be a lot more invested. It's going to make that hick town. Double it in size. You tell him if he can't get it stopped I'm going to have a little talk with the Twin Buttes Chamber of Commerce. They're supporting this project and they're not going to look kindly on a sheriff who has his nuts cut off. I want those renegades stopped."

Sheriff Marsden had felt the pressure and one day he'd gone to Spirit Mountain in an unmarked car with his two deputies, Maxfield and Miller. They were armed with shotguns loaded with buckshot and on that morning two unarmed renegades, thinking these were more of Cotler's investors, rose up in front of them to count coup. The sheriff and his deputies captured them and hauled the two of them in. They were George Ghost Bear and Henry Ghost Bear, his brother, charged by the sheriff with disturbing the peace, trespassing, and assault and battery. Without bail or lawyers they pled guilty and were sentenced to a year in the county jail.

Then the sheriff had gone to Spirit Mountain driving Cotler's Jeep station wagon again to surprise the renegades. This time he captured Charlie Redtail and Harmon Looking Horse. The sheriff leveled the same charges against those two, but they pled "not guilty" and were released for trial when Abner Hill put up their bonds. At the time of trial Ava Mueller offered a plea bargain to Hill. She had an important county condemnation trial coming up and had no time to fuss around with Hill for a week over the case and on the day before trial she agreed that the two could plead guilty to disturbing the peace and be released on their good behavior.

The sheriff couldn't stop the renegades. Even when Cotler would call the sheriff to accompany him the presence of the sheriff and his deputies, all fully armed, created an atmosphere of danger and the investors asked a lot of questions and the answers Cotler gave often didn't mollify the concerns of smart men asked to dump big money into a deal.

After Charlie's arrest, the renegades had reasoned that their leader should no longer attend the demonstrations at the foot of Spirit Mountain. If the sheriff captured him again Mueller would never offer another plea bargain and the judge would give him the maximum—a year, as he had for George and Henry Ghost Bear. With Charlie in jail, the movement would dwindle and they would eventually lose Spirit Mountain.

Willow joined in. "You are the warrior," she had said. "But you are also the spiritual leader and the protector of Spirit Mountain."

"I have to go out there," he said. "A leader who is afraid is not a leader."

"You are not afraid," she said. "A leader who is a fool is not a leader. I'll go in your place."

"You disgrace me," he said. "No man can have his woman fight for him." And after they argued he left her at the old man's place and was gone for three days.

When Cotler had thought the way clear he brought his latest New York investor to view Spirit Mountain. Just to be safe he had taken Dean Miller along, "just for the ride," as he had told the investor. Dean Miller in the tenth year of his service to Sheriff Marsden had been promoted to undersheriff.

Cotler had pulled his Jeep over to the side of the road at the turnaround point. He'd been assuring the investor, one Bruce P. Longley, junior partner of Longley and Sons, how the project was an absolute guaranteed gold mine.

"First we make the profit on the land. The land costs practically nothing. Then we make the profit on the homes. We will have the exclusive building contracts. They will be expensive. We will make a continuing profit on the water system. We will own the golf club, the riding stables, the other amenities. The shopping mall, which will be constructed at the conclusion of the project, will have a hundred stores. We'll collect the rent and a percentage of the gross. This place is large enough to expand to a small, exclusive community of ten thousand people, and the right kind."

Cotler had just finished his pitch when suddenly an Indian emerged from the bushes with a loud, high scream. The Indian was brandishing a spear and rushed at Longley as if to stab him. Longley jumped like a gut-shot beast. It was then that Miller pulled his .357 Magnum from his holster.

"Stop right fuckin' there and drop yer fuckin' spear," Miller ordered. "Now lie facedown on the ground." Miller put the cuffs on the renegade, dragged the Indian upright by the chain of the cuffs, and pushed the struggling savage into the backseat of the Jeep. Then he crawled in next to his prisoner.

"There won't be any mistake about who this dog-eater is," he said. Miller took a good look and he saw the curve of her breasts from behind the beaded vest and he put his hands on them to make sure. Then he put his hands there again. A slow smile came over his face.

"Guess what we got here?" he said to Cotler. Miller pulled the vest back, his prisoner's arms still cuffed behind her, and Cotler saw it was a woman.

"Well, what do you know?" Cotler said, turning around from the steering wheel and reaching back. He ripped at her black shirt. The buttons gave way and as he pulled the car back on the road again he jerked the shirt aside to reveal her bare breasts. Then he grabbed one and before the car ran into the barrow pit he squeezed it, the nipples pink.

Cotler took a swig out of a fifth of Jack Daniel's and passed the bottle to Longley, the potential investor sitting next to him in the front seat.

"I could use a little of that," Longley said, taking a long swig himself. "I thought you had these redskins under control." He passed the bottle back to Miller. "Scared the shit out of me."

"They are obviously down to the bottom of the barrel," Miller said. "Sending their women out now. Well, I will tell you one thing," Cotler said to Longley, "you never can tell what color these blanket-asses come in. This is one we oughta teach a lesson to," he said. The bottle was back to him and he pulled another long one from it. "Who wants to be first."

"Nah, I don't think so," Miller said. "I don't want no part a that."

"What'sa matter, you got nuts but no guts?" Cotler said. "Here, have another." He passed the bottle back to Miller. "Helps a man get his courage up. How 'bout you?" He turned to Longley. "Want a little a that?" He nodded toward the woman in the backseat.

"Well, I will have me a free feel," Longley said. He laughed. "After what she put me through I'm at least entitled to a free feel, don't ya think?" and he reached back from the front seat and fondled the woman's breasts.

"You're a bunch of sick fuckheads," Willow hissed.

"She sure got a tongue on 'er," Miller said.

"I like 'em with a little spirit," Longley said. "You like that don't you, honey," he said, the woman struggling against his hands. "You like that a lot, don't you?"

"Now don't come in your pants," Cotler said to Longley. Then to Miller he said, "I think ya oughta reconsider my proposition, Dean. Justice is justice. We can teach this bitch a little lesson ta fuck around with my project and we can get ourselves a little at the same time. Now that's my idea of justice. Nothin' gets wasted. What do ya say?"

"Well, okay," Miller said. "You can pull off over here. Good spot down by the river."

"You game?" Cotler asked Longley. He handed Longley the bottle.

"I dunno," Longley said.

"Who the fuck is going to talk? The undersheriff here is the law in the county."

"Ya sure?" Longley said.

Then Willow said, "You sons of bitches," and when she tried to bite Longley's arm, Miller slapped her hard. It was then that Longley pulled his hand back from between her bare legs.

"What's she got down there?" Cotler asked.

"You sons of bitches," Willow said. Then she tried to bite Miller again and he slapped her again.

"Wild bitch, ain't she?" Miller said.

"They're the best kind," Cotler said.

Then suddenly the investor said, "Well, you boys have your fun. I got work to do."

"Work will always hold," Cotler said.

"I think he come in his pants," Miller said. And he laughed and they passed the bottle around one more time.

But Longley said no, that they should take him back to the Twin Buttes Hotel, and after that they could do whatever they wanted to with the bitch.

When Longley opted out Miller said they better turn the bitch loose. Even then Colter didn't agree. But Miller said he was only looking for dog-eaters. He pulled the cuffs off her. "Get the fuck outta this car," he said. "You tell them motherfuckers they fuck around with me anymore and somebody's gonna get killed." He shoved her out of the car and onto the road. Then he yelled after her: "An' keep yer fuckin' mouth shut. I got three good citizens in here who'll swear you was tryin' to sell yer ass to us for five bucks."

That had been three weeks before Charlie Redtail was charged with the murder of Ronald Cotler.

17

Undersheriff Dean Miller and Chief Deputy Maxfield had arrived at the murder scene at 8:45 in the morning. The corpse was lying in a heap, the knees up under the body as if it were a fetus fallen in its classic position. Not much blood. Spatters of brains as if they'd been sprayed on the cedar siding of Cotler's ranch house. The magpies were squawking in the apple tree north of the porch.

Miller brought his Nikon, took photographs from a variety of angles, scratched his head, and then began his search for the bullet. Maxfield held a tape in one hand and a clipboard with blank paper in the other. He set the board down and began to examine the siding of the house carefully.

"Get a picture of this brain stuff over here?" he asked Miller.

"Yeah."

"I don't see no bullet hole over here," Maxfield said.

"Bullet blew all ta fuckin' hell when it hit. High-speed cartridge," he said. "Look here. Here's a little piece of lead." He pointed to a shiny metal fragment stuck in the wood, which he retrieved and stuck in his handkerchief. Then they measured the distance to the road and found that the distance was exactly nine hundred and eighty-one feet, which reduced to three hundred and twenty-seven yards. The tire marks in the snow had been obliterated by other passing vehicles. "Musta been Charlie Redtail," Miller said.

"How ya figger?" Maxfield said as if he didn't know.

"Well, you don't have ta be a fuckin' genius ta figger that un out," Miller said. "Put out an APB on that blanket-ass."

Dr. Billingsley, past retirement, had threatened that this would be his last autopsy performed for Fetterman County. He'd lately made such threats over the body of each new cadaver presented to him. "I've done enough a these. Why, if ya stood these stiffs on their feet and had 'em join hands, you'd have a line of the dead reaching from here to Harvard and back. Pretty goddamn scary sight, right, Elmer?"

Elmer Johnson, working on Jimmy Cisneros, who'd died the night before of gunshot wounds in a fight at the Harvard Bar, mumbled, "Right, Doc."

"Can't hold this goddamned saw steady anymore, Elmer," Billingsley hollered above the racket of the devise. "Not a hell of a lot to saw on here," he said. "Haven't seen anything like this since that girl Yellow Calf, back in seventy." He stopped to wipe the bone dust off his glasses. "This is the last one of these I'm gonna do for ya, Elmer." Elmer Johnson didn't answer. "You'll either have ta tell these people to quit killin' each other or you'll have ta bring in some doc from Casper ta do this. 'Bout had it."

Dr. Billingsley surveyed his work. "Now I will tell ya this—this Cotler fella musta been born without a brain."

"How ya figger?"

"Looky here, Elmer. Come on over here. See! There ain't a smatterin' of cerebral tissue left in this skull. Never seen anything like this before, except that Yellow Calf girl. I always thought somethin' was strange about her—maybe the magpies got ta peckin at 'er before we got to 'er. Magpies can fuck up a man's diagnosis."

Elmer looked. "Well, I'll be!" Elmer said. He backed off as if to get a better view of the mangled, dissected skull lying before them.

"Now this guy was shot with a high-powered rifle. No question about that or else somebody gave him some nitroglycerine for a mouthwash. Dean Miller said Colter's Mexican maid found him lyin' on the porch this morning. No time for the magpies. Coulda been some rats, but I don't see any evidence of that. This was a force that blew outward. And it took everything in its path. Never knew what hit 'im."

He opened the stomach cavity and laid his hand against the liver. "Can't say much in my report 'cept he was shot last night sometime. Maybe two-three in the morning from the feel of the liver here. Still a little warm. Dean Miller said the porch light was on when they found the body, so whoever shot him coulda done him in from the road. Had to be a damn good shot, I'll say that much. Miller said the maid never heard a thing. Just found him laying there in the morning when she let the dog out."

The old man examined the hands of the cadaver, as was his custom. He uncurled the fingers on the left hand, one at a time, and turned the hand over and examined the palm. He picked up the right arm of the corpse that had been hanging over the table and looked at the hand. "Well, looky this, Elmer!" the old man hollered. "Looky here. Somebody cut the tip of this guy's little finger off!"

"Jesus!" Elmer said. "What'd he do that for?"

"Damned if I know," Billingsley said. "Maybe it's the way them Indians do their scalpin' nowdays."

Seventeen days later Abner Hill slammed his black Stetson against his pant leg to knock off the snow and stepped into the courthouse, the old heavy smells still offensive to his nose. The passing of more than a decade had not left a conspicuous record on his face, the signs of aging visible but not easily isolated. Perhaps his temples showed more gray, the few gray hairs in his eyebrows, the skin a bit more coarse, like leather ages.

He had climbed these same stairs up and these same stairs down many times and for what? Perhaps, he thought, he was but a climber of stairs, his journey down to the jail to meet his desperate clients, his journey up to the courtroom in search of the jury's faded sense of charity, there to also argue fervently for the judge's mercy, that nearly forgotten word in the English language. But he had never believed he would be called upon to defend Charlie Redtail for murder.

The dispatcher behind the counter looked up from his reading. "Hiya, Ab. Ya have ta wait 'til Dean gets here 'fore ya can go see 'em." The dispatcher turned back to his reading, his lips forming the words from a page of *True Detective.* When Hill made no response, the lawyer quietly standing there watching, the dispatcher looked up again. "'Spose ya think ya can get Redtail off of this un," the dispatcher trying to be friendly, the front teeth gone. He spit a stream toward the spittoon at his feet. "We got 'em this time fer sure. But we ain't found the girl yet." He turned back to his magazine.

"When did you pick Charlie up?" Hill finally asked.

"Week ago yesterday."

"Why didn't you call me?"

"Redtail didn't wanna call nobody. Finally I called his ma myself. Felt sorry for the poor sum'bitch."

Hill sat down on the wooden bench to await the arrival of Dean Miller. Over the years he'd tried to make jurors understand how it was to be a Native American, to be degraded in one's own eyes. Crime, he argued, was often nothing more than the weak responding to the prior crimes of the powerful. When a client robbed the liquor store, his motive only to ease the incessant nagging to quiet the pain, was he not responding to the earlier crimes of the white man? But too often the jurors thought they had a duty to put criminals, Indian or white, away.

Hill leaned up against the wall in the sheriff's office. Behind the wall he could hear the prisoners hollering in their cells, the sounds penetrating ʿ ıe concrete, the words lost in the concrete, desperate sounds, the sounds of caged animals, of beasts, he thought.

Then a thin man in a tan sheriff's uniform swaggered in, a brass badge on his jacket and a small belly that in his midforties he had begun to hold in. His brown hat was too large and pressed at his ears with slight malevolence.

"Well, I 'spose ya wanna see 'em," Dean Miller said. He threw his hat on the counter. His red hair was trimmed up high around the ears with a short forelock that slanted to his right eyebrow. "We got 'em this time, counselor." He shoved his key into the door of the outer jail perimeter and Hill followed down the long hall past the small cells on each side.

In some of the cells the drunks lay sobering up on bare mattresses with dull, gray stripes. Some of the inmates, their hair standing on end like the manes of wildebeests, held onto the bars and with wooden eyes watched the two men walk past. One, his face streaked with dirt, the skin yellowing beneath, reached out his hand for Hill like a monkey in a cage. Hill stopped, took it, gave the man a sad smile, shook it, and went on. The place smelled of Lysol over old vomit.

At the end of the corridor Miller stopped at a small cell occupied by a figure in orange prison coveralls. He was barefooted. His hair was black and a single braid extended down his back nearly to his waist.

"Hey, Redtail, somebody here ta see ya," Miller hollered. He selected a large key from his ring of keys and shoved it into the lock. The sound of steel on steel echoed across the concrete when the cage door opened. The man standing in the shadows of the cell turned, saw the two of them, and when he saw Abner Hill his eyes grew gentle like a child's. Then the prisoner asked in a voice as soft as a whisper, "Did they find her yet?"

"No," Hill said to Charlie Redtail. "They must be hiding Willow out there someplace."

"Yeah," Charlie said as if he knew. "I surrendered on my own. Figgered if they got me that'd be enough for 'em. Maybe let her go. But Miller says they're still lookin' for her."

As Hill grew accustomed to the darkness he could see that both of the man's eyes were blackened, the right eye swollen nearly shut. There was a large, running wound over the right eyebrow. The man's nose had obviously been broken and the face was puffy.

"Who the hell beat you up, Charlie?"

"You shoulda seen me a week ago right after it happened," he said. "I was a bad-lookin' mess then." He laughed his high laugh. "I'm lookin' pretty good today." Then Charlie said, "She didn't have anything to do with this."

How could they have charged this man, Hill asked himself? Charlie, the peaceful one, the one with the quiet, measured wisdom beyond his less than thirty years. Some said he was strange and he was to those who saw a world made up of bulldozers and diesel smoke, the annual elk hunt, Coors beer, and graves decorated with plastic flowers on Memorial Day. He was a man with large hands who used them to examine the undersides of wild lilies and spoke to the towering firs as if they were his brothers. He remembered how Simon Yellow Dog had told of the time Charlie had stopped him from killing a rattler.

"It's not the fault of the snake that it strikes to protect itself any more than it's the fault of the man who strikes at the snake for the same reasons. We and the snake were born of the same spirit," Charlie had said.

Simon Yellow Dog, Charlie's best friend and son of his father's best friend, Jacob Yellow Dog, had laughed at that. "Ya musta learned that from old Henry."

But Charlie had stood in front of his friend and Simon Yellow Dog had not struck at the snake with his club and at last the snake had slithered away into the tall grass.

This man wouldn't murder anyone, not even Ronnie Cotler. Others were more likely suspects. Others were better equipped emotionally to kill. What about all of the Native Americans whom Cotler had abused and cheated? Maybe even his bartender. Sometimes in the deep of night when he couldn't sleep, Hill himself had thought how it would be to kill the man. Men think of such things when the mind runs free. The mind thinks of killing because killing is in the genes. Men do not speak of such things, the thin facade of civilization, the silencer. But the mind cannot mute the killer from speaking to the self in the cover of night.

Hill thought of how Cotler had tortured Mary Hamilton, tortured her deliberately. Once he had said to Mary Hamilton, "Somebody oughta kill the no-good son of a bitch." And she had said nothing back from her side of the table. Just looked at him with the sad eyes, holding her tongue as if she needed to preserve all of her strength to get through the rest of the night.

That had been the time when Cotler bought the Redtail shack from Widow Martin who had inherited the property from her husband, Jasper, and the widow, burdened with the widow's commiserating heart, never could throw Mary Hamilton out on the street, not even when Mary got six months behind on the rent. Instead she had sold the property to Cotler, who had offered her half again what the property was worth. Never could understand what the man wanted with the shack. And he had her sign a piece of paper that transferred Mary's debt for past due rent to Cotler as part of the deal.

A few days later Cotler had knocked on the door of the shack and pushed past Mary. "Came to look over my property," he said. Mary stood in the living room staring at the man, not knowing what to say. He'd walked uninvited through the four rooms, stepped into the kitchen, seemed interested in a butcher knife sitting on the counter, inspected it, and set it down again. Then he wandered back to the living room, Mary bereft of speech, following him. He plopped himself down in the old, overstuffed chair, the rips and holes in the worn arms covered with doilies her mother had crocheted.

"I bought this place to help you out," Cotler said. "Knew you were behind on the rent. Thought it'd be better for you if I owned it. Never can tell when Mrs. Martin might move you out," he said and laughed. "She might need the money."

He offered her a cigarette which she refused, lit his own, and blew smoke in her direction. "I been missing you, Mary," he said, the woman still standing there staring down at the man in disbelief. "Aren't you glad to see me?" The smart-ass smirk. She hadn't answered. "You're still in love with me, aren't you?"

Still no answer.

In the penetrating discomfort of her silence Cotler had finally gotten up. Then he shrugged his shoulders and opened the door. "I'll be back," he had said. "But don't wait up for me. By the way, Mrs. Martin gave me her key to the place." He laughed and then walked on down the broken steps.

*   *   *

"I'll get a doctor in here to sew you up, Charlie," Hill said. "Shoulda had a doctor a week ago. Gonna send in a photographer. Cooperate with the photographer, Charlie. Don't answer any questions for anybody but me, understand? Don't talk to the sheriff or anybody else."

"She didn't have nothin' ta do with it, Abner," Charlie said. "I came in on my own."

"What did they do to you, Charlie?"

"They said they were having a conversation with me." He laughed his high laugh. "It was funny. They had me in cuffs and were beatin' on me. Tryin' ta make me confess." He laughed again. "The sheriff was hollering at me. Said, 'You know I got an election comin' up, you fuckin' dog-eater,' and then he said, 'You killed Cotler because he was cutting up Spirit Mountain.' Miller hit me with his gun butt and Maxfield was hitting me with his stick. Hit me in the ribs. But the more they hit me the more I laughed."

"Why did you laugh, Charlie?"

"Wasn't it funny?" he said. "They had all the power and they had no power. They looked silly poundin' away and hollerin'. They knocked me out," he said. When I came to I was lying on the floor over there in the granary behind the jail and I was laughing and they were still cussin'."

The powerlessness of power. Hill had seen it many times. He had seen the judge with all of his power still incapable of providing justice. He had seen it when the white man had tried to exterminate the spirit of the American Indian. Yet the spirit kept popping up like pesky dandelion sprouts in the spring.

"They took my rifle," Charlie said as if he had mentioned a irrelevancy.

"What kind of a rifle was it?"

"A .30-.30 Winchester carbine. Belonged to my father."

"Had you shot it recently?"

"Yes, I took a dry doe the day before and gave half of it to the old man and the other half to my mother."

Abner Hill sat down by the man on the steel cot. "Can I get you anything, Charlie?"

"They took my shoes."

"I'll take care of it," Hill said.

"If they catch her ya gotta protect her, Abner. I'm looking to you for that," and for the first time Hill saw fear in the man's eyes. "Can't protect her, Abner. Not with me in here."

"Are your feet cold, Charlie?"

"I 'spose," he said.

Then Abner Hill hollered, "Jailer," and the inmates down the line hollered after him, "Jailer," the echoes against the concrete walls, "Jailer! Jailer!" And after a while Abner Hill heard the outer perimeter door slam open and closed again and Miller's pounding boots approaching.

"I'll get you some shoes," Hill said.

"Can't have no shoes," Miller said, who had just arrived. "Might try hangin' himself with the laces."

"I'll get ya some warm socks," Hill said.

"Can't have no more socks. This silly sum'bitch give his socks to another puke. Puke left with 'em when we turned him out."

"Well, he's gonna have some warm socks," Hill said, "or you and I are goin' upstairs and have a talk with the judge." It was as if he'd lived his entire life in this cell, as if the inert concrete that had soaked up the blood of the father had the power to absorb the blood of the son. As Abner Hill stepped out of the cell Hill heard the words escape his lips.

"This is where I found your father, Charlie."

"I know," Charlie said. "I been talkin' to him."

Over the passing years Abner Hill had sat at his end of the kitchen table, the coffee brewing on the stove, the pine table with the straight, square legs, the boards pounded together by some impatient carpenter. Many a night he'd worked on the table, his papers spread out on the red-and-white checkered oilcloth, the woman at the other end quietly watching, her questions sometimes breaking the silence. She was a brave woman, he thought, alone, and in ways helpless although she would never admit to her helplessness, and with those two small boys.

He'd been attracted to the woman from the beginning, her easy laughter, the joy she showed in small things, the woman with good spirits when his were not. She was braver than he. As brave perhaps as his mother. As beautiful as his mother, and in the same way, the dark hair, the blue eyes, the tight, lithe body, at times the impenetrable seriousness and the devotion to her sons. He had wanted to help her. That she could not pay him seemed a bothersome irrelevancy, something that plagued her, not him, that caused her often to apologize for her poverty and to express feelings of guilt over the charity she received from him.

Sometimes she hadn't called him when her need for him was obvious. She said that to ask for his help made her feel cheap. She didn't like to be indebted to anyone. Yet it was he who came knocking at her door claiming he had only dropped by for a cup of her good coffee and to see the boys. Then he always inquired of her well-being. And sometimes she didn't tell him, but that day, after Cotler had moved her out into the street, she found herself talking to Abner Hill, he fiercely intent on her words.

She told him how Cotler had visited her the second time as promised. Her day off, the boys grown and gone, Billy in New York making millions, she said, and Charlie living on the reservation with the old man. Even though it was early afternoon Cotler had been drinking. He unlocked the door with his key and burst in, his eyes wild like they had been that night at the drive-in. Without saying anything he'd grabbed her, pulled her to him, and tried to kiss her. He put his hands on her buttocks and pulled her into his groin. She tried to pull away.

"I love your ass," he said.

"You're drunk, Ronnie," she said, still struggling to pull away.

"You've wanted me all this time. Why don't you admit it?" He tried to kiss her again and this time she'd been able to escape.

She ran to the kitchen, Cotler following. She grabbed the butcher knife and he laughed when she tried to stab him. He grabbed her arm with one hand and put his other hand in the place. Then he held her there for what seemed a long time, her arm in the air like the Statue of Liberty, the knife in her hand. And she began to tremble.

Finally he said, "Don't you think you owe me something?"

"You must be crazy," she said.

"All I want is what's comin' to me," he said. He twisted her arm and the knife fell to the floor.

Then she said matter-of-factly, "Are you going to rape me?"

"No," he said. "I just want to collect the rent." He turned her free. "We could make a beautiful couple," he said and laughed again. And when she told him to get out, before he walked through the door he said, "In case you change your mind, let me know. Otherwise the sheriff will be here in the morning. It's called 'forcible entry and detainer.' Ask that two-bit shyster of yours what that means."

The following morning Miller and Maxfield knocked on the door and when she refused to answer they broke it down—couple of kicks was all it took. Miller swaggered in and the two began to throw her things out. They started in the bedroom first. Miller opened her chest of drawers and removed a pair of panties and was holding them up and twirling them over his head and laughing and making remarks.

The sheriff's men had moved the chest out to the curb and had taken her things from the closet in large armfuls when Cotler drove up in his Eldorado convertible. "I can stop this for you, Mary," he hollered.

Then she called Abner Hill.

In minutes he was there. "What's going on here?" Hill asked, jumping out of the pickup, Mary standing helplessly at the curb watching the deputies dump her clothes on the ground.

"They're moving me out," she said.

"What's this about?" He walked over to Cotler, still sitting in his convertible. The smirk. Cotler reached over for his .45 automatic lying on the front seat.

"Wouldn't stick my nose in it if I were you, counselor," Cotler said.

"I'll stand good for the rent," Hill said.

"Hundred fifty-seven dollars, counselor."

"I'll write you a check."

"I don't take checks from shysters," he said, Miller and Maxfield moving in. Hill pulled out his checkbook, wrote the check, and tore it loose. He held it out to Cotler but Cotler left the man holding the paper in his hand.

"Good," Hill said. "I tendered the money." He put the check back in his pocket. "You throw her out now and I'll have a lawsuit on you in the mornin'. Maybe end up ownin' that shit pot you call a bar." He stood at the convertible's door staring down at Cotler, Cotler's hand still on the pistol. "You want to shoot me for tendering a widow's rent?"

Dean Miller stepped up. "Come on, Ronnie. This ain't the time or place for any action. The whole fuckin' neighborhood is watchin'. Later, maybe, huh?" He winked at Cotler. Then Miller turned to Hill. "Give me the fuckin' check." Hill handed Miller the check. "Let's get the fuck outta here," Miller said. That had been two weeks before the deputies found Ronnie Colter's body on his own front porch, the magpies squawking in the apple tree, waiting.

18

The geraniums in her window had never bloomed but she had not given up on them, not in all of the years Hill had known her. He poured in the milk from the Carnation can and stirred again, the steam of the coffee in his face.

"Don't worry," Hill said into the cup. He looked up at the woman. "He's innocent and like they say, 'the truth will out.'"

"I have never seen it will out yet," Mary said.

"They got nothin' on him. Just suspicion. You can't put a man away on suspicion. Gotta prove it beyond a reasonable doubt. They got no proof."

"They never had to have proof yet," she said.

"This is different, Mary. This is murder."

The words shocked her. She had never let the words creep into the ear of her mind. Finally she said, "I got two hundred dollars in the can to bail him out."

"Can't bail him out this time, Mary. No bail for murder."

"He'll go crazy in jail," she said. "You 'member the last time."

He looked at the woman as he had always looked at her—across that ineffable barricade that on the one side demanded that the lawyer care about his client and, on the other, that the lawyer not care too much, that he not fall into entanglements of the heart that might disable the lawyer from saving his client from entanglements of the law. Sometimes through the barrier he saw her as a woman and that had made it harder.

Abner Hill knew the rules and he was a man who played by the rules. They were silent for a long time, as if the stirring of their coffee could not be disturbed.

"He didn't kill Ronnie," she said. Then she thought for a moment. "I wouldn't blame him if he did. I tried to kill him myself." Then she said, "Charlie told me he was going to kill Cotler."

"You never said that to me," Hill said. "I never heard that, you understand?" He looked at her a long time. "For Christ's sake, if they call you as a witness . . ."

"It was just a passing thing," she said. "A manner of speaking. It was when Cotler threw us out in the street. He found out about it. But Charlie would never kill anybody. You said yourself you ought to kill Cotler."

"I know," Hill said. "That was just a passing thing, too." She sat in an old cane café chair, one she'd bought at a Methodist church rummage sale for a dollar. She watched him blow at his coffee and sip.

"They've always been after the Redtails. You know that, Abner. They gotta get somebody for the murder," she said, still watching him. "They're trying to stop those renegades on the reservation. If they get Charlie they get the leader. That'll probably end it." Then suddenly she said, "What about Willow?"

"Went out to see Henry Old Deer myself. Claims he doesn't know where she is."

"She was always with Charlie," Mary said. "We gotta find Willow. Did you ask Charlie where she is?"

"Charlie won't talk about it. I'll go see Henry again," he said.

She saw the deep worry in the man's face, the eyes not wanting to look at her, the mouth held hard. She thought he looked like a small boy near tears and she wanted to go around the table and hold the man, comfort him, this man who had been the only man who had always been there for her and who was there for her now, this man always on his side of the table.

Then after a long while he said, "I was wondering if you could get me a pair of Charlie's socks. Wool ones, if he has any."

After Charlie's arrest Ava Mueller conducted Charlie's preliminary hearing in Justice of the Peace Benny Kelso's small courtroom. Some claimed Benny Kelso had graduated from the eighth grade, but no one knew for sure. Benny never spoke of his education, it being nobody's business. Furthermore, higher education was not a prerequisite for a justice of the peace in Wyoming.

Benny had fitted his garage with the necessary accouterments for a justice of the peace court—a wood-burning, potbellied stove, the stovepipe of which found its way to the roof through a maze of cobwebs that swept from rafter to rafter across the garage's open ceiling. A long metal table served as his desk at one end and as counsel table at the other where Abner Hill sat across from Ava Mueller. Charlie Redtail, in cuffs and shackles, sat next to his lawyer. A wooden, armless kitchen chair was designated as the witness chair, which Judge Benny Kelso had placed closest to the wood stove. "Put a little heat on them witnesses," Benny liked to joke.

Judge Kelso had been justice of the peace in Fetterman County going on thirty years. The county paid him twenty-five dollars a month rent for the use of his courtroom and ten dollars a case. In support of the arrangement he argued, "I'm here, day or night, whenever I'm needed. The witnesses can wait in my kitchen, for which I get no compensation whatsoever, and the wife pours 'em coffee, for which I also get no compensation whatsoever. Then we call 'em out to the garage as we need 'em."

Over the years the judge had tried thousands of misdemeanor cases that had been brought before him, the petty thefts, the simple assault and battery cases, the wife-beating cases, the drunks, the bad check cases. And on a regular basis he conducted the preliminary hearings in the various felony files the county attorney brought before him.

Under the laws of Wyoming any justice of the peace in the county had jurisdiction to hold a preliminary hearing, the inquiry before the justice being whether or not the state had evidence establishing probable cause for the state's charge—in the case of Charlie Redtail, for murder in the first degree. And if in a murder case the justice found that the evidence of guilt was strong, he could so certify and the defendant would be confined to the county jail without bail to await his trial, and, in Fetterman County, usually his conviction.

Considering the fact that Justice Kelso had held hundreds of preliminary hearings over the years and that no one could remember the last time he had dismissed a case for lack of probable cause, it had been no surprise to Abner Hill that Ava Mueller had brought Charlie Redtail's case before the venerable justice. She called Undersheriff Dean Miller as her first witness. He'd been sitting behind Charlie Redtail with a cup of Nelly Kelso's coffee in his hand.

Miller testified that he put out an all-points bulletin for Charlie Redtail because Redtail was the leader of a gang of thugs on the reservation who were constantly attacking and intimidating Cotler and that he, Miller, had personally heard Charlie Redtail threaten the deceased.

"How did that happen?" Ava Mueller asked.

"Why, I was sitting in the Big Chief bar about two weeks ago and Charlie Redtail come in and walked up to Cotler sitting at the bar, mind-ing his own business. I was havin' me a beer after my shift. Redtail saw me and give me no heed whatsoever. He walks up to Cotler and jabs his finger into his chest. Damn near knocked the man off his stool. I gets up and starts over there and that's when I heard Redtail say, 'I am gonna kill you for what you done to my mother. An' one thing more, motherfucker'—pardon my French, but that is exactly the word he used—'you ain't gonna know when or where it's comin' from.' That there is why I put the APB on Redtail. But he come in on his own."

Charlie whispered to his lawyer, "That's a total lie, Abner. I haven't been in that place since they killed my father there."

Then Miller told how he had taken Charlie's rifle, which he said Charlie always kept in the rack across the back window of his pickup. "I took it in conjunction with the arrest," he was quick to add in order to make the search legal. "And I also took a paraffin test of the defendant's hands and sent it and the rifle to the state lab."

"And what were the results," Ava Mueller asked.

"Objected to as hearsay," Hill said.

"You know better'n that, Abner," Judge Kelso said. "Hearsay is always allowed in these proceedin's. Always has been."

Miller said, "He had powder residues on both his hands and there was powder residue on the gun. In case you wanna know, I got the lab report right here in my pocket." He started to reach in his jacket, but Mueller moved on to the next question.

"What is the significance of gunshot residues on the defendant's hand, Undersheriff Miller?" Ava Mueller asked.

"I know what it means," Justice Kelso interrupted. "It means that the defendant here shot his rifle in the last twenty-four hours. That's what it means. See it all the time."

"Right," Miller said.

Ava Mueller looked at Judge Kelso as if to ask if he needed any further evidence and in response the judge said, "That seems ta me to be sufficient. I bind the defendant over fer trial to the district court, the defendant Charlie Redtail to be held without bond because I find that the evidence is strong that the defendant committed this killin' with premeditated malice." He cleared his throat in order to get a fresh start. "If ya wanna know why, it's pretty obvious. Ever'body in Twin Buttes knows what's been goin' on out there on the rez. Those Arapahoes have brought the so-called Spirit Mountain Project to a screechin' halt and that is not good for the community. You can't have progress facin' what I like ta call 'the new-age Indian wars.'" He paused and leaned back in his chair and thought for a moment.

"This defendant has been before me before. I can take judicial notice of that." Hill had twice defended Charlie in Judge Kelso's court for disturbing the peace when the renegades were demonstrating in the streets of Twin Buttes over Cotler's development of Spirit Mountain. And twice Hill had paid Charlie's fine when he couldn't come up with the money. "My charitable contribution for the year," Hill had said, shrugging his shoulders.

"So them are my reasons," Judge Kelso said, "and they are plumb sufficient under the law, I'll guarantee ya that. Next case."

Although most of Charlie Redtail's misfeasances were minor, there'd been that one time three years earlier when he'd been charged with assault by deadly weapon and after he had been bound over for trial to the district court by Justice of the Peace Benny Kelso, Hill's arguments to Judge Hankins in the district court were for reason and understanding.

"Charlie Redtail was never a violent youth. You know that yourself, Your Honor," he said, making his arguments in his quiet, thoughtful way. Reason, he believed, was the tool of the lawyer, mercy the gift of justice. "Your Honor saw him in combat on the basketball court. He was always the last to foul out. He has never been a violent man. But on this one occasion, Your Honor, he took matters into his own hands. Are we not all human, all of us?" Hill had waited for the judge to think about it. Everyone knew of the judge's own imperfect past, his whoring and fighting and bootlegging before he'd married the widow from Alabama, Matilda Jane Redford. The townspeople had given her full credit for having put the man on the straight and narrow that had launched his career in Twin Buttes, first as a successful lawyer and later his election and every six years thereafter his reelection to the district court bench.

"Charlie Redtail was goaded beyond the endurance of a saint," Hill argued to Judge Hankins. "Goaded by a bully who wouldn't stop taunting the boy about his being a breed."

"Is the boy an Indian?" the judge had asked. He looked sleepy.

"His father was Arapahoe, Your Honor. You must remember his mother, Mary Hamilton."

"Does the fact that your client had an Indian for a father make him Indian?"

"Perhaps that is the root of the problem, Your Honor. He sees himself as Indian."

"A pity," the judge said. "I should think he could as easily be white. Perhaps we should give him an extended opportunity to reconsider his allegiances."

"The man was a small man," Ava Mueller interrupted.

"Bullies come in all sizes, Your Honor," Hill said back. He walked over to the prosecutor's table and smiled at Ava Mueller. "The prosecutor is right, Your Honor. When Charlie threw the man through the door it broke off both of the door's hinges. But we've made restitution," Hill again having tendered his personal check.

Then Hill looked down at the seated prosecutor and gently laid his hand on the counsel table where she sat. "I have always found Miss Mueller to be a reasonable woman, but she has been misguided in this case. Surely she understands that the defendant's conduct amounts to nothing more than a simple assault and that one cannot be charged with assault by deadly weapon simply for throwing someone through a door."

Ava Mueller was on her feet interrupting. "That man is a walking menace," she cried, pointing to Charlie Redtail. "That man is good with his hands. You saw him yourself. He could hold a basketball with one hand and throw it the full length of the court. This is no ordinary man with ordinary hands. Any man who can throw another man through a solid wooden door has dangerous hands. They constitute deadly weapons, Your Honor."

Judge Henry Hankins interrupted. "Can't you children agree? You both allegedly passed the same bar exam. A man throws another man through a door. Under such circumstances are the perpetrator's hands dangerous weapons so that the perpetrator can be charged with the felony of assault by deadly weapon rather than the simple misdemeanor of assault and battery? I order both of you to trot down the hall to Miss Mueller's office and settle this matter while I take my afternoon nap in chambers. As you know, I'm a cranky old jaybird when I wake up." He put on a severe look, delivered it to both lawyers, and then disappeared from the bench like the passing shadow of an afternoon cloud.

They had gone to Mueller's office, she behind her plain oak desk, Hill in an equally plain wooden chair facing her. Hill had started off with a humorous volley.

"Listen, Ava," he said. "I'll kiss your fanny all the way out the front door to the street *and back* if you'll drop the charges."

"If I were in the mood, that isn't where I'd want to be kissed," she said. "Let's get serious or the judge'll throw us both in jail."

Then Hill's face got very solemn and he said, "Ava, you know it's not right to charge Charlie with a felony when a misdemeanor will do."

"I have to stop people from throwing other people through doors. That's my job," she said.

"The only thing injured was the door. The so-called victim just had his feelings hurt. What's more important, a door or a young man's good record?"

"The community peace is what's important. You always represent those rowdies, those ruffians . . ." She was looking for the word. Then she came up with it. "Those renegades." She stopped for a moment. "For a peaceful man, Abner, I have never understood how you could represent those people with such passion."

"*Those* people?" he said, which she ignored.

They argued for nearly an hour until the clerk hollered at the door that the judge was ready for their agreement. It was then that Hill said, "I'll plead him guilty to simple assault and battery."

"All right," she said, "I want six months."

"Ten days, and no more," Hill said. "And I'll take you to dinner."

"You can't buy me," she said. "Thirty days and we have a deal."

"Deal," Hill said. They shook hands on it and hurried to tell the judge they had reached an agreement. And when he heard it he approved it without question, congratulated them both in an unconvincing voice, and left the bench like a vanishing sleepwalker.

During his ninth day in jail Charlie had begun pacing the floor. The pacing went on, day and night—four steps to the right and turning sharply, four steps to the left, back and forth again and again, hour after hour, all day and all night like a caged animal at the zoo. He had stopped eating. His mother brought him fresh corn on the cob, his favorite vegetable, and roasted elk loin that his friend Simon Yellow Dog had poached, brought it served on a pretty red plate to brighten his day and that she'd kept warm with double layers of aluminum foil. But often Miller and the dispatcher ate it. "Spot check," Miller called it, smacking his lips and laughing. "Makin' sure she ain't slippin' him somethin' ta break out." And when the deputies decided to deliver the food to Charlie they brought it on old newspapers, which according to Miller was to prevent him from breaking the plate to make some crude weapon, the food was always cold.

When Mary inquired as to the condition of her son, Miller told her that Charlie was eating regularly and that he was as strong as a bull and that she should keep on bringing him his supper. But when she was finally permitted to visit him, which was at four o'clock in the afternoon on the second Friday after his incarceration, she saw that her son was withering. And when she tried to talk to him he would say nothing, just pace the floor back and forth as if he had gone mad.

"He's completely lost it," she told Abner Hill, holding back the tears. "You have to get him out or he's gonna die for sure."

After that Hill had gone to see Charlie. The young man looked sick and wouldn't speak to him and wouldn't eat, and by the twenty-second day Hill found Charlie lying on the floor, unable to walk and unable to get up. Hill made an immediate visit to Ava Mueller.

"You have to do this for me, Ava," Hill had said. "You have to let Charlie out. I'll owe you a big one. But you have to do it. We're gonna lose this kid. And he doesn't deserve it, not for a simple assault and battery."

"I can't just turn criminals loose on the street because they get a little stir crazy," she said.

"Please, Ava. Do it for me. This kid means a lot to me."

"What am I supposed to owe you, Abner?" she asked, and that had stopped him and he couldn't think of what to say. "All your cases hurt you, Abner. Hasn't anybody ever told you, you get too close to your clients? Especially this one."

"I've been taking care of Charlie since he was a little boy." He spoke as if he were speaking to no one. Finally he got up and when he did he didn't look tall anymore, his complexion gray, the slump at his shoulders. He turned slowly and started for the door when Ava Mueller stopped him.

"Okay, wait a minute, Abner," she said. "Draw up the stipulation. I'll present it to the judge." And that was how Charlie Redtail was released on his twenty-second day of a thirty-day sentence in the Fetterman County jail. After that Abner Hill took him home and helped him into his mother's house, but even then Hill had known that was only the beginning of his trouble.

19

It was another of those short, sharp, cold days when the winter sky was as blue as blue bottles and as cloudless, the sun low in the south but as high as it could rise. The air had lain so heavy on the valley that the wind was smothered under the weight of it and the land was as silent as diamonds. But in the sunshine the world was bright and brittle and the day worth grasping. Abner Hill did not see the day.

They sat at the old man's shack, Henry Old Deer in his woolen army shirt and denims, stiff and dirty, the worn moccasins on bony feet, his beaded vest, the geometric designs of the Arapahoe in blue, white, and yellow.

"If they catch her, Henry, they'll jail her and force her to say whatever they want," Hill said. "I've seen 'em do it before." The old man listened, his hand cupped to his ear. "We gotta find her first," Hill said. "We gotta find out what she knows and what she saw."

Having shaken the fire like a naughty child the old man came back to the table, his eyes with the milky rings around the irises. But in the dark room with the one small window and the winter sun setting in the late afternoon there was a brightness in his eyes. "How come you don't ask Charlie what she knows?" Henry Old Deer said.

"Charlie's protecting her," Hill said. "I can't get him to talk about her."

"He didn't do it," the old man said.

"How do you know?"

"I taught him better." Then Henry Old Deer said, "You ask him?"

"Didn't ask him."

"You want to know, but you don't want to know. The white man is crazy."

"I may want Charlie to testify."

"So you want him to lie if he has to, but you don't want to know he's lyin'," the old man said.

"You don't understand."

The old man squinted his eyes. "You lawyers have a license to trade in lies."

Hill was silent.

"To not know because one does not wish to know is the same as a lie," the words coming from the face of many wrinkles. Then the old man laughed. "But whatsa difference? Everybody lies in the white man's court. We lie in the white man's court. It is good medicine to lie to the white man."

He swatted lightly at the rump of a skinny cur that had been begging at his lap to be petted, the dog's tail pounding the dirt floor. "Get!" he said to the dog. "Can't you see I'm talking to this here lawyer?"

Then the old man turned to Hill. "If we tell the truth the white man kills us. If we tell the truth he puts us in the pen. If we tell the truth he takes our land. If we speak to him from the heart he laughs at us. If we cry out he puts more wood on the fire of our sorrow. We told him the truth for many years and he lied to us and slaughtered our people and our buffalo and stole our land. So we lie to him and it is good medicine. Sometimes we tell him two lies. Sometimes two lies make the truth. Ha," he said without laughter.

"If we can just find the girl," Hill said, trying to keep the old man on the subject.

"If you find the girl what will you do with her?" the old man asked.

"I'll ask her what happened."

"What if she tells you that Charlie killed the man?" He peered at Hill as if he had caught the lawyer in the crux question. "Will you ask her to lie?" Henry Old Deer asked.

"No."

"I can ask her to lie," the old man said. "Truth is no good without justice."

"I can't ask you to ask her to lie," Hill said.

"You don't think straight," the old man said. "You don't know if it is necessary for her to lie. You don't know if I will ask her to lie. You don't know if she will lie. You don't know nothin'. Yet you act as if you know everythin'. You are a confused man."

"Right," Hill said. "You tell the truth. I am."

"You white men are all fuss and feathers about how you do somethin'. You should be fuss and feathers about what you do, not how you do it. If you care more about how you get justice than you do about getting' justice then you will never get justice. Do you understand?" the old man asked.

Hill nodded.

"You do not understand. You have thought too long in the wrong way."

The old man got up and went to a wooden box on the floor and with great care lifted the lid and rummaged around in the box. Shortly he came up with a Snickers bar, unwrapped it, and broke the bar in two. He handed Hill the half that was slightly smaller and bit off a piece from his half with his side teeth.

"In the white man's court the rules aren't the same for both sides," Hill said. "The cops make people lie. And the cops lie. I see it all the time. They want your people in prison."

Henry Old Deer took another bite off the Snickers bar and after the bite was half-chewed he said, still chewing, "We have been prisoners for a long time. We are prisoners here on the reservation. The difference is small." Then he held up the candy in front of him and said, "This is the only thing the white man gave the Indian that is good. This is very good," he said. "Ha."

"Can you find the girl?" Hill asked.

"You should not ask the question," the old man said. "I will clear the room of the question." He waved his arms in both directions as if to clear the room of the evil. "If you do not ask the question I do not have to lie to you. Sometimes the truth only gets in your way. The truth will not set you free, as the white man likes to say. The truth can put you in prison. And so you have not asked the question." He took another bite of the candy. "Ha," he said.

"Then you understand," Hill said. "I didn't ask Charlie the question either."

"Justice is always better than truth," Henry Old Deer said. He threw a crumb from his Snickers bar to the dog, who grabbed it in midair. "I have thrown this dog the crumb. The truth is the dog likes Snickers, too. But truth does not feed a dog. Justice is when the dog is fed. Do you understand?"

Ace Yokum was carrying on in the back room of his garage with a thin-faced brunette over a bottle of Old Cabin Still. She was wearing one of those short, tight, jersey dresses with the wild designs like something painted by Mondrian and was sitting on the couch, her legs crossed. The woman was the wife of the local veterinarian.

"They sure got the wrong man this time, Ab," Ace said as Abner walked in.

Hill nodded at the woman and plopped down on the opposite end of the couch where she was sitting. "Knowin' they're innocent makes it worse. If you know they're guilty and lose you can at least handle that."

"I told ya I'd take care of the bastard," Ace said. "Cotler had it comin'. Easy shot from the road with my .270. Blew hell outta things."

"Don't even kid like that," Hill said.

Ace poured the woman another drink and filled a glass for Abner Hill. "When I pulled the trigger it was pure pleasure seeing the bastard's brains scattered all over the countryside."

"Wish you'd stop that," Hill said. He turned to the woman. "You know he's kidding, Mildred."

"He's very funny," she said. She giggled and gave Ace a look.

"Where's Doc tonight?" Hill asked of her husband. Shouldn't have asked.

"Takin' care of a sick horse," she said, crossing her legs in the opposite direction, "like always."

Hill sat looking into his glass. The magic eraser he called its contents. Sometimes it could wipe away the fear in the belly. He emptied the glass. He saw Ace laughing, talking to the woman, the kind of talk men make when they have that in mind. Ace had the courage he never had, Hill thought. The man wasn't afraid. But he, Abner Hill, was always afraid, an unqualified coward, he thought. And there was no room for cowards in this deadly business.

Ace went over to the woman, lifted her off the couch, bit her on the neck lightly, and said he would call her in the morning. He closed the door behind her protests and poured Abner another drink. Double.

"You wanna talk?" Ace asked.

Hill nodded and looked back into his glass. Didn't know how to start. "I got no business in this case," Abner said.

"Why the fuck not? Who else cares about Charlie like you? No-fuckin'-body, that's who."

"That's the point," Abner said. Suddenly his tears surprised him. He looked back into the glass. He was stirring the whiskey with his finger.

Ace sat down on the couch and hit a fist on Abner's thigh. "It's okay, man."

After a while Hill was able to say it: "Who could I send him to? There aren't any other lawyers in town who can try a case. Not even the simplest drunk driving case." And he didn't know the other lawyers around the state except Harold Yancey and a couple of other insurance company lawyers from Casper. There were good lawyers around, he knew, and maybe he could find one. But Charlie didn't have the money. If the judge appointed a lawyer it would be someone who had neither the interest or the experience to get Charlie justice. He felt trapped. Ace poured him another shot of Old Cabin Still.

Yet there was something to caring, a power in it. He cared about Charlie Redtail and about Charlie's mother—more than he should. How could any lawyer ask a jury to care about his client, to care about justice, if the lawyer didn't care? And one thing he knew: Caring was contagious in a courtroom. Yet the law didn't want a lawyer to be involved. He might care too much and step over the edge or he might care so much his judgment would be impaired. Some lawyers made arguments like that.

As he stirred his whiskey the demons began to make their showing—Charlie being escorted into the gas chamber, the same stoic statuary for a face, the mother weeping, the sobs echoing out to the stars and the empty stars silent. He saw the mother looking at him when the cyanide pellet was dropped into the acid in the gas chamber and her look accused him of the murder of her child and he had no answer.

"I care too much," he heard himself saying out loud.

"They got a case against him, Ab?"

"No," Hill said. "They have lies. They have circumstantial evidence. But he's already convicted. Their case is simple: He's an Indian—a breed, which is worse. He was the leader out there on the reservation."

"But you have a jury, Ab, and sometimes you do pretty good with a jury."

"If you think I have a conflict, think of the conflict the jurors will have," Hill said. "Number one: They all think they're going to get rich in one way or another from the Spirit Mountain Project. Number two: They hate Indians, but they are all too fucking sanctimonious to admit it. Number three: Their survival instincts are at work. That's the most pernicious. They already think he's a murderer—the idea that 'where there's smoke there's fire.' Even if I establish reasonable doubt they'll

184 • Gerry Spence

refuse to acquit. You don't turn someone you suspect of murder loose on yourself and your family because you harbor a fucking reasonable doubt."

"Maybe you should get a change of venue."

"I filed a motion yesterday. But remember, the judge is part of the same pack."

"Trial by a jury of your peers," Ace said. "Let's drink to that."

They lifted their glasses and after they drank, Ace filled Abner's glass again. Hill felt tipsy. He cherished the feeling, the relief. Perhaps at that precise moment wisdom would make its brief appearance on the stage.

"A trial by one's peers is a farce," Hill said. "Your peers do not know you. Your peers do not love you. Your peers are afraid of you." He laughed. "Your peers want you dead." He was pacing the floor. "It appears that your peers mirror your fears."

"They got the woman," Ace said. "Heard it on the radio a few minutes ago. They got Charlie's girlfriend."

Hill jumped to his feet and staggered for the door as if the place were on fire.

"Don't worry, Ab," Ace Holkum hollered after him. "When the time's ripe I'll come in and confess the fuckin' murder. Give me somethin' ta do besides fuck all these lonesome women."

20

Abner Hill ran up the icy path to the courthouse, fell once on the ice, and picked himself up again without brushing off the snow. He waded though the snow to the back door, the entry to the sheriff's office in the basement. The dispatcher was on the police radio hollering over the static.

"I know ya scoured the rez and all lookin' fer her, an' the rez is as clean as a scrubbed duck's ass and that ya still can't find 'er—the reason bein' we got 'er here."

Came the reply through the static, "Well, how come ya never tol' us and left us out here all night in this fuckin' cold lookin' under ever rock for the bitch. We been out here mor'n two weeks."

"Ya never asked," the dispatcher said.

"Kiss my hairy ass," at the other end of the static.

"Ten-four," the dispatcher said. He turned to Abner Hill. "What can I do for ya?"

"I want to see Willow Hodges." Hill tried to be calm. "I hear you finally got her."

"She ain't here."

"Where is she?"

"She's bein' held elsewhere," the deputy said. "We ain't got no facilities for women prisoners."

"Don't feed me that crap. You've got separate cells in there. Where is she?"

"No cause ta argue with me," the dispatcher said. "I jus' work here."

"Well, you get hold a the sheriff. And tell him I'm on my way back to the office to draw up papers for a writ, and unless I get a call from the bastard before I get the papers typed up, and I'm a pretty fast typer, his ass is going to be in front of the judge."

"Ya don't need ta get pissy about it," the dispatcher said. Then Hill whirled and ran into the doorjamb going out. "An' ya ain't gonna type too fast in yer condition," the dispatcher yelled after him.

She could have held out longer in Simon Yellow Dog's root cellar. Already she'd been there for over two weeks. She'd nearly frozen along with the parsnips in the sand barrel and half a venison hanging from the log beam at the ceiling. The cellar was lit by a small, neurotic candle. Sometimes she had slept not knowing whether it was night or day. But mostly in the flickering candlelight she stared at the logs holding up the dirt roof and against the logs she saw the visions.

In the morning Simon had come with breakfast, venison fried in lard. The meat made her sick. He brought her a root beer and that made her sick as well. She was sick especially in the mornings. She knew why but she hadn't told Simon Yellow Dog. He sat down on a box to watch her eat, she on the army cot huddled over the tin plate.

"They're probably beatin' the shit outta Charlie tryin' ta make him talk," Yellow Dog said. "I seen 'em beat people 'til they was unconscious. I seen 'em torture 'em by taking their clothes off of 'em in that jail. Never left no marks on 'em," he said. "But pretty soon they get so cold they get to shiverin' and after a while they go outta their minds and they talk. I seen it coupla times before." Then she saw Charlie laying naked on the jail floor and she was cold to the bone. Suddenly she knew she had to give herself up. Simon had driven her to the sheriff's office that same day. Told the sheriff he found her walking down the road and gave her a ride in. Didn't know where she'd been hiding.

The sheriff, William Marsden, was a flat-faced man with a thick, graying mustache that covered his entire upper lip. He was stocky, of medium height, in his late fifties, and wore a tan sheriff's jacket covering one of those cop bellies, his hanging over a silver rodeo buckle.

He'd put cuffs on Willow and led her to what appeared to be an abandoned frame building behind the courthouse. The place smelled of grain. A mouse-eaten burlap sack half-full of oats sat in the corner of the room. A set of old harnesses hung on a wooden peg, the leather blackened from decades of horse sweat and dirt. The old granary had become the sheriff's interrogation room when he had run out of space in the courthouse.

The sheriff walked over to the portable gas heater hissing on the other side of the room where the woman sat, its blue flame licking the sides of the heater door. He turned up the heat. The woman was staring at her small hands, the fingernails cut short, the eyes frightened, large and brown. She folded her hands across her sheepskin jacket. It was hot and the room was bright from a set of twin floodlights that were shining in her face.

"Do you understand what I mean, cooperate?" the sheriff said. "Maybe you can explain to her what cooperate means." He was speaking to his undersheriff, Dean Miller.

"Ya fuckin' right. It means if you don't talk to us they will throw yer ass to the gas, too. Ya understand what I mean, sister!"

"Ever see some puke in the gas chamber?" the sheriff joined in. "They gasp in there and they turn blue and they holler, and nobody can hear 'em because the fuckin' place is soundproof and they fuckin' gag in there an' it takes a hell of a while for 'em to die. That is what the fuckin' gas chamber is about. An' that is where your ass is headed if you don't cooperate."

Small beads of sweat were budding on the young woman's forehead and along the sides of her cheeks. Her blond hair was in two braids. She said nothing, her eyes still on her hands.

"Look at me!" Miller hollered. "Look at me, sister!"

"You're too ugly," she said, which was the first thing she had said.

"Why you bitch," Miller said. He jumped up and started for her, but the sheriff stepped in front of him.

"We don't want her messed up. Not yet."

"And your breath is bad," she said to the sheriff.

The sheriff pulled his face back from in front of the woman. He squinted his eyes, looked at her, and without taking his eyes from her lit a cigarette. "You hot, sister?"

She didn't answer.

"Why don't ya take yer coat off?" Marsden went around behind her and reached down for the coat as if to help her off with it. He pulled the coat open against her folded arms and saw that she was good behind the black cotton shirt and again he pulled against her folded arms. But she held her hands tightly together. "All right," he said, "roast to fuckin' death. Just as well roast now as later. Right?" he asked Miller.

"Right," Miller said, lighting a cigarette of his own.

Then Sheriff William Marsden said to the woman, "You think you're being so fuckin' loyal to that breed boyfriend of yours, well, let me tell ya: We got his statement. So if ya wanna make it easy on yerself, you'll just lay it out like it happened. We know ya was with him. Just spill it so we can all go home. The old lady's waitin' supper on me."

"Where's Charlie?" she asked. "I want to see him."

"He sold you down the river," the sheriff said. "Never can trust one a them Indins."

The sheriff had stopped hollering at her long enough to pick up the ringing phone.

"I don't give a shit if he does get a writ," Sheriff Marsden told the dispatcher over the phone. "By the time the judge signs it we'll have what we want from the bitch."

After that he took off his tan jacket with the sheriff's emblem on the shoulder, threw it over a chair, and turned up the heat again. He was still wearing his silver-belly Stetson, but he pushed the hat back off his forehead. He was sweating.

"I have to go to the bathroom," she said.

"Ain't got no bathroom here," the sheriff said. "I'll take ya to the bathroom as soon as you talk to us. Get it *all* off yer system at once." He looked over at Dean Miller and laughed at his own joke. "Trade you a load off yer mind for a load off yer bladder."

"You sons of bitches," she said.

"Cussin' won't get ya nowheres," Miller said. "Didn't yer momma teach ya no manners?"

"Come on, honey, I'll take ya over to the bathroom as soon as ya talk to us," Marsden said.

"I gotta go pee myself," Miller said. " 'Scuse me while I go take myself a nice long pee." He laughed. Then he stepped outside and emptied in the snow. When he came back he said, "Now, that felt sooo good. How about you?" he said to Willow Hodges.

"You tell us what we wanna know and we'll take you to the bathroom. We won't even watch."

"Right," the sheriff said.

"Well, looky there!" Miller said. "I'll be go to hell. The bitch wet her pants! Jesus Christ, didn't yer momma teach ya nothin'?"

21

Miller had dragged her up in cuffs and chains through the morning light to the office of the county and prosecuting attorney, the long ordeal in the granary of the night before at last over.

"Take the cuffs and shackles off the woman," Ava Mueller said.

"This is a tough bitch. Ya sure ya know what yer doin'?" Miller asked.

"You can wait by the window outside my office and watch the grosbeaks at the bird feeder," she said. She smiled at Willow.

"I got plenty a birds down in the jailhouse ta watch and a whole lot more of 'em actin' up on the rez." Miller closed the door and the two women sat across the desk from each other, the prosecutor in her tight jeans with the man's white shirt open at the neck and Willow in her orange jail coveralls. The room had one of those old, high ceilings. Through the transom Willow could hear the secretary pounding away on an ancient Smith-Corona, the sound like the malice of machine guns in the street.

She had felt fear before, but never the fear of helplessness. In Mueller's office she could scream and no one would care. They'd only haul her back to the cell. She could swear and Miller might slap her around or put his hands on her again. Make her sick like she was sick for a week the last time. It wouldn't do any good to scream. The sheriff and Miller had worked her over in the granary. Never touched her, not so as you could see it. She had told them nothing. She lay in the bunk all night, shivering and wet. Then in the morning the dispatcher threw a clean pair of orange coveralls through the bars. Said he didn't want her stinking up the place.

"You look pretty good in orange," Mueller joked.

"Thanks," Willow said. "My favorite color."

"How they treating you down there?" The prosecutor had eyes that didn't squint or turn cold and empty as she talked.

189

"I'm all right," she said. She could feel the warmth of the room but she was still cold. In her cell she had tried to warm herself in the single army blanket, but the blanket smelled of old vomit. When she asked for her sweater Miller said it was against the rules. "This is a fuckin' jail, sister, in case you have forgotten. We ain't runnin' no sorority house here."

"It's cold down there in the cellar," she said to Ava Mueller. "I was hoping you could get them to let me wear my sweater."

"I'll see what I can do," Mueller said.

She felt the chair warming her buttocks, felt it through the coveralls. Then suddenly she began to shiver again.

The prosecutor got up, went to her closet, and took out a red ski jacket. Willow put it on. "Now you are quite the bright sight," Mueller said. "We should send for the fashion photographers." Then she said, "I want to talk to you about this case."

"I suppose if I don't talk you'll take the coat away from me," Willow said to the woman. "Don't I need a lawyer?"

"I thought a couple of girls could talk with each other without some smart-ass lawyer sticking his nose into things."

"I don't have a lawyer," she said, suddenly, not realizing why she said it and pointing to the door where Miller had exited. "That son of a bitch who brought me up here is a son of a bitch. I don't mean to be redundant."

"He's a creep," Mueller said.

"Ever put the moves on you when you were in handcuffs?"

"That's not my thing."

"It's not mine either," Willow said.

"Was Cotler with Miller when he had you in the cuffs that time?"

"I think I should have a lawyer," Willow said.

"Have you called your parents?" The prosecutor struck at her short hair to push it over her ear. She wore a pair of small ruby earrings.

"I want to keep my father out of this," Willow said.

Arvid Hodges had inherited the family fortune, but he was not one of those with old money who frittered his life away. He ran the business, managed their properties, and was an avid hunter. A crack shot, he hunted anything that would run or fly. He'd been a sober, loving father. The abuse Willow suffered was at the hands of her mother, whom she adored.

Before her mother swallowed the lye, she wrote a note claiming that she was killing herself because Henrietta Norman had cheated at bridge and won the tournament, that life had proven to be unbearable because she had thought that bridge, a mere game, was the only honest part of life she had encountered and if her best friend had cheated at bridge, there was nothing left in the world that was honest and she could not bear the pain of a totally dishonest existence.

In truth, poor Henrietta had neither cheated nor won the tournament. Later the family lawyer, Jarred Holloway, had remarked to one of his partners that since the death of Victoria Hodges had been founded on mistake it should have been revocable under the law. He laughed. "But God does not follow the law."

Despite the horror of her mother's insane tantrums, Willow had loved her, for behind the screaming, dish-throwing, window-breaking, deranged episodes of unrestrained violence in which Victoria Hodges threatened to kill anyone who came within focus, especially her husband, there was a tenderness that the woman revealed only to Willow, quiet times when the child gained a sense of her mother's fragile heart that hung to the dangling threads of Victoria Hodges's exquisitely painful love of her child. At last this crippled love had proved more precious to the child than her father's steady, quiet, unemotional presence.

When her mother was calm, she and Willow spent hours together in the garden talking to the daylilies and identifying the songbirds. But when her mother was on a violent, psychotic rampage, the girl did not exist. Then the mother, her eyes red and wild and protruding as if some inner pressure caused their bulging, her hair as wild, would run through the house, sometimes naked except for her silk stockings bunched at the ankles. She would brandish a brass candlestick or a butcher knife and threaten to murder any and all whom she might encounter. Once she cornered the chef, who was obliged to stave her off with a broom handle as if he were engaged in a fight with a deranged swordsman. On such occasions Victoria Hodges would run past Willow as if the child were invisible, all the while screaming at the top of her voice that the place was populated with plotting murderers and rapists who were infected with a pernicious disease she referred to as the "mucky-green plague."

Then, at the hall clock's strike of noon, she would ascend the long stairs to her bedroom, make herself up and dress perfectly, and the chauffeur would drive her to her bridge game where she was the darling of the party. Sometimes in defense of themselves, the staff set the clock up an hour, and, sure enough, when the clock struck twelve she would revert to her predictable calm and return to her bedroom to prepare for the afternoon.

Willow was at her boarding school when her mother died. No one called her. They buried Victoria Hodges without the girl knowing it, without the girl having had a chance to say good-bye or to lay a daylily on her casket. Victoria Hodges had been in the ground a full three months before someone sat Willow down to tell her and even then it hadn't been her father, who himself could not bear to bring the girl the news. Instead Mattie Hornsburger, the family's maid of more than twenty years, told Willow that her mother was really not on an ocean voyage with her friends, as her father had several times reported when Willow asked of her. Her mother was dead.

"Your father could hire the best lawyer in the country for you," Ava Mueller said.

Willow was still cold. "I was wondering if you had a cap I could wear?" she said. "You lose most of your body heat through your head, you know."

"No," Ava Mueller said. "I never wear a cap. I wear a hat, if that would help." She got up and went to the closet and brought back her silver-belly Stetson with the small brim. "Here," she said handing the woman her hat. "You're welcome to wear this." Willow put the hat on. "You're quite the sight, if I do say so myself," Mueller said. She laughed and her laugh was full-throated and not held back.

Ava Mueller walked over to where Willow was sitting. She pulled up a chair beside her prisoner and looked into her eyes. "You were with Charlie Redtail when he shot Ronald Cotler. We know that," Mueller said.

"I think I should have a lawyer," Willow said. "Couldn't you get me a public defender?"

"At the arraignment the judge will appoint somebody for you—one of the locals in Twin Buttes. Richard James Everhart is up next. Used to be a football coach. Says he couldn't stand the stress of coaching so he went into law. Now he stays home drunk half the time."

"Isn't there anybody else?"

"None of them ever try cases. They get appointed and plead their client guilty, collect their hundred dollars, which is all the county allows for a felony trial, and go on with their business. Only one who tries any cases is Abner Hill. But he's representing your boyfriend."

Mueller walked over to the closet and extracted a Winchester carbine with a red tag attached to the lever. She handed the rifle down to Willow, who held it away from her body with both hands like a filthy stick. She pushed the rifle back to Mueller but the prosecutor left the rifle in Willow's hands.

"Ever see that gun before?"

"How would I know? I've seen a lot of guns," she said. She could smell the perfume from the woman drifting down.

"At least you aren't a liar. This was the gun Charlie carried in the rack in the back of his pickup." Then she said, "I hear you're pregnant."

"How did you know that?"

"Smart guess," Mueller said. "It would be a shame to have your child born in the pen. I don't believe I could bear that. You know Charlie confessed?"

"Charlie didn't have anything to do with it," she said. Her breath came in short gasps now. She saw her mother standing naked on the front verandah crying, begging to be killed, sobbing like a small child, hollering down to the people passing on the river in their boats, "Kill me! Kill me! Please, kill me!" And Willow had run to her mother and put her arms around her mother's naked leg and her mother quit crying and had reached down and touched the child's head. "Don't pay any attention to me, Betsy," her mother said, which was what her mother sometimes called her. "Nobody will kill me. They're all too cowardly to kill me," and in the same breath she had said, "and I love you very much."

Willow was still holding the gun in both hands. Then she said, "I shot the son of a bitch. So kill me!" she shouted. "Kill me! You are too fucking cowardly to kill me."

Ava Mueller picked up the phone and asked her secretary to come in with her notebook.

Abner Hill pulled open the courthouse door as if to punish it and ran down the steps two at a time. When he arrived at the cell behind Miller's jangling keys he saw the man inside the cage pacing. Charlie stopped his pacing when Miller unlocked the cell.

Charlie saw the look on his lawyer's face. "You heard," Charlie said like a child.

Hill said nothing, the silence like drums in the ears. At last he said, "You tryin' to kill yourself, Charlie?"

"She confessed to somethin' she didn't do," the man, sitting on the steel cot looking at his big hands, his eyes like the eyes of a horse that had been ridden too far. "She's always tryin' ta fight my battles for me."

"She confessed because they told her you'd already confessed. Jesus Christ." Suddenly Hill felt old and beaten.

"They are always lying," Charlie said.

"That could be the name of this case," Hill said to no one.

"Miller come in here laughin'. He was hauling in that guy over there." He pointed with his eyes to the man in the cell across the walkway. The man was sitting quietly in the shadows. Hill couldn't see the face. "The guy was drunk."

"Yeah?" Hill listening.

"An' Miller hollers in, 'We got your ol' lady, Redtail. She spilled her guts.' Then he stuck his nose in and says, 'She is gonna fry, motherfucker.' That's what he said, and he was laughin'."

Hill got up, walked to the bars of the cell, and held on to them, his head against the steel.

"I told him she didn't have nothin' ta do with it. An' Miller says, 'Well, I suppose the motherfucker killed hisself. If she didn't kill 'im, who did?' and I says, 'I did.' An' he says, 'That is just so much bullshit hearsay ta me, Redtail. Ya want me ta call in the court reporter for a statement?' I told him I didn't know, and he says, 'You are a dumb motherfuckin' dog-eater. You're all alike. You don't know shit,' an' I said, 'Bring the reporter then,' an' so he brought the reporter an' I told 'em."

'Why didn't you call me?"

"Didn't have a chance ta call ya. He brought the reporter in and Miller asked a bunch a questions an' I told him I shot him."

"Shot who?"

"You know who. Don't like ta say his name. Name's bad medicine."

A heavy weariness washed over Hill. Maybe Charlie was providing Hill an escape. How could Charlie expect any lawyer to defend him in face of such evidence now sealed with a confession?

"What am I supposed to do now, Charlie?"

"I wanna plead guilty," he said.

"What are you talking about?"

"She has my baby in her."

*　　　*　　　*

Hill had read the confession many times. Perfectly drawn, he saw the imprint of Ava Mueller on it, the simple language that gave it authenticity, the motive clearly stated, the act of murder laid out in understandable language without an excess word where a defense attorney might burrow in for an attack. It was Ava Mueller's confession, he thought. Not Charlie's. But it was Charlie's signature at the bottom.

He'd gone to the books to determine if a prosecutor who knew the defendant was represented by an attorney was obliged to call the attorney when his client wanted to confess. But Mueller had known the law, knew it before Hill did, knew that if the accused wanted to confess and claimed he did not want his attorney present, it was his right to do so. He read from the case of *Yeary v. State of Wyoming*, Judge Horace Blakely holding forth in a case that was "on all fours" with Charlie's, as lawyers like to say: "Although the accused is entitled to an attorney during every significant step in the process, he is still a citizen endowed with all the rights of a citizen. As ill-advised as it might be, he has, among other rights, the right to demand that his confession be given without the advice of counsel."

Hill looked at the confession yet again. He saw no holes.

STATEMENT OF CHARLIE REDTAIL
December 22, 1989

I, Charlie Redtail, wish to make this statement. I have a lawyer, but it is my desire to make this statement in his absence. I do not need a lawyer. I need to make this statement. I make it freely, without promise of leniency or reward. I know that I could face the death penalty and that by signing this statement it could lead to my execution. Nevertheless, I want to get this matter off of my conscience.

On December 13, 1989, I was in the Big Chief bar. I had my .30-.30 Winchester carbine rifle in my pickup. It was fully loaded with the kind of soft-point ammunition I use to hunt deer. Ronald Cotler, the owner of the bar, had purchased Spirit Mountain. This is a sacred Indian mountain. He has been attempting to cut it up and destroy it. I came into the bar to ask him to stop. He laughed at me. I went out to the car and sat there a long time thinking. I waited for the bar to close. Then I drove out to Cotler's place and waited for him to come home.

I was hiding about twenty-five yards from the front door of his house. The porch light was on. When he walked up on the porch in the light I hollered at him and he stopped. Then I pulled the trigger. He fell in a heap and I took off running, got in my car, and drove out to the reservation.

I had had two drinks of whiskey that night. I was not drunk. Elizabeth "Willow" Hodges had nothing to do with this. She did not know I was going to kill Ronald Cotler. I have read this confession and it is true. I freely sign it knowing the consequences of my act.

> (signed) Charles Redtail
> Witnessed: Dean Miller, Deputy Sheriff
> Randy Hall, Court Reporter

At first Hill had spoken quietly to the man, this man who was like his son, this man, the murky enigma, and at the same time the boy with a soul as clear as a late summer creek. He felt the raw, primal feelings of a man losing his child. It was as if he were watching the murder of Charlie Redtail, the murderer without a face, without form, with no soul, descending upon Charlie Redtail. Then suddenly Hill screamed at Charlie.

"If you go down for this killing, your fight for Spirit Mountain is over. You've lost. Look, Charlie," he said, pacing. "Look. The bulldozers are coming. Look. They're tearing up the mountain. Look. They're making room for white men's houses. They're cutting up the land to make golf courses. They're making trails for fat bankers to ride their fat horses on. Maybe you don't understand." Hill was out of breath.

Charlie put his head into his hands. After a while he said, "I should have been like Billy. He could buy the mountain if he wanted to. If I was like Billy I wouldn't be here. They don't do this to rich people."

Hill began anew, this time speaking slowly and in a quiet voice. "When Cotler was killed, his interests in the property went to his estate. His murder doesn't stop anything. Spirit Mountain will be sold, maybe this time at public auction, and whoever buys it will carry on the project." Charlie came up from his hands.

"What do you mean, it will go on?"

"Did you think that if Cotler was killed, that would save the Mountain?"

"What do you mean that it will be sold to others?"

"Did you think that if you sacrificed yourself in this thing that the mountain would be saved?"

Charlie Redtail didn't answer. He sat like a man suffering from great exhaustion. He got up and walked over to where Hill was standing.

"I want to plead guilty," he said. "Want to get it over with."

"You must be crazy," Hill said. "I'll plead you not guilty by reason of insanity."

"It's ruined."

"It's not over yet. Not 'til the jury says it's over."

"Trials in the white man's court are not for justice but for the white man's purpose."

"You're not making a speech to your renegade friends, Charlie. You're talking to me, Abner Hill," he said, beating his chest.

The man went on as if he didn't hear his lawyer. "These trials in the white man's court are games white men play. They play for money. The old man was wrong. Money is not a pile of jackrabbit turds. Money would buy the mountain. It would buy those town people. They want the money. I should have gone with Billy. We had scholarships, you know, to play at Kentucky. But I didn't want to play the white man's game."

Hill was silent for a long time.

They could hear the snoring of the man in the cell across from them. Finally Hill walked over to Charlie and put his hand on the man's shoulder, the man's back to him, the man holding on to the bars. The lawyer spoke softly. "Charlie, don't you owe me something after all of these years?" Nothing back from the man, his back still to his lawyer. "They will kill you. They will march you into the gas chamber and kill you if you plead guilty. I don't think I could stand that."

"Is it not better sooner than later?" Charlie asked.

"Think of your mother."

"I have thought of her much."

"Think of the old man."

"I have thought of him much."

"Think of Willow."

He was silent.

"The child, Charlie."

Hill heard the soft sobbing down the walkway in the cell beyond them. Then Charlie said, "That man down there wants to die but he cannot die," the sobbing of the man like the long sobs of a beast caught in a trap.

"When one is trapped it is not bad to die," Charlie Redtail said. There was a finality in his words, as if they were the man's last, as if he was waiting for the jailer to bring him his last supper.

"It would be different if you killed him, Charlie." Hill put his arm around Charlie's shoulder and turned the man to face him. "Charlie, it would be different if you did it." He looked Charlie in the eyes for a long time. Then Charlie looked down, turned away, and there was an awful silence in the cell.

22

When Mary Hamilton with her son, William R. Hamilton, walked into the sheriff's office, Dean Miller greeted the man and ignored the woman.

"Hiya, Billy," Dean Miller said. He wore the shiny badge over his left breast and a silver bar on his epaulet as if he were a lieutenant. "Ain't seen ya since the last time ya was my guest here." Miller laughed.

"We came to see Charlie," Hamilton said. Mary fumbled with her fingers. Then Hamilton took her hand and they followed Miller into the jail.

"Like old times, huh, Billy?" Miller said, shoving his key in the lock. Then before Hamilton could answer, Miller asked, "Could you give me a ride in yer airplane, Billy? Never have rode in one a them jets before."

As they approached the cell Hamilton could see Charlie sitting hunched over on the steel bunk.

"Always knew you was gonna be big-time, Billy, but not this big-time." Miller laughed. "Figgered you was gonna be a big-time crook, ta tell ya the truth. Too smart to be one a them turdballs."

As they walked into the small cell, the mother quickly squatted to look into her son's face. "I brought you some fresh rhubarb and straw-berry pie, Charlie," Mary said. She handed him the plate covered with foil.

"Call me an' I'll come let ya out," Miller said. "Let ya out a here more'n once, huh, Billy?" He locked the door behind them, the sound of his boots echoing down the concrete walkway.

Hamilton took two steps to where Charlie was sitting. Charlie got up and embraced his brother, Hamilton stiff in the embrace but pat-ting Charlie hard on the back.

Then Hamilton looked around, a gesture with open palms at the rusting bars, the concrete ceiling. The concrete floor with the stains of blood and vomit that could never be erased. "Great place for a family get-together," Hamilton said.

Mary sat down by Charlie and took his hand with hers. Hamilton said, "We're going to get you out of here, Charlie," Charlie's eyes on his brother. "Brought along the best mouthpiece in New York. Got me out of more than one tight place." He slapped Charlie on the leg. "Hey, man, you think it's hard getting by out here. You ought to be on Wall Street. Like piranhas. Strip you clean to the bone and then start chewing on the bones." He took a closer look at Charlie.

"They never could beat my boys," Mary said. "Not when they were pulling together. 'Member how you used to win all of the basketball games?" Her eyes more accustomed to the darkness she said, "You look so pale, Charlie."

"He's finally growing into a pale face," Hamilton said.

"Yes." Charlie laughed, his small, high laugh that surprised from the usual deepness of his speaking voice. "Yes. I'm like the flower that lives under a board."

"Hardly," Hamilton said.

Then Charlie laughed his high laugh again. "But I don't smell like a wild rose," and they both laughed. Then he said to Mary, "The concrete here is sick." He looked at the floor with pity. "These bars are sick. The people who work here are sick. They can't escape the sickness. But I am only pale." Then he laughed once more, but his laugh was not so high.

"That's good," Hamilton said.

"I weep for the concrete that it should be wasted on such misery. But I can fly out of here whenever I choose."

"How's that?" Hamilton asked.

"The hawk flies," he said.

Hamilton and his lawyer, Anthony Russo, occupied the back booth in the Buckhorn bar, the arraignment of Charlie and Willow before Judge Henry Hankins but a week away. It had been a quick trip. "I wanted to look in on the kid," Hamilton had said.

The noise of the crowd and the beat and sob of the western band made the men speak on the edge of shouting.

"I got a lot of investors' money locked up in that project and a lot of my own money," Hamilton said, paying the waitress. Left a five-dollar tip.

"Not to mention my money," Russo, his lawyer, said.

"You can't even guess how much it takes to turn that fucking sage-brush into golf courses, tennis courts, and swimming pools."

"What about Charlie?" Russo asked.

"He was leading that bunch of war-whoops who never earned a fucking dime in their lives."

"Does he know Spirit Mountain is your deal?"

"No."

"How about your mother?"

"No."

"Maybe you ought to tell them."

"Too late now," William Hamilton said. "Just fuck things up between us." He emptied his glass.

"Kid's in big trouble," Russo said.

"I hated this little armpit of a town. Couldn't stand it here. Every-body's either dumb or dead in their heads. But they have something." He didn't say anything more for a while. "Something," he said again.

"Right," Russo said. "They have every petty prejudice known to man." Russo watching the people dancing, bumping, and jumping.

"Sometimes I wish I'd never left. The people here don't kill each other over a couple of bucks."

"No, but they'll kill your brother."

"If I hadn't left, Charlie wouldn't be in this trouble."

"If you hadn't left you'd still be selling magazines instead of banking new companies. And when Charlie got his ass in this jam you wouldn't have been able to hire a stuttering shyster, much less me."

"Money isn't everything," Hamilton said.

"You must be drunk," Russo said. He hollered to the bar waitress to bring them another round.

"Look at these people," Hamilton said. "They're happy. They live in Nowhere and haven't got a pot to piss in."

"They're drunk, too."

Suddenly Hamilton's eyes got hard. "I told Cotler to handle things. If he was going to front the deal he had to handle those fucking rene-gades out there raising hell and running off all my prospects."

"You don't put some two-bit promoter from Podunk in charge of the World Fair."

"I knew the son of a bitch from way back. Charlie saw the son of a bitch and a couple of deputies kick our old man to death."

"Pretty good motive for murder I'd say: Kid kills his father's killer."

"The Arapahoes were all over Cotler out there. He couldn't raise another fucking dime. His creditors were jerking him into the bankruptcy court. He calls me. Said I was the only person he knew with the kind of money he needed."

Russo waited.

"Cotler needed killing."

"Yeah?" Russo said.

"You can kill a son of a bitch with a gun. But more men been killed in money deals than with guns. I decided to take his project over, kill the son of a bitch a little at a time—enjoy it. Promised to pay off his debts and give the asshole a bonus based on a percentage of net if he'd front the deal. Didn't want my name mixed up with Spirit Mountain. Besides, there was a fortune laying there." Hamilton took a long drink and spoke to the glass. "Charlie was always more honest than I was."

"So?" Russo said.

"So I let Cotler twist a long time. Made him beg for every penny. Gave him barely enough to keep his fucking head above water. Killing him a little at a time. Maybe Charlie was more kind. Did it all at once and painless."

Russo waited.

"Son of a bitch deserved killing. Set our mother out in the street once when she couldn't pay the rent and she wouldn't fuck him for it."

"Another pretty good motive for murder," Russo said.

"Yeah," he said. "I wish the kid would have let me do it my way. No law against killing a man in a money deal."

"You get respected for that," Russo said. He laughed.

"If I hadn't taken the deal the bankruptcy court would have sold the mountain to the highest bidder and a lot of sleazy scavengers would have chopped it up into cheap home sites and dumped trailer houses and prefabs all over it."

"You did the right thing," Russo said.

"Cotler was a dumb son of a bitch!" Hamilton said. "Got himself killed, got my brother charged with murder, got my investors running like a bunch of cats with their asses on fire. Good thing the son of a bitch is dead or I'd have shot the son of a bitch myself."

Abner Hill first met Anthony Russo at Hill's office the following morning, the dark man with slick, thin black hair waiting at Hill's office door when Hill arrived, the man in a pin-striped navy blue suit, white shirt, a blue silk tie sporting small red checks.

Russo held out his hand. His shirt cuff revealed three buttons, his initials, *AR*, embroidered in old script.

"Name's Anthony Russo." Hill took the hand. Soft. Small. "Hamilton asked me to come along. Said maybe I could be of some assistance. I'm a member of the New York Bar. Had some experience in these cases."

He followed Hill into his office. Without an invitation he took a chair and lifted his feet up on Hill's desk. Wore those loafers with the little doodads that flopped when he walked.

"I'm told you've never tried a death penalty case," Russo said. "Lawyer shouldn't be learning to try a death penalty case on somebody he cares about."

Hill watched the man. Hard face like someone who sold bad cars, the teeth yellowing. Russo took out a cigarette from a gold case and lit it. Blew blue smoke out the side of his mouth.

"Death cases are the hardest. Hard to find a juror nowadays who doesn't want to stick it to somebody. People like it when the state gives 'em a chance to kill—legally. We're all killers at heart."

Hill waited.

"I stacked up the corpses of my clients, one after another, until I finally learned how to try a death penalty case. Most of 'em needed killing." Then Russo added, "Nobody can teach you how to beat those death penalty cases. Most lawyers got no stomach for it."

Hill waited.

"When your client gets the chair—even if he's raped and murdered for the kicks—you get sick. You can't sleep. You want to quit the practice. The only way you can get over it is to go back to work and defend another one." He waited. Then he said, "You haven't paid your dues yet, Hill. You haven't stacked up enough corpses."

"Right," Hill said.

"So how you got this one figured?" Russo asked.

"Charlie thinks he's going to save the girl. His life is all tied up in that Spirit Mountain thing Cotler was promoting."

"Bunch of bullshit," Russo said. "If you want to cause trouble all you have to do is claim the land is sacred and that your ancestors are hanging around there. I saw it out in the Monterey Bay Area. The Ohlones claimed that the whole fucking Bay Area was their sacred hunting ground. Give 'em a case of Thunderbird and they'll forget it."

"As the Arapahoes saw it, Cotler was invading their holy land," Hill said. "Something like the Christians would feel if somebody built a five-star hotel in Bethlehem over the birthplace of Christ. You a Christian?"

"Raised in the Catholic church."

"You believe in that business about the Father, Son, and Holy Ghost?"

"I suppose," Russo said. "Man believes what he's been taught."

"Then you might understand how Charlie and his friends believe in the spirits on Spirit Mountain."

"Still think it's a bunch of bullshit," Russo said. Then he said, "The cheese is getting very fucking binding in this case. You're looking at a trial and pretty quick if my guess is right."

Hill nodded.

"They tell me the state's got a confession from both Charlie and the girl and each of 'em claims they were solely responsible for the murder. Christ. Never saw anything like it." He pulled his feet down from the desk. "If Charlie pleads you could probably talk the prosecutor into a deal to save his life."

"Yeah," Hill said. "He can sit in the pen for fifty years thinking about how he lost the home of his ancestors, his woman, and his child."

"If Charlie loses, he'll probably get the death penalty. I been checking. People are really pissed over all of that Indian trouble. Only one chance," Russo said. "Gotta set aside the confession." Then he added, "Well, there is one other way if you know what I mean." He looked around. "Is this place bugged?"

"I don't want to hear it," Hill said, getting up from his chair.

"Suppose a little deal could be made with a juror. I'm just talking in the hypothetical. I don't mean anything by it." He was still looking around. "Not proposing anything."

"Not interested," Hill said.

Then the New York lawyer said, "By the way, does Charlie know anything about his brother's investments?"

"Charlie's not into financial stuff."

"His girlfriend needs a lawyer," Russo said. "Somebody pretty good. Somebody we can work with."

Hill was quiet for a long time looking up at the ceiling. Suddenly he picked up the phone and dialed the number. "Who'll pay his fee?" Hill asked.

"I suspect Mr. William R. Hamilton will pick up the tab if I ask him."

"Good," Hill said, and when the secretary answered on the other end Abner Hill asked to speak to Harold Yancey.

Ava Mueller's eyes made tears when she told Willow she couldn't stand seeing her go to the gas chamber.

"Think of the child," she said. "Hear the child saying, 'My mother died in the gas chamber,'" her beseeching eyes still on Willow. "Sometimes a woman has to make hard decisions. A woman always decides for life over death. That's how women are different than men."

Mueller came from behind her desk and took a chair next to her prisoner. "It's one thing to have all of those romantic ideas about love. But what we're talking about is the life of your child. I can save you so you can save your child."

"You want me to testify against Charlie—that's what you want, isn't it?"

Mueller's voice was easy. "Somebody has to pay for Cotler's death. If it's you, you punish an innocent child. How could we be parties to that?"

She'd waited for Willow to answer.

Then Mueller pressed on. "Why should this child be sacrificed for what was going on at Spirit Mountain?"

"Charlie had nothing to do with it," Willow said. "You want me to lie?"

Mueller watched the woman begin to shiver anew, watched her stare into her hands. Then after ten minutes of silence she called for the deputy.

Willow sat in the darkness of her cell, the cold, the sound of the prisoners yelling, cursing back and forth, the one who sobbed continuously, the cell doors slamming, the prisoners rattling the bars, the sound of men pacing, a shuffling sound like old men. And she had cried out for Charlie but he could not hear her. Then she began to shiver again and after a while, she could not remember for how long, she was lifted up into a warm place, onto a sunny slope of the mountains, and Charlie was there.

They were walking through the forest on a small game trail, Charlie in the lead through the tall, fecund growth of fresh forest grasses, the wildflowers in profusion. He stopped in the trail and pointed to a wild geranium, its pink petals fresh and open as young souls.

"You have to stop and look at the flower," he said.

"Why?" She was laughing.

"Because this flower has struggled all winter to survive and has fought the last frost of spring." He held it gently between his fingers but he hadn't picked it. "And it has gone through great pain to bloom and it's shouting at us, 'Look at me! See how beautiful I am?' If we don't see it, its struggle and pain will have been wasted." He laughed his high, small laugh. "Flowers have spirits," he said.

"How do you know that?" she asked. She closed her eyes and ran her fingers lightly over the bloom. "It feels very soft. It feels like your skin," the filtered light through the forest softly etching the edges of his hair. "How does the spirit look?"

"The spirit looks like you," he said. "The spirit has your voice." Then he had touched her lightly and they had walked on.

On the day of the arraignment the courtroom was only half-full, the hard pews occupied mostly by reporters conditioned to long waits on hard seats. The townspeople had little interest in the formality. Everyone knew Charlie Redtail and the Hodges woman would plead not guilty, that they would be held without bond awaiting trial, a date that Judge Hankins would one day set. Then, as everyone supposed, Redtail and the Hodges woman would be convicted, which would end the angst and anger of the citizens.

The breed, Charlie Redtail, with the long braid and the calm face, still in his orange prison coveralls, was shackled. His lawyer, Abner Hill, sat beside him. Behind them stood three armed deputies that included Miller and Maxfield.

The woman, Willow Hodges, sat at the adjoining council table with her lawyer, Harold Yancey. She, too, wore the orange prison coveralls but she sat without the shackles and the cuffs. A large woman dressed in a sheriff's uniform stood behind her, the woman's powerful arms folded across her chest.

Willow leaned around her lawyer to get a glance at Charlie. He looked pale, she thought. He looked thin, the once beautiful skin like old, yellowed paper. She tried to catch his attention, but the woman in the sheriff's uniform stepped in to block her vision.

As they approached the bench Willow tried to find Charlie's eye, but he didn't looked in her direction. The pain of it, she thought, the deep pain of their separation, their entrapment like animals. She remembered how Charlie had spoken to her of traps, that the coyote in the trap gnaws off its leg and the beaver in the trap drowns itself.

Down in her cell she had told her lawyer, this Harold Yancey, that she was in a trap, that she was in it with Charlie Redtail. She told Yancey the prosecutor had wanted her to lie.

"Well, my lady," Harold Yancey had said, "you didn't leave yourself many choices after you signed that confession."

"I signed it without the advice of a lawyer," she said.

"The confession recites very plainly that you were advised you had the right to a lawyer and that you waived that right." He put the confession in front of her so she could see the place.

"I was crazy," she said.

"You want me to plead you insane?"

"No," she said. And when her intense staring at the concrete floor produced no answer, she said, "Let them kill me."

She saw her mother standing naked on the verandah crying to the passing boats for someone to kill her, and for the first time she understood her mother, and she understood the coyote and the beaver in the trap. She looked at Yancey, who was leaning up against the bars at the corner of her cell surveying her with a small smile on his face. She disliked the man. She got up from the cot and walked over to him. "Let them kill me, Mr. Yancey. If I lied for Mueller I would become what Charlie calls the walking dead. Let them kill me and get it over with." Then the deputies led her up to the courtroom.

Judge Henry Hankins read the information, the reporters listening, taking their notes like schoolchildren. The judge was not a good reader, not out loud. He stumbled over some of the words and with a small smile of apology, reread the words. The words charged Charlie Redtail with first-degree murder—a killing "with malice aforethought." Then he looked down at the man standing before him.

"How do you plead?" the judge demanded.

Charlie Redtail stood mute.

"I asked you, how do you plead, sir?"

The man didn't answer.

"Counsel," he said, glaring at Hill. "Does this man understand English?"

"Yes, Your Honor."

"Is he in possession of his natural faculties?"

"Well, Your Honor—" Hill began.

"Can he hear?"

"Yes, but to be honest with you—"

"You should be honest with the court at all times," the judge said. "Now, don't play games with me, counsel." His face was red. "Is your client going to plead insanity?"

"I don't believe so, Your Honor."

"Is he going to enter a plea?"

"You will have to ask him," Hill said.

The judge turned to Charlie and shouted, "How do you plead?"

The man stood mute.

"Well, then, I will do as the law directs and enter a not guilty plea for you," the judge said.

The judge turned to Willow, Yancey standing next to her, and he read an identical information to her. She stared up at the judge but she did not see him and when he asked her how she pled she said in a voice that sounded as if it were drifting into the courtroom from a distant place, "Not guilty."

Once more she tried to catch Charlie's eye, but Yancey led her back to the table.

The next morning in the chill of the Fetterman County jail Willow tried to feel the child in her belly. She closed her eyes and concentrated. It is a boy, she thought. He will have the eyes of his father and his skin will be like the sago lily and his small hands will be very fat, of course. She couldn't see the face. But when she sat up she knew that the child was no larger than her thumb.

That something so small should have such power, she thought, like the small bulb in the forest. Sometimes Charlie's eyes grew tears when he spoke of it, the bulb no larger than a thumb he'd said, and having survived the winter, how it fights for its life. At the first hint of spring, the first dripping of the frost from the pine needles onto the soil, the bulb, in the belly of the Mother begins to stir.

"Oh, how it fights!" Charlie said. "It pushes up with a magical power. The gravelly earth is rough against its tender shoot. Often it cries out, but no one hears it in the Mother's belly. Still, it pushes harder, and when it edges up through the earth and the early light touches it, it is frightened, for the sprout has never seen the light. Then the grazing elk steps on the tiny sprout and it is hurt badly, but still it fights and suffers much pain."

She saw his face, the man on his knees holding a small white sprout between his fingers.

"At last," Charlie said, "it finds the strength to grow again, but the deer nips it. Still the bulb does not give up and still the sprout comes on, for nothing can stop it. It is new life."

"How do you know all of this?" she asked and she was laughing. She threw her arms over his back and held on to him.

"I know it because the Old Man of Much Medicine told me," he said. "There is much power in small things."

"And what is the power?" She was still laughing.

"The power—" he said, "there is no word for it in the Arapahoe language."

The dispatcher brought her supper. Two meals a day, one at eight in the morning and one at five in the afternoon, times that matched the shifts of the deputies. The sheriff's wife, Jane Bell Marsden, did the cooking, the antelope and deer meat confiscated by the game wardens from poachers.

She chewed at the boiled meat. It tasted rank. She tried to swallow, gagged, and finally spit it on the tin plate. The half a potato was also boiled. No salt and she ate that. Then she laid back on the cot and pulled the army blanket over her head so that the ghouls could not get in, her nostrils accustomed to the blanket's smell of old vomit. Once more she began to shiver. Then she saw the coyote in the trap, and she could smell the breath of the coyote.

23

The blond man was leaning up against the bar, the man with the cold, blue eyes, like a blue-eyed snake some said. After nearly a decade, the gray at the temples was beginning to show. He was still flat-bellied and wore the same khaki army jacket and high, flat-heeled black boots. He walked down the bar where Abner Hill was drinking alone. "Name's Emmett," he said. He didn't offer a hand and spoke to the back bar, not to the man.

"I remember you," Hill said. He looked at the blond man and turned back to his drink. He was tired. Not in the mood for conversation.

"You aren't going to win the case," the blond man said.

"How do you know?" Hill said, irritated. He picked up his glass as if to move down the bar.

"You don't win cases like that. You try cases like that. Cry over cases like that. You don't win them." Emmett laughed. "And your client isn't guilty."

"How do you know so fucking much?" Hill said, turning straight on to the man.

"I know because I killed Cotler," he said, the voice void of the sounds of life.

"You another of those loonies?"

The blond man laughed. "I shot him."

"Why?"

"His time," he said. "Besides I liked to see his brains spatter all over. It was very amusing."

"You murdered a man for no reason?"

"Have you forgotten, there's no logic in the universe," he said.

"Why are you telling me this?"

"Doesn't it interest you?"

"You'll take the stand, of course, and testify?"

"Of course not."

"You want me to go to the sheriff?"

"Makes no difference to me. I'd deny I told you anything. Your word against mine. Cops would laugh at you. They're laughing at you now, aren't they?"

"What's your gig, asshole?" Hill said.

The blond man laughed again. "I'm a mercenary for the universe. I'm in tune with the universe."

"You're one crazy son of a bitch." Hill started to leave.

"Perhaps you're suggesting I don't know the difference between right and wrong. That's how you lawyers test for insanity, isn't it?"

"I said, you're nuts."

"I know the McNaughten rule quite well, counselor. And you're right. I do not know the difference between right and wrong. Right and wrong don't exist in the universe. The idea of right and wrong is an insane concept in itself. What's right one place is wrong in another."

"What are you talking about?" said Hill, irritated, yet listening to the rigid, measured voice.

The man laughed again. "The one towering evil in this society is to kill an innocent man. Yet we kill millions of innocent people around the world in wars and those who kill them are hailed as heroes. Yes, you're right. I don't know the difference between right and wrong."

Something about the man made the room turn cold. Hill looked around him. He saw the people in the booths, others standing at the bar, all drowning in a vague sense of futility in their foaming mugs. He saw the women, their faces painted and drawn, their mouths laughing at nothing, the high cackling through the dense haze of blue smoke, the men laughing at everything.

He saw the flashing beer signs and heard the cash register ringing, jeering at the imbeciles whose tokens of labor the cash register swallowed.

Suddenly the strange man, this man who confessed he was Cotler's killer, seemed the sanest of all.

Then the blond man said to Hill, "Do you think you can save your client?"

"If the system works. He's innocent," Hill heard himself say.

"That's why they'll convict him." The man laughed again. "And why do you care?" The man looked at Hill for the first time, the empty eyes.

"Why do you ask?" Hill asked.

"I could have killed you instead of Cotler," Emmett said.

"Where are you from?"

"I didn't kill you," he said with a faint sound of regret in his voice as he looked away.

Hill stared at the man.

Then like an impatient child the man asked again, "Why do you care?"

"Why do you ask?" Hill asked again.

"Caring is a random thing also."

"What do you mean?"

"You could have as easily cared for me," Emmett said. Then he walked out of the bar without having touched his beer, the foam already flat.

24

Anthony Russo wore a pair of cowboy boots and a black cowboy hat—
"fresh bought," as the cowboys liked to say. They laughed as they
watched him try to walk in the boots, his ankles giving way so that he
wobbled like an old man.

"She is full of romantic, heroic ideas," Yancey said in Hill's office as
he slipped off his four-buckle overshoes.

Russo hung up his new hat next to Hill's on the hat rack.

"She insists she killed Cotler. Tells a good story. But I happen to
know she didn't," Yancey said.

"How do you know?" Russo asked.

"I asked her how you shoot a .30-.30. She didn't know. Asked her
how to put a fresh shell in the chamber. She couldn't, and gentlemen,
the old cartridge case had been ejected and a live cartridge was in the
chamber when the cops took the rifle."

"She gonna stick?" Russo asked. He lifted his new boots up on Hill's
desk, the snow dripping, making small puddles on the oak top.

"As the trial date creeps up, little by little people change their minds
and she'll change hers," Yancey said. "She's got that baby coming, you
know."

"These two aren't ordinary people," Hill said.

"The survival instinct is at work in all of us," Yancey said. "Keeps us
breathing. It's imbedded in the soul." Yancey sat down, this time talking to the ceiling. " 'To be or not to be' is not the question. 'To be' is the
only question. It's the mammalian imperative. And don't forget: she's a
pregnant mammal."

"We can't rise above our instincts?" Hill asked.

"This is all so much bullshit," Russo said. "He says he did it. She
says she did it. If they both go to trial the jury'll convict 'em both.
Something has to give here."

"Maybe the jury would acquit 'em both," Hill said. "Who really did the killing? Reasonable doubt."

"Dream on," Russo said back. He took a cigarette from his gold case and tapped the butt on Hill's desk. "Reasonable doubt is for law books."

"Let's be practical," Yancey said, turning to Hill. "It was your client's gun and your client's fingerprints on the gun. It was your client with the gunshot residues on his hands. It was your client's cause—that mountain, you know. Your client confessed it. Miller will testify that he heard your client threaten Cotler. So how does anybody come up with the idea that my client did anything?"

"Miller never told the truth in this life," Hill said.

Russo looked at Yancey. He took long drags from his cigarette and at last pulled his boots off the desk. "Well, boys, it looks like the game has just been called. The name of this game is every man for himself, right?"

"I have to represent my client," Yancey said. "That's the first rule of ethics. I wasn't hired to mollycoddle a romantic-minded woman who has yet to come to her senses. Once that baby asserts itself she's going to sing a different tune. My job is to see that she isn't convicted."

"We're playing into Mueller's hands," Russo said. "Get us at each other's throats and she gets us both. I thought we were going to have a little cooperation here. As a matter of fact, I thought that's why Abner suggested you represent the woman."

"Just how would you like me to cooperate?" Yancey asked. He raised an eyebrow and waited.

"We need a fall guy," Russo said. "Cotler had a lot of enemies out there."

"I wouldn't take part in such a thing," Yancey said, wrapping his red, woolen muffler around his neck. "It's unethical." Then he pulled on his four-buckle overshoes and buckled each buckle carefully.

"Ethics usually provide the sellout lawyer an excuse," Russo said.

"See you gentlemen in court," Yancey said, and walked out the door.

When he was gone Russo said, "If I'd known you were going to pick a white-laced motherfucker like that to represent the woman I'd never told Hamilton to pay his fuckin' fee."

"She's entitled to a good defense," Hill said.

"*She* isn't our worry. Our worry is Charlie. Our worry is the fuckin' gas chamber. And that holier-than-thou prig has the easy case. That's why he's so fuckin' self-righteous. He knows that nobody wants to send a woman to the gas chamber." Russo was silent for a moment. "I'm starting to smell the gas already."

Hill looked down on the street from his window. He watched Yancey slide into his three-holer Buick, pull out from the curb, and drive slowly away. He turned back to Russo. "It isn't as simple as finding a fall guy. One thing Charlie won't do—he won't lie."

"Not even to save his ass from the gas?"

"No."

"Not even to save her?"

After a long time Hill started to speak. Then he said nothing.

Russo looked at the man and saw the worry in his eyes. "Don't worry, pal. I have a whole bag of tricks. So let Uncle Tony here ask you a few questions: Is the judge solid?"

"A little strange sometimes, but honest."

"Nobody's honest," Russo said. "Judges are people and people are only honest when it's easy. Does he spend a lot of money? Is he behind on his house payments? I mean, what's the deal with him? Every man has a 'tender.'"

"The judge's wife has money. And I'd have no part in—"

"What about the prosecutor? What's her 'tender'? Who's she got the hots for? Her old man's a rancher. Is the bank breathing down his neck? What's in her closet? She's got hormones like everybody else. She been fucking the deputy sheriff? Maybe she likes to fuck young boys. Or does she have the hots for girls?"

"This has gone far enough," Hill said.

"This a good man you represent?" Russo asked.

"Yes."

"Worth saving?"

"Yes."

"Even if he shot Cotler?"

"Yes."

"You want to save a killer?"

"If he killed he had good reason."

"Spirit Mountain's a good reason?" Russo asked.

Hill didn't answer.

"You're concerned with the means, Hill. I'm concerned with the ends," Russo said. "You're against a little 'side play,' shall we call it. I'm against a good man breathing in the gas. Think about that."

216 · Gerry Spence

"I don't have to think about it," Hill said. "I've been thinking about it every day for months."

"You got this situation, counsel: You got a good man and he's going to the gas. He's got an honest man for a lawyer. The cards are stacked against the lawyer. The prosecution is going to put on perjured testimony and they're going to convict him. Then they're going to drag this honest lawyer's client into the gas chamber, strap him to the chair, and then they're going to drop the pill in the acid while everybody watches. You need to think about *that*."

Hill was silent, pale, his eyes on Russo. He got up and walked to the window and looked down on the street. The people were talking in small groups. Some were laughing. An old woman with a cane was hobbling, carrying a small bag of groceries and a couple of kids were swinging their lunch pails as they waded in the gutter's water and slush.

Russo got up and walked over to the window and stood by Hill. They watched the kids playing boats with small sticks. Then he put his hand on Hill's shoulder and said, "It isn't easy. A man has to think these things through. We still have time."

Hill was silent.

"When they haul Charlie out of the gas chamber what's going to be the condition of your soul when you know that you could have saved him by doing a little deal somewhere? Think about that. What's more important, Yancey's little rules of ethics or the life of Charlie Redtail?"

Mary thought it was her fault. She should have let Ronnie Cotler have what he wanted and kept her mouth shut about it so that Charlie never knew. She hadn't wanted Charlie to kill Cotler and when Charlie had said he was going to kill him, she'd said, "No, Charlie, killin' only brings on killin'. Don't ever say that to me again."

It was her fault. She should never have let Charlie go out there with the old man. Put a lot of crazy ideas in the boy's head. And now they wanted to kill Charlie. If they killed him she would die. She couldn't live with the pain of it. She couldn't stand the sound of her own weeping in an empty house.

That night Abner Hill had been at the table again, Mary Hamilton sitting across from him in the same way, him peering into the coffee, the darkness of their voices, the shadow of heavy spirits, the fear like murky waters rising.

He spoke as if speaking to himself. "Suppose she was telling the truth? Suppose she shot Cotler like she said and Charlie's covering for her."

"He can tell the jury the truth," Mary said.

"He won't do that. Wants to save his woman and his baby." He looked at Mary. "Your first grandchild, Mary."

She began to weep softly. "You have to do something, Abner." She went on as if speaking to herself. "You have to talk to Mueller. You have to make a deal—give 'em somethin'. I got two hundred dollars in the grocery can." She reached for the coffee can on the shelf. "An' I could go to work for Mueller. Do her housekeepin' or somethin'."

Hill listened, still stirring his coffee.

"I would work for nothin.' I would go to work for the sheriff for nothin', work the rest of my life for 'em. I'd give them whatever they want." She began to cry. She turned away from Hill. "I don't have nothin' to give, nothin' anybody wants."

He wanted to put his arms around the woman to comfort her. He sipped at his coffee.

"I always tried to think positive," she said. "But they are gonna kill my boy." She looked around the room in panic as if to find the answer somewhere, on the barren walls, on the floor. Suddenly she said, "They should both lie. No use givin' up a good life to even the score for somebody like Cotler. 'Scuse me for speakin' ill of the dead, but he was no good. They should both lie."

"If a lawyer knows his client is going to lie he can't put take part in it," Hill said.

"Well, *they* lie whenever they please. They lied against Charlie already. Why are you always so righteous about everything? They are gonna kill my boy, Abner," she said. "Don't ya understand that? Isn't it all right to lie when they are lyin' to kill your boy?"

Hill thought about it, but only for a moment. "A lawyer's ethics says if you know your client's lying and you put him on the stand and take part in the lying by asking questions, and you know the answers are going to be lies, you're guilty of suborning perjury."

"Ethics!" she cried. "Ethics! What about the ethics of killin' an innocent man?" She picked up the fly swatter from the cabinet top by the stove and struck at the empty wall with a vengeance.

"We gotta have rules, Mary, or we'd be worse than savages."

"Rules are for killin' innocent people. Why doesn't the law put those lyin' cops away?"

He tried to calm the woman, to reason with her. The law is designed to keep order, he told her, to preserve a system based on truth. You can't have justice without truth.

"That isn't so," she said. "The truth is that Cotler shoulda been killed a long time ago. I shoulda killed him myself. If I had it to do over again I would."

"We have to play by the rules, Mary," he said again.

"Seems like if you're in a war, that whatever weapon they use, you can use. They lie. We lie."

"Only one trouble with that," Abner Hill said. "You might talk me into lying, but nobody can talk Charlie into it."

"Unless it's to save his woman and his baby," Mary said. "We'll lie to save our own. I done it more 'an once." Then she sat looking at the man across the table from her and she kept her eyes on him for a long time.

Again the following evening he'd seen the man, Emmett, at the saloon. In fact Hill had gone there hoping to find him. Maybe he could discover something more, develop the fall guy Russo suggested. He saw the man standing alone at the far end of the bar. He offered to buy him a beer. The place was noisy. The man didn't look at him, silent, the man staring at the back bar, the bottles in long rows, the mirror with a beer sign flashing in blue neon.

"What's with you and the necklace?" Hill said in a taunting voice.

"I keep track with it," the man finally said.

"You got a bead there for Cotler, right?" Hill said.

"What are you talking about?" the man said. "Get out of here."

"You don't remember? You told me last night you liked seeing his brains splattered all over the place. Thought it amusing."

"I've never seen you before."

"I'm not wired," Hill said.

"If you don't mind," the man said, turning away from Hill.

"Wait a minute," Hill said, crowding closer. "You told me you killed randomly, like the universe."

"Do I have to call the bartender?" Emmett motioned for the bartender and after that Hill walked away.

Then as suddenly Hill turned back and said, "You must be a very lonely man."

The blond man looked at him for the first time. "Why do you say that?"

"Do you have any friends?"

"Cotler was a friend of mine," he said. "Somebody murdered him. I think you know who did it." The cold, blue eyes on Hill. "Do you want to tell me about it?" the man said.

"You're crazy," Hill said.

"Someone shot my friend with a high-powered rifle. I intend to find out who." Then the blond man walked out of the bar, his beer still untouched.

He had gone to see Ava Mueller, that woman with the power of life and death over Charlie. He tried to dismiss the conversation he'd had with the blond man who called himself Emmett, but he could erase neither the vacant sound of the man's voice from his ears nor the deadly, flat eyes from his mind's eye. If he mentioned the conversation to Mueller she'd think it was a pitifully devised ruse to aid Hill in his defense. He had no witnesses to the conversation. He had no evidence. Yet the man knew that the rifle had been a high-powered rifle and that information had not been spelled out in any of the news stories. True, he could have gotten the information from one of the deputies and in a small town there are no secrets. And if he were the only witness to Emmett's confession he'd have to testify, which would disqualify him as Charlie's lawyer. A lawyer can't be both a witness and counsel in the same case. Ava Mueller knew that. She was a smart one. She might put Hill on the stand for no better reason than to get Hill off the case.

This woman had come out of a place Hill didn't understand, this woman seeking to kill Charlie Redtail, not with a gun, but with the lethal weapon of the law, with words that kill as deadly as any bullet. Ava Mueller had all the weapons in her hands and she'd aimed them at Charlie Redtail when she announced she would seek the death penalty.

How could she ask for the death penalty? The history of the human race was a history of killing, but the killing was done by men while women buried the dead and, gathered together in small tribes, kept the fires warm for the warriors when they returned. They took care of the children, raised the boys to become men, and the boys, once men, became killers like their fathers and their grandfathers and the children of the boys would be killers after them. But this woman—how did she come to this killing? And with such fine devotion? Perhaps her insistence on the death penalty was only a strategy intended to force Hill to plead his client guilty so that in exchange for a life sentence Charlie Redtail would not risk the gas.

Hill trudged up the courthouse steps once more to see Ava Mueller, to reason with her, because on rare occasions she had listened to reason. Yet Charlie Redtail had not agreed to any deal and even if he were able to make a deal, probably Charlie wouldn't take it. But what else was he to do in the face of Charlie's confession and Mueller's easy case against him?

Her office adjoined the judge's chambers like a daughter's room next to the father's, like one large, happy family up there, Hill thought, the sheriff, the eldest son, in the basement. Those two, Judge Henry Hankins and Ava Mueller, were in fact like father and daughter, the judge and his wife having been childless.

And fathers do not decide against their daughters. Hill could not remember the last time the judge had held against Mueller even when it was plain that he should. Still it had taken some time and some adjustment on the judge's part to accept this woman as a competent lawyer. Women were women. When they operated outside of their assigned role they became insufferably difficult and ineffable. Once during a hearing Mueller seemed tense and distant and the judge called her to the bench, Hill standing there.

"Would you like to postpone this hearing to another time, Ava?" the judge asked, with that diffident look.

"Why?" she asked.

"Well, you seem a little cranky today. Sometimes when Matilda got that way," referring to his wife, "I knew why and I made certain accommodations." He raised an eyebrow at the woman to accent his joke, but Ava Mueller had not laughed. Instead, she had backed up from the bench so she could hold the man squarely in her eyes. Her eyes got very narrow and her mouth hard so that it was easy to see that beneath the benevolent surface lay a woman the judge had not reckoned with. She had not taken her eyes from the judge, her eyes contemptuous slits, until the judge cleared his throat and looked away.

On another occasion the judge had called her *girl,* as when he said, "Listen, girl, you don't need to respond. Just hold on there, girl." The eyes had narrowed again and she had said, nearly in a whisper, "I am not your girl or anyone else's girl, Your Honor. I would like to make that very clear." And although the judge didn't apologize, he nodded his head, and went on as if nothing had happened.

But in time the two grew to be friends and they made no apologies about their friendship. In the fall they went duck hunting together on the North Fork of the Twin Buttes River. As the story went, she shot her limit of mallards and the judge's as well. And sometimes on the weekend they went to her father's ranch and rode horses, the judge and her father having been old friends who had served in the same outfit in Italy in the Second World War when the reserve was called to active duty.

Abner Hill, his hat in his lap, sat across from Ava Mueller, her papers neatly stacked at one side, she in the same boots and Levi's and the man's white, starched dress shirt open at the collar. Hill had never brought it to the surface of the mind, but he liked the way she looked, crisp, clean, the good face, the leanness of the woman, but still the woman.

He fiddled with his hat, trying to think how to start this conversation. An errant word slipping out from some hostile place could set the egos at each other and ruin any hope of settlement.

He asked about her father and the ranch and her favorite quarter horse, Ike, whom she had named after the late president. Finally he began cautiously.

"I was wondering, Ava, if there was something we could do in the Redtail case."

"Glad to have you on the case, Abner," she said, putting her feet up on the desk, a faint, greenish remnant of the horse barn stuck to the underside of her heel. "You want to plead him guilty?"

"Well, no," Hill said. "I don't think he's guilty, Ava."

"I have a confession that says otherwise. If I thought he wasn't you know I wouldn't charge him, Abner." She had a pleasant smile. "This man has been raising all kinds of hell out there on the reservation for years. He's the leader of that bunch of renegades who've been terrorizing the whole county."

Hill nodded, careful not to argue.

"Now we've got him in a cold-blooded murder, Abner. And he's got a record about a mile long." She handed the lawyer several sheets of paper with hard-to-read printing. "His rap sheet," she said. "But you know what's on it. You were on every one of his arrests, if memory serves."

Hill left the papers in her hands. "No felonies, Ava. Worst thing there is that one simple assault and battery conviction we both remember."

"He was lucky on that one," she said. "This man is a violent breed.

The bunch he hangs with have all been in and out of the pen. And he's been charged with everything but a felony. I tried to give the boy a chance once, Abner." She gave him the good smile again. "And what do I get in return? A premeditated murder. That's the thanks I get."

The woman was the kind who could make you forget she was a woman. But if you looked her over with even passing interest it was easy to come back to the realization. Still, Hill thought, when you were with her the tension men felt around other men wasn't there, that competitive thing like dogs sidling up to each other with the hair up on their backs and their tails wagging in those tight, little hostile wags. People liked her. Juries liked her.

Mueller went on. "This time Redtail ambushed the victim. His girl-friend saw it all. She wants to take the blame, but we both know Charlie Redtail did the shooting. Then he mutilated the body, cut off the finger of the deceased. After that the two of them tried to escape to the reservation. You know the rest, Abner. Simple case. Not much to mitigate the death penalty."

"If I could talk him into a guilty plea, could you consider dropping the death penalty?" Hill heard himself finally ask.

"I have an open and shut case on Redtail," she said. "I have a confession. I don't need a plea bargain, Abner."

"But you have a confession against the Hodges woman, too."

"Right," she said. "She's just trying to save her man. She'll get over that after awhile."

"What if Charlie confessed to save his woman?"

"That's passed my mind," she said. "But Redtail had threatened the life of the deceased before. What more do I need?"

"Miller lied," Hill said, almost as if to himself. "You know that."

"That can be your defense then, Abner," she said. "Make the jury believe Miller lied. Make them believe the gunshot residues were from having shot a deer the day before."

Hill was silent for a moment, the woman watching him like a swordsman waiting for his next thrust with a broken sword. Finally he said, "Your case is all circumstantial, Ava. You're not going to put a man in the gas chamber on circumstantial evidence. No eyewitnesses. Cotler had a lot of enemies."

"The graveyards are full of felons executed on less evidence than I have in this case," she said. "I have enough on Redtail to convict him a dozen times."

"Like what else, Ava?"

"Like you'll see," she said. "But I'll tell you this much: Your client shot a leading citizen in this community. Shot him in cold blood—an arrogant, purposeful, intentional, evil execution. Then he mutilated the body. The county's up in arms. The president of the Chamber of Commerce, Ernest Pillsberry, told me that some of the business men are talking about an old-time lynching, that they're not about to let a bunch of renegades from the reservation terrorize Twin Buttes. They're angry out there." She pointed in the direction of the street. "I told Ernest the law would take care of it. The Indian wars are over, Abner."

"Maybe I should call you as my first witness on my motion for a change of venue," Hill said. He wished he hadn't said it. Then he knew the negotiations in Charlie Redtail's case were also over.

Mueller leaned back and looked at Abner Hill and her eyes got narrow. "I'll see that your client gets a fair trial—before he goes to the chamber. That's where he belongs—in the gas chamber. Sorry, Abner."

He let a little time settle in, he looking down at his hat, turning his hat slowly around by the brim. He doubted that Ava Mueller had ever seen a man strapped to the chair in that small, iron room with only the one glass window like a square porthole in the side of a ship, doubted she had even imagined seeing the cyanide pill drop into the acid. Nor had he before this case. Yet now he could see the gas rolling up, filling the small chamber, the man struggling against the straps, holding his breath.

For Abner Hill the gas chamber was the kind of cruel and unusual punishment proscribed by the Constitution because the condemned must kill himself. No executioner released the trap door or pulled the trigger or pulled the switch. No, the condemned was free to kill himself, at his leisure—whenever he chose. He could breathe the deadly fumes now or he could breathe them in twenty seconds, even a minute later while the people outside watched in macabre anticipation.

At last Hill came up with the only argument left. "Ava, the Arapahoe people are behind my client. You wouldn't want to stir up a lot of race riots." He spoke softly. "And what would happen if the Arapahoes boycotted Twin Buttes? What would Ernest Pillsberry say then?" He was still fiddling with his hat brim. The woman noticed.

"In the first place, none on the reservation supports Redtail except the renegades. In the second place, the Indians are not about to drive to Casper to spend their government checks. Their cars wouldn't get there." She laughed. Then she got up, extended her hand to Hill. "Sorry,

Abner. See you in court. You know I like you. We'll have a good trial."
He took her hand, and she gripped it hard like a man shakes hands, and
after she pumped it a couple of times she let it go and he turned and
went out of the room.

Then she hollered after him, "Abner, you shouldn't be in this case!
You know that, don't you?"

The lawyer walked slowly back to his pickup. He felt the warm, fresh
air of a false spring in his lungs. Both life and death can be inhaled
through the same lungs, he thought. "Death came from words," Hill
said the words aloud as he walked though the slush to his pickup.
Small words have great power—power over life. And the power would
be in the woman's words. Then he thought what he had thought before:
that Ava Mueller had ambitions, maybe to be governor.

That night Hill found Mary Hamilton wearing a new dress. He couldn't
remember when he had ever seen her in a new dress, this one a simple
black cotton with a low front that clung in good ways to her body. She
was wearing a string of dime-store pearls around her neck. Claimed
people couldn't tell the difference unless they got their nose in there, and
she wasn't going to let them get that close to her anyway.

"You're looking good," Hill said across the table, she leaning over
him to pour the coffee. "What's the occasion?" She was wearing a new
pair of black high-heeled pumps.

"Nothing special," she said. "I figgered with the kids grown and all I
didn't need more than a hundred in the grocery can." Then she gave
him a different sort of look.

They had nothing in common, he thought. To his knowledge she
had never read a book, at least none he'd read. She had no interests
other than her children and her work, which was important only
because it had always provided, if only piteously, for her and the twins.
Yet she had uncommon good sense and he found himself talking about
his other cases with her, she sometimes offering suggestions that
seemed eloquently simple. Often he thought of her when he was select-
ing a jury because juries possessed those surprising pits of wisdom that
escape the lawyer. And he always came back to her bravery. She was
brave, he thought, and he wished he were as brave as she.

"We been too tied up in Charlie's case," she said, "too sick and
scared. I thought it would be good if we lightened up." She smiled, something sad in the eyes. "We gotta lighten up to get through this."

"Well, yeah," he said.

"We can beat ourselves to death. We can make ourselves sick," she said. "Maybelle at the restaurant said I gotta lighten up. Nothin' I'm gonna do is gonna change things. Person's gotta make it through an' I'm gonna make it though this one, one way or another."

Abner Hill thought she was right. They had to lighten up, a long, hard road ahead. He knew that much.

"I always think that when bad things are happenin' it's like a person bein' thrown in the lake," Mary said. "You hold your breath and close your eyes. And pretty soon you come to the surface and you better start breathin' and paddlin' or you'll drown. We can drown in this, Abner," she said. "We gotta start breathin'." She started over to where he sat. "We gotta get new air in our lungs."

"Right," he said. "I'm not too good at that."

"We went dancin' once," she said. " 'Member?"

"Yeah, I remember," he said. He gave her an embarrassed smile. "I remember."

"They're having a dance at the Elk's Club tonight."

He looked at her in surprise. He had never taken her anywhere, their lives together having been lived across from each other at the kitchen table. Then he got up and he said, "All right. Let's go."

He stumbled through the dances, her leading most of the time. They danced the fast ones and the slow ones. The people watched and some talked about the Indian lawyer who was dancing with the mother of the breed charged with murder. Something wrong there.

Buddy Forsythe at the organ was playing an old tune, "The Missouri Waltz," and Abner Hill did not know how to waltz, but that made no difference. She was up close to him in her new dress. They didn't move their feet much, only their bodies and their feet once in a while, and Abner Hill could feel her through the smoothness of the cloth. He pulled her into him at the small of her back, and her hips moved with the music, and some of the people were still watching from their tables around the dance floor.

After the music stopped and Buddy Forsythe took a break, they went back to their table and ordered another round of drinks. She was drinking pink ladies and his, Jack Daniel's and soda. Hill looked at the people looking. Some would probably be on Charlie Redtail's jury, some with the wrong idea about the lawyer and the mother. They talk in small towns. Jim Peterson, who ran the county title company, said it once: "Why, they know when your wife missed her monthly afore you know it."

After a while Mary said she was getting tipsy, and that he should take her home.

He awakened in the morning. He opened his eyes without moving, the woman in his arms, her naked body against his, the feel of her flesh, and her fake pearl necklace still around her neck. He looked up at the sagging ceiling with the leak marks on the plaster board and he saw the single cord hanging down with the small shade around the bulb. Suddenly he felt the cold stab of reality. This was his client. He tried to think, lying very still, her breathing against his chest. Then suddenly he broke out in laughter.

"What's the matter? Why are you laughing?" she asked, her voice sleepy.

He laughed more. Then he said, "But you, you!" He leaned up on an elbow and looked down at her. "You are so beautiful."

She laughed, too, and he pulled her too him.

She got up and made the coffee. "You don't look so good," she said. She smiled to cancel her words. She brought the coffee to him and, already in her cotton housedress, she sat down on the bed and ran her fingers through his hair as if to comb it. Then she leaned over and kissed him lightly on his lips, hers still warm from the coffee.

Suddenly he jumped out of bed, grabbed at his pants, pulled his boots on, and ran out the door. "I got work to do," he said.

25

The Old Man of Much Medicine put another cottonwood log on the fire and prodded around in the potbellied stove with a poker. He nodded at the stove, slammed the door shut with his moccasined foot so as not to burn his hand on the handle, shooed the skinny cur off the bed, and motioned for Hill to sit where the dog had lain. Then he pulled up a wooden chair so that his face and Hill's face were close. He squinted at Hill to make out his features and when he was satisfied that they held each other's attention, he cleared his throat and spoke.

"So you came to find out about that night," he said without asking. "I know all about that night." He spoke slowly as if the words were laid down one at a time like building a wall with bricks. "They were here that night," the old man said.

"All night? Both of them?"

"All night. They slept where you're sittin'. But the white man will not believe it."

"Why not?" Hill asked.

"Because the white man believes what he wishes to believe. He will not wish to believe it."

"Will you testify?"

"Yes, I will speak the truth. But the white man will not believe it." The old man looked into Hill's eyes. "You must have more. You must have great liars. The white man only believes great liars."

"Charlie confessed," Hill said. "He's trying to protect Willow."

"That's because he's in that stage of life. We are all in stages. Ha."

He nodded to the stack of cottonwood logs piled up next to the stove. "You cannot tell the cottonwood tree not to bud in the spring. You cannot say, 'Cottonwood tree, do not bud. Do you not understand how foolish it is? Your buds will turn to leaves and your leaves will turn yellow in the fall and float to the ground and your limbs will be barren again. It is all a waste of time, cottonwood tree. Do not be so foolish as to bud.' So you cannot tell Charlie Redtail anything." The old man whispered, as if he were revealing a great secret. "Love is a very strong thing. I knew it once myself. Almost did me in. Ha," he laughed again.

The room began to warm from the better fire in the stove and the old man threw off his blanket and leaned in closer to Hill. "So you cannot tell Charlie Redtail anything."

"Willow is protecting him, too," Hill said. "She says she shot Cotler."

"That white woman must have Arapahoe blood in her," he said. "She will protect her man. But they will not believe her. She is not a great liar."

"Neither is Charlie," Hill said.

"If the Indian says he killed a white men, the white men will believe him. That's so the white man can kill the Indian. If Charlie says he killed the white man they will believe Charlie."

Hill nodded. Something in the high, flat sound of the voice like the distant chant of a monk who said words he intended no one to hear.

Finally Hill reached out for the old man's hand. The hand was bony and cold and shook slightly. "We need witnesses," he said.

"I know of such persons," the old man said.

"But somebody has to tell the truth or Charlie Redtail is going to go down."

"No," the old man said. "The white man flinches from the truth like a horse flinches at flies in fly time. The truth drives the white man crazy. Ha."

Suddenly the old man got up and began jumping around, first on one foot and then on another, swinging his hands around his body like the tail of a horse. "The white man cannot stand the truth. 'Get the truth away from me.'" The old man danced in a frenzy, swatting, brushing his face against the flies, and all the while jumping from foot to foot. Then he stopped as suddenly, sat down again, and once more leaned close to Hill's face. He was breathing hard and Hill could smell the old man's breath, but it was not unpleasant. "Do you now understand?" the old man asked.

Hill stared at the old man without answering.

"I will send you some people," the old man said.

"Will they tell the truth?"

"The white man always talks too much," the old man said. "There is a time to come and a time to go." And with that the old man got up and opened the door for Hill to leave. "When you come back the next time bring me some Snickers bars." And as Hill walked out the door, the old man hollered after him, "And a can of Spam!"

Ava Mueller called the meeting, the sheriff in attendance, of course, along with deputies Miller and Maxfield. For want of a conference room they met in the granary.

"Used to come here as a kid with my father during the Fourth of July celebration," she said. "All the ranchers met back here after the parade. Tied their horses to the rail outside. County provided the oats for the horses and they all chipped in for a keg of beer. I liked the smell of this room. Still do."

The sheriff nodded. "Let's get to it. We got an open and shut case against Redtail. We got his gun and his prints on the gun. State lab found gunshot residues on his hands and the gun. We got him threatenin' Cotler. Miller heard it himself. We got his confession. We got his motive—tryin' ta stop the Spirit Mountain Project. I mean what the fuck—'scuse me for cussin'—what more do we need?"

"Small problems," Ava Mueller said. "He'll claim he shot a deer with the gun the day of the murder. We can't disprove that. His fingerprints should be on the gun. The gun belongs to him. He can deny the threats. No one heard them except Miller and Cotler is dead. And the confession? Hill has pictures of him taken a week after his arrest. He still looked like a piece of old hamburger. They'll claim you beat the confession out of him."

"That's bullshit," Miller said. "You know better'n that. "Son of a bitch was already beat up when he come in."

"And he turned himself in. That's consistent with innocence," she said.

"Don't ferget, he run first, he and that girl. There was an APB on 'em before he come in."

"He'll claim he didn't know about Cotler's murder and that he and the girl simply went home that night."

"You cannot satisfy this woman," Miller said as if joking.

She turned to Miller, her eyes squinting. "I will tell you something, Deputy Miller . . ."

"Undersheriff, if ya please," he said. "I worked ten years fer that."

"I will tell you something. This is a murder case. I have asked for the death penalty. I expect to get it. And I expect you to do your job in presenting the necessary evidence to get the conviction."

"Well, don't you fret none now, lady. I will have you a couple more witnesses 'fore the end of the week. I am workin' on 'em now."

"What do you mean, 'working on them'?" she asked. "I want truthful witnesses."

"Now, lady," Miller said, "you know I never bring in witnesses that lie."

"That hasn't been my experience," she said. "What about the witness you brought in against Lone Bear? We found out later he hadn't been within a hundred miles of the murder."

"That was a surprise to me," Miller said. "Anyway, what difference did it make? Lone Bear was guilty."

She didn't answer.

"You get all riled up over little details. The big thing is we gotta get these killers put away. I bring you the witnesses. You think they're lyin'? Well, think about this: Which would be worse—you putting on a witness that is colorin' the truth a little or not bein' able to prove your case against a murderer an' the next day after the jury turns him loose he rapes an eight-year-old girl and strangles her to death like that Huffsmith did over in Colorado that time? How would that suit yer conscience?"

After Ava Mueller left the meeting Miller said to Sheriff Marsden, "Them fuckin' prissy women. If ya let 'em have their way we wouldn't get the first fuckin' conviction. This place'd be run by the criminals and the pukes and we'd all be out of a job."

Hill sat at the kitchen table and after she brought him his coffee she sat down beside him. It was as if his end of the table were being invaded, and the invasion changed everything. He wondered how it would be if she were living with him in his small log cabin by the river, the logs echoing other sounds, another voice, a woman at his stove and in his refrigerator, a woman sharing his bathroom.

Women rearrange things. He'd have to share his closet with her, maybe have to move things out to the shed. He'd be pushed out of his house. He had felt deeply for this woman, but if he loved her he wouldn't say it, not to himself, nor to her. Love was a risk he wasn't prepared to face. Not now. People set themselves up for their miseries, he thought. He had seen it with his mother, the wounds that never healed that she carried in her eyes even when she was laughing. He had wanted to keep his life simple. He had said that much to himself many times and he was not going to let the idea of love into the private play yard of his mind.

But there she was, at his end of the table. Her presence made him uncomfortable despite her familiar good smell, the soft sound of her voice. Perhaps her presence reminded him he had violated what to him was the first rule of ethics: he had crossed the barrier between lawyer and client. It was one thing to care about one's client, but another to have taken this woman into the conjugal bed, and after that, to be called upon to make decisions that could be stained with his need for her or that could be influenced by her hold over him. Out of the bed rises great power—the grapple that drops deep into the inner self and drags up Lord knows what. And still more, the power generated in the loins that clouds the mind like fish that take the bait with the hook plainly in sight.

He did not wish to give her such power, nor to wield it himself out of his need. He had tried to stay above it and yet, standing above it, he had felt lonely. He remembered his fortieth birthday. Still alone he had looked in the mirror and had said aloud, "Abner Hill, you are the incomplete man. You are like the spermatozoa that have not coupled with the egg. You are nothing until you are coupled with the egg." Then he had laughed at such silliness.

But that she should now come to his end of the table uninvited supported his view. What happened that night endowed her with new power. She reached over and squeezed his hand and her hand was strong and warm. At first he had wanted to pull his hand away, but he did not. Small things can be seen as rejection. It was only after her hand had been on top of his for a long time that he said anything and when he spoke her hand was still there.

"Do we need to talk?" he finally asked.

"Do you need to talk?"

"I'm feeling a little confused," he said. And then she squeezed his hand again and it felt good. "I've done the wrong thing," he finally said, "you know, as a lawyer. Sometimes being a man and being a lawyer get in the way of each other."

"Why?"

"A lawyer shouldn't be with his client like I was with you."

"Aren't lawyers supposed to be human?"

"Not with their clients."

"Charlie is your client," she said softly, "not me."

"I know," he said. "A lawyer shouldn't represent his own family. Everybody knows that." She took her hand away and the top of his hand where hers had lain felt cold and he had wanted her hand back.

"Are you sorry about what happened?"

"No," he said.

"You *are* sorry."

"I don't know."

"Did it ruin us?" she asked.

He didn't answer.

"Did it really ruin us?"

"No," he said.

"It ruined us," she said.

Then he got up as if to go because he couldn't think of anything more to say. As he got to the door he said, "I'm confused, Mary, that's all." She stood watching him leave and when the door opened the great cold from the outside drifted in, and she put her arms around herself standing at the open door, watching him tromp through the snow. Then she saw him climb into his old pickup and after that he was gone into the white of the night.

Charlie was sitting on the steel cot, but he got up to greet Hill when Miller let him in.

"I saw Willow's cell when I came by," Hill said. "It's empty. She musta made a deal with Mueller."

"She'll be all right then. The baby will be all right. It is good," Charlie said.

"It's not good, Charlie."

"Better for the baby and for her. She is out of the trap. I'm glad."

"You don't get it."

"You worry too much," Charlie said. "These things are not in our hands."

"The trial starts next Monday morning," the sound of worry in Hill's voice. "The old man told me you and Willow were with him all night that night."

"Yes," Charlie said. "But they will not believe that. And she must say different now."

"The old man will testify."

"They will not believe him."

"You can testify," Hill said.

"They will not believe me."

"Will you let me at least try to defend you now that Willow is safe?"

Charlie saw the pain dulling the face of Abner Hill, the pain of the father who stands helpless to save the son. His life did not belong to him. Even his own case did not belong to him. Finally Charlie nodded as if in surrender. "But the witnesses must speak the truth."

Then Hill quickly hollered for the jailer to come as if to stay longer or if he said more Charlie Redtail might change his mind.

That same day Hill got a call from the old man, some of the younger men having taken the old man to the telephone at Hiram Falls and dialed Hill's number for him. Hill recognized the voice.

"One of my people, they see Miller drivin' Charlie's woman off in the patrol car."

"Where did he take her?"

"We don' know where he took her. Them young renegades is lookin' everywhere for her."

"Why, Henry? Why are they looking for her?"

"They say they got business with her."

"What do you mean, Henry? What kind of business?" But Henry Old Deer had already hung up.

Then Hill had called Anthony Russo and they met that same afternoon in Hill's office.

"The renegades are lookin' for Willow," Hill said.

"Maybe they know what to do with a witness who's forgotten her loyalties. Sounds like certain people I know back home."

Hill looked at the man with that puzzled look of his, as if the man's meaning had not been clear. Then, suddenly, he got up from his chair and grabbed his hat and his coat. "I gotta find the girl," he said.

"Good luck," Russo said. "You go look a lot so later you can at least tell yourself you tried to find her. But you aren't gonna find her. The cops got her stashed away good."

"What about Yancey?"

"She probably signed papers firing him. What does she need a lawyer for? They dropped the charges against her in exchange for her testimony. They always needed an eyewitness, now they got one. She's a free woman. That's better than any lawyer could have done for her. Who can complain?"

"She's free? But they have her hidden? Doesn't sound like she's free to me," Hill said, pulling his hat down low and starting for the door.

"The papers she signed will read that she's been threatened by certain persons, that she wants protection and authorizes the sheriff to provide it for her."

"What are we going to do?" the two walking down the hall fast, Hill in the lead, Russo trying to keep up. The new boots.

"I don't know what you're going to do," Russo hollered. "But I got a call or two to make to some friends who owe me a favor."

He sat at his end of the table as usual. Then as usual she poured his coffee. The man seemed distant, she thought, like a stranger. She sat down at her end of the table, sat looking at the man for a long time, he stirring the coffee, the man looking down into the cup without looking at her. After a while he said, "I got bad news."

"I've had enough bad news for a while," she said.

Finally he looked up at her. "Willow turned on us. Made a deal with Mueller. She's out of jail."

"Well, she shouldn't have been in jail in the first place, her with that baby an' all."

"You don't understand," Hill said. "To get out of jail she had to agree to testify against Charlie."

"Willow would never do that," Mary said.

"She has the baby coming. I gotta find her. Don't know where to start." He got up from the table and headed for the door, but when Hill walked past her, Mary was already up and standing in front of him. She put her arms around his neck and pulled him to her, but he pulled her arms away by the wrists and held on to her wrists. He wanted to tell her that fear trumps all a man can feel. What he said instead was, "I have to go, Mary." He tried to smile at her. "I have to find Willow."

"I'll go with you," she said. And before he could say anything she had grabbed her coat and had tied her scarf over her head. Then they walked out into the snow that stuck to their faces and made their faces wet even before they got to his pickup.

The old pickup bounced through the drifts and sometimes Hill demanded more speed of the truck before hitting a drift so that the momentum pushed them through. Then the wind began to blow so that what was road and what was prairie could not be told. At last he was following only the tracks of some other fool who had preceded them, perhaps only minutes before. But even then, the tracks often disappeared.

The road led to the reservation but they could not see the shacks along the side of the road. The sky was lost in the storm, and the earth was lost in it, and the places where the families on the reservations huddled together by their fires were lost. The lights of the truck shone only a few feet ahead and often he had to slow because he couldn't see, his driving becoming that precarious balancing act—if he slowed too much the old truck would be stuck and if he drove too fast he would likely drive off the road. He pushed his face to the windshield, his nose nearly on the glass. He strained his eyes against the snow trying to see, Mary wiping furiously at the frost with her scarf.

Sometimes he drove on blindly, holding the truck steady so that it did not veer in either direction, and once in a while he would see the track ahead before it disappeared again into the whiteness.

"We're a couple of fools out here," he said. "I think the old man's place is up around the next curve, but I can't see the curve."

"Never been there," she said.

"The old man knows somethin' I don't know," Hill said against the windshield. And when the truck slowed through the next drift he hit the accelerator to force it through. But the rear end of the truck began to spin around and finally the truck would not move either forward or backward. They got out and but for their own tracks could not tell from which way they'd come.

They spent the night huddled together, their bodies close. Sometimes they laughed at themselves and then snuggled closer to keep warm and he felt her strong body next to him. Even then she was brave.

"It's a good thing you came with me," he said. "I would have been out here alone and probably gone wading off through the snow looking for the old man's place and gotten lost and they'd find me in the spring when the thaw came." Then he realized that for the first time since he had left home as a boy, out in that storm, in that pickup with this woman, with the snow slowly covering them he felt complete.

In the morning the snow plow came. The operator had stopped and waded over to the pickup to look in. He brushed the snow off the driver's window and saw them huddled together, her head on his chest, his arms around her, and he thought for a moment that they might be dead, but he yelled just the same.

"Hey, you in there, are you all right?"

Abner Hill raised his head from the top of her head. "We're perfect," he said.

"Well, ya wan' me to pull ya out?"

"Not really," Hill said. Then he got out of the pickup and helped the operator hook his chain to the old truck's rear axle.

26

After the storm and once more in his office, Abner Hill came to his senses. The night harbored insane spirits. In the bright light of day he felt a dull foreboding, lost as he was in a hopeless case. The next morning he had driven on the freshly plowed roads to see the old man and had waded through knee-deep snow to the old shack. In response to Hill's knock Henry Old Deer flung the door wide open and stood there squinting out into the sun and snow.

"Never know what the storm blows in," he said. "Did you bring any Snickers bars?" Hill handed him a box of the confection as if it were the price of admission. The old man opened the box reverently, unwrapped a bar, and after having chewed for a while, as if the candy had provided the vision, and without the question having been asked, he said, "I don' know where the girl is."

He closed his eyes and held out his arms like antennas. Finally he said, "They have her hidden in a far off place. She is not here. She is by a big river," he said. "That is all I can say."

Hill had called Willow's father, who claimed he had not heard from his daughter for six months and was worried sick, had a team of private investigators looking for her, and if they turned up any leads Hill would be the first to know.

Charlie Redtail called on his friend Simon Yellow Dog to find Willow. The renegades were still searching for her and some threatened that if they found her they would tie her to a cottonwood log and throw her in the river to slowly perish as was the custom of one of the northern tribes when a member had betrayed them. But Charlie said no, that it was his wish that they find her and cherish her and that if they touched a hair on her head in anger, they would be striking at him. Simon Yellow Dog had delivered the message and most said they would honor the wishes of their leader. But they held grave doubts as to his wisdom in matters of love.

"Spirit Mountain is a sacred place," Charlie told Simon Yellow Dog. "We cannot dishonor the mountain with killing. That is why we did not kill the white investors. That is why I did not kill Cotler. If blood is shed over Spirit Mountain it will no longer be a holy place and we can no longer meet our fathers there."

Still Charlie paced his cell endlessly like a bear in the zoo and on each of Hill's visits the first thing Charlie asked was whether Hill had heard anything of Willow. Hill would reassure him: "If anybody in this case is safe, she is. Mueller needs her."

In ways Hill was grateful the woman could not be found. If they could not find her neither could anyone else who might have dark intentions against her. When Ava Mueller called her to the witness stand, perhaps the jury could see it—this woman forced to lie in order to save her child. And he could suggest it in his cross-examination, raise the specter of a mother held captive by the prosecutors, testifying before the jury as they demanded.

The case against Charlie would be a case of lies that Hill could never penetrate. Miller would lie on the stand. Hill knew that much. And he thought Ava Mueller knew he would lie. She was disarming, but elegantly cunning. Mueller would put on whatever hapless snitches the officers dug up who would testify to whatever facts Mueller wanted in exchange for whatever meager reward she offered. And she would call witnesses to show how Charlie had led the renegades in their protests and threatened innocent people who had come to Spirit Mountain to make legal investments in a development that was vital to the growth of Twin Buttes and thereby she would touch the sensitive economic soul of the jurors.

At the most propitious time, perhaps just before the evening's recess, she would introduce Charlie's confession, read it slowly to the jury in a sad voice, her standing there close to the jury looking into their open faces. When she came to the horror of it she would pause and in a near whisper read the words: " . . . when he walked up on the porch in the light I hollered at him and he stopped. Then I pulled the trigger. He fell in a heap and I took off running . . ."

After that she would walk slowly back to her table.

And Willow? Mueller would hold her for her dramatic last witness. The woman would take the stand in a sedate maternity smock, the jurors looking her over, a pretty, intelligent woman of good breeding who had somehow gotten mixed up with a breed. Some would feel shame for her, some pity, but they would all believe her. She would weep as she told the story she had agreed to tell. That would put the dramatic cap on Mueller's case. Then turning her back to the jury Mueller would give Hill that quick, slightly malevolent smile that meant, "You have been mortally wounded. Now I shall sit back and watch you bleed to death."

He had been in nearly hopeless cases many times, but there had always been something to argue, a conflict in the testimony, another possible but honest scenario he could paint for the jury from the evidence. Reasonable doubt. God bless reasonable doubt. But there was no defense here. No reasonable doubt. All he had was a client whom the jurors would hate, this stoic killer who stood as the symbol of the enemy, this strange man who was neither white nor Indian whose only help to Hill had been to say, "You worry too much. These things are not in our hands."

Hill thought the night with Mary had made it worse, and after that, the night in the storm. In the light of day he tried to throw off the power of those nights. The storm had covered the world with ice and had frozen the countryside. But in that same storm his own secure wall of ice had melted. The cursed storm. Why had he let her come with him? He usually made his decisions carefully, thoughtfully, with precision. Yet despite his regret for these nights, he felt somehow complete. Then he realized what he had known all along. He would not say the words, not even to himself. And Ava Mueller wanted to kill her son who, over the years, had become his son as well.

Alone in his cell Charlie Redtail both laughed and wept. He wept for those who were trapped, for those who had loved and had been caught in traps. He wept for the coyote and beaver and the great lynx who had been trapped for the furs on their backs. He wept for those who would trade a holy mountain for the white man's money. He wept for those who were worse than blind, whose eyes could see but who could not behold the evil and who were trapped in their own blindness.

At other times Charlie wept for his woman who was suffering alone, his child in her belly. He wept for her wretchedness, for the incontinent guilt he knew she was suffering. He wept because he could not reassure her that he was glad she had made the deal with Mueller, that she must lie against him, lie well, to save their child and to save the mother for the child. The child could live without a father as he had lived without a father. But the child could not live without the mother.

At times he laughed. Yes, the prosecutor, that Ava Mueller, had done him a great favor without her knowing it. She had saved his woman and his child and by saving them she had saved Charlie Redtail.

Hill filed his motion for change of venue and accompanied it with affidavits from the few in the community who would sign them, Ace Yokum for one. Yokum claimed he asked every one of his customers at the gas station whether they thought Charlie Redtail killed Cotler and everyone, except one, said they believed it. The one who said she didn't know was an Arapahoe. Hill had argued to the judge with a vivid intensity he had rarely called up in the past.

"To let this case go to a jury of Fetterman County citizens is like you trying the guilt or innocence of the thief who broke into your house and stole your silverware, Your Honor."

"How so, Mr. Hill?" That afternoon the judge seemed amused.

"The people of this community have a vested interest in the Spirit Mountain Project, Your Honor. Going to give them jobs. Make them rich. This desperate little town is going to grow and amount to something and my client was the renegade who was allegedly out there stopping it, taking money out of their pockets and who, in their eyes, killed the project's owner."

Of course, Ava Mueller had resisted his motion and had argued that the matter could be handled at the time of the voir dire examination. If they couldn't find twelve jurors from the panel who were not prejudiced then they could consider moving the case to another county.

"That is a splendid idea, Ms. Mueller," the judge said. "I have always had faith in the jurors of this county to deliver justice and I will not meddle in the well-established procedures of this jurisdiction by traipsing off to some far place to try this defendant. Your motion, Mr. Hill, is denied."

Hill's motion to set aside Charlie's confession was also denied, Miller testifying that Charlie had already been beaten up before his arrest.

"He likes to fight, Your Honor," Miller testified. "I knew him since he was a boy and I knew his father. It's in their blood. Nobody touched him. But like I told the sheriff, he sure as hell will claim we beat him up. Pardon the French, Your Honor."

Hill also lost his motion to require the prosecution to advise him in advance of the witnesses the state intended to call. Otherwise, Hill argued, the state could surprise him and he'd have no opportunity to prepare his cross-examination. But the judge followed well-established authority that reasoned if the state were required to reveal its witnesses before trial there was too much opportunity for witness tampering by the defense. "On balance," Judge Hankins ruled, "justice requires some protection be granted to the people."

Hill had considered asking Judge Hankins to step down from the case and assign another judge—citing the judge's close relationship to Ava Mueller and her father. But Hill knew such a motion would only intensify the ire of the judge, who was already irrevocably entrenched in his distaste for Abner Hill, a lawyer who on a yearly basis brought the judge more trouble and caused more discordance in his court than all the rest of the bar combined.

At last, having overruled all of Hill's motions, the judge smiled at Ava Mueller and swept himself off the bench like an incarnate March wind. The trial would begin first thing the following Monday.

Part III

27

Abner Hill hurried past the old, rusted cannon, the courthouse in front, his pace fast, the steam of breath marking his path through fresh snow that melted as it fell. His briefcase was swinging, but his steps were forced. Hill stamped the snow off his boots.

Inside, the air of the courthouse was thick and muggy, the smell always repulsive to the lawyer. He claimed he could smell the terror that had been exhaled from the lungs of five generations of wretches tried in the courtroom above and and all but a few found guilty.

He stopped in the foyer not wanting to mount the stairs. He could hear the sound of the crowd above him eager for court to convene, the prospective jurors, the onlookers, the court officials, all buzzing and excited like a mob gathered at the gallows. He started toward the noise and saw the people at the top of the stairs, their cigarette smoke turning the air blue. He saw George Penny, a small rancher from Horse Draw. The man looked down at Hill and turned away without nodding.

Never told you in law school you might have a day like this. If you begged for the life of your client the jury would kill him. If you fought for his life too hard the jury would kill him. If you failed to fight hard enough the jury would kill him. And mercy? Yes, mercy was a word lost to the English language.

He topped the stairs trying to look confident. With nods and small smiles he pushed through the overflow crowd standing in the hallway. Knew them all. And they thought they knew him. Lives in small towns cross one another like chickens passing in a chicken yard.

"Got a tough one, eh, Hill?" Old man in a heavy blanket coat, the new snow melting on his shoulders, Leslie Bloomenberg his name. Had a sheep ranch out on Elk Meadows.

"Layin' any money on yer case?" fella named William Overton asked, his winter's beard already begun. He laughed and poked his neighbor in the ribs with his elbow. Then Hill noticed the blond man with the empty blue eyes standing up against the wall. The man stared at Hill. And when Hill turned to enter the courtroom door, the man laughed.

Hill pushed through the crowd. He saw that the sheriff, William Marsden, already had Charlie sitting at the defense table, the man still in handcuffs and shackles, sitting straight, staring out across the room while three stiff deputies stood behind him. Charlie glanced at his approaching lawyer but gave no sign of recognition. Hill moved slowly through the crowd toward his table. He passed where Mary sat with Billy, his arm around his mother, the woman covering her pain with a small, tight smile when Hill passed. He reached over and touched her on the hand, Billy nodding without speaking as if they were in attendance at a funeral waiting for the preacher to enter. Anthony Russo sat slouched next to Billy looking out of place, the black, slick hair, a sharp suit like nobody in Twin Buttes ever saw except in the magazines.

Hill dropped his briefcase on the table and put his hand on Charlie's shoulder, Charlie looking straight ahead. To represent an innocent man and then after the long weeks of trial and the jurors having deliberated to hear the clerk announce that the jury had reached a verdict, to see the jurors march into the courtroom, their heads down, not wanting to look at the face of the accused as the clerk read the verdict—that was the nightmare of every lawyer who'd ever represented the damned. What would he say to Charlie? How could he bear to see the sheriff lead him off to that place? In a few minutes the judge would call the court into session. Then Charlie would be in his hands again, as helpless as the small boy he'd held in his arms many years before.

He reached out for Charlie's hand and felt its warmth, this large hand, not the hand of a murderer, not the hand of one who'd even pick a flower in the forest. Hill shouldn't be in the case. He'd known that all along. Yet he'd made arguments to himself. What surgeon would stand by and watch his son die of a ruptured appendix when there were no other qualified surgeons around? That was how he tried to think of it.

Hill turned to the deputies standing at attention behind them, smiled and nodded. They were armed with their .38 Special Smith & Wessons carried in regulation leather holsters strapped high at their waists. But the people's eyes were not on the deputies. The people's eyes were on Charlie Redtail, for few had ever seen a murderer, not one in the flesh. And there the murderer calmly sat, his face barren of any expression, his face as cold as a murderer's face should be, the deputies ready to save them should the murderer bolt.

Jim Hudson, the physical education teacher at Twin Buttes High, leaned over to Hugh Simmons, the high school's physics teacher. "Never could figure out how an ethical lawyer could stand up in court before God and everybody and try to get a murderin' breed off and then go about his business like nothin' happened," Simmons said. "Those kind of lawyers are worse than the criminals they represent."

"Everybody's got to make a living," Hudson said. Then they both laughed.

The seating in the courtroom was as provident as the townspeople, the old wooden benches like church pews with their torturous backs, which some insisted was the intention of their design. On that morning the benches were packed, the ranchers, and the farmers who sought to look like ranchers, holding their hats on their laps, their women with legs duly crossed, the people apologizing as they crowded together, not risking to leave their seats for fear someone else might claim them under the revered adage that possession is nine points of the law.

Wilber Hennisey, the farmer with the sunburned face and the white forehead, laid his Sunday hat on the adjoining seat, thereby reserving it for his wife, Madeline, who'd be following in after the chores. Hennisey leaned over to Fred Hobbs, owner of Twin Buttes Elevator, the man in the forest green shirt with PURINA FEEDS embroidered in red over the pocket. Hobbs had an older silver-belly on his lap, the brim dirty and rolled to a point in the front. He was on the bank board.

"I'll tell ya one thing," Hennisey said to Hobbs. "Them blanket-asses damn near did the county in with all that trouble out there at Spirit Mountain. Sheriff never could get 'em stopped."

Hobbs said, "I never had any use for Ronnie Cotler. Some folks say he deserved bein' killed. But ya don't go around killin' people 'cause you got a beef over a piece a real estate."

"Them Main Street boys was really mad 'bout them dog-eaters fuckin' up their project," Hennisey said. "They think they're gonna get rich when all that eastern money comes rollin' in. Ya could bring in a train load a that eastern money. Don't raise the price a alfalfa none." Then he looked at Hobbs, who bought Henissey's barley in the fall. "Or the price a barley neither."

"Right, Wilbur," Hobbs said.

Over the years the courtroom walls, once of white plaster, had grayed from the leisurely accumulation of grime. The bench and the jury's box were of cheaper ash in place of walnut, the ceiling embossed tin, and on top of the tin and between the rafters the packrats often raced.

Sometimes between silent spaces in the proceedings when some poor devil had ended his plea for mercy, and before the judge had begun his sentencing, one could hear the tiny, apocalyptic scraping of rat claws on tin. And although the judge had repeatedly ordered the rats exterminated and had threatened to hold Hernando Martinez, the custodian, in contempt for his endless failures in that regard, each of which the judge took as an act of defiance by the custodian, nevertheless the rats had managed to accomplish what few other living beings had— the avoidance of a lawful order of His Honor, Judge Henry P. Hankins.

Madeline Hennisey, a heavy woman with a powerful bosom, came pushing up the stairs through the crowd. When she reached the foyer she saw the blond man with the empty blue eyes leaning up against the wall. She stopped, startled, disbelieving. The man stared back. They stood like that for a moment, her not knowing what to do or to say, and he, his eyes on the woman as if to subdue her. Then she bolted by him, spotted her husband seated near the center of the courtroom, said her pardons to the people as she slipped by their knees, lifted her husband's silver-belly hat off the seat he'd saved, and took the seat.

"They started yet?" Madeline Hennisey asked her husband, breathing hard.

"About to choose the jury," Hennisey replied to his wife. "I see ol' John Oakley sittin' over there. They get him on the jury and he'll either hang the jury or hang that Indian, one or the other."

Suddenly, without announcement, Judge Henry Hankins took the bench, pounded his gavel, looked out at the assembled crowd, and when they quieted at the sound of his repeated rapping he called the court to order. Biggest crowd he'd witnessed during his nearly twenty years as the district judge. Up for election again next year. Success in life is mostly due to good timing, he thought, and this case couldn't be coming at a better time. He turned to the file he'd carried to the bench and read aloud the caption of the case, "State of Wyoming versus Charlie Redtail, defendant."

The judge looked in the direction of the prosecutor. "Is the State ready?"

"Ready," Ava Mueller answered. She wore one of those severe gray suits with the knee-length skirt, nothing to distract from the business at hand. No rings on the fingers. No red polish. No jewelry. No bright lipstick emphasizing the lips that when pulled tight exposed her slightly crooked lower teeth.

"Is the defense ready?" Judge Hankins inquired in the direction of Abner Hill without looking at the lawyer.

Abner Hill rose from counsel table. "Defense is ready," Hill answered, the judge busy thumbing through the file.

"Don't sound like he's ready to me," Wilbur Hennisey whispered to Fred Hobbs. "Sounds like he's 'bout done in."

"The clerk will draw twelve names," Judge Hankins ordered and one by one the names of twelve citizens were drawn from the box and announced by the clerk. After the twelve prospective jurors had taken their seats, Ava Mueller began her voir dire examination—her intent to qualify the jury to render the death penalty.

The jurors in hard oak swivel chairs sat as ready and duteous as members of the choir prepared to stand and sing, all except the farmer who slouched low in his chair as if about to slide the rest of the way to the floor. But when Ava Mueller began to interrogate him he eased himself to an upright position and, as if to hide his protruding belly, crossed his arms against his freshly ironed bib overalls.

"Mr. Oakley, could you, in the appropriate case, render the death penalty?" Ava Mueller asked, her hard eyes taking in the man.

"Do it ever' day," he said.

"What do you mean?" Mueller asked. The floors of narrow oak boards had soaked up the remnant dirt of time and creaked and moaned as she paced in front of the jury.

"I mean I render the death penalty to the rooster for Sunday dinner, an' I kill the calf for our locker at the locker plant. I send 'bout fifty head a pigs to the market ever' year an' I—"

"I got it," Mueller said, smiling. "But I take it that a man is not in the same category as a chicken or a pig."

"Some are and some ain't."

Laughter.

Judge Hankins's gavel.

"I see," she said. "And you have no religious or philosophical beliefs against the death penalty?"

"I never give it much thought."

"Well, I'm asking you to think about it now," she said in a friendly but businesslike way. She was young in the face and in the presence of the working folk she seemed harmless enough. Yet she spoke with the authority of a woman of maturity.

"I never kilt nobody," Oakley said.

Laughter.

"Order," the judge demanded with a hefty slam of his gavel.

"None of us have killed, I hope," Mueller said.

"Well, it seems ta me that if ya can't cure 'em from killin' ya ain't got no choice."

"This is not a case to cure someone," Mueller replied. "This is a case to convict a murderer."

Abner Hill jumped to his feet. "I object to that, Your Honor. I want the jury instructed to disregard the prosecutor's remark. My client has not been convicted of anything and as he sits here he's presumed innocent."

"Sustained," the judge said, already sounding sleepy.

Russo leaned over to Hamilton and whispered, "Hill doesn't know what the fuck he's doing. He should be moving for a mistrial. Now he's waived it."

"Maybe you could go up to his table and tell him. Maybe slip him a note or something," Hamilton whispered back.

"Too late," Russo said, shaking his head. "You have to be on your feet or it's too fucking late. Good thing you brought me along."

"I didn't bring you to kibitz," Hamilton said. "If Abner's screwing up the case, you better do something."

"Already done something, if you know what I mean."

Hamilton put his arm around his mother again. Mary was huddled in her old winter coat, biting at her lower lip and staring at her feet. Hamilton pulled the woman closer to him, but she didn't look up.

The preacher in his black preaching suit, second from the end in the back row, having been accepted as a juror by Ava Mueller, was answering questions for Abner Hill. When Hill began his interrogation Charlie Redtail focused on the man as if to peer into deep places.

"You say you believe in the Old Testament?" Hill began.

"Yes, indeed," the preacher said.

"The Old Testament speaks of an eye for an eye and a tooth for a tooth."

"That is true."

"Do you believe in that?" Hill asked.

"I believe in the Bible."

"Everything in the Bible?"

Judge Hankins popped up from his slump at the bench. "We are not going to go into everything in the Bible, Mr. Hill. You can find prostitution, fornication, sodomy, mayhem, murder, profanity, wife beating, child beating, stabbing, stoning, water walking—you name it—it's in the Bible."

Laughter.

"Preacher Howe," which, as everyone knew, was what the man preferred to be called, "do you think that 'an eye for an eye' means that if someone kills another the appropriate penalty is to kill him back?"

"That's what the Bible says."

"Would you permit me to differ with you?" Hill asked.

"Of course," he said. Then the preacher raised his nose a fraction and glared at the lawyer.

"The Old Testament speaks of an eye for an eye, not a life for a life."

"You can logically extend the meaning."

"Only if you are inclined to kill. Do you harbor such an inclination?"

"No, of course not."

"Do you think it is all right to impose the death penalty in some cases?"

"Yes, I do."

"You recall the Scriptures, of course, 'Vengeance is mine, sayeth the Lord'?"

"I am one who believes we were given a mind by God and it is our responsibility to make judgments that provide a safe and orderly society in which to live." He moved his head back and forth to indicate his was the final word.

"I take it that in seeking a safe and orderly society you cotton to the idea that some killing is all right?" Hill asked.

"I do not. I believe exactly the opposite."

"Then we agree," Hill said. "I, too, believe there should be no killing of any kind in a safe and orderly society." He smiled at the preacher. "That would include the state's killing, too, would it not?"

The preacher was silent and stared at the lawyer.

"The state is merely the people," Hill said. "So does it not follow that if we are against an individual killing, we must also be against many individuals killing in combination, namely as the state?"

"I'd have to think about that."

"Would you think about that, Preacher Howe, before you, as a member of this larger combination called 'the jury,' agree to kill Charlie Redtail?"

"Yes, I would think about it," the preacher said.

"Generally you think it wrong to kill?"

"Of course."

"Would you impose the law if you thought the law was wrong?"

"Mr. Hill, the law is the law. Killing is wrong. The death penalty is imposed for that crime."

"So should we, ourselves, also commit the wrong of killing a killer for his wrong?"

"You are trying to confuse me. You are playing a lawyer trick."

"The ideas we hold as true can be tricky as well," Hill said. "Do you believe that redemption is, in the eyes of God, the ultimate goal of man?"

"It's right up there with our other goals," the preacher said.

"If that be so, how does one have the opportunity to achieve redemption if one is first murdered by the state?"

Mueller was on her feet. "I object, Your Honor. The death penalty is not murder. It's *punishment* duly imposed by law. I ask that the jury be instructed to disregard Mr. Hill's uncalled-for remark."

"To the point, Your Honor," Hill said. "The genocide of the Jews was duly imposed by the law in the Third Reich. Still it was murder. In America we are given the right to question the state's conduct. That's all I'm doing with Preacher Howe."

"I thought we were taking a trip through the Bible," the judge said. "Proceed, Mr. Hill."

"You will note that my client, Charlie Redtail, is a Native American."

"That is not accurate. I know his mother well. She sits over there with her son, Billy. Her name is Mary Hamilton and she is not Native American."

"His father was Joseph Redtail. So, Preacher Howe, what would you call Charlie Redtail if not Native American?"

"I would call him . . ." The preacher stopped. "I would call him . . ."

"A breed?" Hill prompted.

"That is your word, not mine."

"What is your word?"

"I don't see what relevance it has."

"Does God love breeds as much as full bloods?" Hill waited. "Or only half as much?" He waited.

"That is an impertinent question, Mr. Hill. I have known the Red-tails for many years. I have had them in my church, although not often enough, I must say. I baptized Charlie as a boy."

"Could you impose the death penalty on someone you baptized as a boy?"

"I would find it very difficult, Mr. Hill. I would pray on it. And in the end I would do whatever my duty appeared to be."

"You would have to ask God?"

"I would speak for myself," the preacher said.

"What if you and God didn't see eye to eye on this matter?"

"What do you mean?" the preacher said.

"What if you render the death penalty and God is against it?"

"This is silly."

"Which is silly, your rendering the death penalty or God's position against it?"

"Do I have to answer that, Your Honor?" the preacher asked, turning to Judge Hankins.

"No," the judge said. "Move along, counsel."

"If God is against killing his children for punishment and if you have misinterpreted 'an eye for an eye,' do you think God might conclude that *you* were guilty of murder if you rendered the death penalty in this case?"

"Do I have to answer that one, Your Honor?"

"You'll have to admit, he got ya on that one, preacher," the judge said. "Now Mr. Hill, what if God gets angry at you for pushing one of his preachers around like that? Don't you think we have to be careful how we call up God in a case like this?"

"Preacher Howe," Hill continued. "We punish people so that they will learn their lesson and do better, is that not so?"

"Yes, of course."

"God sometimes punishes us so that we may learn and do better?"

"Yes."

"How then can one who is gassed to death in the gas chamber learn anything from that?"

Preacher Howe didn't answer.

"And how, after having been gassed to death, can he do better?"

"I leave that to the judge to figure out," Preacher Howe said.

Then Judge Hankins called a recess.

*   *   *

At the recess Hill watched the deputies put the cuffs and shackles on Charlie. Hill followed them out the back door of the courtroom and down the stairs to the jail.

In his cell, his cuffs and shackles still on, Hill asked, "What do you think, Charlie?"

"Think we should get rid of the preacher," Charlie said.

"Why?" Hill asked.

"He has the wrong spirit."

"How do you mean?"

"He may be crazy. Maybe doesn't know the difference between right and wrong."

"What do you mean," Hill asked.

"When we were kids, our mom sent us to church. Preacher Howe was teaching us the Ten Commandments. 'Thou shalt not kill,' he told us. He told us that God's law was the only law. Today he says it's right to kill if it is according to man's law." Charlie laughed his high laugh. "So, you see, he doesn't know which is right and which is wrong. Maybe he's crazy."

Suddenly Charlie's voice got childlike. "Some men do not have the good spirit in them, Abner. That's why some men need to preach to others."

When Hill had returned from Charlie's cell he found Russo waiting for him at counsel table, the court still in recess.

"Listen," Russo said, "I've done a little investigating. Keep the preacher and get rid of the farmer."

Hill was still peering at his yellow notepad.

"Those farmers kill all the time," Russo said. "Man hanging from a rope is like a carcass of beef hanging from a hook in the cooler. You heard him say so yourself. Get rid of him."

"I've known old John Oakley for twenty-five years. Good ol' boy," Hill said.

"Good ol' boys kill," Russo said. "I found that out to my sorrow in the first dozen death cases I lost. One thing you have to get focused on, counsel: that Mueller woman has one goal-to see your client choking in the gas. Get that picture in your mind when you're thinking about 'good ol' boys'."

Hill looked up, surprised. "Get focused on that, Hill, not on the fact that the son of a bitch is a good ol' boy."

"Judge'll be comin' in a minute," Hill said.

"Another thing: These jurors are already prejudiced against Indians," Russo said. "Remember, prejudice trumps logic. Prejudice trumps the truth. Give me a jury without prejudice and you can trust them. But if there's prejudice you can never win with 'em, even if you're right. And there's plenty of prejudice around here."

"What about the preacher?" Hill asked. "Those preachers will say a prayer over Charlie and then offer to pull the switch."

"I haven't got time to explain. Just take my word. No matter what, keep the preacher," Russo said.

When it came Hill's turn to examine the schoolteacher, Thelma Melbourne, he asked, "Ms. Melbourne, you knew Charlie Redtail?"

"Yes, and I knew his brother, Billy, too." She pointed to Hamilton. "His name was Billy Redtail before he went back East and took his mother's name."

"How did you know them?"

"They were students of mine. Billy was a very bright little boy. But Charlie never seemed to care much about what we were trying to teach him. Some thought he was slow, but I knew better."

Then Hill asked, "What did you think of Charlie?

"I thought Charlie had no clear role model. And, of course, his mother didn't help."

"What do you mean by that?"

"She worked down at the hotel. Waitress, you know. Never there when the boys got home. I took Billy under my wing." She looked over at Hamilton sitting next to his mother. "Billy went to Harvard, you know, and made a lot of money. Big success. But Charlie didn't fit in. He claimed he was Indian, but everybody knew his mother was white. He was lost from the beginning, I'd say. A pity."

"Does that mean that if you found Charlie Redtail guilty of murder you'd vote for the death penalty no matter what other facts were presented?"

"I've tried to follow the law all of my life and I've tried to teach my children to follow the law. I hope you will follow the law, too, Mr. Hill. If you know your client is guilty you should say so right now so we can get this over with," which last offering by Ms. Thelma Melbourne was followed by loud clapping from some of the audience.

The judge rose up from behind the bench and hit his gavel. "There'll be none of that," he hollered, "or I'll clear the courtroom. Proceed, Mr. Hill."

"Jesus Christ," Russo whispered to Hamilton, "Hill should be moving for a mistrial again. I'm telling you this guy is a fucking joke."

Abner Hill focused again on the teacher. "What is it you want to 'get over with,' Ms. Melbourne?"

"This whole maudlin affair."

"Wouldn't you say that even a guilty man is entitled to a fair and full trial before he's gassed in the gas chamber?"

"Waste of time, if you ask me," she said. "If he's guilty he's guilty. What's to try?"

"Ms. Melbourne, I take it that you believe guilty persons should be executed and that only innocent persons should be tried by a jury."

"You are trying to trap me," she said. She stared at Hill over her rimless glasses.

"Don't you think that the state should prove its case, even against a guilty person?"

"I have never had to think of such things. I taught English."

"If the state doesn't have to prove its case in every trial, guilty or not, how can any of us be protected against the state?"

"I'm not going to argue with a lawyer," she said, and after that Abner Hill struck Miss Melbourne from the panel.

"Jesus Christ," Russo whispered to Billy Hamilton. "He knocked off the schoolteacher. Those tough, old bitches are the best kind. She wasn't about to kill one of her kids, no matter what."

The Swedish salesclerk who worked for the Twin Buttes Lumber Company agreed with Ava Mueller that he could render the death penalty in the right case. He was a serious man who sang his words, each with the same tune, one that was soft in the middle. Abner Hill walked up to the man, looked at him for a moment as if he didn't know what to say. Then he finally came out with it.

"How does it feel, Mr. Swenson, to be asked for permission to kill another human being?"

"Don't know what you mean," he said.

"I mean Ms. Mueller, on behalf of the state, is asking you if it is all right with you that the state kills my client."

"I object!" Ms. Mueller said, her voice sharp and strong. "I certainly do object."

"Why?" the judge asked. He had risen up from a deep slump. "Why? This is exactly what you're doing. You are asking if it's all right with the juror that the state kill Mr. Redtail. Overruled."

Then Hill said, "As His Honor has said, you are being asked by the state to take part in the killing of my client. That is premeditation. I was wondering last night as I lay awake, thinking about this case, what it must feel like to have someone ask me to premeditate the killing of another person. Have you thought about that?"

"No, sir."

"What do you think about that now?" Hill asked. "Have you ever thought about killing a person before?"

"That's objected to," Mueller shouted.

"Shouting doesn't carry any more weight with me than a civil tone, Ms. Mueller. Overruled." The judge slumped once more to the point that only the top of his bald head was visible.

"Ever been asked before to premeditate a killing?" Hill continued.

Russo was whispering to Hamilton again. "The guy's doing all right now. Never heard that one before. Learn something every day, even from incompetents."

"The state invites you to premeditate a killing here," Hill pushed on. "Must feel terrible."

Swenson looked embarrassed.

"I will fight against it, Mr. Swenson. I will be fighting against the state trying to make a premeditated killer of you," Abner Hill said.

"You pushed that one just a little too far, Mr. Hill," the judge said, popping up again. "The problem with lawyers is that they don't know when to leave well enough alone. Now, Mr. Swenson, you are not being asked to be a premeditated killer. You are being asked to follow the law. Can you do that, sir?"

"Yes, sir," Swenson said like a private responding to a general.

The examination of the jurors extended into the next day, both sides attempting to condition the jury to their theory of the case, Ava Mueller for the state seeking to create a vigilante attitude in the jurors and Abner Hill first attempting to identify those jurors most danger-ous to him and after that to open them to the idea of reasonable doubt. Then the name of a prospective thirteenth juror was called, one who would sit on the jury as an alternate if one of the jurors became ill or was disqualified. A Mexican American sheepherder named José Sanchez was drawn.

He swaggered up to the jury box with a big smile, several of his front teeth missing. He smiled at the judge, who glared back, and he smiled at the prosecutor, who jumped to her feet to examine him.

"Do you speak the English language?" she asked.

"Wha' you say?" he asked.

"Do you speak the English language?" she repeated as if his answer either way would incriminate him.

"Tha's right," he said.

"What's right," Mueller demanded.

"I spick the good English," Sanchez said. He wore new black cowboy boots with pointed toes. His black hair looked as if it had been slicked down with egg whites and he wore his black shirt buttoned to the top.

"Can you read and write the English language?" Mueller demanded.

"All the time," he said.

"Well, read this," she said. She approached the juror waving a copy of the *Twin Buttes Times*. "Read the headline." She took long, intimidating steps toward the little man.

Jury Called to Try Redtail Case.

"I don't read no papers, señorita," the herder said. "I read my paycheck," and then he offered a small, embarrassed smile and stared back at the prosecutor with his mouth half-open.

Judge Hankins slowly raised his white hand with stubby, crooked fingers. "That's good enough," he said, and with that the Mexican herder was seated.

After both sides had concluded their questioning, and the last of the preemptory challenges had been exercised by both sides, the twelve remaining, along with the alternate, were sworn as the jury. They included the farmer Johnathan Oakley; the salesclerk Swen Swenson; Jane Pickering, housewife and mother of five; Sam Nance, lineman for the telephone company; Bill Hammer, who ran the local dairy; Harold Yeckersly, a farmer out on the government project; Jim Buford, a rancher from Hat Creek; Jim Jessep, another rancher over by Big Hollow; Holly Barbeenela, a farmer's wife; Harmon Watson, manager of the Farm Loan Board; Maude Miller, secretary for the Twin Buttes Water District; and Martha Romney, a dental assistant and wife of Jim Romney, bishop of the Morman church. The alternate juror's chair was occupied by the sheepherder, José Sanchez.

Abner Hill watched as the jurors were sworn by the clerk. He watched their mouths say the words and he saw them nod their heads in the affirmative when they were asked if they would render a true verdict, their faces serious, some frowning, some appearing as harmless as dead fish on the beach. Already he saw them not as jurors but as the enemy. Suddenly he had wanted to run up to them and shout in their faces that they, too, would soon be murderers.

You, a member of a mob of twelve, will kill Charlie Redtail.

You will kill him because you will be told lies.

You will believe the lies because you will be more comfortable with the lies than with the truth.

You have not taken your seats to try the case, as was your oath. You have taken your seats knowing in the shadows of your mind that you have come to kill this man. And you will be proud that you have done your job.

Anthony Russo waited by the old cannon for the courthouse to empty. When he saw William Hamilton coming down the way, his arm around his mother, Russo turned to meet them. Hamilton saw Russo and hurried ahead of Mary.

"I hope you got things in hand," Hamilton said.

"Bad news," Russo said. Russo looked to see that Mary was still out of earshot. "That dumb hick Hill kicked off the preacher."

"So?" Hamilton said.

"I gave the preacher some of your money."

"How much?"

"Twenty-five."

"For Christ's sake, you could have done it for five. Five grand's a fortune out here."

"I wanted it to stick," Russo said. "You don't bribe preachers. You buy 'em churches. Gave him something for his building fund." Russo laughed. "I told Hill to leave the fucking preacher on, no matter what, and he knocked him off."

"Go get my money," Hamilton said.

"That money's long gone," Russo said. "I'll ask him to give you a bronze plaque to hang inside the vestry." Russo laughed again.

"I bring the smartest criminal lawyer in New York all the way out to this two-bit-wide spot in the road and he can't even fix a jury. Now what do we do, hot shot?"

28

Ava Mueller made her opening statement without notes. Its brevity and want of passion had surprised Hill. Not much he hadn't anticipated. She mentioned the threats "and other motives." Nothing specific. She gave a sanitized summary of the murder scene, the gun and gunshot residues, of course, and witnesses who she said would establish Mr. Redtail's guilt beyond a reasonable doubt. Her opening took less than five minutes. She stood in front of the jury speaking without palpable emotion as if she were reading from a police report. At the end she said simply that it would be the unpleasant but clear duty of the jurors to render the ultimate penalty for this vicious crime. When she sat down, the judge smiled at her as if approving the businesslike economy of her presentation. Then he turned with a scowl to Abner Hill, inviting him to step forward and do the same.

Once more at that moment and facing that jury, Abner Hill knew he should not be in the case. He felt paralyzed. Always before in his opening statement he laid out a defense—whatever he had—so that the jury could compare the facts the prosecutor presented against the facts he offered to prove on his side of the case. In Charlie's case he had worked on his opening for days, but each time he had discarded his latest effort. The tone was too angry or was too marinated in emotion. Sometimes the facts as he presented them sounded concocted. At other times exaggerated. This strange-looking man with the long braid down his back had killed no one, threatened no one, and was capable of killing no one. All of the witnesses were lying. Yes, to believe his defense the jury had to find that not one of the state's witnesses, but all, were liars, and that their own Ava Mueller, this darling of the prosecution who led the ticket every time she ran for reelection, had put before them a case based on lies.

Many a night in the privacy of his cabin Hill had practiced his opening. Now, if he stood up to speak, when he opened his mouth nothing would come out except, "My client is innocent. I have no defense. But please don't kill him."

"I reserve," Hill said. The calmness of his own voice startled him. If he were ever to make an opening it would be later, after the state had rested its case in chief.

"You reserve?" the judge asked incredulously.

"I reserve," Hill said again.

Russo exploded so that his words could be heard through the entire courtroom. "He's incompetent. Nobody reserves anymore."

Judge Hankins scowled at Russo. Realizing his outburst he looked down with embarrassment. "Well, then," the judge said turning to Ava Mueller, "call your first witness."

Ava Mueller walked to the lectern, laid out her notebook, and said in a clear voice, "I call Mary Hamilton as my first witness."

"I object, Your Honor," Hill said and jumped to his feet. "This woman knows nothing. This is an attempt by the prosecution to prejudice this jury."

"Overruled," Judge Hankins said. "If Mrs. Hamilton knows nothing she can say so. The jury will decide."

Russo and Hamilton sitting together began a frenzied whispering. As she got to her feet Hamilton whispered to his mother. Then she rose and walked sedately to the witness chair. She wore an old pink sweater over the black cotton dress she had on the night of the Elks dance.

She held on to her hands, her head down. She looked frightened. But Mueller started her questioning in a kindly manner. Mary admitted that her son's father was Joseph Redtail, a full-blooded Arapahoe who had died in the county jail some years ago.

"You, of course, didn't want your boy Charlie to go the way of his father," Mueller said.

"I tried to keep him from goin' out there. But I couldn't," she said.

"He took up the Indian way?"

"More or less," she admitted.

"You knew the deceased, Ronald Cotler?"

"Yes."

"And your son Charlie told you he saw Cotler kick his father to death, isn't that true?"

Hill, on his feet, shouted, "That's leading and it's hearsay."

"Sustained," the judge said.

"You brought a suit on behalf of your boys and against Mr. Cotler for the death of the boy's father?"

"Yes."

"That suit was dismissed by His Honor who sits here in this case?"

"Yes, but that was because we didn't want Charlie to testify," she said. "He was just a boy."

"Why didn't you want Charlie to testify?"

"Irrelevant!" Hill objected.

"Overruled."

"We didn't want him to testify because we didn't want him to relive what he saw."

"And what did he see?"

"He was there when his father was beaten and kicked to death."

"Where?"

"At Cotler's bar."

"And your son has harbored hatred for Cotler all of these years?" Mueller spoke slowly, softly.

"Leading, without foundation and based on hearsay," Hill shouted.

"Sustained," the judge said.

"There came a time when Mr. Cotler purchased your home."

"Yes."

"And you owed a good deal of back rent?"

"Yes."

"Mr. Cotler finally ordered you to pay the arrears or he would move you out?"

"He tried to collect it in another way," Mary said.

Ava Mueller was obvious in her surprise. "What do you mean?"

"Irrelevant," Hill objected.

"Overruled."

"I don't want to answer," Mary said to her hands.

"How did he want to collect the rent, Ms. Hamilton?" Mueller insisted.

"I'm not sayin'." She began to cry. Finally she said, "He wanted me to do something for the rent."

"Did you?"

"No."

"What did he do when you refused?"

"Moved me out on the street."

"Did Charlie know about this?"

She didn't answer.

"Did Charlie know about this?"

"Answer," the judge ordered.

"Everybody knew. I told everybody."

"What did Charlie say when you told him?"

She didn't answer.

"Answer," the judge said.

"He said he should kill him, but he wasn't that kind of a boy. He didn't mean it. That is the truth. He wouldn't kill a fly. And that is the honest-to-God truth."

"No further questions," Mueller said.

Abner Hill was on his feet, his mind blank, his mind racing wildly to form the first question as he walked to the lectern. He stood staring at the woman, this mother, this woman he had those feelings for.

Then Hill said, "How does it feel to be asked by the prosecutor to testify against your son?" Hill pointed at Mueller.

"I feel sick," she said.

"Why did you say your son wouldn't kill a fly?"

"Sometimes he says things, gets it off his chest, but he never does it. He said killin' would ruin Spirit Mountain."

"What did he mean by that?"

"The place was a holy place. Killin' Cotler would ruin it."

"Thank you," Hill said and sat down.

Mueller was quickly at the lectern again. "You say Cotler owned Spirit Mountain?"

"Ever'body knows that."

"And he was cutting it up into some kind of a development?"

"Ever'body knows that."

"And Charlie was the leader of a group of young Arapahoes who were trying to stop the development?"

"Yes," she said. "But they didn't kill anybody. They only scared 'em."

"Cotler called the sheriff on your son for his involvement out there, didn't he?"

"I bailed him out," Mary said. "But I know he didn't kill anybody because killin' would ruin the holy place, he always said." She spoke like a child trying to make a parent believe her.

"Of course," Mueller said. "Thank you. That's all. I'm sorry I had to call you, Ms. Hamilton."

As Mary Hamilton was taking her seat Charlie leaned over to Hill. He whispered, "This is why I didn't want to take part in the white man's game. See how she tried to have my mother kill me? When I am convicted she will believe it's her fault and she'll die a slow and painful death from it. I want to plead guilty now."

Charlie started to stand up and when he did the deputies behind him pushed him down again, and one began to put the cuffs on him, the jurors watching, their eyes wide, some shying back.

"Please, Charlie," Hill whispered, the jury still watching. "What's been done to your mother has been done and can't be undone."

Before Charlie could answer, the deputies still holding him firmly in his chair, Ava Mueller called Undersheriff Dean Miller, who swaggered in hard steps to the stand.

Once more he swore that the day before the murder at the Big Chief bar he'd heard Charlie Redtail threaten to kill Cotler. "He said it like he wanted me to hear and he laughed in my face after he said it and walked out. The girl was with him. He said, 'We are gonna kill the bastard' and she laughed, too."

"That's a lie," Charlie whispered to Hill. Once more he insisted, "We were never in the place."

"Were they drunk?" Mueller asked.

"Looked plumb sober to me," Miller said. "An' I seen a lotta drunks in my day."

Then Mueller had Miller establish the facts of the murder scene. He identified the color photos he'd taken of the deceased in the fetal position in a pool of blood on his front porch. The photos were handed to the jury, the men peering at them, some for a long time, the women quickly passing them on after a glance as if they were too painfully gruesome for tender eyes. Miller told how he had put out an all-points bulletin for the arrest of Charlie Redtail, but that Redtail had come in voluntarily. They'd done a paraffin test on Redtail's hands and sent the paraffin and the rifle he took from Redtail's truck to the state lab to determine if the defendant had recently fired a weapon.

On cross-examination Hill began matter-of-factly: "The bar was full of people on the night you claim Charlie and his girlfriend made this statement to you, isn't that true?"

"Sure. Always a good crowd there."

"I suppose you claim no one else except you heard what you claim Charlie said."

"That's right, counselor."

"They just walked over to you, cold sober, and said that in your face so that they'd be the first persons you'd look for after they killed Cotler."

"Argumentative," Mueller said in a clear, solid voice.

"Sustained."

"They told you they were going to kill Cotler so that you'd be able to testify to their threat and convict both of them of murder, right?"

"Argumentative," Mueller objected.

"Sustained."

Russo whispered to Hamilton, the disbelief in his voice, "He's making a pretty good go of it."

"Do killers usually come up to you and tell you they're going to kill the person they intend to kill?"

"Not too often," Miller said. "But this guy was somebody who might do anything. I knowed him a long time."

Russo whispered to Hamilton, "Jesus! One question too many. An amateur doesn't know when he's ahead."

Then Hill asked, "Could you tell from the wound what kind of gun killed Cotler?"

"No. Any high-powered rifle woulda done it. He was shooting a .30-.30. That woulda done it."

"Ever see a cranium emptied of its contents like that from a .30-.30?"

"Never have. Most people don't get shot in the head with a .30-.30."

"Did you ask Charlie if he had shot the gun recently?"

"Yeah, he told me he shot a deer the day before."

"Did you check to see if he had?"

"Why should I? That's what them redskins always tell ya."

"Did you ask him where the carcass of the deer was?"

"No. They always have a deer or elk hanging someplace."

"You could have told a fresh kill from an old one, undersheriff?"

"Not in the dead of winter."

Russo whispered, "One question too many again."

"And when Charlie Redtail heard there was an all-points bulletin out for his arrest he came in voluntarily?"

"Probably figgered we would catch him anyway. Probably figgered it would look good fer him if he come in by hisself."

"His voluntarily coming in is consistent with innocence, isn't it?"

"Not necessarily. I know plenty of 'em who was guilty as hell who give themselves up." He looked over at the jury and grinned as if to emphasize his winning answer.

"If he hadn't come in and you had arrested him after a chase, you would be arguing that such conduct was evidence of guilt, isn't that so?"

"I don't know what I woulda argued. It never happened," Miller said and gave a quick grin to the jury again.

Robert Jamison from the state lab testified that the paraffin taken from Charlie's hands contained barium and antimony in sufficient quantity to establish that the defendant had probably fired a rifle recently. He found the same substances on the rifle and was able to conclude that the .30-.30 in question had likely been fired by the defendant during the day preceding the murder of Ronald Cotler. Hill asked only a few questions on cross-examination.

"You understand that we admit that this rifle was fired at a deer the day preceding the murder?"

"Yes."

"Your tests do not tell us what the rifle was fired at, isn't that true?"

"That's true."

"And if you had done the same tests on any one of dozens of hunters who shot their rifles on that day you would have gotten the same results?"

"I suppose."

Then Ava Mueller called Dr. Billingsley. The bailiff toddled out of the courtroom to fetch the doctor, who had been waiting in the foyer. The old doctor strolled with great dignity to the witness stand and made groans too loud for the occasion as he settled into the chair. He put on his half spectacles ready to read from the report he held in his hand. Yes, he had done the autopsy on Ronald Cotler.

"Did you examine the brain of the deceased?" Mueller asked.

"Wasn't any brain to examine."

"What do you mean?"

"The brain had been blown out."

"Was that consistent with a shot from a high-powered rifle?"

"Wouldn't have been done with a BB gun, I'll tell ya that."

"What did you establish as the time of death?"

"Couldn't say for sure. Anybody tells you otherwise is stretching the truth. I say he was probably shot about two, three, maybe even four in the morning from the feel of the liver. Still a little warm."

"Anything else unusual about the condition of the body when you examined it?" she asked.

"Well, I would say! Somebody cut off the tip of his right finger and nobody could find it out there."

"Had it been a fresh cut?"

"Yes. Raw wound. But no blood. Finger was cut off after death."

Russo said to Hamilton, "Hill should let well enough alone. Can't get anything out of that old bastard that'll help. And he's dangerous. Jury likes him."

Hill got up from his table and walked to the lectern, "You say there wasn't any brain to examine. Do you mean *none*."

"I mean none."

"Have you in your forty years ever seen a skull before in which the entire brain had been blown out?"

"Seen it once. But I figgered the coyotes got to her before I did."

"Have you seen brains shot with an ordinary hunting rifle?"

"Yes, a few."

"Did they look like the one you saw in this case?"

"No," he said. "The whole side of this skull was blown away and all the brain tissue with it."

"Would that be consistent with a bullet from a .30-.30?"

"More consistent with a 12-gauge shotgun at point blank."

"Did you tell Ms. Mueller that?"

"No. She never asked."

"I didn't think so," Hill said. "About the finger. Do you know anyone who is collecting fingers these days?"

"No, I don't."

"Did Ms. Mueller inquire of you concerning your theory about the missing finger?"

"Yeah. She asked me an' I told her that finger would show up some-day. Somebody took that finger ta prove they did the killing."

"Thank you, doctor. I have no further questions."

Mueller ran to the lectern.

"Your report doesn't say anything about a 12-gauge shotgun, does it?" she was shouting. Strange to hear her shout, Hill thought.

"Nope. I wasn't asked what kind of a gun it was and I wasn't going to guess."

"You can't say for sure that this wasn't a shot from a .30-.30, can you?"

"Well, you can't say nothing for sure in this business. Anybody says you can is stretching the truth, if you know what I mean."

"Were there coyotes in the vicinity of the Cotler residence?"

"I don't know. It was out in the country a little ways."

"Magpies?"

"Probably."

"Ever see a skull in which varmints of this kind had cleaned out the tissue?"

"Never seen it," he said. "I suppose it could happen."

"Thank you, doctor," Ms. Mueller said. And sat down.

Hill got up once more and walked slowly, as if he were thinking as he approached the lectern.

"Is it your opinion that varmints cleaned out that skull?"

"Could be."

"The whole left side of the skull was missing, wasn't it, doctor?"

"Yeah."

"Did you observe any teeth marks on the skull?"

"No."

"When was the last time you heard of a coyote coming onto the porch of a resident and eating off of a dead man before the body had cooled?"

"Never heard of it."

"Did you go to the scene to determine if there were pieces of skull available for your further inspection?"

"No."

"Any provided for you by the deputies?"

"No."

"Did you go to the scene to determine if there was any evidence on the front porch of magpies or other birds having been there?"

"What kind of evidence?" the doctor asked with a thoroughly elfish look on his face.

"Magpie droppings."

"If there was any there I wouldn't know. Deputies go to the scene. I just cut up the corpses and write my reports."

"Thank you, doctor," Hill said.

At 4:30 the court had called a recess for the day, the courtroom slowly emptying, the people not wanting to leave. Too early for the farmers to go home to their chores and no other place handy to the courthouse for people to gather. The sheriff's deputies had taken Charlie back to his cell in shackles and cuffs and Russo had come to the counsel table as Hill was stuffing his papers into his briefcase.

"Your client's mother, Mary, doesn't follow instructions very well," Russo said. "I told Hamilton to tell her to get up and walk out of the courtroom. They didn't have her under subpoena."

"Better she didn't," Hill said. "Not in front of the jury."

"We could have got her the hell out of Dodge," Russo said. "Hamilton could have flown her anywhere. If you're in the big leagues you have to play big league. Too late to cry about it." He started to walk away. Then as if it were a second thought, "Overall, you're doing pretty good."

"Tryin' for reasonable doubt. That's all we have to go on right now."

"Like I told you before, Hill," Russo said, "you can't win a murder case on reasonable doubt. No jury's going to turn a killer loose on reasonable doubt because they're turning him loose on themselves."

Hill listened.

"Jurors go into these cases believing that where there's smoke there's fire. A little reasonable doubt doesn't change that. The burden's on you."

"The burden's on the prosecution," Hill said.

"Jurors don't follow the law. What they see is a killer killing again after they turn him loose on reasonable doubt and them trying to explain to themselves that it's all right because they followed the law. Who you got to establish Charlie's innocence?"

Hill told him the old man would testify that both Charlie and Willow were with him that night. Russo laughed. "No one is going to believe the old man," he said. "He'd lie to save the kid. So would most any Indian out there. Have to do better than that."

"Like what?" Hill asked in deep skepticism.

"Let ya know," he said. And after that he and Hamilton left.

Hill reached out for Mary as she walked out of the courtroom. She turned and offered a remote smile, her eyes still soft from the tears, the shoulders drooping.

He went back to his table, the courtroom empty by then. He sat there for a long time trying to think, but he was too tired to think. Then he heard the voice.

"You're pretty good," the voice said. It was the blond man named Emmett.

"What are you doing here?"

"Watching the show."

"You could save me a lot of trouble if you'd take the stand and tell the jury you shot Cotler."

"I shot him all right," he said, laughing. "Old Doc never saw a skull blown out with a rifle like mine." He laughed again.

"Yeah?" Hill said. "What kind of a rifle was it?"

"It was a boom-boom gun," he said like a little boy. "The gun went *boom boom*."

"Why are you telling me this?"

"I am what is known as a voluptuary."

"What's that?'

"Look it up in the dictionary like your mother used to tell you." He laughed again. "There's nothing more entertaining than to watch a lawyer try to defend an innocent man when the prosecution knows he's innocent."

"What do you mean the prosecution knows he's innocent?"

"They know that a .30-.30 wouldn't blow all that brain tissue out. They know your client is not the kind to kill. They know he's innocent or they wouldn't be about to call a witness they know is lying."

"How do you know what witness they're going to call?"

Emmett started for the door. "I know because they're going to call me."

"What are you talking about?" Hill shouted. "Why are you telling me this?"

"Adds to the drama, counselor. Life is but a drama written by the great playwright up in the sky, the universe." He laughed again and walked on out of the courtroom door. Then he turned back and said, "But the playwright is crazy," his laughter on down the stairs. "The playwright doesn't know the difference between right and wrong."

29

Ava Mueller called Willy Hogan to the stand. He was a young, sunken-chested witness, pale with a fresh haircut and an ill-fitting secondhand suit, the padding at the shoulders sagging, the pant cuffs almost dragging the floor. His hair was greased down in a futile attempt to hold it in place. He took the oath by nodding his head. No one noticed.

He said he had been incarcerated in the Fetterman County jail on burglary charges and that his cell was across from Charlie Redtail's.

"Me an' Redtail got to be pretty good talkin' buddies," he said.

"That man is lying," Charlie whispered to Hill. "I never talked to him once. He tried to speak to me one time, but I never said anything back."

"What did you talk about," Mueller asked Hogan.

"Ya know. 'Bout life an' all. 'Bout girls and 'bout how he killed that fella out there."

"What fella out there?"

"Fella that was cuttin' up some land the Indins thought was holy. Said he didn't like ta do it, but the spirits tol' him to."

Charlie said to Hill, "He's making that up."

"Did he say how he killed the man?" Mueller asked.

"Yeah, he give me a lotta details. Never heard nothin' like that before. Run the chills up my spine. Said he hid in the bushes. His girlfriend was drivin' his pickup. Said it was dark and he waited 'til the guy come home after the bar closed. Said it was like pickin' off ducks in a barrel. Only 'bout ten yards away. Said the guy just folded like one of them puppets when ya cut the strings."

"Have you been promised anything for your testimony."

"Nah. Just tryin' ta be a good citizen fer a change." He laughed and looked over at the jury and the lady in front smiled back at him.

Mueller gave Abner Hill a look that said she had laid the last shovel on the grave of his case. "You may examine."

Hill stood staring at the man until the silence became embarrassing. Finally he heard himself saying, "Mr. Hogan, you burglarized a house?"

"Yeah."

"Whose house?"

"Some woman down on Fifth Street. I was drunk."

"You hurt her?"

"No."

"Touch her?"

"Well, they claim I pushed her 'round a little."

"How old a woman?"

"Don' know."

"Would that have been Mrs. Lacey?"

"Heard the name."

"She's past eighty."

"Maybe. Don't 'member much about it."

"Did she go to the hospital after you 'pushed her around'?"

"Somebody said so. Didn't mean ta hurt 'er."

"What did you take?"

"Some silverware. Jewelry."

"You've been in trouble before?"

"Some."

"Been in the penitentiary before?"

"Yeah."

"How many times?"

"Twice."

"For what?"

"Bad gigs. Never done what they said."

"What did they say you did?"

"Hearsay!" Mueller objected.

"Overruled," the judge ruled.

"Said I done a robbery up by Middleton. Never done it."

"What else."

"I forgot."

"Were you in for rape?"

"Nah."

"How many years did you spend in the penitentiary altogether?"

"'Bout fourteen."

"What's it like in the pen?"

"Whadda ya mean?"

"What is a typical day like?" Hill's voice was quickly soft, kind, as if he were a doctor talking to a patient.

"Get up, eat breakfast, go to work at yer license plate press, eat supper, and lock up."

"Have any family?"

"No."

"Any kids?

"Had some but I ain't seen 'em for a while."

"How long?"

"Never seen 'em since they was little."

"Have a girlfriend?"

"No."

"Anybody care about you?"

"Well, I don't know about that."

"Mother?"

"She died while I was in Rawlins."

"Father?"

"Never did know him."

"Want to go back to the pen?"

"Ain't so bad."

"Want to go back there for life? You're what they call a 'habitual,' isn't that true?"

"Dunno."

"Did you talk with Ms. Mueller before you came in here today?"

"Yeah."

"Where?"

"In her office."

"When?"

"This mornin'."

"Did she show you some pictures?"

The witness looked over at the prosecutor, who stared back at him without any sign.

"Well, I don' 'member."

"You don't remember?"

"No."

"She might have shown you some pictures?"

"Objected to as speculative," Mueller said.

"Well, hardly," the judge said. "Answer the question."

"Maybe," the witness said.

"Did you see this picture?" Hill handed the witness a photograph of the deceased crumbled on his front porch. The witness took the picture and glanced at it quickly.

"Seems like I seen that before," he said.

"And did she tell you anything about the charges she's brought against Mr. Redtail?"

"Don' 'member."

"It was just this morning."

"Don't 'member."

"You claim Mr. Redtail told you a lot of details concerning the killing."

"Yes."

"You remember those?"

"Yeah."

"But you can't remember what Ms. Mueller told you this morning in her office?"

He shrugged his shoulders.

"Charlie Redtail must have really trusted you."

"Dunno."

"You must have told him your secrets. Like how you beat up that old lady and stole her silverware and jewelry."

No answer.

"Well, did you tell him those kinds of secrets?"

"No."

"But he told you his secrets?"

"Yeah."

"Did Ms. Mueller read you the confession the sheriff took from him?"

"I don't know what you mean."

"Did she read to you from a piece of paper?"

"She read a lot of stuff."

"And then she said something like, 'If you say the right things we'll help you,' isn't that true?"

"No."

"She told you to deny that if I asked it, didn't she?"

"No."

"This is the judge who will sentence you." Hill pointed to Judge Hankins, who was staring down at the witness. "Are you willing to tell him now that you do not expect any consideration for your testimony here and that you will accept none if offered by Ms. Mueller at the time of your sentencing?"

"Objected to," Mueller said.

"Sustained," the judge ruled.

"How did you get word to Ms. Mueller that you had something to tell?"

"Told the deputy."

"Didn't the deputy come to you first?"

"Wadda ya mean?"

"It was Undersheriff Miller, wasn't it?"

"I don' know his name."

"The one over there." Hill pointed to Miller seated behind Charlie Redtail.

"Yeah."

"And he told you how you could help yourself a little, isn't that true?"

"No."

"What did he say to you?"

"'Don't 'member."

"We all have to take care of ourselves, Mr. Hogan. You've done the best you could to take care of yourself by your testimony here today, isn't that right?"

"Dunno whatcha mean," the witness said. Then Hill walked back to his table and sat down.

"He's lyin'," Charlie said.

Suddenly Hill was on his feet again. "One more question of the witness," he said as Hogan was being marched out of the courtroom by Sheriff Marsden. Hogan turned and came back to the witness stand.

"What day was it that you went out to the scene of this murder?"

"Assumes a fact not in evidence," Mueller objected.

"Sustained."

"Did you go to the scene of the murder?"

"I thought there was going to be only one question," Mueller said.

"Overruled," the judge said. "Answer the question."

"They took me someplace."

"Who is 'they'?"

"The deputy over there and another guy."

"Did you go to the place where they found the dead man?"

"Don' know."

Hill handed him the photograph he had previously seen. "Did you go to this place?"

"Yeah."

"That's where you got the details you've testified to, isn't it?"

"No."

"You didn't get the details from Charlie Redtail. You got them from Undersheriff Miller, who took you to the scene of the murder itself, isn't that true?"

"No."

"I have no other questions," Hill said.

Mueller looked up at the judge as if looking for guidance. Finally she got up and walked to the podium.

"Did I tell you what to say?"

"No."

"Did Mr. Miller?"

"No."

"Have you been promised anything?"

"Not really."

"I have nothing further," she said.

At the noon recess the jury was served lunch in the back room of the Twin Buttes coffee shop where the Kiwanis Club met on Tuesdays. But Ava Mueller and the three members of the sheriff's office, Miller, Maxfield, and Sheriff Marsden, had lunch brought to them in Mueller's office. The prosecutor turned to the sheriff. "I think I'll rest my case as soon as I put Redtail's confession in," she said.

"What do you mean?" Miller said. "I got the witness you was askin' for. You ain't got a case. That Hill has turned ya ever' way but loose."

"How do you see it, sheriff?" she asked.

"Sorta agree with Dean. Don't know if the confession'll do it or not. Hill's got them pictures of his face all beat to hell."

"Well, did you beat him?"

"You know better'n ta ask," Miller said.

Mueller said, "If I put the confession in, Redtail will have to take the stand to tell the jury you beat him up. And I can cross-examine him. Otherwise he may not take the stand at all."

"When ya callin' the girl?" Miller asked.

"I'm holding her back for rebuttal. She'll be our last witness."

"What if she turns on ya?"

"She won't."

"I wouldn't be too sure," Miller said. "She is one tough bitch."

"You might watch your language," Mueller said.

"Beg yer pardon, ma'am," Miller said. He threw a smirk at Marsden. "I'll tell ya what I would do if I was you," Miller said, biting into his ham sandwich and talking while he chewed. He swallowed the bite with a large swig of Coca-Cola. "I'd put on the witness I brung ya."

"I don't believe that witness is going to tell the truth," she said.

"He's tellin' as much truth as the one ya just put on."

"I didn't know you'd taken him out to the murder scene and pumped him full of facts. One witness like that is enough."

"Lady," Miller said, "if you are hanging your case on that bitch— 'scuse the language—and she backfires on ya, it'll be too late. Time ta make hay is when the sun is shinin' and the sun is shinin' now. I got this witness who seen the two of 'em speed off in the car after the shooting at two-thirty A.M., a live, breathin' eyewitness."

"I don't believe you anymore, Dean. Tell me this is a bona fide witness."

"'Course, he's bona fide. But 'spose for argument sake he's lyin' through his teeth. So what?"

"So what?" she echoed. "That's putting on perjured testimony. It's a felony, in case you've forgotten."

"Well, lady, you ain't thought about this clear though. You know Redtail killed Cotler, right?"

"Of course."

"You know it because he had the motive, he had the just cause to kill the bastard. You know it because the bastard—'scuse the French— tried to put the make on his old lady. You know it because the bastard kicked his father ta death. You know it 'cause he's all hung up like some screw loose over that mountain an' Cotler was in his way. So you know it, right?"

She stayed silent.

"No doubt in yer mind. Now how will you feel if the jury turns him loose?" Miller asked.

"You don't need to cross-examine me, Dean. You know I'm committed to bring justice in this county."

"I been in this business fer a long time," Miller said. "The first killin' fer the killer is the hardest. After that he knows his soul is goin' ta hell anyways and the next ones come easier." Miller continued, his sandwich nearly consumed during his argument. "Now 'spose ya decide not to put this witness on, on 'counta all of those purty ethics of yours. Jus' tell me this: Which is worse, to give the jury a little confidence in what they're doin' by givin' 'em somethin' ta hang their hat on or lettin' a killer kill again?"

"I've heard that argument from you before," she said. "But our system of justice is based on the truth. If we can't prove it, we can't put people in prison because some undersheriff wants them there."

"That there is so much bullshit, with all due respec'," Miller said. "Now 'spose it was your son instead of Cotler."

"I don't have any children, Dean, as you know."

"Jus' 'spose it anyway. He's been shot by this Redtail. How ethical you gonna be under them circumstances?"

"I wouldn't be in the case. I would be disqualified to try it."

"Well, if the sheriff here messed with the case a little to put the bastard away you wouldn't be too upset, would ya?"

"I can't imagine," she said.

"Well, you met Cotler's mother the other day. How ya figger she'll feel if Redtail walks outta here?"

"That really shouldn't be my concern."

"It should be if you're as hot on bringing justice to Fetterman County as ya say ya are. Cotler's mother is entitled to justice, too."

She hadn't touched her sandwich. "I think this has gone far enough. I'm not going to call your witness. I'm going to rest my case."

"Don't ferget yer up fer reelection next fall. How ya think the people of Fetterman County are gonna vote when they 'member that ya let Redtail walk 'cause ya refused ta call my witness? They're gonna say you was bought off or you woulda called him. They ain't gonna ferget that you let them renegades take over private property and you wasn't man enough to shut them bastards down. An' they ain't gonna ferget because what you done was take money right outta their pockets. If you was half as ethical as ya claim ya are you'd at least talk to the witness."

"All right," she said. "Bring him up here. I'll talk to him."

Abner Hill, alone at his table in the courtroom, was eating the peanut butter sandwich he'd brought with him. Russo came by.

"You're doin' good." Russo sat down. "But you're not going to win this case without a witness that blows the prosecution the hell out of the water. You got an alibi for Charlie. Nobody believes alibis. They got the girl stashed away somewhere. She's going to take the stand, her belly about to pop, and she's going to cry and the jury is going to love her. And who knows what other eyewitnesses they've conjured up who'll take the stand before this is over?" He moved closer to Hill. "I been talking to the old man. Says he has some witnesses. Says they'll come to your office in the morning before court to talk to you. You better listen to 'em."

"I'll listen to them," Hill said. "They better be tellin' the truth."

"Oh, of course!" Russo said. "It's always better to let an innocent man suck the gas than to feed the jury a lie or two and save him. Don't you agree?"

"If a lawyer puts on perjured testimony maybe the lawyer's as bad as the killer," Hill said.

"But your man Charlie isn't a killer. I always thought winning for an innocent client was the best ethic," Russo said. "You saw what Mueller did. Brought that lying piece of shit Hogan to the jury. I know and you know they put that story in his mouth."

"And the jury knows it, too," Hill said. "That's what cross-examination is for. Ferrets out the truth."

"Only people who believe that are law professors who never tried a case."

Then he walked off and Hill watched William Hamilton, his arm around Mary, leave the courtroom with Russo. He felt alone.

Following the noon recess the judge came sweeping onto the bench like a black winter storm.

"Call your next witness," he ordered.

The blond man with the cold, blue eyes walked down the aisle in smooth, precise steps and took the witness stand.

"Your name, sir," Muller asked.

"Emmett, people call me. Emmett Jones."

"Where are you from, Mr. Jones?"

"Billings, Montana."

"What do you do?"

"I sell encyclopedias. I come through here occasionally. I was at the Big Chief bar having a beer or two on the night of this murder."

"Did you see the deceased, Ronald Cotler, there that night?" Muller asked.

"Yes, I did."

"Did you have a conversation with him?"

"Yes." The witness's answers were given as if his words when dropped would shatter like a crystal glass.

"What was your conversation?"

"I was explaining to him that he should buy our encyclopedia. He had a young nephew he was fond of. I made a sale to him at about closing time and I knew I'd better get him on the dotted line and get his check. People change their minds sometimes in the light of day. So I was following him home after closing. Said he was going to give me his personal check."

"Did you follow him home?"

"Yes."

"What time was it?"

"Little after two in the morning."

"Did you know where he lived?"

"No."

"So you followed his vehicle?" Her questions were fast and hard without a hint of emotion.

"Yes."

"What were you driving?"

"A Jeep station wagon. Carry a lot of sales supplies in it and a full set of encyclopedias for demonstration."

"Did you follow him to his house?"

"Yes."

"How far ahead of you was he driving?"

"I'd say a block or two. I saw his car turn into his place."

"Did you see anything unusual as you approached his house?"

"Yes. I was about to turn into his house when I saw this old Ford pickup sitting there on the road about fifty feet north of the turnoff to Cotler's house. Looked like it was stuck. Lights were off. Didn't see anybody in it. Never thought anything of it until I started to turn in. In my headlights I saw this big man running toward me carrying a carbine."

"Were you able to recognize the man?"

"Yes."

"Do you see him in the courtroom today?"

"I do."

"Would you point him out to the jury?"

"The man sitting next to Mr. Hill."

"Let the record show the witness has identified Charlie Redtail, the defendant," Mueller said.

"And what did you do after you saw the man?"

"I drove on down the road at a slow rate of speed trying to think what to do, and then this same Ford pickup that was parked came speeding by me. In my headlights I could see there were two people in the pickup."

"Did you get its license number?"

"Yes, I did. It was Wyoming twenty-four-four-eighty-six."

"How did you happen to remember it?"

"I have a memory for numbers."

"And what did you do after the man passed you?"

"I drove on back to my motel."

"Why didn't you go in to meet Mr. Cotler as planned?"

"I thought something was off kilter there. I didn't want to get mixed up in it. A sale wasn't worth it. I thought I'd see him the next day."

"How did we learn of your testimony?"

"When I discovered that there had been a murder there I was shocked and I thought I should tell the police what I saw. I contacted Undersheriff Dean Miller."

"Thank you," Mueller said. "Your witness, counsel."

Abner Hill approached the bench and asked Judge Hankins for a recess.

"We need recesses only for the court to take care of a cranky bladder," the judge said. "That's why all judges should be over sixty years of age. Otherwise there'd be no need for recesses at all. All right, counsel, I'll give you a recess." Then he whispered to Hill, "I suggest you have a talk with Ms. Mueller and see if you couldn't work out a genial deal, maybe keep Redtail out of the gas chamber. That would be my idea of wisdom under the state of this record."

After the judge and jury left the room Hill went to where Russo was sitting in the audience and whispered, "Could you go outside and find this guy's Jeep? It's sitting around out there someplace. Get me the license number and look inside and tell me what's in it. Then find out who the Jeep is registered to. And hurry."

When the court was in session again Hill stood looking at the witness, the witness with the cold blue eyes staring back. The noise of Hill's heart was in his ears. It was as if his child were drowning and there was no time to think. He had to dive in.

"Where in Billings, Montana, do you live?" his first question.

"Live in an apartment at forty-four West Second Street."

"How long have you lived there?"

"Year and a half."

"Where did you live before then?"

"Calgary."

"Where in Calgary?"

"On Beaty Street."

"What address?"

"Twenty-four-twenty-five Beaty Street."

"What's your supervisor's name?"

"Jim Wilson."

"What's his telephone number?"

"I don't know it."

"Don't you talk to him on the phone?"

"No."

"How do you report to him?"

"By mail."

"What's his mailing address?"

"One-two-four-eight-seven Hammond Boulevard, Calgary."

"When is the last time you were in contact with him?"

"I sent material to him last week."

Then Russo came into the courtroom panting, obviously having run up the stairs. He motioned to Hill, the jury watching.

"The Jeep's license is Michigan thirty-four, forty-seven sixty-nine," Russo whispered. "Nothing in the back of the Jeep except a rifle case and one small duffel bag." Hill tore a sheet off of his yellow pad with the name and addresses Emmett had given. "Check these out. Find out who the Jeep is registered to. I'll keep him busy up here as long as I can."

Hill went though a long cross-examination of the man's entire history for the past ten years. He claimed to have lived in Hartford, Connecticut, where he worked as a vacuum cleaner salesman. He wasn't married. Sold magazines door to door in Omaha, Nebraska, and feed to farmers in Broken Arrow, Oklahoma. He was, he admitted, a sort of gypsy. Lived in his car most of the time.

"You sleep in the car?"

"Sometimes."

"Are you sleeping in your Jeep now?"

"No. I have a hotel room at the Twin Buttes Hotel."

"Do you have your supplies up there in your room?"

"No."

"Where are they?"

Emmett face suddenly grew grave. His eyes narrowed. "I sold my last set of encyclopedias to a farmer outside of Billings."

"What's his name?"

"This is all irrelevant," Mueller objected.

"Yes," the judge said. "Proceed, counsel."

"Where is your sleeping bag?"

"I didn't bring it this trip. I was offered a hotel room by the sheriff's office."

"What do you have in your car?"

"Irrelevant," Mueller objected.

"Do you have a rifle in there?"

"Yes."

"May we see it?"

"I object," Mueller said.

"What is the relevance, counsel?" the judge asked.

"The relevance is that this man was at the scene of the murder on the night of the murder. He owns a rifle. We're told that the deceased was killed with a high-powered rifle. We're entitled to have the rifle examined."

"We are not going to go astray here, Mr. Hill. About everyone in these parts owns a gun of some kind. Proceed."

"What is the license number of your Jeep?

"Don't remember."

"Didn't I hear you testify that you had a memory for such numbers?"

"Don't pay any attention to my own."

"Don't know your boss's telephone number nor your own license number?"

"That's right."

"Have we met before?"

"Not that I know of." Then on second thought he said, "I do believe I saw you at the bar the other night."

"Did we have any conversation?"

"No. You tried to talk to me, but I didn't want to talk to you, if I remember correctly."

"Did you tell me that you killed Ronald Cotler?"

"Objection, Your Honor," Mueller shouted. She rushed toward the bench. "I must approach the bench."

At the bench the judge, his face tight with anger, said, "What cheap trick are you trying to pull, Mr. Hill? You know better than that. I'm going to instruct the jury to disregard your last question as utterly improper. And I am going to report your conduct to the bar."

"Do as you wish," Hill said. "But I had a conversation with this man two nights ago at the bar. He told me he killed Cotler and laughed in my face about it. I'll file an affidavit to that effect."

"For what possible reason would this man kill Ronald Cotler?" Ms. Mueller asked.

"He told me he killed him because he was in tune with the universe, that the universe killed helter-skelter and so did he. He said it amused him to see Cotler's brains spattered all over the place."

"Why didn't you report this to me?" Ava Mueller asked.

"Because you wouldn't believe me then any more than you believe me now."

"Do you intend to testify to this conversation, Mr. Hill?" the judge asked.

"Haven't made up my mind," Hill replied.

"If you decide to testify I'll declare a mistrial. You can't testify in my court and act as an attorney at the same time."

"I'd like a recess to consider this matter further, Your Honor."

"Very well, we'll be in recess until nine A.M. tomorrow. Better get this matter figured out, Mr. Hill," the judge said and flew from the bench like a black-winged apparition.

Sometime before sunup Judge Henry Hankins received a telephone call from Sheriff William Marsden. The substance of the call was that the farmer on the jury, John Oakley, had awakened to find his wife on the living room couch with a knife in her heart. It appeared she'd been raped. But Sheriff Marsden was questioning the evidence. He thought her cut panties, which she clutched in her right hand, and her half-naked body could be an attempt by the husband to misdirect the sheriff in his investigation. The sheriff had Oakley in custody for questioning and asked the judge if he thought this would affect the trial in any way.

"You have a juror in custody?" Judge Henry Hawkins asked through his sleep.

"That's right, judge," Marsden said.

30

The brothers faced each other in Charlie's cell, the one well-tanned, his hair cut by one of those eastern stylists, the other pale, his hair in the one long braid. Their eyes seeing each other looked at themselves. Their eyes saw the separated egg. And there was a longing that the egg join in its separate parts and become whole again. But the egg no longer existed. And the longing to come together was all that remained.

The men, Charlie Redtail and Billy Redtail—that's who they were, the Redtail twins, nothing more, were as different as the two sides of the hand and yet the hand. They had always felt it, but they had not been able to speak of the longing. They had come together best on the basketball court, the rhythms of the game playing the simultaneous music in the separate, beating hearts.

Yet they repelled each other like the opposite poles of a magnet.

In the cell, Billy Retail looked at his brother. "I'm going to get you out of this, Charlie," he said. Then he laughed and slapped his brother on the leg. "You always were a pain in the ass."

Charlie said, "You can't get me out of this one. It is not in your hands," but his voice was not sad.

"A man can do whatever he wants," Billy said. He was quiet for a while. "I'm not poor anymore."

"A man can be poor in different ways," Charlie said.

"I'll never be poor again. The worst of all crimes is to be poor."

"Is it worse than murder?" Charlie laughed.

"Nothing is worse than being poor," Billy said.

Dean Miller came tromping down the walkway, the mean sound of the boots on concrete. At Charlie's cell he hollered in, "Time's up, Billy."

Hamilton reached in his pocket, peeled off a hundred from a roll, and handed the bill to Miller. "We're talking," Hamilton said. "Can't you see? We're talking."

"Sorry to have interrupted you," Miller said taking the bill and then they heard his boots retreating and the perimeter door slam behind him.

"When I get you out of here I want you to promise me something," Billy said.

Charlie waited.

"I want you to leave Twin Buttes. This is no place for you. Come to New York with me. I'll send you anywhere you want to go. But leave this hole."

"I'm not leaving," Charlie said. "I can't."

"They'll kill you here, Charlie."

After that Charlie would say nothing more.

He was that way, Billy thought. The kid, as Billy called him, had been traumatized all right. He had to make room for his injury—seeing the old man kicked to death. But people have to rise above their injuries. People can write their own tickets. Charlie had the same brain. The kid was smart. But he did nothing with it. Poor as a poor pissant, Billy thought. And he wouldn't work. Christ, his mother worked. Worked until she dropped in her tracks. But would Charlie work? No. Too fucking good to work.

The son of a bitch had no pride. All he wanted to do was cause trouble out there on the rez, fuck up the project, and fuck the girl with the big tits called Willow. Not a bad life. But he was still poor and amounted to nothing, a walking zero.

Billy remembered when he had tried to get Charlie to go to school. Got a scholarship for him. He would have helped him through like he always did. But no. He wanted to hang out with the old man. Play Indian. Talk to the fucking flowers. Hug the fucking trees. Jump like a fucking jumping bean to the tom-toms. The kid never grew up. Locked in his psychological pen when the door was slammed shut on him at ten years of age when he saw the old man kicked to death. Door stayed locked.

Yet there were times when Billy thought Charlie knew things he didn't. The kid radiated peace, sort of Buddhist-like. Everyone said so. Maybe Billy hadn't hugged enough fucking trees. But what could you buy with it? Wouldn't pay the rent. Wouldn't buy a nickel's worth of fuel for his jet. You can't have peace sleeping under the bridge. Happiness is never generated from a shrunken belly. He never knew a shivering man who was happy. His mother had never been happy. That beautiful woman tied up in knots of poverty that even he couldn't untangle. Poverty killed. If it didn't kill the body, it killed the soul.

Sometimes he had nightmares about being poor. In his dream he'd lost it all. The banks would loan him no money. His safety deposit box was empty. No one would even give him the price of a meal. He was on the road, hitchhiking. He was cold. No one gave a shit. No woman. No friend. No one. He was alone. He woke up, afraid, the pall of the dream hanging over him for days.

No, he would never be poor again. And another thing: He had too much money tied up in that project. After Cotler had been murdered he'd had to fuck with a bunch of phony trustees trying to keep his involvement undercover. Why should he be afraid to let the world know that he, William R. Hamilton, was the CEO of the Spirit Mountain thing? The townspeople would kiss his ass, anoint him as king, hold him up as brilliant. Call him beautiful. Money stood for every virtue. He could own the town and twenty like it. But something caused him to hold back. The Indian thing. He was part of the fucking Indian thing. It was like a birthmark. You could cut it off the hide but it would grow back, only bigger. The only thing you could do was cover it. Money covered things.

And after Charlie was charged with the murder of Cotler the guilt filtered in. If he hadn't put the heat on Cotler maybe Charlie wouldn't have killed the bastard. That was something he would never understand—how someone who talked to flowers could blow the brains out of a man. But maybe Charlie was innocent. You could never tell by looking at a man's face. The murderers and the saints all looked alike. He knew a guy down in the Bronx once who spent his life administering to the poor, a regular saint, and he looked like the meanest hit man in town.

No, Billy thought, he was not guilty. If Charlie killed Cotler, he could have had a lot of reasons other than Spirit Mountain. What he did to their mother was enough of a reason. Sometimes he thought that if he had the guts he would have killed Cotler himself. Should have. Charlie was right.

But a businessman cannot tolerate a psyche laced with guilt. If you want to fuck up a good deal, let the guilt seep in. Guilt for making a good deal. Guilt because the other guy didn't. Guilt for being successful. Guilt because the world is poor and you're a rich son of a bitch. Guilt because you sit on the soft lap of luxury and the others out there are starving to death. Fuck guilt. And one other thing, he thought. If he got Charlie out of this mess he was not going to have him fucking up his project.

"Charlie," he said again, "I'm going to get you out of this and when I do, I'm taking you out of here. That's one thing for sure." Then he called for the jailer to come.

After Billy left his cell Charlie Redtail saw the spirits. His father, among them, came to the cell, Joseph the father and Charlie still the child. The father did not come until Billy was gone. It wasn't that the father did not love Billy. Fathers love their children. It was, Charlie thought, that they were not of the same spirit. The white man called it soul. There is flesh and blood and spirit. There is the world of the flesh and the world of blood and the world of spirit. Billy Redtail, his twin, were of the blood, and of the flesh, but not of the spirit. But still, he thought, Billy longed to be of the spirit.

Charlie walked to the bars of his cell, held on to them, and watched his brother retreat down the walkway, the left foot turning in slightly. It was his walk, all right, nearly identical bodies walking. The paths different, he thought. Yet, he thought, if I were not so poor, if I were of a different world I would buy Spirit Mountain and return it to my people. In that way, he thought, I have failed. If I were not so poor the people would embrace me and I would buy my woman and my child. The people would believe me. The jury, too, if I were not so poor. Poor people are not to be believed. Then he laughed. And why he laughed he did not know.

That night Anthony Russo and William R. Hamilton were seated once more in the back booth of the Buckhorn bar. After a couple, Hamilton said, "I had a good talk with Charlie."

"Did he tell you anything?"

"I didn't ask him," Russo said.

"How come?"

"Didn't want to know."

"How come?"

"I'll tell you something," Hamilton said. "I want that kid out of that mess. I don't care what it takes. I don't care how much money you spend. Take care of it. And when we get him out, I want him the fuck out of here. I got a project out there that's blowing up in my face. If he stays, he'll fuck it up for sure."

"What if he won't leave?" Russo asked.

"I want you to talk to him."

"What if he won't listen?"

"Then maybe we better let Mueller have him."

"What are you saying?" Russo asked. And after that they drank some more in silence. Then Russo said, "I think you're a little fucked up, Hamilton."

"No," Hamilton said. "It's the kid who isn't thinking straight. And I'm not responsible for people who don't think straight."

31

Abner Hill watched from the window as the two Native Americans walked with long steps through the snow, young men, one in a faded denim jacket, hardly ample for the weather, the other in an old green parka with the hood thrown back. Their heads were bare, their braids down the back betraying them as new-age Indians. These were the renegades who had taken on the style of their ancestors. They were not of their fathers; not the obsequious imitators of the white man who wore the white man's cowboy hats and boots and cut their black, straight hair short so that it stuck out in all directions. The braids down the back, one wearing a beaded headband, said they were of their ancestors and to be reckoned with.

Abner Hill knew the taller one, Simon Yellow Dog, the protruding cheekbones as if they had been pushed too far up in the making. He didn't recognize the other man. They entered the street-level entrance of the building and he heard them climbing the stairs. He went to his office door and watched them come down the long hall toward him, the hall too narrow for two men to walk comfortably abreast, the one in front, Simon Yellow Dog.

Hill nodded to Yellow Dog and stepped aside for the two to enter. Yellow Dog sat down, the other man stood by the door as if to guard it. Yellow Dog shifted in his chair and without looking at Hill began to speak. "The spirits come to me in my sleep last night. Tol' me ta come an' tell ya."

"Tell me what?" Hill asked.

"Tell ya what I seen that night when Cotler was killed."

"You were there?"

"Yeah, me an' Quinten here. We was at the Big Chief bar and ol' Miller, that sheriff, was there. Him and Cotler got into it. An' I heard

Cotler sayin' not ta fuck with him or he'd have Miller's nuts cut out and have 'em shoved up his ass."

"What time of the night was that?"

" 'Bout closin' time. They was havin' trouble over some girl there. White girl named Caroline. Never seed her before. Then I seed ol' Miller leave. An' after that they closed up the bar an' kicked us all out."

"Did you see Charlie or Willow there?"

"No, they was with the old man."

"Did you see a blond guy there, guy who wears army clothes?"

"No. Never seen no white guy in army clothes."

"What did you do after they kicked you out at closin' time?"

"Percy Old Man had a bottle and we was tryin' ta get a drink offa him, an' he wouldn't give us none, so after a while we decides to go home."

"Then what?"

"We was headed home. We al'ays drive by Cotler's place 'cause its on our road and we seed the sheriff's car there."

"What time was it?"

" 'Bout two-thirty probably. Never had no watch. Hawked it over at the Big Chief pawn shop las' Christmas."

"I wasn't drunk, neither," Quinten See Hair said. "I run outta money 'bout five in the evenin'. I was drivin'. I seen the sheriff's car there myself. I says to Simon, 'I better slow way down. I wonder what that bastard is doin' there this time a mornin'?'"

"How much had you had to drink that night, Simon?" Hill asked.

"I run outta money 'bout eight. Roger Black Eagle bought us a bottle of tokay, but we drunk her up by midnight. I was sober. Plumb sober an' I seen that sheriff's car there."

"Anybody in the sheriff's car?"

"We drove by real slow so as not ta cause no trouble. There wasn't nobody in the car."

"You sure this was the night of the murder?"

"Yeah. An' I says to Quinten, 'Back up. Les' see what's goin' on there. I said that on accounta the sheriff woulda drove in to Cotler's place if he had business there. Thought we might get us a radio or somethin'."

"You were going to steal a radio from the sheriff's car?"

"No, I was jus' thinkin' about how funny it would be an' all."

"He ain't tellin' ya the truth," See Hair said. "He was gonna steal the whole car. Thought it would be a big-ass gas to steal the sheriff's car an' go drivin' 'round the reservation at two in the mornin', raisin' hell with the siren goin' an all."

"Nah, I wasn't gonna do that. I was jus' bullshittin'. Ol' Quinten here was backin' up to the sheriff's car when ol' Miller comes runnin' up to his car. He's carryin' a shotgun. An when he sees us we take off like a bat outta hell, an' that there is all we seen."

When the news got out that Katy Oakley, the buxom farmwife of the juror John Oakley, had been murdered, nearly everyone but Abner Hill had already heard about it before the judge called the lawyers into his chambers. Hill could tell something extraordinary was afoot. Ava Mueller, pale and looking as if she had spent a sleepless night, would not look at him. The judge himself seemed strangely preoccupied.

Judge Hankins cleared his throat. "We have a serious matter to consider." Then he told the lawyers what he knew about the murder, which was nothing more than what the sheriff had already relayed to him by phone in the middle of the night. "The question before the court is what shall we do?"

The lawyers were silent. Then Hill said, "I don't believe this."

Finally Ava Mueller said, "I think you must declare a mistrial, Your Honor."

"Why?" the judge said. "We have an alternate juror."

"You know I tried to get that man off the jury. He can't read or write," Mueller, said referring to José Sanchez, the Mexican American sheepherder who sat as the thirteen juror.

"There's no arduous reading going on here, Ms. Mueller," the judge said.

Then Hill said, "I think I should join Ava in her motion for a mistrial."

"On what grounds?" the judge asked.

"Some jurors will argue that Charlie's friends killed Oakley's wife as a message. They'll interpret this murder as a serious threat to their safety and the safety of their families, and they'll rush to convict the defendant in retaliation or to protect themselves."

Ava Mueller pondered what Hill had said. "I think to the contrary. I think that the jurors could be frightened by this. They could come to the conclusion that the murder of Oakley's wife was, indeed, a message and that if they convict Charlie Redtail they and their families will all be in danger. Out of fear, and without regard to the evidence, they might acquit him to save themselves."

The judge said, "I believe this is merely a coincidental intrusion into our case. I have not been shown there's the first connection between those renegades and this murder. In fact, the sheriff told me the juror himself was a suspect."

Without more the judge ordered them into the courtroom saying that since both had moved for a mistrial it looked to him like the playing field was level. "Besides," he added, "we have a lot of time invested in this case already. I am not going to have it wasted. Matilda and I have had our vacation planned for well over a year. Cruise to the West Indies. If you possess an ounce of compassion you wouldn't wish to unleash Matilda's wrath on me should her vacation plans be foiled." Then, as if in afterthought, the judge turned to Hill. "Have you decided to abandon your attempt to pin this murder on Emmett Jones?"

"I can't prove what he said to me," Hill replied. "It would be his word against mine."

"Very well," the judge said. "Let us hear nothing more of it."

Once more the man who called himself Emmett Jones took the stand dressed as before in his army fatigues and black polished boots, both feet flat on the floor, his weight slightly forward, his hands on his thighs like a man readied to move instantly in either direction. As Hill approached, the man's eyes followed his steps to the lectern. Once there he kept Hill intensely in focus like an osprey on a limb above the ripples where the trout gathered in the late summer.

But before Hill formed his first question the judge turned to the jurors and said, "Ladies and gentlemen, yesterday you heard Mr. Hill make reference to an alleged statement by this witness concerning the murder of Ronald Cotler. You will disregard that question and any implications from it." The jurors in front nodded and smiled at Emmett. The Mexican, José Sanchez, was sitting in John Oakley's chair at the end of the jury box next to the witness stand.

Hill looked over at the witness staring at him. "This Jeep you're driving is your vehicle?" he asked.

"Of course,"

"To whom is it registered."

"To me."

"I've checked the registry. It's registered to William Knudson?"

"Yes. I bought the Jeep from Mr. Knudson recently. Likely the title transfer hasn't appeared yet on the records. They're slow about that."

"Where did this sale take place?"

"In Billings."

"You bought a Michigan Jeep, registered in Michigan, in Billings, Montana, and have not changed the Michigan license plates or accomplished the registration in Montana. Is all of that correct?"

"Of course."

"Where is Mr. Cotler's house?"

"It's out on the road."

"Yes, of course. What road?"

"The road that leads to the reservation."

"What color is the house."

"I don't know. It was dark."

"But the porch light was on. You could see it from the road."

"I paid no attention to the color of the house."

"There is no office for Encyclopedia Britannica nor phone number for your boss, Jim Wilson, in Calgary. Do you have an explanation for that as well?"

"The company's headquarters are in Providence, Rhode Island. Mr. Wilson's name is Richard J. Wilson. He goes by Jim. You will find a listing for him at the address I gave."

"You claim that Cotler was going to pay you with his personal check?"

"Yes, that's what he said."

"Did you know he has no personal checking account?"

"That wouldn't surprise me. We are often misled."

"What kind of a rifle do you have in your case."

"It is only a .22-caliber rifle. I use it to shoot varmints. It's my hobby."

"May we examine it?"

"I've already ruled on that," Judge Hankins said.

"Did you see the defendant, Charlie Redtail, at the Big Chief bar that night?"

"Yes."

"What was he wearing?"

"He was wearing what he's got on now."

"Would it interest you to know that the clothes he's wearing I myself bought him for this trial."

"Looks like what he was wearing that night."

"Was he with anyone?"

"Yeah. Some girl."

"What color were her eyes?"

"Don't know. Never looked into her eyes. You wouldn't either if you'd been there and her boyfriend was that man over there." Some of the jurors laughed. Out of habit the judge, hearing laughter, struck his gavel.

"What was she wearing?"

"Can't remember."

"What time was it when you saw them there?"

"They were there to about closing time."

The court had called a recess. To gather their forces, the witness, Emmett Jones met with Ava Mueller and Dean Miller in Mueller's office. She was pacing the floor. The blond man stood leaning against the wall, the sole of one black boot against the wainscot. He seemed amused.

"Emmett there done real good," Miller chortled.

"They're checking the listing for Encyclopedia Britannica in Providence and for Richard J. Wilson in Calgary as we speak," she said. Turning to Emmett she said, "You are very facile. But lying under oath is known as perjury, and if I know it, we would both be guilty of felonies." She stopped her pacing and looked at Emmett, walked up to him, and stood squarely before him. "I therefore do not want to know if you've lied or not. All I want to know is what your answers are going to be in the event Hill discovers there's no Encyclopedia Britannica in Providence and no Richard J. Wilson in Calgary."

Emmett looked at the woman without moving from the wall. He gave her a dead smile. "Would you prosecute me for perjury?" When she didn't answer he added, "How about for murder?" She walked to her desk and fell into her chair.

Miller said, "All he has to say is he's an undercover agent for the gom'ment—shit like that."

The bailiff knocked on their door, his quivery voice hollering, "Time's up."

The blonde man walked to Mueller's desk where she sat and dropped three small turquoise Indian beads on its surface. "These are for good luck," he said. Then he laughed and followed her into the courtroom.

Mueller picked up the beads, examined them closely. Then she watched Emmett Jones leave the room, the beads still in her hand.

*   *   *

Calmly enough, Hill continued in his cross-examination. "Mr. Jones," he began, the witness peering steadily at him, "where did you go during the last recess?"

"To Ms. Mueller's office."

"Who was there?"

"Ms. Mueller and Undersheriff Miller."

"What did you talk about?"

"Ms. Mueller said she wasn't feeling well. Undersheriff Miller offered her some aspirin. She said she was coming down with a cold, but, frankly, I think it's the strain she's under in this case."

"Did you talk about the case?"

"Quite to the contrary. We were careful not to, because we all knew you would ask me that question."

"You of course know that the home office of Encyclopedia Britannica is not in Providence, Rhode Island."

"Is that so?" he seemed amused again.

"You find that amusing?"

"I find it predictable. I should have thought you would check that out during the recess. I commend you."

"Nor is there a Richard J. Wilson listed in Calgary."

"Well, well," Emmett said. "What should we do about that?"

Something in the way the man answered the question. Hill suddenly turned and said, "No further questions."

Mueller was on her feet.

"Have you lied to this jury?"

"Intention is a necessary part of perjury as you know, Ms. Mueller," Emmett said matter-of-factly. "I have told you all I can tell you about myself and my work in conformity with the instructions I have received from my superiors. I have not intended to mislead, nor have I misled, concerning any material facts about what I saw that night."

"What's this business about instructions from your superiors?"

"I have nothing further to say about that," Emmett said.

"You work for a secret government agency?" she asked.

"I refuse to answer," Emmett said.

The jury was locked on the man, the eyes of the twelve a single eye. "You may examine," she said to Abner Hill

"I have no further questions," Hill said. Then the blond man walked from the stand with a stride and rhythm that seemed in harmony with the endless cosmos. The back of his eyes were as if they reflected the empty stars. As he exited the courtroom door he turned to Ava Mueller and said across the audience, "I hope your headache is better." Then he disappeared down the stairs.

Russo whispered to Hamilton, "What the fuck is going on? Hill let that son of a bitch go. He should have moved the court for an order of contempt." Russo jumped to his feet and ran to Hill's table. "Order the witness back, for Christ's sake. Follow up on who he is and what he's doing. He's a lyin' motherfucker. He just shoved this case up your ass." Before Hill could respond Ava Mueller called Dean Miller back to the stand.

"I hand you this instrument marked state's exhibit seven. Could you tell us what it is?"

"The statement of Mr. Redtail."

"How did it come about?"

"He was in jail downstairs. He calls me. Said he wanted ta make a statement. Surprised me. He wouldn't talk ta us earlier. I said, 'Okay, ya sure?' An' he says, 'I am damn sure.' An' I says, 'Ya better call Mr. Hill. He's yer lawyer.' An' he says, 'I don't need no lawyer. They jus' get in the way. I got somethin' on my chest I wanna get off, an' Hill will try an' stop me. So I wanna do this.'"

"So what did you do?"

"I says, 'Ya want me ta call in the reporter?' An' he says, 'Whatever.' So I calls in the reporter and he makes this statement, an' the reporter types it up, and Redtail, he signs it in front of me and the reporter, and that there is what this paper is-his statement."

"Did you tell him this statement could be used against him?"

"No."

Confounded, Mueller asked, "Did you hear my question? Did you tell him this statement could be used against him?"

"No. He tol' *me*. He says, 'I know you are gonna use this against me and what not, but I gotta get it off my chest. So les' go.'"

Then Mueller offered Charlie Redtail's confession into evidence, the court reserving its ruling until after Hill had completed his cross-examination.

"I take it, Mr. Miller, that you got this statement voluntarily from Mr. Redtail," Hill asked on cross-examination.

"Absolutely."

"I show you defendant's exhibits three, four, and five. Do these correctly reveal the condition of Mr. Redtail's face a week after his arrest?"

"Well, yeah. I remember that." Hill offered the exhibits into evidence without objection from the prosecutor, the jurors passing the photos to one another down the line.

"You claim you had nothing to do with the beating he obviously took?"

"No. He was that way when he come in."

"You and Sheriff Marsden beat this defendant, isn't that true?"

"No. You are makin' that up like ya made up a lotta other stuff in this case," Miller said.

"I move to have the witness's answer stricken," Hill said.

"The last part of the statement can be stricken," the judge said. "The jury is instructed to disregard it."

"He signed that so-called confession only after you told him that the woman he loves was going to go to the gas chamber, isn't that true?"

"That is not true."

"He signed it on the day she was brought into the Fetterman County jail, isn't that true?"

"Maybe. Don't remember the day she come in," Miller said.

"Are you telling us Mr. Redtail used the exact language contained in this statement?"

"Practically," Miller said. "That there is a summary of it. He rambled on fer a long time an' used a bunch a profanities about how he hated Cotler, and how Cotler tried ta rape his mother, and how Cotler was destroying them Indians' holy mountain an' how Cotler had it comin'. He said a lotta stuff like that but we jus' put it down nice and straight like—kept all that other stuff out so as he could get hisself a fair trial." Miller looked over to Ava Mueller and raised an eyebrow.

After Miller stepped down from the stand Ava Mueller walked to the front of the jury box. She waited until all of the jurors' eyes were on her. As she took in the whole panel she said the words with a movement of her head that said she had proven her case beyond a reasonable doubt.

"The State of Wyoming rests its case."

And with that Ava Mueller whirled and returned to her place at counsel table after which the judge recessed the trial until nine the following morning.

When Hill returned to his office that afternoon he found Anthony Russo with a tall, lean stranger waiting outside his office door. The guy wore army fatigues like Emmett Jones's.

"Good news, Abner," Russo said. "We've found a witness who'll finally lock this case up for us. Meet Bill Jordan."

"What kind of a witness?" Hill asked, his question soaked in skepticism. They followed Hill into his office. Took chairs like they owned the place, the man named Jordan looking tough. Man about forty, tanned. Hard face. Short hair. Thin with a lot of muscle. Guy sat there saying nothing.

"One of our guys found him. Billy sent his plane after him last night. I haven't mentioned it but we've had seven operatives working on this case trying to solve this murder. We think we've got it solved." Russo paused to light a cigarette. "Best operatives in the business, the ones I use in New York. They know how to get to the bottom of things."

"Well?" Hill said.

"One of our operatives came on to Bill here. Bill happens to be a friend of Emmett Jones—or a sort of friend. Jones isn't the kind who makes many friends, if you know what I mean."

"Yeah," Hill said, listening, watching, the man never taking his eyes off of Hill.

"And Bill here knows what happened to Cotler. He'll testify that he and Jones were working for the government as undercover agents, the department of the army. Cotler was a target for the army. The army offered Cotler a cool million for Spirit Mountain. They wanted to make a military base up there. Cotler turned them down. Thought he could make a lot more money in the development. Jordan said he and Jones had orders to clear the way for the army anyway they could. Jones had decided to do it easy and quick, if you know what I mean. Bill here bailed out."

"Who's going to believe that story?" Hill asked.

"The jury," Russo said. "If they believe Jones's testimony that he was working undercover for some government agency, they'll believe Bill."

Hill turned to Jordan. "Is your testimony true?"

"We're all adults here," Jordan said.

"It's beautiful," Russo said. "They bring in this lying sack of shit Jones to pin a murder on an innocent man, and we bring in a witness to pin the murder on the lying sack of shit. What could serve justice better?"

"Jones did kill Cotler. I'm convinced of that," Hill said.

"Right." Russo laughed. "Wonderful twist of fate that we found Bill."

Then Hill turned to Jordan. "How much did they pay you?"

Jordan didn't answer.

"Look," Russo said. "You either ask the wrong questions or you're talking when you should be listening. Now this guy can pin the murder on the real killer. What more do you want?"

"I want the truth."

"I want my brother acquitted," Hamilton said.

"What you got goin' here won't get Charlie off," Russo said. "Too much prejudice. Remember what I told you: prejudice trumps logic. It wipes out common sense. When a jury's prejudiced it takes a lot of help."

In the morning the *Twin Buttes Times* carried the latest news concerning the murder of Katy Oakley, the wife of the juror John Oakley. Oakley had been in custody, but the sheriff reported that their investigation now revealed certain evidence pointing to the involvement of unidentified Native Americans. The *Times* reported that a confidential source in the sheriff's office said that a number of small turquoise beads were discovered implanted in the body of the deceased. The source said, "These beads, which are common ceremonial beads used by the Arapahoe people, could only have been placed there intentionally." The sheriff said his investigation was continuing. The funeral for Katy Oakley would be held on Thursday.

32

That morning Hill pushed the *Twin Buttes Times* over to Russo.

"What do you make of this?" Russo read the headline: "Indians Involved in Killing, Source Says."

Russo read the article, threw the paper back across the desk to Hill.

"I'd say our witness Bill Jordan got here just in time. Ask the judge for a mistrial. Put the paper into evidence to support your motion. The judge'll deny it, but we'll have your motion in the record in case we have to appeal. Then we put Jordan on and walk out of the courthouse with Redtail. Hamilton can fly us all to the Big Apple for a celebration."

At nine o'clock sharp the bailiff called the court to order. The judge turned to Abner Hill.

"You may make your opening statement, Mr. Hill," he said, looking bored.

"I waive my opening," Hill said.

Russo jumped as if he were shot. He whispered to Hamilton, "He waives his opening? Christ!"

"Call Ace Yokum," Hill announced from counsel table.

The gangly man wearing his Skelly station uniform came ambling down the aisle following the bailiff. "If he were any skinnier he'd fall through his own asshole," Bill Harrison used to say. He played basketball with Yokum on the Junior Chamber of Commerce team. Yokum was carrying a gun case in his right hand. When he got to the witness box he sprawled out on the chair. Looked like a dead lobster, legs all over the place. Yokum laid the gun case across his lap and grinned over at Hill.

"How have you come to testify here today."

"You served this paper on me."

"What is the paper?" Hill asked.

"It's a subpoena. Says I have to come or that old geezer up there will throw me in jail."

The judge, turning red, said, "Are you looking for a contempt citation, Mr. Yokum?"

"No, sir. Just tryin' ta tell the truth like I promised ta do."

More laughter. The judge struck his gavel.

"What do you have in that gun case?" Hill asked.

"Got a rifle." He unzipped the case and withdrew a heavy-barreled rifle with a large scope.

"Where did you get it?"

"Out of a black Jeep station wagon bearing Michigan license plates, thirty-four, forty-seven, sixty-nine. Guy named Emmett Jones supposed to own it."

"When and how did you acquire this rifle?"

"I did a little jimmy trick of mine. People always locking their keys in the car. I got me a set of jimmies. I jimmied the lock on the Jeep and brought this rifle to court."

Judge Hankins jumped up from the bench. "Sheriff, arrest that man!" the judge hollered. "We have just heard an in-court confession of a felony." Undersheriff Miller jumped forward.

"Just a minute, Your Honor, I'm not through with my questioning," and before the judge could say more Hill asked Yokum, "Did you intend to steal this rifle?"

"No, sir. I intended to bring it into court and turn it over to His Honor as evidence."

Hill looked up at the judge. "This could hardly be a crime since Mr. Yokum possessed no felonious intent." The judge waived Miller back.

"Who asked you to do this?" Hill asked.

"No one."

"How did you happen to do it?"

"You and me were having a beer and you were whimperin' about that old bagger's . . ." he stopped. "You were complaining about the judge's refusal to let the jury see Emmett Jones's gun. So I decided to help the court out a little on my own."

"When did you get the rifle?"

"While Jones was testifying yesterday afternoon."

"Is it in the same condition as when you first obtained it?"

"Right."

"What kind of a gun is this?"

"This is one of those .22 Super Swift Magnums. It has about the same amount of load in it as a .30-.06 but the bullet travels three times as fast and when it hits the bullet explodes and flies apart. Bursts into a thousand little pieces. Blows the hell out of things."

"Watch your language there, mister. I am on the verge," the judge said. "I can be tipped over with one more word."

"I've seen ya tipsy before," Ace said. He threw the judge a big smile. Laughter.

"Will you please proceed?" Judge Hankins begged.

Hill had the clerk tag the rifle as an exhibit and offered it into evidence.

Mueller was on her feet. "I object," she said. "This exhibit has no relevance to this case. Moreover, it was taken from Mr. Jones in violation of his Fourth Amendment rights against unlawful searches and seizures."

"Well, isn't that interesting," Hill responded. "For the first time in my career I hear a prosecutor trying to protect a citizen's Fourth Amendment rights. But in this case she seeks to protects them in order to convict an innocent man."

"You can argue this later," the judge said, "But Mr. Jones is not a suspect in this case and therefore the proscription against unlawful searches and seizures is not applicable. Wouldn't that be true, Mr. Hill?"

"I think Mr. Jones is a suspect, so far as we are concerned," Hill said. "But if he's not a target for the state, then you're quite correct, Your Honor." Hill bowed slightly.

"Your objection is sustained, Ms. Mueller. I don't see the connection between this crime and this rifle. You haven't laid a sufficient foundation, Mr. Hill."

Hill had anticipated the judge's ruling and immediately called Dr. Billingsley to the stand.

"Have you seen this rifle before?" he asked the doctor.

"Yes. Ace Yokum asked me to do some experiments with it," the old doctor said.

"Did you?"

"Yes. I took it out and shot it. It is one sweet-shooting little Betsy. With that scope you can shoot the gonads off of a fly at a thousand yards."

Laughter.

The doctor turned to the judge. "Gonads is a proper medical term, Your Honor."

"I see," the judge replied.

"I shot some pumpkins I had stored in my basement and at three hundred yards they blew to smithereens—into a thousand little pieces."

"Move to have this testimony stricken as irrelevant," Mueller said.

"I'll hear it out of respect for Dr. Billingsley," the judge said. "I've known him a long time. He's testified in my court about a hundred times, haven't you, doc?"

"That's right, Your Honor. Then I shot a pig in the head at three hundred yards and it blew the whole back side of the pig's skull out."

"You shot a live pig?" Hill asked.

"Yeah. Farmer friend of mine was gonna butcher it anyway. And then I shot another one of his pigs, same size, with a .30-.30 up close, and even up close and with soft-point ammunition like was in Charlie Redtail's rifle, it left an exit hole about the size of my thumb. I bought that pig and took it to the locker plant for my private use." The doctor smiled up at the judge. "Shootin' a pig in the head doesn't hurt the bacon any."

"So from your experiments with this .22 Super Swift Magnum compared to the .30-.30 what are your conclusions?"

Mueller was on her feet. "I object to any conclusions by Dr. Billingsley concerning matters of ballistics. He has not been qualified as an expert in ballistics. He's a physician. He has no more expertise in ballistics than anyone else who shoots pigs and pumpkins."

"Sustained," the judge said. "You may step down, doctor. Give my regards to Mary Jane." Then the judge turned to Abner Hill. "Do you have any further witnesses?"

It was then Hill told the judge that he was unable to present any further witnesses that day for reasons he was not at liberty to share with the court and he asked to be given until the following morning to present the remainder of his case.

"Approach the bench," the judge said.

At the bench the judge asked Hill in a whisper, "Is the defendant taking the stand? I've always found it advisable for the defendant to testify, if you don't mind the advice. If you don't put Redtail on, the jury will think he's guilty or he'd testify. Any man charged with a crime that he didn't commit would demand to take the stand to clear himself," the judge whispered.

Ava Mueller was listening intently. She said nothing.

"Right," Hill whispered back, "and if Charlie takes the stand, the jurors will believe he's lying through his teeth to save his own guilty hide. And when a good cross-examiner like Ms. Mueller gets through with him every juror up there will be convinced he's lying even if he's desperately telling the truth in every detail."

"Have it your way," the judge said aloud.

That night they sat across the table from each other. She seemed distant. She poured his coffee and he stirred in the cream and sugar and looked into the swirl for something to say. They'd not been together much, Hill preoccupied with the trial, and although he'd missed the warmth of her body and the comfort of her presence and had given her words of encouragement in the hallway of the courthouse and at recesses, he'd not wanted to burden her with his worries.

Billy had been with her and he seemed to bring her comfort. As he saw it, they each had their burdens to carry. If he could only hold up his perhaps they could get through it.

Then she said, "I'm glad you came here tonight, Abner. I've missed you."

He nodded.

"A hundred times during the trial I've wanted to run up there and throw my arms around you and hold you. You look so alone." Then she said, "You're a very great lawyer."

"I don't know what to do," he said.

She got up and walked behind where he sat and put her arms around him and her cheek was against his. "I love you very much," she said. But Hill could not say the words back.

Then he heard himself saying what he had promised himself he'd never reveal to another person. "Mary, Russo has a witness. Name's Bill Jordan. He'll testify Emmett Jones killed Cotler. Working for the department of the army. Killed him because the army wanted Spirit Mountain for a base and Cotler wouldn't sell."

"Oh, my God, thank God!" She began to cry and she wept for a long time. When she had been able to gather herself, she said, "I knew somethin' would happen," she said. "I knew that dreams come true."

This was the time, he thought. The inevitable crossroads one comes to and nothing is the same after that. He could stand at the crossroads, say nothing, do nothing, but even refusing to decide which road to take, in refusing, he'd still have made a decision.

"I been dreamin', Abner, that when this is over maybe we could take a trip together."

Hill sat looking at the woman. She began to weep again softly as if the joy were too painful. Then she dried her eyes on her apron, and Hill, wanting to escape the place he was in, said, "Where would you like to go, Mary?"

"I was dreamin' we could go to San Francisco or someplace like that. I never been to San Francisco. I never been on a train."

"What would you like to do there?"

"In my dream, Charlie is free, and he's happy out there on the reservation with his woman and I am buyin' some little booties for their baby. Maybe it will be a boy. I dream, Abner, that it'll be a boy and he'll look like Charlie, and he'll be a very smart child and he'll call me Mimi. I don't want him to call me Grandma. I'm not old enough to be a grandma, do you think?"

"No," Hill said. "You are not old enough."

"And when we get to San Francisco, maybe we could get on one of those boats and take a little trip on the ocean. Just around the bay or somethin'. I never have seen the ocean. Billy wanted me to take a trip once. Sent me the money but I sent it back. It wasn't for me to take his money like that. I always been independent like that." She laid her head on Hill's shoulder, their chairs together, his coffee cold. Then she said, "With that Jordan witness maybe my dream'll come true. I always believed dreams could come true."

"Mary, I can't put the witness on," Hill said.

"Why?" She held on to her chest.

"Russo bought him. He's a paid perjurer." He let the words sink in.

"Well, they're tryin' to kill my boy with lies. Never could understand why ya can't tell a lie if they're tellin' lies."

"Two wrongs don't make a right, Mary."

The pain returned to her voice. "I know, but the wrongs aren't the same. Them killin' Charlie with lies is worse than our lyin' ta save him. Isn't that true, Abner?"

"Mary, the jury's supposed to decide. The jury heard my cross-examination of Jones. They have to decide if he's lying. It's our system."

"The system left my boys without a father. The system left my boys without justice. The system forgets folks like us."

"If I put perjury into the case you'd never respect me, Mary."

"What am I gonna think about you if you let 'em kill my boy?" she said. Her face was drawn, her eyes fierce. "The law is s'posed ta be just." She thought for a while and wiped her hands on her apron. Then she said, "Maybe you could go to the judge and tell him how they been lyin'."

"The judge wouldn't believe me. He'd say, 'Prove it.' I can't prove it."

"So if we don't put on this Jordan fella and if we stick to the truth on our side, we'll end up lettin' the truth kill Charlie. Truth can't stand up against lies," she said. She thought for a moment. Then she said, "If you saw somebody aiming a gun at Charlie, and they were about to pull the trigger, would you shoot the man if you had a gun in your hand?"

"Yes, I would," Hill said.

"Well, that's the way it is. They have a gun pointed at my boy with those lies. You have a gun in yours. You can save him."

"I never thought of it that way," Hill said, "but Charlie wouldn't want us to use lies to save him. He told me that from the beginning."

"How can you say it's up to Charlie?" she said. "If the man was about to shoot Charlie you wouldn't ask Charlie's permission to shoot the man, would you?"

"This is different," Hill said.

"How can you say it's different? It's life or death."

He saw the woman's pain, her fighting for any logic that might save her son, this woman he felt such things for that he could not say them, this mother of Charlie Redtail, this son who was not of the blood nor of the flesh.

"You know how I feel about you, Mary," he said softly.

"How do you feel?" she asked. Then she looked away.

"Mary, you didn't lie for your son when you were on the stand," he said. He saw the hurt in her eyes.

She began to cry again. "Wasn't smart enough," she said.

He put his arm around her but she pulled back from him. Finally Hill, speaking more to himself than to her, said, "I'm a lawyer. It's the ethics of my profession. If I put on perjury I'd be no lawyer anymore. I'd be nobody."

"You're somebody," she said. "Always have been ta me. But I never figgered you were one who'd let that ethics stuff kill an innocent man. Who ya gonna be when they take Charlie into the gas chamber?" She'd stopped her weeping. Instead she got up and poured him some fresh coffee.

"Mary, I got to weigh things," he said. "Got to see how things balance out."

Then she laughed a funny little laugh he'd never heard before. "They say these trials are for findin' the truth. The truth is that Charlie's innocent. Looks ta me like you can't get to the truth without a little lyin'."

33

When Hill got to his cabin he found the two men sitting in the car waiting for him, the motor running, the heater going. He climbed into the car.

"It's against everything I've been taught," Hill said to Russo.

"Got no choice," Hamilton said. "They're going to convict Charlie."

"It's a religion to me," Hill said. "Never have put on perjured testimony—never knowing it, anyway. Could have a lot of times. I've lost some cases on account of it. But I sleep at night."

"How well are you going to sleep when they pour the gas to Charlie?" Russo said.

"I been through this with you before," Hill said. "If every time you're afraid you're about to lose a case you put on lies, where would we be?"

"Ask Mueller that question," Hamilton said. "I want my brother saved. I don't give a shit how he's saved. Have you forgot who we were together? A family."

"Not quite a family," Hill said.

"Let's go through this one more time," Russo said. "You need to see where you're going. Charlie's in the gas chamber. They drop the pill—"

"I don't need to go through it again," Hill shouted. "I go through it every night in my dreams. But there's a whole road of appeals open to us before that happens."

"You haven't reserved any appealable error," Russo said. "Been asleep when you should have been talking and vice versa. When Charlie's gasping his last breath and looks out the window of the chamber and he sees you sitting there, you know what he says? He says, 'Thank God I had an honest lawyer.' Isn't that what he says, Hill?"

Silence in the car, the sound of the motor, the small vibrations through the seats from the running engine. Hill opened a window to let the cigarette smoke escape.

"I believe in juries," Hill said. "How could they trust Emmett Jones after Ace brought that gun into court and after Dr. Billingsley's testimony? And I'm gonna call the old man. Charlie has an absolute alibi." I can win without Jordan's testimony."

"You sure?" Hamilton asked. "You better be sure, Abner."

The windows were fogged inside the car.

"Nothin' is sure in a trial. Like throwing the dice at Las Vegas," Hill said. "But I have the dice in my hands. Looks to me like the odds are in my favor. Gotta play the odds but you gotta play it straight."

"They don't play it straight in Las Vegas—not for the big money," Hamilton said.

"You don't sound like the kid I knew a long time ago, Billy," Hill said.

"You never knew me, Abner," Hamilton said. "I won. Something about losing that repels me."

"What are you going to say after you rest your case and they call the girl?" Russo asked. "They're going to call the girl. You can bet your ass on that."

"Let's get to it," Hamilton said. "Either you agree to put Jordan's testimony on or we have to stop the trial."

"How are you going to stop the trial?" Hill asked.

"You don't want to know," Russo said.

No sleep for him that night, the ghouls screaming, their echoing voices like voices in the fever dreams of his childhood. He awoke sweating. He sat upright in bed.

For the moment he couldn't remember where he was and when he found himself in his bed, he sat there for a long time trying to chase out the sounds with the music of the river.

He tried to imagine himself a ripple in the river. The sounds made by the ripples were the same, but at each instant the sounds were different. He listened for a message from the river. The only message was that the river rolled on without a message. He lay back down on the bed and stared up at the ceiling.

After a while the sound of the ripples became the cold words escaping the lips of the blond man, Emmett.

"There is no right and no wrong in the universe," the ripples said and he saw Emmett laughing in his face. "Right and wrong are fictions of man," the ripples said. He sat up in bed again.

The questions were so profoundly simple. Is it right to save a man's life with the crime of perjury? No. He would not do it. But when judgment was passed upon him he heard the words of the judgment: "You cared more for the religion of the law than for the life of your woman and the life of Charlie Redtail."

And he heard the laughter. But it was only the sound of the river.

He listened like a lost child listening for the distant voice of his mother. He listened, his ears straining and then he heard the ripples say, "We find you guilty. You let an innocent man die when you knew you could save him. You are guilty of murder."

"I had no choice," he said aloud. "I'm bound to the system."

"You premeditated the killing." He put his hands to his ears but the words came even louder than before. "You knew that without a just lie Charlie would die."

"A *just* lie?"

"Lies that do justice are just lies," the voice said.

"Who lies the best. Is that what it's all about?"

"So it has always been."

"I am a lawyer. I've taken an oath to uphold the system."

"That was your first lie."

"I've tried to uphold my obligation to the system."

"Your obligation is to your innocent client. Not to the system."

He jumped out of bed and ran into the bathroom. He jerked the light cord above the mirror and peered into the glass. His eyes were swollen and wild. The lines along his cheeks had deepened and his hair stood on end.

"You are the murderer," the madman screamed.

"No, I am insane. I don't know the difference between right and wrong." He took comfort in the words. He felt saved in his insanity. Then he crawled back into his bed and pulled the covers over his head to block out the sound of the river. But still he heard the ripples and under the bedclothes they sounded even louder.

"Insanity is a legal fiction," the voice said. "The law is a fiction."

"I know."

"A fiction is a lie."

"I know."

"The law is a lie."

"I know."

"The lie of the law prohibits other lies to compete with the lies of the law."

"I know."

Then in the night he saw his mother and he wept for his mother, who had lived the life of a lie and had lived alone. And he wept for Charlie Redtail, who would die in the gas chamber. And he wept for himself, for his fragile shell that had burst.

In the bright light of day when the ghouls had faded into the morning light, Abner Hill walked up the steps to the courtroom. He walked mechanically like the mad walk down the long, gray walls of the asylums. When he walked through the foyer adjoining the courtroom he saw Simon Yellow Dog and Quinten See Hair standing there. He nodded to them.

"We come ta help ya," Yellow Dog said.

He walked into the courtroom and saw the old man sitting in the back row next to the bailiff and when the bailiff brought the court to order and the judge had taken the bench, Abner Hill had called Henry Old Deer to the stand.

"On the night of the murder did you see my client, Charlie Redtail?"

"Ya," he said. The old man wore the same cloths caked with dirt, the beaded vest. He looked the same except he had an eagle feather hanging from the braid down the back of his head.

"Where did you see them?"

"They was at my house."

"Where in your house?"

"There is only one place for them. Tha's where the dog sleeps. Ha," he laughed.

"What do you mean?"

"I mean the dog, he sleeps on the bed. An' when they come I kicked the old dog offa the bed and he was mad as hell."

"Watch your language," Judge Hankins warned.

"He was one mad son of a bitch," Henry Old Deer said.

"That is my second warning, Mr. Old Deer," the judge said.

"Well, I will ask you right to your face," Henry Old Deer said, looking up at the judge. "Ain't ever' male dog a son of a bitch?"

"And who took the dog's place?" Hill asked.

"Charlie and the girl. I turned out the lights."

"What do you mean?"

"Them two was in love. A man shouldn't keep the lights on all night when they is two people in love in the bed in the same room."

Laughter.

The judge's gavel.

"How do you know they were there all night?"

"I got ears."

"What did you hear?"

"Heard a lotta things."

"Like what?" Hill felt as if he were outside his body watching the lawyer ask questions.

"Like it ain't none a your business and it wasn't none a mine. It was their business. They was in love."

"Do you know if they were there all night?"

"'Course."

"Were they there in the morning when you got up?"

"Yeah. They was there. They was sleeping finally. They slept 'til 'bout ten in the morning."

"Did they leave during the night?"

"No. They didn't leave."

"You may examine," Hill said.

Ava Mueller walked quickly to the lectern.

"Do you remember when Mr. Miller, the undersheriff, came out to see you?"

"Right. I never liked the man."

"You refused to talk to him."

"This here is America."

"I know it's America, but you refused to tell him anything about that night, isn't that true?"

"Yeah. He lies a lot. Ever'body on the reservation knows that."

"Did Mr. Hill tell you not to talk to him?"

"No. Me, I got sense enough myself not ta talk to the man."

"Do you remember telling Arnold Blue Horse that you were glad that Mr. Cotler had been murdered?"

"Ever'body was glad. He was a no good sum'bitch."

The judge was silent.

"Besides," the old man continued, "Arnold Blue Horse is a Shoshone and ya can't believe nothin' them snakes says."

"And did you tell him that Charlie Redtail and his girlfriend were out all night the night of the murder, but that you were going to fix an alibi for them?"

"That there sounds like a white man's lie ta me. You ask Arnold Blue Horse if I said it."

"I shall," Mueller said.

"Ya can't believe nothin' them snakes says anyway," Henry Old Deer says.

"Can we believe you?"

"I never lie to the white man," he said. And when Hill said he had no more questions, the old man stepped down from the stand, his old bowed legs carrying him up the aisle to the courtroom door, the eagle feather in his braid marking each step. As he walked out the door he turned and said across the audience to Abner Hill, "I guess I told her." Then he walked on out the courtroom door.

At the noon recess Hill followed the deputies down to the jail with Charlie and he ate his sandwich in Charlie's cell. He sat next to Charlie on the bunk.

"The old man was telling the truth," Charlie said. He laughed. "He always told me to lie to the white man. He said they take the truth and turn it into lies. So he thought if you lied they would turn the lies back into the truth. He's very wise."

"Your friend Simon Yellow Dog is up there waiting to go on the stand. He wants to tell the jury he saw Miller running out from Cotler's place the night of the murder. Said he was carrying a shotgun. Said Miller and Cotler had been fighting over a white woman. I don't know if it's true or not," Hill said. "But Miller could have shot Cotler. Wouldn't bother him a bit. Doubt if he'd kill him over a woman though. But who knows? I've seen stranger things."

"Might be telling the truth," Charlie said. "But Simon'd lie if he thought it would help me."

"I think the old man sent him," Hill said. "But Doc Billingsley said the wound in Cotler's skull mighta been from a shotgun."

"Miller always carried a shotgun in his patrol car," Charlie said.

"Shall I put Simon on?"

"It's his right," Charlie said.

"What do you mean?"

"Man's own case doesn't belong to him. It belongs to those who care about him. Belongs to my mother, to the old man, to Simon. This case is their case, too. They have rights."

"Do they have a right to lie, Charlie?" Hill asked.

"Not if I know it," Charlie said. "Not if I could stop it."

*　　　*　　　*

After that, Simon Yellow Dog took the stand, his face as solemn as rocks. Like the old man, an eagle feather dangled from the braid. He folded his hands, his eyes on Hill as he approached the lectern.

"Your name is Simon Yellow Dog."

"Yeah," he said in the flat sound of the Arapahoe.

"You are a friend of Charlie Redtail?"

"Yeah."

"You have something you want to tell this jury?"

"Yeah," he said.

"All right, Mr. Yellow Dog, what is it you wish to say to the jury?"

"I had this dream," Simon Yellow Dog began.

"Objected to," Mueller said. "Dreams are not evidence."

"Sustained," the judge ruled.

"And this mare fell on me."

"This is irrelevant," Mueller said.

"Sustained. I don't want to hear anything more about your dream, Mr. Yellow Dog," the judge said.

"Them dreams is important," Simon said.

"They may be important, but they are not evidence," the judge said.

"Well, this white woman's hand came in where my head was. It was between the horse's hind legs. An' the hand pinched the mare and made the mare kick."

"Is that all you have to say?" the judge asked.

"No. I seen that Miller over there come runnin' from Cotler's house on that night an' he was carrying a shotgun."

"That's a goddamned lie," Miller hollered from behind Charlie Redtail.

"Order! Order!" the judge hollered, pounding his gavel. "Escort that man out of this courtroom!"

"I am in charge of security here, judge. You can't order me out."

"I order you to keep silent," the judge said. Then the judge turned to the witness. "Do you have anything more to say?"

"Yeah. I know that Charlie and his woman was at the old man's that night."

"How do you know that?" the judge asked.

"I object to the court conducting this examination," Mueller said.

"Overruled. Somebody has to do the yeoman chores here. How do you know that Charlie and his woman were at the old man's that night?" the judge asked.

"On accounta my brother Herbert tol' me and he was there."

"That's hearsay," Mueller said.

"Sustained," the judge said.

"An' that there is all I gotta say," Yellow Dog said.

Mueller stepped up to the lectern and began her cross with the simplest of questions.

"What time did you see Mr. Miller at the Cotler residence?"

" 'Bout half hour after closin' time."

"What time was closing time?"

"Two clock."

"Was his sheriff's car parked nearby?"

"Yeah. By the road there."

"How do you know it was a sheriff's car?"

"That light on the top. Black and white. Seen it. Says 'sheriff' on the side."

"Do you own a 1964 Chevrolet pickup truck?"

"Yeah."

"Where was that pickup at two-thirty in the morning on the night of this murder?"

"Was out there where I said. I drove it out there."

"Have you forgotten that your pickup was in the sheriff's custody at the time?"

"Wha' ya mean?"

"I mean it had been repossessed the day before. I have the sheriff's receipt here in my hand." She handed a paper to the witness. "Does this paper refresh your recollection?"

Simon Yellow Dog handed the paper back. "That there paper is lyin'," he said.

"I see," Mueller said.

"Were you drunk that night?"

"Nah."

"You were in the custody of the sheriff that night, right here in the jail downstairs, isn't that true?"

"Nah."

"I hand you a copy of the jail record to refresh your recollection. You were picked up on Main and Second Street on the afternoon before the murder by Officer Maxfield. You were arrested as drunk and thrown into the Fetterman County jail. Doesn't this record refresh your recollection?"

"That there record lies," he said.

"I see," Ava Mueller said. "I have no other questions."

Charlie Redtail whispered to Hill, "The cops never had him or his pickup. I saw his pickup at the old man's that night before Simon and Quinten left for town. Said they was goin' ta the Big Chief for a party. I told him not to go. But I guess he did."

Then Hill called Quinten See Hair to the stand.

See Hair swore that he was with Yellow Dog on the night in question, swore they were driving Yellow Dog's blue pickup and that Simon Yellow Dog was not in jail that night. He gave the same story concerning Undersheriff Miller—that they had seen him running from Cotler's house carrying a shotgun.

"Them papers lie," See Hair said of the jail record and the sheriff's repossession receipt. "They is always lyin' in the sheriff's office. I had 'em lie against me before," he said.

Mueller was ready. "Have you ever been convicted of a felony, Mr. See Hair?"

"Wha' ya mean?"

"I mean have you been in the state penitentiary?"

"Yeah."

"For what?"

"I got drunk one night and stole a car. Never kept it. Left it in the mornin' at the sheriff's office or they woulda never caught me."

"I see," she said. "But that was your first offense. You were convicted of car theft after that, weren't you?"

"Once," he said.

"I don't have anything more," she said.

On redirect Hill asked, "Mr. See Hair, the next morning you left that second stolen car at the sheriff's office, too, didn't you?"

"Yeah, or they never woulda caught me neither," See Hair said.

"You're a slow learner, I must say," Hill said.

Laughter.

"Are you telling the truth about seeing Miller at Cotler's house that night?"

"Yeah."

"Have you learned to lie?" Hill asked.

"Yeah."

"So how do we know you're not lying now?"

"I never lie to the white man," he said.

*　　　*　　　*

Judge Henry Hankins called the lawyers to the bench. "Kiwanis Club is having its annual eyeglass carnival this afternoon. I always act as the judge of a kangaroo court. Had plenty of experience, don't you think?" No smile. "You know, they bring people in from the street an' I order 'em hanged if they don't put up five dollars for the kid's eyeglasses. We got ourselves four hundred and fifty dollars last year at the carnival. So I'm going to order a recess here until nine in the morning."

Then the judge turned to the jury. "I will remind the jury that the Kiwanis Club is having its annual eyeglass carnival this afternoon," the judge said. "Invite all of you to attend." He smiled at the jury. Then whispering to Abner Hill at the bench he asked, "Are you going to call your client to testify?"

"Haven't made up my mind, Your Honor," Hill said.

"Well, heed the advise I've already given you," he said. "Do you have any other witnesses?"

"Don't know," Hill said.

Then Judge Henry Hankins fled the bench like an burglar in the dark of night.

34

That same afternoon Hill visited Charlie in his cell, the cell cold, the officers having returned him to his orange coveralls, his wool socks on his feet. Hill sat close to Charlie and talked quietly in his ear, not confident the cell hadn't been bugged.

"You understand there's considerable risk in putting you on the stand. The biggest risk, Charlie, is you," the man sitting on the edge of his bunk, listening like a small child.

Hill had watched the jury. He thought they saw him as honest, perhaps even marginally competent. He had hoped they would trust him. Indeed, he had never broken their trust except, perhaps, for the testimony of the Indian boys and even then he had sent a clear signal to beware. He had taken only a small part in the presentation of Yellow Dog's testimony. The judge had mostly done that for him. The same with Quinten See Hair.

His defense was not the powerful defense he had wished for, but the evidence taken together told the jury that someone else had murdered Cotler, that the killer had shot something other than a .30-.30, a more powerful gun, perhaps the .22 Super Swift Magnum of the blond man, or the shotgun of Miller. That was reasonable doubt. He had not been able to establish a motive for either Emmett Jones or Dean Miller, but motive is not a necessary element of murder, and he would ask the judge for an instruction to that effect.

Even though the jury might not believe the testimony of Yellow Dog and See Hair, their testimony sat there "like a turd on a wedding cake," as Judge Robert R. Rose of the Wyoming Supreme Court liked to say off the record. No evidence could remove the visual of Miller running from Cotler's house with a shotgun in his hand. And it was for the jury to decide if the sheriff had been fiddling with his own records that said

Yellow Dog was in jail on the night of the murder and that the sheriff had possession of his truck.

He had established an alibi for his client. The alibi was the truth. The old man's testimony was undisturbed except Henry Old Deer had a clear motive to lie. Hill had been able to undermine Emmett Jones's testimony but the jury might believe he was a government agent, a matter Hill could never disprove given the disposition of Judge Hankins to preserve the safety of government agents and the national security. More crimes, he thought, had been committed and gone unsolved in the name of national security than anyone knew. But in these backwoods there might be some on the jury who didn't trust the government, especially the ranchers.

Although Dr. Billingsley wasn't offered as an expert, nevertheless he left the jury with another visual: of pumpkins blown into little pieces with Emmett's gun and a pig with the entire back side of its skull blown away from the same weapon. Hardly sounded like Charlie's .30-.30.

Still Charlie's confession was the most dangerous part of the case. He turned again to Charlie Redtail.

"Charlie, what will Willow say when she's called to the stand?"

"She'll tell the truth," Charlie said. "But I don't want her to testify. I don't want them to put the twist on her."

"But she had to make a deal to get out of jail. And they've had her hidden for a long time."

"I know," he said. "But I talk to her every day."

"How?"

"We have our ways though the spirits. We always talk. That's why I never went crazy in here like a horse on locoweed." He laughed.

"What will you say if I call you to the stand?"

Charlie didn't answer.

Suddenly Hill stood up and walked around to face the man. "Most lawyers are afraid to put their clients on the stand because they're afraid they'll lie to save themselves. I'm afraid to put you on the stand for fear you'll lie to save Willow."

"Willow and the child come first," Charlie said. "It is the law of the Great Mother."

"What about Spirit Mountain. What about your ancestors, your father? The mountain is the hub of the tribe. If you're convicted the tribe will lose the mountain. You can lose the tribe as well, Charlie."

"If I lose Willow and the child I am worthless to the tribe. I cannot lead them in the fight for Spirit Mountain. It will all be lost anyway."

"How can Willow be in any jeopardy? She made a deal with them."

"Who knows?" he said. "They have their ways to destroy. It'd be better for me to confess this thing again. If I confess they will leave her alone."

"You won't let me put a witness on who lies. Yet you will lie? You will confess a crime you didn't commit?"

"The truth cannot serve the wrong master," Charlie said.

"You are not thinking clearly, Charlie. We have to think with our heads, not our hearts. Hearts don't think clearly."

"I trust the heart," Charlie said. "Sometimes the truth lies. But hearts do not lie."

"If I put you on the stand and you tell the truth, you'll tell the jury that you were with Willow at the old man's place. But Mueller will cross-examine you. She'll ask you all of the questions about how you saw your father kicked to death by Miller and Cotler. She'll ask questions about your lawsuit against Cotler when you were a boy and how you were cheated out of justice. She'll lean heavy on the time Cotler moved your mother out into the street because she wouldn't give him what he wanted."

Charlie nodded.

"If you tell the truth, you'll admit that you told your mother you were going to kill Cotler."

"Yes," Charlie said.

"Then Mueller will spend hours showing the jury what went on at Spirit Mountain. She'll have you tell how you counted coup with the others, how you were their leader and how you and the others threatened Cotler's life."

Hill peered out through the bars as if he could see into the courtroom from there. "Then she'll bring the gun over to you and get you to admit it's your gun. She'll say, 'This was your father's gun, wasn't it?' 'Yes,' you'll say. 'This gun has the spirit of your father on it, doesn't it?' she'll ask. 'Yes,' you'll say. 'This gun was the gun that killed Ronald Cotler in your attempt to preserve the spirit of your father on Spirit Mountain, isn't that so?' she'll ask. 'No,' you'll say. But the jury may believe the logical suggestion she has made.

" 'Willow was with you that night,' " she'll ask. 'Yes,' you'll say. 'And she drove your pickup that night?' 'No,' you'll say. 'She drove the getaway vehicle for you, isn't that true?' 'No,' you'll say again. Then she will say, 'You cut the man's finger off after he was dead, isn't that true?' And you will deny it. Then she'll ask, 'What did you do with the finger?' I will object, of course, but the jury will believe you know even after the judge sustains my objection.

"Even if you say only the truth, Mueller will convict you on your own testimony," Hill said.

Charlie laughed. "The truth tells great lies."

Hill began pacing the cell. "The jury has seen those pictures with your face all beat to hell. The jury can surmise the confession was beaten out of you." He thought for a long time.

Hill was about ready to leave when he told Charlie of the witness, Bill Jordan. Whether he should call the witness was a decision Charlie should make, Hill said.

"Is he telling the truth?" Charlie asked.

"I haven't asked him many questions," Hill said without answering him. "Let's assume for the moment he isn't, that your brother paid him. Mueller put Jones's lies on and Miller's, too. Jordan's testimony would even the score a little."

"Every man has to die sometime," Charlie said.

"Yes. It's too soon for you to die."

"A man must die with honor or his spirit will not live after him," Charlie said. "If I take the stand and confess, my lies for Willow and the child are lies with honor."

Hill didn't answer.

"My father, he died in honor. He was trying to save his friend, Jacob Yellow Dog. He died in honor."

Hill watched the man, his voice soft.

"I saw the deputies and that Cotler kick my father to death. I saw this and I have kept it in my heart. Never have I spoken of it to my mother, and never to my brother, who thinks he does the right thing. But he does not understand about honor. If I let a man lie for me who gets paid for his lies with the white man's money, there is no honor."

Hill asked, "Would you rather die?"

"I do not wish to die. But if I live because a man lied for me for the white man's money my spirit would not live and I could not join my father."

"This case belongs to all of us," Hill said. "You've said that yourself. Think about your mother. This case belongs to her, too. If you die she'll die."

"I've thought on that much. But a mother cannot have honor when her son is without honor and a mother without honor is no mother at all."

"She would rather have a son without honor than no son at all. I know that much about your mother," Hill said.

"That is the way of all mothers," Charlie said. "But a son who loves his mother would save her such a fate."

"What's right and what's wrong are ideas created by man," Hill said.

"I do not believe in that way," Charlie said. "I was taught by my father, Joseph Redtail, and by the old man, Henry Old Deer, that the Great Spirit is of the universe and that we are of the Great Spirit and the Great Spirit is not evil."

Then before Hill left he said he'd look into the truthfulness of Jordan's testimony and if he believed Jordan was lying he promised Charlie Redtail he would not call the man to testify. That was Hill's solemn promise.

Hill built a fire and heard the river rippling by, the sound of the pine logs snapping at the flames. He put on a pot of coffee and opened a can of Campbell's tomato soup. Made him think of his mother on a cold winter's night, soup and some hot chocolate, and to bed in the thick covers. He tried to outline his case again, to see it emerging from the writing on his yellow legal pad, but the words seemed disconnected and the conclusion was in his heart, and he could not trust his heart.

In bed he was helpless to sort it out. Again he lay on his back looking at the ceiling, his hands folded on his chest. He thought that was how he'd one day lie for eternity or at least until his bones rotted to dust. He unfolded his hands and turned on his side, but he couldn't sleep. Then he got up, dressed, and drove to Mary Hamilton's place. It was nine o'clock. Her lights were out. He knocked on the door and when she turned on the light and opened the door he walked directly to the kitchen table without speaking. Soon she poured the coffee from the pot.

"Can't sleep," he said.

"Couldn't either." She was in the long, terry cloth robe and the slippers Billy had bought her one Christmas when he was a boy.

Finally Hill said, "Charlie doesn't want me to put on any testimony that's false, Mary. I promised him I wouldn't."

"He was always this way," she said. "Him not lettin' us put on Jordan's testimony is like suicide. If you see somebody who wants to commit suicide do you let 'em?"

"He says it will ruin his spirit so he can't join his father."

"We gotta save him, Abner." Then she thought for a minute. "Do you know for sure Jordan's lyin'?"

"Yes, I know. Billy hollered at me that I'd already cost him twenty-five thousand dollars for the preacher he'd bribed—the one I kicked off the jury. He said, 'Now I suppose you're going to waste another fifty grand. That's what these good witnesses cost nowadays.' That's what he said to me, Mary."

"They fought sometimes. But down deep Billy always did love his brother," Mary said.

The testimony of Yellow Dog and See Hair on one hand and this Bill Jordan on the other were inconsistent. Jordan would say that Emmett killed Cotler, while the Indian boys claimed Miller had.

Perhaps he should leave it to the jury to sort out the perjury. Jurors had the nearly magical ability to recognize the lie—nothing logical, nothing they could put a finger on, but a sense of it that came out of primordial places. The human was the only creature on earth that could lie. Detecting the lie provided the species with the biological advantage of saving itself from the dangers of deceit. That's why juries were trusted to find the truth.

Yet the sense of the lie that the juror could feel when assaulted with the lie could never penetrate the shield of prejudice. "Prejudice trumped truth," Russo had said. He was right. The jurors would believe Emmett. The jurors, burdened with prejudice, would not believe Simon Yellow Dog. The choice between the perjurers was clear. If they believed Emmett he could call Bill Jordan to the stand.

Yet, Hill thought, the law provided honest tools to deal with perjury. The law provided the most powerful weapon in the courtroom— cross-examination, the right to test the testimony of the opponent. But, as Russo said, prejudice always trumped truth.

When he returned home Hill again found the two men waiting at his cabin, Russo at the wheel, Hamilton in the passenger seat. Hamilton was the first to speak.

"We can't put this off any longer, Abner. Timing is the first rule of business. This is business. I got money invested in that project. I got money invested in this case. We are going to lose this case. No one is going to believe those fucking Indians."

"Right," Russo said. "Mueller scalped 'em up."

"I don't think so," Hill said.

"You see this testimony through your own prejudice. You're an Indian lover," Russo said. "The jury has a different prejudice. The jury knows they're lying."

"No time left to argue about it," Hamilton said. "Jordan goes on or we stop this trial."

"You can't stop the trial," Hill said.

"You don't think so?" Hamilton said. "That lying bitch of a prosecutor. The trial can't go on without her."

Hill looked at Hamilton in disbelief.

"Jordan is ready," Hamilton said.

"This isn't you, Billy."

"The boy you knew never let his brother down. The boy you knew never let them touch a hair on his brother's head. The trial is going to stop or Mueller is going!"

"You never said that. I never heard it," Hill said.

"What's the matter with you, Abner. She deserves to go," Hamilton said. "She's trying to kill an innocent man. That's murder. This is self-defense."

"I promised Charlie I wouldn't put on any testimony that I knew was not the truth."

"You lied," Russo said. "Everybody lies."

"You can lie to Charlie after it's all over. He'll never know," Hamilton said.

"I'll know," Hill said, his mind racing. Then he heard himself say, "Everybody'll think Mueller was killed by the Indians."

"Exactly," Hamilton said. "After that I shouldn't have much trouble out there with those renegades."

When the court was called to order the next morning the judge turned to Abner Hill.

"Call your next witness, Mr. Hill."

It was then that Abner Hill announced to himself and to the world the course he had chosen. As he got up from counsel table he heard the sound of the river in his ears. The sound of the ripples had turned to the roar of the rapids and he shouted over them, "Defense calls William J. Jordan."

"Is he going to tell the truth?" Charlie asked as Jordan strolled easily to the witness chair.

Hill nodded without looking at his client.

The man took the stand and settled into it as if it were his throne.

"Your name?"

"William J. Jordan. I live in Chicago."

"What do you do?"

"Various things. Mostly, I'm retired. I was a special agent for the department of the army until I resigned. I buy and sell antique firearms. Make a few dollars. My hobby as well. I'm an expert in ballistics. Worked in this field for the army about twenty years." The man spoke in a stiff way but he seemed to have a solemn believability about him, the way he answered the questions, not volunteering too much, but enough so that his testimony came to the ears in the right way.

"Tested firearms?"

"Yes, many. All of the major calibers."

"Tested the .22 caliber Super Swift Magnum?"

"Yes, the army gave this weapon a good deal of consideration. Some thought the weapon, light as it was, would be ideal for ground troops on arduous expeditions. Its single flaw was that it could explode without much penetration. For example, it might hit a twig and because of its enormous speed it might explode."

"What would happen if it hit a human skull?"

"Likely blow the entire side of the skull off. There was a great deal of resistance by NATO against the rifle—humane arguments and the like. The decision eventually went against it, although with the proper optics it is the most accurate weapon on earth."

"Do you happen to know a man by the name of Emmett Jones?"

"I know him, of course. He goes under a number of names: Hollister Franklin, Herman Grieder, Hans Lockhart, Robert Henderson, to name a few."

"How did you happen to know him?"

"We worked together as special agents for the department."

"What, in addition to ballistics, were your duties?" Hill asked.

"We did undercover work."

"Did you and Mr. Jones do work for the army in Fetterman County?"

"Yes. We were to obtain title to what is known as Spirit Mountain. The army had plans to put a base there. Perfectly situated inland for a strategic training operation. Isolated. Hard to get to. Up high with good visibility all around. Virtually impossible to approach without being detected."

"Did you know Mr. Ronald Cotler?"

"Oh, yes. I knew him very well. Emmett and I spent many an evening with him trying to acquire the property for the army. We offered him more than a million dollars. He turned it down."

"Do you know why?"

"Said he could make twenty times that amount with his development. The army wasn't budgeted to meet his demands. We were instructed to accomplish our mission in any way possible."

"What do you mean by that?" Hill asked.

"I mean, frankly, we had full discretion to do what we saw fit to obtain title to this property for the army."

"What did you do?"

"I did nothing. Emmett—he was going by Hollister Franklin at the time—said he was going to put his .22 Super Swift Magnum to work. He liked to shoot things. Killed cats, dogs, anything that moved—people. He would brag about it. He said he could buy the property from Cotler's estate for its appraised value, which would be a lot less than a million. I told him he'd have to do it without me. I was ready to retire. Twenty years in that business was long enough for me. I took retirement. Then one day I read in the *Denver Post* about Cotler's murder."

"Thank you," Hill said turning to go to his table.

"One other thing," Jordan offered. "He told me he had something worked out with Dean Miller from the sheriff's office. They seemed to be good friends."

"Did he say what it was that he and Miller were doing?"

"Said Miller would back him up. But Emmett was like that. He made little deals with people. Always covered his tracks. Never knew him to even get arrested."

"Thank you," Hill said. He walked back to his table without looking at Ava Mueller. "You may examine," he said.

She asked for a recess. William Jordan was a surprise witness, Mueller argued to the judge. "Frankly, I think he's a perjurer and I intend to prove it, Your Honor. This just goes to show you what money can buy in a case like this. They spread that money around, and you know Billy Redtail has plenty of it, and they bring in these false witnesses!" She was pacing back and forth in front of the judge in his chambers, Hill sitting quietly by.

"Is this perjured testimony Mr. Hill?" the judge asked.

"Why would you ask that, Your Honor?" Hill asked back. "You made no such inquiry of Ms. Mueller when she put Emmett Jones on the stand."

"I'll admit Jordan's testimony sounded pretty good to me," the judge said. Then the judge granted Mueller's motion for a recess until the next morning when Jordan again took the stand and comfortably sat down as if he were about to carry on a conversation with an old acquaintance.

Mueller was beginning to show fatigue, the puffy dark under the eyes, the face slack. Been up all night, Hill thought. So had he. As he watched her approach the lectern he suddenly felt tight in the belly. He wished he'd never put the man on the stand. If she could convince the jury that this was perjured testimony Charlie was on his way to the gas chamber. Juries had no tolerance for murderers who lied to cover their crimes. More men were executed for lying about the murders they committed than for the murders themselves. It was too late.

Mueller approached the lectern, a large pile of notes in her hand.

"When did you retire from the department of the army, Mr. Jordan?"

"Little over two years ago."

"Who was your immediate superior?"

"Someone who called himself Jade."

"Jade?"

"Yes. We had code names at that time."

"Would it surprise you to know that the army has no records of your service?"

"Wouldn't surprise me in the slightest."

"How do you get your retirement check?"

"It's sent to my box number made out 'payable to bearer.'"

"What was your code name in the department?"

"It varied from time to time. I was known as Panda. I was known as Tulip Blossom. I raise tulips. I was also known as John Wayne. No likeness, as you can see." He smiled like a bashful boy at the jurors and several women smiled back.

She was searching through her notes for her next question when the witness interrupted her shuffling. "May I ask you a question, Ms. Mueller?" Before she could answer he said, "Did you try to find out if Mr. Emmett Jones had any records in the department? Didn't you discover that he, too, was a 'missing person,' as we secret agents liked to call ourselves?"

She was obviously taken aback. Finally she said, "Is William Jordan your correct name?"

"Of course," he said, giving her a quick smile. "It's as correct as Emmett Jones's was correct for him. Perhaps you could find something under his favorite code name—the Snake."

"What's your legal name?" she said.

"William Jordan," he said. He pulled out his driver's license and flashed it to the Mexican herder sitting closest to the witness chair.

She turned from the witness, grabbed her papers, and headed back to her table. "That will be all," she said.

Then Judge Hankins called both lawyers to the bench. "You mean you have no more witnesses?" the judge whispered to Hill.

"Yes, Your Honor."

"You mean you're not going to put your client on the stand?"

"That's right, Your Honor."

"Why not?" the judge asked, confounded.

"My client says he doesn't wish to take part in the white man's game."

"Very well, Mr. Hill. But I think you're making a serious mistake."

When he arrived at his cabin the same car was waiting for him in his parking place. Hamilton and Russo seemed happy to see him, friendly even. Hamilton was in a good mood. "You did well today, Abner. You were the kind of lawyer I've always thought you could be. Your examination of Jordan was superb."

"I agree," Russo said. "Congratulations! Jesus Christ, did you hear that bullshit about Panda and John Wayne and the Snake? The son of a bitch knew how to talk to the women—likes to raise tulips, for Christ's sake? You can see why this bastard cost fifty grand. He's good. And the nice thing about him is he just disappears. It'll take seven of our operatives to find him again.

"And," Hamilton added, "you are a hero. You saved not only Charlie Redtail, but you saved Ava Mueller as well."

Hill got out of the car and stood watching as they drove off. Who was he? What kind of a soulless bastard? Where he had hesitated to put on perjury to save Charlie Redtail, he had willingly put it on to save Ava Mueller? And he cared nothing for the woman. Then he stood there for a long time listening to the river, the ripples, the river flowing without answers.

35

"We are prepared to proceed with our rebuttal," Ava Mueller announced coolly, as if she were traipsing above the combat in the courtroom. "We have but one witness. We call Elizabeth Hodges."

The jurors turned to see the woman as she walked to the witness stand, a slight sideways waddle in her late pregnancy. She wore a blue maternity smock of plain cotton material and a white blouse with a large round collar.

Abner Hill thought her face looked swollen. Her blond hair was neatly braided and in a bun at the back of her head in the same style that his mother had worn hers. When she took the stand she glanced nervously over at Charlie Redtail, whose eyes were alight but troubled and whose mouth was tight as if sealed. She gave the man a small, nervous smile and before they could speak further in such manner, Ava Mueller asked the first question.

"You are Elizabeth Hodges."

"Yes." Her voice was far off.

"Some in these parts call you Willow?"

"Yes, that's the name my people have given me."

"And who are your people?"

"The Arapahoe people."

"Have you agreed to testify in this case in exchange for immunity?" The question sounded harmless enough, the jurors' faces calm in response.

"Yes."

"Will you tell us the truth?"

"Yes."

"Are you acquainted with Charlie Redtail, the defendant?"

"Yes."

"How did you come to know him?"

"We worked together in his cause for Spirit Mountain."

"I see you are expecting a child."

"Yes."

"Did Mr. Redtail have anything to do with that?"

"Yes, he's the father."

"Have you ever been married to Mr. Redtail?"

"No." She stared down at her knees, her lap filled with her pregnancy. She glanced over at Charlie again. He was gazing at her, his eyes focused on her like the red-tail hawk, but the eyes were not of the hawk but of the man and the man began to tremble. She saw the trembling and she began to weep, sobbing softly into her hands. He started to get up, but the deputy behind him pushed down on his shoulders with both hands.

"Are you familiar with the activities of Mr. Redtail leading to the protests against the Spirit Mountain Project?"

"Yes," she whispered, the jurors straining to hear her.

"Why did he engage in this unlawful activity?"

"He believed that the mountain was holy."

"Do you believe that?"

"Yes," she said.

Mueller looked at her for a long time as if in disbelief. Then she said, "You must have come to that conclusion of late?"

"No. I have always believed it holy."

"Where have you been in the past months?"

"In a place you sent me to in Minneapolis. I've been a prisoner there since this occurred."

"Aren't you aware that we sent you there for your protection and at your request?"

"I needed no protection. I needed to be with my man." She began to weep again.

Mueller stopped for the moment, surprised. She cleared her throat and looked at a paper she held in her possession. She lifted the paper and began to read from it. Then thinking better she said, "Well, Ms. Hodges, let's get to this as quickly and painlessly as possible. Were you with Mr. Redtail the day of the murder?"

"Yes."

"Were you with him all day?"

"Yes."

"Were you with him the night of the murder?"

"Yes."

"What did the two of you do that night?"

"We went to the old man's house where we stayed all night. His name is Henry Old Deer."

Mueller took the woman in with hard eyes. "This is not what you told us before. Perhaps I should refresh your recollection. I know this has been a very difficult time for you. Didn't you tell us that you'd been at the Cotler residence with Charlie Redtail at about two-thirty in the morning of the murder?"

"I don't remember."

Mueller was pale. Her words came slowly as if she couldn't bring up the next question. Finally she said, "Here, read this and see if it doesn't refresh your recollection."

Willow took the paper and read it swiftly. "I don't remember reading anything. You just told me to sign it. I signed it."

"You signed it because it is true, Ms. Hodges, isn't that correct?"

"No. I signed it because our child would have died in your jail. I was bleeding. I needed medical attention. You said if I would sign the paper you would help me save the child."

"Have you forgotten, Ms. Hodges, that you signed this confession before Dean Miller and the court reporter who was taking all of this testimony down the same as we speak here today?"

"I did what you told me. And you did what you said you would do. You got me to a doctor and our child was saved."

"The bargain you made was to tell the truth."

"Yes, I told you I would tell the truth, and I *am* telling the truth."

"But your confession states that you were the driver of the pickup truck following the murder of Ronald Cotler by Charles Redtail and your statement is under oath."

"Yes," she said. "I lied, but I did not intend to lie. I did not read the paper. You remember, I'm sure. I was so cold. I was losing blood. And you said just to sign it and that you would take me to a doctor. You were very kind. And that is what I did and that is what you did."

"I see. So you recant this statement?"

"I didn't make it of my own free will," she said. "I made it to save our child."

"You were with Mr. Redtail when he killed Cotler that night, weren't you?"

"No. That's a lie."

Then Mueller's lips pulled thin and her eyes as well, and she said, "Ms. Hodges, you would do anything and say anything to save the father of your child, isn't that true?"

Willow's eyes grew very large as she realized the truth borne of the question. She cleared her throat as if to speak and then held back. Finally she said, "Yes, I would lie to save Charlie, but I'm not lying."

Mueller moved toward the witness a few steps. "You would lie about murder to save him, wouldn't you?"

Willow grabbed the arms of the witness chair as if to hold on to her life. Then she said, "I might lie about murder. I might. But I don't have to lie. You made me lie," she said. "I lied to save our baby."

"You would lie to save yourself, wouldn't you?"

"Maybe," she said looking down but still holding on. "Wouldn't you?" Charlie was struggling to get up, but the deputies, one on each side of him, had their hands pressing hard on his shoulders, holding him in his chair.

"So we know we have a liar among us," Ava Mueller said. "All we have to determine is when she is lying, indeed, if she has ever told the truth here; wouldn't you say that about sums it up, Ms. Hodges?"

Hill was on his feet. "This has gone far enough, Your Honor. I object to this line of questioning as being argumentative. She's impeaching her own witness."

"Well, we have to sort this out," the judge said. "Overruled."

"So how can we tell when you are lying and when you are not?" Mueller said.

Silence.

"Do you give us certain clues we can look for? Do you hold your mouth in a certain way or refuse to look us in the eyes or what?"

"I haven't lied, except in that paper. You made me lie in the paper."

"Let us see what we can agree on: You are in love with this man charged with murder."

"Yes. But he's innocent."

"You were with him the night of the murder?"

"Yes. But—"

"And you would lie to save him," Mueller said, as if to cap off her argument.

It was then that Charlie Redtail stood up, the deputies hanging on his shoulders and around his neck like small children. Charlie Redtail spoke in a strong straight voice. "Leave the woman alone. She speaks the truth. You white men do not know the truth when you hear it, because you do not want to hear the truth." As he spoke the deputies were on him, four of them, and still he stood there, the old bailiff toddling down as if to assist, the judge pounding his gavel and screaming, "Order! Order!" and in the pandemonium the jurors, not sure whether the man would break loose, had risen from their seats.

Over it all the voice of Charlie Redtail could be heard: "You do not seek the truth! You are the killers!"

"Order! Order! Remove that man from this courtroom," the judge shouted. "And you sit down, Mr. Hill. Unhand that deputy this minute."

Willow took a hesitant step from the witness stand and as soon as she felt the floor under her feet she ran for Charlie Redtail and threw herself into his arms, the deputies wrestling Charlie, the deputies helpless to stop her. He shook them off and then he held her close to him, Dean Miller hitting Charlie over the head with his sap and, although his knees buckled, he held onto the sobbing woman. Then, while he held her Miller put a choke hold on Charlie with a nightstick and still Charlie held her. Another deputy put the shackles on him and finally two deputies grabbed hold of one of his arms, pulled it from around the woman, and at last they had the cuffs on him.

Then Miller dragged Willow back to the witness stand, but before she sat down Ava Mueller, as if nothing had occurred in the interim, said, "No further questions."

Abner Hill rose to question Willow but Charlie, still in cuffs and shackles, said aloud: "Leave her be, Abner. She's been hurt enough," and after Hill sat down Dean Miller pulled the woman up the courtroom aisle toward the exit. She was weeping and holding back, looking back at Charlie Redtail, and as Miller dragged her through the door of the courtroom she cried out, "I will take care of our child, Charlie," she said through the weeping. "I promise you, Charlie. I will take care of our child."

Then, still as if nothing had happened, Mueller called Dean Miller back to the stand. He calmly testified that he'd been present during the entire transaction between Ava Mueller and Elizabeth "Willow" Hodges and that the Hodges woman read the confession carefully, changed a word or two in it—he pointed to her initials over two crossed-out words on the document. "She wasn't forced ta do nothin'," he said. "She said she wanted ta get the thing offa her chest. It was awful what

Charlie done, especially cuttin' off the dead man's finger like that, an' that she was glad to help the law." Then Ava Mueller abruptly announced that the state rested its case.

Three hours and twenty-three minutes later the bailiff advised the court that the jury had reached a verdict.

The courtroom had filled again with the spectators, the halls were filled, the overflow sitting on the stairs. Surely they hadn't reached a verdict of guilty so soon, so easily. Hill had seen the jury march in and he had hope. They must have decided for Charlie. Yes, he thought, some at first were afraid to look at him, but he saw as they marched in that others glanced at him and they seemed happy enough. And happy jurors meant an acquittal. His heart was pounding, the fast beat in his ears. He could not breathe. He sat down as the spectators took their seats at the judge's command. Then he had seen the foreman, Harold Yeckersly, a farmer from the irrigation project, rise from the back row, the verdict in his hand and, in response to the judge's inquiry, announce in a proud voice that the jury had reached a verdict.

Hill had argued the case out of his heart, not his head. He had argued that the evidence was not complete, that it could not be believed, that reasonable doubt marched through the case from beginning to end. That was the function of reasonable doubt—to warn the jurors they were about to convict an innocent man.

"Who can prove oneself innocent?" Hill had asked the jurors. "Don't you recall as a child being accused of something and you were innocent? Don't you remember that you were helpless to convince your parents you were innocent, that the more you protested your innocence, the more guilty you seemed? Yes, did not Shakespeare tell us, 'The lady doth protest too much me thinks'?"

He had not argued the testimony of Simon Yellow Dog. He mentioned only in passing the testimony of the Old Man of Much Medicine. He was an old man, too old and too wise to lie, Hill said. Surely they had seen the truth in his eyes and heard the love of justice in his voice. And Charlie's confession—how could that be believed? Hadn't the jury seen the love of the man for his woman, his willingness to lay it all down for her and she for him? Neither of the confessions were the truth. His confession was his gift of love to Willow and hers the gift back and for their child.

The truth lay in the belly of the Snake he had argued, the Snake and his rifle that could blow out the side of a man's head. The truth was that

Charlie Redtail's .30-.30 was incapable of the damage they had seen. It was Emmett Jones's rifle fulfilling whatever motive he had for the killing.

He, Abner Hill, had become a criminal trying to save one wrongly charged of a crime, he had said to himself. He was the only criminal at the defense table. But he had not argued Jordan's testimony as he had argued the other facts of the case. The fruits of the perjury had to stop somewhere—his relying on the perjury, his arguing it, his demanding an acquittal based on it. It was as if, having introduced the disease into the body of the case, it was his duty to stop its spreading. So he had not argued the testimony of William Jordan.

Worse, Charlie had believed that Jordan's testimony was truthful. He had whispered to Hill when he came back to the table, "I knew there was something strange going on there. Now I know." He seemed relieved. And Hill's lie to Charlie laid heavy. Still he'd finally concluded he must commit the crime to prevent the greater crime. He had to commit the crime to save the lives of Charlie Redtail and the woman who was bent on killing him, Ava Mueller. And having committed the crime, win or lose, it would rot in his heart.

Hill heard the clerk reading the verdict. He read the entire caption of the case, even the case number, the reading consuming an eternity, Hill's breath not coming, his hand squeezing at the arm of Charlie Redtail, the man relaxed and as unimpassioned as the wooden Indian. At the end of the eon the clerk had finally gotten to the words, "We the jury find the defendant, Charlie Redtail, *guilty* as charged." Hill fell to his chair and could not get to his feet again.

He did not hear the shouting and clapping of hands from the spectators, the happy, excited people congratulating one another as if the case had been their own. He had struggled to his feet to say something to Charlie before the deputies dragged Charlie off, and as they did, the prisoner's chains rattling, Charlie Redtail looked at his lawyer, and said, "It was good, Abner," and the big man had laid his hand on Hill's shoulder, his eyes soft, and then they had taken him away.

Struggling through the crowd he had tried to reach Mary Hamilton before she had been hurried from the courtroom by Billy and Russo. He'd wanted to take her into his arms and soak up her tears, but he had been unable to reach her. He fell into a front pew, too grieved, too wounded in the heart, like the sword that pierces the heart but the victim does not yet know he is dead.

Then he drove to her house. She was alone, having told Billy she wanted to be left alone. They sat at the table, she at her end, he at his. She was silent, drowning in the deep underwaters of her grief.

"How could they have done that?" she finally asked. He could barely hear her voice. "I thought Willow done 'em a lotta damage. I figgered they'd turn Charlie loose for sure after she got done with 'em."

"They thought she was lying to save her man," Hill said as if talking to himself.

"How could they?" Mary said, staring at Abner Hill at the other end of the table, waiting a long time for his answer.

And around the table in the jury room, the rancher Jim Buford had said, "I wished I had me a woman who'd fight for me like that." He laughed.

"Yeah," the telephone lineman, name of Sam Nance, said. "If I had me a woman like that I could get away with murder myself." He laughed, too. "Like the prosecutor said, that Hodges woman would do anythin' for her man."

"Well, I woulda done the same thing," Jane Pickering, the housewife, said. "I thought the woman was very brave. I hope they don't prosecute her for lying."

"We could put that on the bottom of our verdict here," Nance said. "Just as a recommendation, you know."

"Right," Jane Pickering said, and with the consent of all she had written the words in her precise hand, "We recommend that the Hodges woman not be prosecuted for anything."

"That should do it," Sam Nance had said.

Then after the body of the verdict had been read by the clerk and Abner Hill had heard the single terrible word, *Guilty*, the word that could extinguish the life of Charlie Redtail and that would irrevocably change the lives of the innocent, the clerk had come on to the handwritten words of Mrs. Pickering and the clerk hesitated. He walked up to the judge and asked the judge if he should read the words at the bottom of the form and the judge nodded. Then the clerk read the words aloud and the people hearing the words concerning Willow had shouted their approval, the judge, of course, pounding for order.

*　　　*　　　*

The two of them sitting in her kitchen were silent for a long time. He'd thought the woman would surely cry and that he would go to her end of the table and hold her. But she didn't cry. Seemed as if she was like the twisted sage on the prairie in the dead of winter, alive but dead in the cold, alive but no moisture in the brittle stems, no tears, the bones brittle, the eyes dried and sunken.

She said, "Charlie shoulda testified. They woulda believed Charlie."

"At the last he refused to take the stand, Mary."

"He should have," she said. "Charlie tells the truth and people know when other people are tellin' the truth."

"Right," Hill said softly without anger, "that's why the jury believed Dean Miller and Emmett Jones. That's why they didn't believe Willow. Prejudiced people believe what they need to believe."

Around the table in the jury room the wife of the Basque sheep man, Holly Barbeenela, had said, "I wish they woulda put that Indian on the stand. Like ta hear what he had to say. Hidin' behind a woman like that. Coward, I say."

"Yeah," Harold Yeckersly, the foreman said. "Hope we can get this over with afore too long. I got chores ta do."

"He didn't have to testify according to the Constitution, and the judge told us to make nothing of it," Jane Pickering said from the other end of the jury table.

"That is just lawyer talk," Jim Buford said. "But I will say that a man might not want to testify if he wasn't good at talkin'. Now that breed might not been too good at talkin'."

"He's good at talkin' all right," Sam Nance said. "He's the leader out there. I say we got a clear duty to put a stop to all of that horsing around."

"What about that other Indin, that Yellow Dog?"

"He's just 'nother a those war-whoops out there," Harmon Watson said. "They'll say anythin' to save one of their own."

The wind had begun to blow and the glass rattled in the window. Mary Hamilton pulled down the shade on the south-facing window and after the shade was pulled it flared out with the gusts. She went back to the kitchen table and wearily fell into her chair. "I never did understand about guns," she said. "I told Charlie he shouldn't carry that gun around, that it would jus' get him inta trouble. But it was Joseph's gun and he liked to have it with him," she said.

Hill said, "Charlie's gun never killed Cotler. They should have at least believed Doc Billingsley."

Around the jury table in the jury room Jim Buford said, "I got me one a those .22 Super Swift Magnums myself. Shoot prairie dogs with it. An' I'll tell ya one thing: When ya hit one of 'em they plum disintegrate."

"Ever shoot one with a .30-.30 from ten yards out?" Harold Yeckersly asked.

"No."

"Wouldn't be much left of him if ya did," Yeckersly said. "Remember. The killer went up ta the body and cut off the little finger. What else did he do? Maybe done somethin' to the skull while he was up there. Maybe cleaned things up."

At the kitchen table Mary Hamilton said, "I don't know how they could believe that Emmett Jones, 'specially after Bill Jordan talked to 'em. He was the best witness in the trial." She began to sob quietly to herself. Hill could hear the clock ticking on the shelf next to the stove, the wind still rattling the window on the south. He wanted to go to her, but he couldn't think of the words. He started to get up, but had slumped down again in his own exhaustion.

Around the table in the jury room Jane Pickering sat up very straight. "I don't know," she said. "Seemed a little strange to me that the defense just happened to find that Jordan fella hanging around someplace. I had a strange feeling about him. Too smooth or something. I didn't trust him."

Then José Sanchez spoke up, the Mexican American herder having sat silently by himself at the far end of the table, his eyes very large, his mouth slack. "He was lyin'," José said.

"How ya know?" Bill Hammer said.

Sanchez seemed too timid to say it. "He couldn' been in the army twenty years."

"How do you know that?" Yeckersly asked again.

"That driver's license. He was born the same year as me. Seen it on his license. Make me fifteen years ol' if I was in that armys twenty years."

"You saw his driver's license?" Jane Pickering asked.

"Yeah. He stick it in my face. Pay no 'tention ta me."

"An' that means just one thing," Yeckersly said. "If he was lyin', Red-tail done it."

The jury was silent for a long time. Finally Jane Pickering said, "What about Jones? He gave me the creeps."

"Well, I don't think Ava Mueller would put on false testimony," Martha Romney said. "I've known her since she was a little girl. Know her father."

"I know her, too," Sam Nance said. "But just to be sure I say we cross Jones out and we cross out that Jordan fella and we sure cross out Yella Dog."

"Gotta cross out the girl, too," Bill Hammer said.

"Yeah, an' the old man. He's jus' another A-rap tryin' ta save another Indin," Yeckersly said.

"So what we got left after we cross all of 'em off?" Nance asked.

"We got our common sense," Yeckersly said. "When ya get rid a all the liars what ya got is an Indin. The Indin had the best reason ta kill him. They was all out there tryin' to screw up that project. An' he confessed ta the killin'. An' then ya got the mutilation. Indin's like ta do that. We all know that. Besides, look what Cotler did to Redtail's mother."

At the kitchen table Mary said, "I don' know how they could do what they did." She put her face into her hands. "There was reasonable doubt all over the place."

"I thought so, too," Hill said, but his mind was blank and that was all he could say. He was slumped in his chair, the life emptied, the heart gone, the head lost in a white storm of bewilderment. He could think no longer. Yet he heard himself saying, "We have to stop thinking about this, Mary. Tomorrow we have to save Charlie's life. The death penalty phase of the case starts at nine." The words sounded strange in his ears. He hadn't planned this phase of the case. He hadn't been able to make himself believe the case would ever come to this.

Finally Hill had said to Mary, "I never did one of these death penalty hearings before. I guess I'm going to call you to testify about how he was as a boy, all about how his father was killed and all. And I'm going to put the old man back on. The jury liked the old man. And I'm going to pray for the first time since I was a little boy. I don't know what else to do. God help us if this jury is a killin' jury." Then he was sorry that he had said it. Too tired, he thought, to edit his words. "We'll be all right," he said, but his voice was without conviction.

He'd gotten the strength to walk around to her side of the table and she had wearily pulled herself up. She stood limp in his arms. He tried to hold her close and she did not resist. He said, "I'm so sorry," but the tears had gone from him as well.

She saw his eyes, the wound in them. She said, "It wasn't your fault, Abner. You did all you could do."

Then he had gone home to face the demons that invaded his cabin, that swarmed in his bedroom through the night, that yowled and laughed and argued. In the morning, after the endless night without sleep, he had trudged to the courtroom, his mission to save Charlie Redtail from the gas chamber.

36

"I feel sorry for any mother who has to go through somethin' like that," Jane Pickering had said to the other jurors gathered in the jury room to determine the fate of Charlie Redtail. They sat around a long oak table, one at which countless juries had gathered before. Round coffee stains marred its surface and some juror in times past had carved the word *justice* into the oak, the word having turned brown with the inlaid scum of the years.

"I don't like this duty myself," Sam Nance said. "Never figgered on having to decide the life or death of a man. I woulda found some excuse to get off if I'da thought it was gonna come ta this."

"Well, it ain't just one of us who is doin' it. It's all of us, if ya can take any comfort in that," Bill Hammer said. "And we swore to do our duty here. I don't like it any better than anybody else."

"I couldn't help but feel sorry for the mother," Jane Pickering said again. "I don't know how she can stand it."

"Well, maybe she shoulda thought about that before now," Harold Yeckersly said. "I will tell ya one thing: I wouldn't a let no kid a mine hang out with those Indins on the rez. Ya reap what ya sow, the good book says."

"What about his girlfriend? How about her? She is gonna have a hell of a hard time when they pull the plug on him or whatever they do," Jim Jessep, another rancher, said.

"Well, we took care of her pretty good," Jane Pickering said. "At least they may leave her alone to raise the kid. That's about all we can do, isn't it?"

"I will say one thing. The prosecutor had it right when she said we had the duty to put an end to this killin'," Yeckersly said. " 'Bout the only way I can see to do it is to let them A-raps out there know that if they are gonna kill they get killed. It's that simple, as far as I can see it."

"If we don't do somethin' they'll be killing one of us. Ya heard about John Oakley's wife. And they found those Indian beads in her and all. That was nothing more and nothing less than a goddamned threat to the rest of us, and I, for one, am not about to be threatened," Nance said.

"Me neither," Yeckersly said. "I said to Helen last night, 'I am gonna see that they don't kill any more juror's wives.' I said, 'I am gonna put a goddamned stop to that bullshit once and for all!'"

"But there isn't any evidence that Redtail had anything to do with the Oakley killing," Jane Pickering said. "How can we put him to death for something we aren't sure he did?"

"Gotta use a little common sense," Yeckersly said. "That's what jurors are for."

"Well, if we send him to the gas chamber aren't those Indians gonna look us up for revenge? I don't know if I can sleep again," Jane Pickering said.

"We all gotta do our duty. If we let 'em intimidate us we are done for. They take over," Yeckersly said. "I say if we don't do our duty here those Indins'll think they can get away with this. We gotta nip 'er in the bud 'fore it gets outta hand."

"I was having second thoughts last night," Holly Barbeenela said. "I said to Leonard, 'What if that Lawyer Hill was right and that reasonable doubt is tellin' us we are about to convict an innocent man?' An' I was wishin' I could take my vote back. But after hearin' his mother I am convinced he did it all right. She told how her boy had seen his father kicked to death by Cotler and those deputies and if anything struck me it was that. Once a boy sees that, the poison just grows until he can't help himself."

"Are you saying that we shouldn't give him the death penalty?" Jim Buford asked. He came forward on his chair, the sound of the front legs hitting the wooden floor making a loud clap.

"Well, I don't think he could help it."

"You wait 'til one of them redskins comes sneakin' up to your house some night and blows off your husban's head," Buford said. "Or maybe one of 'em will come in while he's gone and rape you like they done John's wife and stick a knife in ya when he's through. Then tell me what that breed could or couldn't help."

"I say once they got that blood in 'em you can't never tell," Sam Nance said.

"We aren't supposed to be prejudiced," Jane Pickering said.

"Who's prejudiced?" Nance said. "We were sworn to find the truth and I'm jus' tellin' it the way it is."

"But what about the judge saying we were to weigh the mitigating factors?" the Pickering woman said.

"What mitigating factors? Nance asked. "Like how he waited in ambush for his victim? Like one of his buddies went up and raped the hell outta John's wife, killed her, and stuffed those beads in her to scare us? Like how he cut off the finger of the dead? Mutilating dead bodies is about the worst thing a man can do."

"The Oakley killing isn't in this case," Maude Miller, the secretary for the water district, said. "We are not supposed to consider that. And I don't think it's as bad to cut up a dead body as it is to cut up a live one, as far as that goes."

"I thought that Indian's lawyer Hill done a good job pleading for his client's life. Cried an' all. All for the same money, too," Buford said.

"We are supposed to be weighing the mitigating circumstances against the aggravating circumstances," the Pickering woman said.

"Pretty aggravatin' ta me that they called us here in the first place," Nance said. "Ever'body knows the breed done it. Who else coulda? If there was anybody else that lawyer woulda been all over it like bees on honey."

"Well, I don't know much about the law. I suppose if we are making any mistakes here that the judge can correct 'em. An' they got all a those appeals," Martha Romney said. "I hear it takes 'bout ten years for the appeals to get over. If we do somethin' wrong they'll give him another chance, I suppose."

"I say we vote on this and quit this yow-yowing," Yeckersly said. "I gotta get home and do the chores. An' stretchin' out the misery don't make it go away."

After that the jury had voted, and on the first ballot they agreed that Charlie Redtail, a citizen of Fetterman County, Wyoming, should be put to death in accordance with the laws of the state.

37

Charlie asked that she not come to see him in the prison. It was hard on her, he said. "I know you care and I know you know I'm innocent. That's all that's important. Comin' up here just tears you up, Mom. You shouldn't come anymore."

"How can you say that, Charlie?" she said. "I'm your mother." He was led in cuffs and shackles by two guards to "the visitor's room," as they called it—a space no larger than a closet without windows, the concrete ceiling and walls, the floor also of concrete. "The box," the prisoners called it. She followed, and when the steel door clanged shut she embraced him and held on to him until he finally pulled her away. But she no longer wept when she saw him. He could see she had aged. Her hair black and straight had begun to turn gray and her once smooth skin began to wrinkle like the skin of a pumpkin after it had stood in the window too long.

His own cell was a six-by-seven cubicle without natural light. In the hallway where the guards walked by looking in on those in the small cages waiting to die, the light was on day and night and when he slept, the same light was on as when he was awake. But for the fact that in the summer it was devilish hot and in the winter cold, he could not distinguish the passing of the seasons. For eight years he had not eaten a meal with another human being. For eight years he had waited for the appeals to end, not with any anticipation of relief, but with a detached amusement as to what the white man would do to ensure his execution, maintaining at all cost the appearance of justice.

Billy, of course, had hired appellate specialists. These lawyers claimed that Charlie had not been properly represented, that basic due process guaranteed by the Constitution had not been afforded. "Incompetence of counsel" had been the assertion of the appellate lawyers. Among other charges they alleged that Hill had been incompetent for having failed to demand a mistrial when the wife of the juror John Oakley had been murdered under circumstances that must have intimidated the jury. In addition to a plethora of technical arguments, the lawyers argued it had been gross incompetence in a case suffering from such a paucity of viable defenses not to call the defendant himself to the stand.

The state had switched sides. The Wyoming attorney general had appeared for the prosecution, now extolling the virtues of Abner Hill's representation of Charlie, pointing lavishly to his masterful cross-examination, and holding him up as the paragon of criminal defense attorneys. The attorney general pointed to the affidavit of Ava Mueller, asserting that although the motion did not appear of record, on the morning the murder of Katy Oakley was announced, both Mueller and Hill, in a meeting in chambers, had asked the judge to order a mistrial in the case. The appellate court was swift to dispose of the lawyers' arguments.

"No lawyer should be judged because his decisions concerning trial strategy are placed in question with twenty-twenty hindsight," the presiding judge, Justice William J. Moore of the Supreme Court of Wyoming, ruled. "Redtail had competent counsel. His lawyer had refused to call the defendant to testify, doubtless a matter of strategy. He was provided a jury of his peers, an impartial trial judge that afforded him every opportunity to fully defend himself, in short, he enjoyed the due process guaranteed every citizen under the Constitution."

But how could any judge who had never seen the witnesses, who had never looked into the eyes of Charlie Redtail's mother, who had never seen the unfathomable pain of Willow, who had never witnessed the blatant lies of Dean Miller and Emmett Jones, how could any judge who had not measured the nearly genetic prejudice of the community against Native Americans do more than don his deadly black robe, occupy an easy seat on that high bench, and, as the old man, Henry Old Deer, had often said, "just fart in the wind"?

The judges had never walked through the prisons, never dirtied the soles of their feet on the grime that clung to the concrete floors. The judges, above it, had been placed there by God to peer down from their safe, antiseptic places. They did not want to deliver justice, Charlie said. Were they of the mind to deliver justice, the power of it might open the prison doors to the poor, for the poor occupied most of the prisons' cells. If the justices wanted to deliver justice, especially to the poor, they had all the power they needed to do so. If the justices cared, with all that inimitable intellect, with all that incomparable power, they could have easily discovered the roots of crime, which, Charlie argued, was the punishment of the innocent who were born into the dredges of prejudice and poverty. He argued that criminals only acted out in ways they'd been trained by the system—to strike back, to take back, to hate back. He argued mostly to himself.

In his years in prison, Charlie Redtail had read much and he thought it a humorous irony that he should educate himself only to be put to death. But life was an irony. A paradox. One lived, one learned, and at the peak of one's knowledge, one died. It should be the other way around, he thought. Indeed, it was the other way around. The child was born with all knowledge and it became one's life's work to discover the knowledge born within.

He read the books in the prison library, those on philosophy and politics. History books and books on sociology. He had learned that what most called knowledge was argument. Even the scientists couldn't agree on most things. The politicians and religious writers were bent by their politics and their religions and could not give straight answers.

But the man was not bitter. He was the prairie dog in the hole and he resented neither the hole nor the coyote sniffing at its entrance, sniffing and digging, the coyote after the prairie dog. The coyote was not evil. The coyote was merely the coyote, also trapped in the system. And the judges were merely the snobbish minions of the system who spoke of justice as if it were something unattached to living persons, a pedantic exercise unconnected to the first pain of the people.

He tried to explain it in a kind way to his mother so she would be prepared for his inevitable rejection by the judges. But she would not hear of it and he could not find the words she could understand.

"We are gonna win, Charlie," Mary had said, and sometimes the way she said it made Charlie believe it. "You will see," she promised. And she smiled to herself, because deep in her heart she knew that the judges would see. They were smarter than she and if she knew of Charlie's innocence, surely one of them would discover it as well.

After he was led back to his cell in cuffs and shackles and he heard the prison door slam shut, steel on steel, his mother now on the outside, Charlie fell into his own arguments again: If the judges sought justice, they would convict the system, not the victims of the system. They did not want justice. They wanted to worship old cases and old rules. They would rather cover injustice with long words in their pedagogical opinions than uncover injustice in plain English. When all of the high rhetoric had settled, the justices were no different from the rest of the people from whom they had been chosen. They were good citizens, all right. But in places they never visited in their hearts there was something there that yearned to kill.

The judges were no different than the jurors, Charlie thought. The death penalty, killing without responsibility, was a gift to all who hated, to all who were angry, to all who feared, to all who suffered twisted psyches, to all who did not care because no one had ever cared for them. It was the gift to all who could not love.

Charlie Redtail had expected the decisions of the courts that one after another denied his appeals. Instead, he had hoped that the appeals would be over with sooner. As he saw it they only prolonged the misery of his family. No hope had existed from the start. And hope, unwed to reality, brought pain. Hope had set Willow up for bitter disappointment after disappointment when Charlie's appeals were turned down, first in the state courts and then in the federal courts. Every time an appeals court rejected the arguments of his lawyers, his mother died once more. No, hope was not their friend. Hope, where none existed, was their enemy. Better, he thought, that they come to an acceptance of his execution. An honest acceptance of one's fate, he argued, is better and less painful than a false clinging to hope. Where there is no hope, hope kills.

The appeals were mere window dressing to make the system look good. Yet occasionally someone escaped—usually the rich. Even so those few who escaped kept hope alive so that the lawyers could point to the cases where innocent men were set free. Without hope there would be no jobs for either the judges or the lawyers.

The death penalty, Charlie thought, was an inhuman process created by humans, a process in which the killing was made easy and no one bore responsibility. All the jurors had to do was to say the word *guilty* and someone died. The word killed. The sheriff's officers, the witnesses, the prosecutors, the judges, the jurors, the lawyers, none could be individually charged with his death. The system was like a mob. No one in the mob could be singled out for having struck the death blow and no one in the mob, therefore, need take the direct blame. But mothers did not understand such things. Mothers were of life. Mothers were of the heart. Mothers were not in the head and Mary, his mother, did not understand.

He had thought of calling off the appeals that followed one after another like a long, painful train, appeals that Billy had paid for. Billy had hired the elite of the profession, the New York lawyers from the large firms who said they knew the right people, lawyers who had clerked for the federal appeals court judges sitting on Charlie's case, lawyers who knew the judges like a son knows his father. Billy paid the lawyers' large fees and the lawyers cited the endless cases and precedents that would save Charlie Redtail.

The lawyers talked in elevated language about such things as the sociological impact of the case on a society that had always been insensitive to the struggle of the "American aborigine," and they spoke about civil rights, about the disparagement of minorities, and they employed other brittle words that, when the didactic smoke cleared, left the Arapahoe people worse off than before, because they would learn by the judges' decisions once and for all that the inorganic system, not the people, was king, that it would always be king, and that the people could never walk up and yell into the face of the king and survive.

Mary had begged Charlie not to give up and Willow had begged him, if not for her, then for their son's sake, who would be eight years old by the date then set for the execution. The boy had the coal black hair of his father and the brown eyes of his mother. In the end Charlie had understood, as he had always understood, that his case did not belong to him. It belonged to all the others whose lives would be more affected by it than his. And for that reason he had not ordered the appeals withdrawn.

At the same time he knew that his case also belonged to the state. The state needed to prove to the people that the system was just, that even an Indian had a fair chance at justice and could take his case to the great and erudite who occupied the highest courts of the land. The state needed the opportunity to display the trappings of justice so that the people would not lose faith in the system, for so long as the people had faith in the system, those in power could remain in power. That had been the argument of Charlie Redtail to the last.

38

The execution was set at Rawlins, Wyoming, for one minute past midnight on June 29th, a Friday. Gala preparations preceded the event, especially at the site of the penitentiary's gas chamber, which had seen no use since James Jefferson Bradford had been put to death twenty-three years before. He had murdered a bank president in the town of Wheatland, a murder committed in the act of robbery. The execution had been an event widely celebrated in Wyoming, and Governor William U. Sorensen, a staunch opponent of the death penalty, had failed to recognize how deeply anchored the support for the death penalty was with the citizens. But his opponent, "Plain Bill" Williamson knew. Williamson had gone around the state claiming that Sorensen was soft on crime and that he coddled murderers. "How can the people of this great state trust the likes of a man who wants to save killers? I say we save the citizens," Williamson had shouted up and down the state.

The people had voted their beliefs—that the death penalty stopped murder, that it was just, and Sorensen was defeated for reelection. Victims had rights, too, they argued. Besides that, as Vincent Rathborn, the physical education teacher at Wheatland High argued, "It's cheaper to kill the bastards than to keep 'em around for life."

The warden had ordered that the gas chamber be carefully checked for leaks. It was old and rusted in places and in some places the welds had failed, especially around the single square window through which the gathered witnesses could observe the prisoner suffering in his last throes. The rubber fittings around the door were also suspect and were replaced to assure the safety of those on the outside of the chamber who had come to witness the official business of the state.

The workers replaced the motor on the clearing fan and afterward tested it by locking the door and smoking their cigarettes in the chamber until their eyes watered and they began to cough. Then they turned on the fan and timed how long it took to empty the room of visual smoke.

The phone company installed a private line to the official's booth, a small, enclosed room with a glass window facing the chamber. The phone was white but the warden had it painted red. The warden, with a clear view of the chair, would sit next to the red phone, the phone at his right hand so he could capture any last-minute reprieve from the governor. There were seats for the assistant warden and for representatives from the offices of both the governor and attorney general. Below the officials' booth and to the right of the window the workers had brought in folding chairs for the media from the prisoners' rec room. Although there was no rule set by law, these seats were limited to twelve, passes for which the warden issued to those members of the media who, in the past, had shown no overt enmity toward his administration.

To the left of the window were twenty-five other seats in three rows, reserved for the families of both the original victim and the family of the victim in waiting, Charlie Redtail, and for designated representatives of the several organizations whose members attended such functions as either a celebration of justice or a rebirth of barbarism. The witness gallery had received a fresh white paint job applied by those prison inmates who were trusted beyond their cells so that, all in all, the witnesses in attendance would come bearing a good impression of the prison's administration—a neat, clean, well-run place.

The local paper, the *Rawlins Sun*, put out a special "execution night edition" and sold advertising to the merchants who sponsored it, the edition providing a four-page history of all recorded executions at the penitentiary since 1893, the first execution having been held the year after the penitentiary had been built. In those days the state hanged its victims, not in the traditional style of the public gallows, but by a small, wayward device that sat over in the corner of the prison yard. According to the *Sun*, the machine was ordered abandoned by the state legislature when, on at least three occasions, it had proved unreliable, the last being the state's attempt to hang Big Joe Bailey, who was hanged multiple times before they were able to break his neck—the exact number of attempts having never been recorded.

After what was referred to as "the Bailey bungle" the legislature begrudgingly admitted that the gallows, although traditional in the West, was cruel and unusual punishment and adopted what they thought was the more humane method of exterminating the state's enemies, the gas chamber, then also in vogue in eleven other states.

Five new security guards had been hired for the week of the execution and the parking lot was enlarged to hold the expected influx of people, some to protest, some to jeer at the protesters, and some to simply take in the gala affair, which was more entertaining than the Rawlins Fourth of July Rodeo. Some of the Rawlins townspeople joked that they could double the town's revenues if they were to hold such executions more often.

In the meantime the warden had cleaned out a cell about ten feet by ten feet at the far end of the death row cells. It would serve as the place where Charlie could receive his last-day visitors. In that room, for the first time in his eight years in Rawlins, Wyoming, Charlie Redtail could see out the barred windows into the prison yard and beyond to the rolling, empty hills of sagebrush that extended undisturbed from Rawlins north to Fetterman County and to Spirit Mountain.

39

"It was my fault, Tony," Hamilton said. They were sailing on Hamilton's yacht fifteen miles off shore on a southeasterly course from New York to Bermuda. The two women, "pretty patties," as Russo called them, the ones with the long yellow hair, were up on top sun bathing, earning the brown bellies that looked good in those open midriffs, navels puckered like the tiny mouths of babes. Russo and Hamilton were drinking in the cabin below.

Before they sailed Russo said to Hamilton, "One thing more you could do: Send a bag full of money to Governor Ava Mueller. She's running for reelection," and after that Russo had dispatched a lawyer from his office with a hundred thousand dollars in bills, the lawyer to work out the details of how the money should be divided between Mueller and the party, the funds earmarked for Mueller's campaign.

"Just see she gets the money," Russo told the lawyer. "She'll get the message. She'll find a way to commute."

The following week Russo had wired the governor his request to commute Charlie's sentence, a well-conceived document that spoke in an eloquent way to provide the governor the language she could use in the commutation. Russo had hired Jonathan Steward Lurch, the famed speechwriter for three presidents, to write the body of the document. Mueller could commute, Russo told Lurch, not because she'd been wrong in her prosecution, which she would never admit, nor because she was against the death penalty, which she was not, but because the death of Charlie Redtail would bring irrevocable unrest between the tribe and the people of Fetterman County. In part the petition read:

After considering the consequences of putting Charlie Redtail to death, after weighing the possible disruption of the peace and beneficial interchange between the people of this state and our Arapahoe neighbors and friends, we believe Wyoming will not be a better state because we have put to death one of our Native American neighbors. Enmity between neighbors must cease, and you, the governor, have the power to take the first brave step toward that end. As much as we know you are dedicated to the inherent justice of capital punishment, we believe you will see that wisdom and mercy in this case will best be served if you commute Charlie Redtail's sentence to life without parole.

"She doesn't have to come up with a damn word of her own," Russo said. "The greatest speechwriter in America has done it for her. All she had to do is substitute the word *we* with *I*. Her commutation will be seen as brilliant," Russo said. "The money's in the bag, the milk of human kindness is in her heart, the interest of the people her deepest concern— she's got no choice but to grant the petition."

They were silent for a while, the sound of the yacht's engines a soft blur against the waves lightly washing against the hull, the sailing easy, but not the hearts of the men.

"It was my fault," Hamilton said again.

"Bill," Russo said to Hamilton, "you are full of shit." He laughed and poured Hamilton another scotch. "You did everything you could. Bought the best lawyers in the business, the best witness in the business." He laughed again. "You bought me and even tried to buy the jury. You gave the kid the best money could buy. What more could you have done?"

"I should have known better than to touch Spirit Mountain in the first place. The spirits got back at me," Hamilton said.

"Sure, Bill. Have another drink." Russo poured again.

"Cotler was from the world below."

"You going off the deep end?"

"I killed him all right. He was dead before any bullet hit him. Killed him in the deal. Busted Cotler. I let him curl up and die on the vine. He was begging for money. The people in the town were eating him alive. I was playing with him, watching it, enjoying it. I ended up owning his bar, his house, his old man's pawn shop. I owned all of him. I killed him and if I hadn't kept him in front of the deal this wouldn't have happened."

"All your fault, right? He could have broke you instead of you breaking him."

"But Charlie was in the way. My own brother, for Christ's sake. He and those renegade friends of his."

Then Russo said, "Cotler was an asshole."

"I liked seeing the bastard burn. But when he ends up dead they came after Charlie. Never saw that coming."

"Nobody did."

"I always hoped the kid was innocent. Always told myself he was," Hamilton said.

"Cotler had a lot of enemies."

"But sometimes I wonder if Charlie didn't do it," Hamilton said. "Had every reason to. Probably would have killed him myself if I were in Charlie's shoes."

"Cotler was a sick son of a bitch."

"Maybe just once Charlie succumbed to being human," Hamilton said. "He was always a notch above it. But it's human to kill your father's killer."

"Hill mighta saved Charlie's life if he'd made that argument," Russo said. "It's also human to kill somebody who's shittin' all over a holy place."

Hamilton stared at Russo for a long time. "Maybe Charlie did do it."

"Maybe," Russo said.

"After the trial Willow told me how Cotler and Miller and that little pimp Longley I sent out there as a prospect had messed with her in the sheriff's car."

Russo asked, "Did she tell Charlie about it?"

"She said she shouldn't have, but she did."

Russo nodded and took another drink, swallowed, and wrinkled his face.

"I asked her how she knew Charlie didn't do it and she said 'Because I was with him and because murder isn't in him.' That's the way she put it. I said, 'Bullshit. Murder's in us all.'" Hamilton was having trouble with his words. "I told her I'd thought of murdering Cotler myself. I said, 'Charlie and I have the same blood in us.' 'Yes,' Willow says, 'you and Charlie have the same blood in you, but not the same spirit.'"

Hamilton emptied his glass.

They were quiet for a long time. "I think it *was* Charlie," Hamilton finally said. "Always thought there was a certain credibility in the state's case. What advantage was there for Mueller to put in false testimony?"

"Politics, maybe," Russo said.

"We paid the best lawyers in America to review the record twenty times. How could all of the judges in all of the courts, both state and federal, be wrong? If Charlie was innocent wouldn't some hint of it come through to some judge over these last eight years?"

"Can't judge it by that. The fuckers don't read the record," Russo said.

"I think Charlie did it," Hamilton said. "Never wanted to say it, but I think he did it."

On the Tuesday before the execution William R. Hamilton had flown to Cheyenne to personally talk to the governor. He'd rehearsed the scene many times. As he sat in her office he followed his script perfectly. When they were seated across from each other in the governor's office and after they had exchanged old memories, and laughed, Hamilton finally got to it.

"We provided you with a well-drafted petition for commutation. Did you know that Jonathan Steward Lurch wrote it? It's a perfect way out for you. You'll look better than if you let him die. If you execute Charlie those renegades will be all over Spirit Mountain for the next fifty years. Lot more wars. More killing. I never will get the project completed and the businesspeople in Twin Buttes will be the losers. Commutation in this case is good for business. The people in Twin Buttes will appreciate you for it."

"I'll think about this," she said. "Billy, you know this lays heavy on me. We've known each other a long time." Then she got up and shook his hand, the firm handshake of the politician, friendly, confident, and true.

As he walked down the hall toward the exit he suddenly felt deep panic. Ava Mueller was about to kill his brother. And when she killed Charlie she would kill him. He had the money. He could buy the whole fucking state of Wyoming. He turned and ran back to the governor's office and rushed in past the secretary, Mueller still sitting at her desk.

"I almost forgot something important," Hamilton said.

"What is it, Billy?" She sounded like his third grade teacher.

"I was wanting to contribute a couple million to your favorite project, I think it's the Girl Scouts. You could make a camp for them up in the Twin Butte range. I know just the place."

"That would be very generous of you, Billy. And I will consider your petition for Charlie. I know it means a lot to you. And it lays heavy on me as well," she said again. Then she smiled and shook his hand again.

40

Ava Mueller was the featured speaker at the annual dinner dance of the Cheyenne Chamber of Commerce. It was a semiformal affair, the men in business suits, there being no tuxedo rental in the town, and the ladies in long dresses. The women wore corsages, mostly of white and red carnations, a few roses. The people danced to the music of George Burrows and the Burrows Boys, a bass sax, a piano, drums, and an accordion played by George himself. They played the old music, the kind the people liked to dance to, and the management of the Plains Hotel lowered the lights at midnight. By then most of the people were tipsy from the booze and the music.

At the edge of the dance floor stood a blond man. He wasn't a tall man, but his thin, muscular build provided an appearance of size and importance that was deceiving. He was wearing a black business suit with pinstripes and black, round-toed cowboy boots. He made no effort to dance or to converse with anyone. Several people had noticed him, but none seemed to know him and none had approached him the entire evening.

Ava Mueller, the inveterate politician, had come unescorted to the function. She saw the man and when the lights had been turned down by the management she had walked over to him. She had been dancing with various citizens who had asked her to dance when their wives had excused themselves to go to the powder room.

She held out her hand to the blond man. "I'm Ava Mueller," she said. She was wearing a long, red dress with a high top and a string of small pearls. She wore no corsage. "Are you enjoying the party?"

"I find it amusing, governor," he said.

"I find it so myself," she said. "I would rather read a good book. But we all have our duties."

"Yes," he said. "We all have our duties."

"And what are yours?" She said it in a light, teasing way, the two of them standing next to the wall under the head of a mounted buffalo, fifty years of dust on its beard. He had never taken his eyes off the woman and that had made her only slightly nervous, this man standing there without his hands in his pockets as men do, not looking down, no self-conscious smile pasted to the face, no fawning, as the people did in her presence, the state's famous governor, the only female governor in America.

"I follow the dictates of the universe," he said.

"Well, well," she said, a good-natured mocking. "And what is the universe dictating to you today?" She laughed. She thought she should excuse herself and with that certain grace she'd developed, move on as had become her facile way to cover an entire crowd in an evening. But she hesitated long enough to hear his answer.

"It appears that I have some business with you," he said, the words without lightness.

She wished she had not said it. "And what would that be?" the man's eyes affixed to her.

He took a small step toward her. Then stopped. "You know what my business is," he said.

She started to leave, but he was still looking at her with the strange, blue eyes imposing, but the eyes not betraying the man. At that moment she felt the shiver. Then the man turned from her and walked into the bar. She stood there for a moment. For reasons she could not think of she followed him in.

"I beg your pardon," she said, "but I didn't get your name." The bartender was at the far end of the bar mixing the drinks for the waitress, who was holding out her tray in front of a tired face. "Have I met you before? I apologize but I meet so many people nowadays."

"The name's Jones," he said. "As you know I go by several other names, but Jones will do for tonight."

"I'm sure if I had met you before I wouldn't have forgotten. You would not be an easy person to forget. You may take that as a compliment," and she laughed lightly.

He ordered her a drink. Vodka and soda. He ordered one for himself.

"And what did you say your business was?"

"Same as it always has been," he said. "Sometimes I work out of Calgary selling encyclopedias."

She stood looking at the man for a long time. Then she sat down on a bar stool.

"Here's to your health," he said, lifting his glass.

Her hand around her glass, the glass still on the bar, she said, "Why have you come?"

"My duty to the universe, you know." He laughed but it was not a laugh. "The Indian will be executed tomorrow?"

"Yes, of course. After midnight unless I stop it." She stared at him.

"I came to tell you. I shot Ronald Cotler." He watched her face turn ashen. He watched her pull back from him as if his breath were poison. He smiled at her and gave her a long, low bow. "Governor," he said. He turned and walked out, leaving Ava Mueller sitting alone at the bar, his drink untouched. Then he stepped out into the night, the stars, black holes, and a half-moon shining.

For eight years William R. Hamilton had hired a full-time crew of seven operatives to locate Emmett Jones. They had access to the records of the FBI and the CIA. They had probed deeply into army intelligence. The man had disappeared.

In the morning Ava Mueller went to her office as usual, at the same hour of 8:30, as usual, dressed in her gray business suit as usual. She opened the mail as she usually did and made two piles: one requiring her personal reply and one her secretary could answer for her. Then as usual she saw the first person on her calendar for the day. After she had spoken with William R. Hamilton she scratched some quick notes on a pad and shoved the pad in her desk when her secretary entered. The secretary bore a small, brown envelope. "A blond man was here," she said. "He asked me to give you this. Said he thought you would be 'amused' by it."

The governor took the envelope from the woman and opened it. She saw something in its bottom and carefully dumped the contents on the desk's blotter. The thing appeared to be a small, dried-up fingertip, the nail still clearly visible. Also fallen on the desktop were three small turquoise beads, the kind that had been taken from the body of Katy Oakley, and the kind—she suddenly remembered in horror— Jones had previously left with Mueller during the trial just before he had taken the stand to testify. She picked up the envelope and peered in. There remained a small piece of paper inside. She pulled the paper out. It was the driver's license of Ronald Cotler.

She had lain awake that night, gotten up to look out the window and locked it. The brown envelope was on the dresser. She folded it and stuffed it in the toe of a shoe in the closet, the black pair of high-heeled pumps next to her riding boots. She looked out the window again. The sky had an eerie glow, no stars, the half-moon shining on the roof of the governor's mansion. She began to pace the floor in her long, flannel nightgown. She walked down stairs and checked all of the doors to see if they were locked. Then she locked her bedroom door.

She felt cold. She couldn't think. She was tired, she thought. The people there that day and her meeting with Abner Hill had been distressing. She began to talk aloud as was her custom when she had important decisions to make and there was no one she trusted to whom she might speak.

The man, Jones, as he called himself: This man would never testify or he'd end up taking the place of the Indian in the gas chamber. He didn't strike her as one who would readily take to such a fate. She now possessed the only evidence that could convict him or, for that matter, exonerate Charlie Redtail.

And Dean Miller. He was now the sheriff of Fetterman County. Ran unopposed when William Marsden suffered a heart attack and died three days later. Miller had lied in the Redtail case. She knew that. But his lies, too, would someday be buried with him.

Once Miller had come on to her after she had interviewed a prisoner in the jail; it had been nearly midnight and he'd been waiting for her. Miller had followed her through the back door of the courthouse and once outside he'd stopped her and grabbed her. Said he was in love with her and tried to kiss her. He put his hands on her, but she'd wrestled away from him. She was stronger than he, the little skinny prick with ears.

And the snitch that Miller had brought in, the one Hill destroyed on cross-examination: If he were alive, and that was doubtful for those kind, or if he could even be found, which was doubtful, too, his testimony would make little difference. No one would believe him if he turned again.

The fingertip of the cadaver and the beads—she had them. What was the blond man's game? Why had he given her the only evidence that would acquit the Indian? Then she said aloud, "I can do with it as I please." She felt a certain power.

"Yes," she said, back, "you can do with it as you please."

The next morning she busied herself with thank-you notes to those who were contributing to her campaign and made three television commercials in the afternoon. She sat behind her desk looking very pretty, very official, encased by the American and Wyoming flags.

"Bring the camera in close so they can catch the eyes," she said. "It is all in the eyes, you know. If the eyes don't show it the people won't believe it."

That evening she'd gone home as usual. She poured herself a vodka and soda, sat down before the fire, and gazed into the flames to see if the flames provided answers. Her encounter with the blond man the evening before still troubled her. Why had he told her it was he who murdered Ronald Cotler? What was in it for him? Perhaps someone on Hamilton's behalf had been hired to murder Cotler—and now at the last minute Hamilton had sent him again, this time to save Charlie's life. That night she had called Hardy Fox, the sheriff in Cheyenne, a man with whom she had developed a good relationship. She described the blond man to the sheriff, gave the sheriff his name, and asked him to locate the man, to keep him under surveillance, but not to arrest him.

"What's the matter?" the sheriff asked. "The man after ya or somethin'?"

"No. I just need to know where he is for the next few days," she said. And she had hung up.

The pesky ghost of Ronald Cotler would never die. The lies of Miller and the snitch had been permissible lies—lies to convict the guilty. And now this Jones rose up out of the past's ashes to cause this trouble. She should call off the execution long enough to verify that the finger matched. But it would take an exhumation. A court order. Time. The beads would have to be sent to the FBI for matching. Then she would probably have to testify.

She could see it, the press, the gnawing, hungry press, like vultures on carrion, famished for a story. There would be the questions about her prosecution, this perfect case that had catapulted her to the top, the people cheering, the people adoring her, her easy win in her first term because the people loved her. What if in the ensuing investigation Miller told the media he had advised her from the beginning that Redtail was innocent? That wasn't likely, she thought, but Miller was unpredictable in front of the cameras. And he had always resented her after that night when she had turned him away. "You'll regret this someday," he said.

What would the people say if they discovered she had convicted an innocent man? What if Jones were crazy, which perhaps he was. What if he made a deal for immunity and testified that he gave perjured testimony and that she had known it? That was unlikely, she thought. No prosecutor would make a deal with the killer to get a mere suborner of perjury. But maybe they would charge her as an accessory to murder. She was big game and Jones was no one. The people were like lovers, her lovers. Once a lover gave his heart he would never forgive betrayal.

She had rechecked to make certain all of the doors were locked. Then she tested the numerous windows in the governor's mansion both upstairs and down, the basement windows as well. The housekeeper, Millie Sorensen, had heard her and had gotten up. She found Mueller in the pantry trying the pantry window.

"Are you all right, ma'am?" she asked.

"Fine," Mueller said. "Just checking to be sure we are secure. I check it every once in a while, you know."

"I think we should have a man in the house," the housekeeper said. "It's not good to be at night without a man."

"Never needed a man, Millie," she said.

"This is the night they execute that Indian, ain't it, ma'am?"

"Yes," Mueller said.

"Are you gonna save him?"

"He's a murderer," Mueller said.

"I see, ma'am," the woman said. "Good night then."

There was something in the way the woman had spoken to her, as if she had doubts. How could the woman know anything? No one knew. No one should have doubts. But the blond man?

If she stayed the execution in order to carry on a new investigation she would lose control of it. Even as governor she could wield little control over the Department of Criminal Investigations that would be in charge of the case. But if she buried the finger and beads there would be no proof, just the blond man's word and he would be seen as some psychotic wanting to make trouble, wanting publicity. Yes, she thought, I will bury the evidence.

She got up and dressed in her jeans and a sweater, the envelope clutched in her hand. She walked out to the garage. The wind had begun to blow, the sky clouded over so that the half-moon appeared and disappeared like a child playing. She took a Kerr fruit jar from off the workbench in the garage, poured out the nails that had been stored in the jar, and stuffed in the envelope with its contents. Then she sealed the jar with its lid. She walked out into the night, too afraid to look around her, afraid that if she looked something, some apparition out of dark places, would accost her. She stuck the shovel into the soft dirt and buried the jar in the roses next to the house in the backyard. Then she hurried back inside and locked the door behind her.

But what about the innocent man? "The world progresses on the sacrifices of the innocent," she said aloud.

"Are you all right, ma'am?" It was the housekeeper again.

"Of course," she said. "I needed a breath of air."

"On a night like this?"

"What in the world is the matter with you, Millie?"

"It's the night that Indian dies," she said. "I never did like nights like this."

Mueller hurried back to her bedroom. We made the world free for democracy on the blood of thousands of innocent young men, she argued to herself. War kills the innocent. The innocent are sacrificed every day for the greater cause, and what greater cause in Wyoming than her candidacy? She had been a good governor. She had kept a strict budget. The state was in good financial condition. She had strengthened the Republican Party with her governorship. She had plans for the future. The state was rich in uranium and the state had an honest workforce. She had plans to supplement the state's income with mining. She was a natural businesswoman. At her nomination dinner the state auditor had proclaimed her a genius.

She would provide jobs for the workers and good schools. The companies would flock to the state because she kept the taxes low. She had plans for the tourist industry and she had formed an economic council that, at the beginning of her next term, would present an overall plan for the massive expansion of Wyoming's economic base. She thought of her plans for Wyoming, her career. She could even go to the United States Senate. People were already talking about that. Perhaps she might go further.

People had to be sacrificed. When they built the Arts and Science Building at the university three men had died in the collapse of some scaffolding. They were innocent. She had thought then and she thought now that if she must make a choice between progress on the one hand and the lives of several workers on the other, she must always chose progress. Had she been told by God that three young men would fall to their deaths, she would have ordered the construction of the building to proceed. Innocent workers are always killed. It's part of the cost. Innocent people are killed on the highways going to and from work. It is part of the cost. Should all human activity cease to save lives?

Suddenly she felt the burden lift from her. No, she thought, she should not save Charlie Redtail. He would be the innocent sacrifice, like many young men were innocently sacrificed for the greater good.

"If I saved him I would only be sacrificing myself," she said aloud. "And for what? For an uneducated Indian who has done nothing but cause trouble for Fetterman County? For that breed who has always been trouble?"

She looked at herself in the mirror. She was in her prime. Not too young and not yet suffering the immutable ravishes of time. Timing was everything.

It would be a bad trade for the people—Ava Mueller's career for the life of some Arapahoe breed. She owed it to the people.

The people of the state also had a stake in the execution. They believed in capital punishment. Capital punishment was part of the state's romantic history, the cattle thieves and horse thieves always hanged, even before murderers. The state hanged killers to keep the streets safe for their women and children. Wyoming was a safe place for people to live. If the people began to lose faith in the death penalty they would lose faith in the law, in justice, and if the people believed there was no justice, the whole social structure would begin to fall away. No, the execution must go forward for the benefit of the people. She walked to the window and looked out at the half-moon glaring at her. Then she hurried to her bed and crawled in. It was ten o'clock in the evening. She pulled the bedclothes up around her and soon she slept like a child.

41

The friend is the friend.

After the verdict Simon Yellow Dog visited Charlie at Rawlins whenever he could, which wasn't often. When he came he brought smoked elk meat and smoked trout. He brought him sage leaves to burn that would drive away evil thoughts. That's all he knew how to do. He didn't know how to cry.

He said, "This is the shits, man."

Charlie said, "I'm all right."

"Them white motherfuckers stopped the project up there. We done it."

"That's good, Simon."

"I'll see ya, man," Simon said. "See ya aroun'."

He left nearly as soon as he got to the prison, the man being unable to breathe in the steel and concrete without serious damage to his soul.

On the day preceding the execution, the prison guards led Charlie Redtail to the small room with the window at the end of death row. The sky was blue that day, as blue as a Wyoming sky some would say, this first sky he had seen in eight years.

On the last day Simon Yellow Dog came to see Charlie. It was late in the afternoon. Simon wouldn't look at Charlie. Then Charlie turned back to the window and took in the sky.

"I come to see ya," Simon said.

"Glad you're here, brother."

"Don't know how to say nothin'."

"Don't say nothin' then," Charlie said. "I'll be around."

"I know," Simon said. "I had me a dream," the man still not looking at his friend. "I was ridin' a pure black horse in the night. I was ridin' it fast across the prairie chasin' after a long shadow. I couldn't catch the shadow and the horse stepped in one a them badger holes and fell. Threw me. I was hurt bad. I was laying on my back lookin' up at the sky. There was one a them half-moons, but the stars was black holes. Nothin' in 'em.

"Then the horse started talkin' ta me. Some horses talk, ya know."

"I know," Charlie said.

"It said, 'There is three worlds, Mr. Yellow Dog.' That horse called me Mr. Yellow Dog. Nobody calls me Mr. Yellow Dog. I said, 'I already know that. There is the up world, the below world, and this here one.'

" 'Right,' the horse said. 'But I will tell ya somethin' ya don' know. Them worlds is all the same world.' I says, 'Don' shit me,' an' the horse says, 'I wouldn't shit ya none, Mr. Yellow Dog. I got too much respec' for ya ta shit ya.' An' I says, 'Well, in that case, I will take whatever meanin' there is from it.' An' the horse got up and walked off, and I did, too. I wasn't hurt no more. An' I wasn't drinkin' neither."

"That was an important dream," Charlie said.

"Tha's what I thought," Yellow Dog said. "I brung ya some elk jerky." He handed Charlie a small, thin package wrapped in newspaper. "Figgered ya might need it for the trip."

Charlie took the package and nodded his thanks.

"We'll be ridin' that black horse together?" Simon asked.

"You can ride up front," Charlie said.

"No, you was always up front, man." They were silent a long time. When the guard came Simon Yellow Dog looked at his friend for the first time and he said, "See ya, man," and he had walked on out behind the guard looking straight ahead.

42

The woman is the woman.

After the verdict Willow Hodges had been held in the Fetterman County jail until Ava Mueller made up her mind. Should she lodge perjury charges against her? Mueller said she had been extremely distressed that Elizabeth Hodges should come into court and recant a confession that Mueller herself had taken. She'd been kind to the woman. Mueller said so right off to Judge Henry Hankins the following Sunday when she and the judge were visiting Mueller's father at his ranch.

"I should charge her," Ava Mueller had said, "if for no better reason than she embarrassed the law." They spoke to each other in the barn, the good smell of the horses, her favorite quarter horse, Ike, in the stall.

"If every witness who lied got convicted of perjury we couldn't build the pens fast enough to hold 'em all," the judge said. He poured the oats in the feed trough.

"That may be so, judge, but I'm not responsible for all the lying witnesses. I'm responsible only for those who lie in my cases. This woman lied. It's my personal, moral responsibility to uphold the law." She threw her saddle up on her horse.

"She embarrassed *you* more than the law," the judge said as he reached under her horse's belly and pulled the cinch up.

"Yes, she embarrassed me. After all I did for her—accusing me of coercing her confession to save her child."

"Desperate people do desperate things, Ava," the judge said. "You did all right. You got the breed convicted. You're the hero of Fetterman County, the toast of Wyoming and, I predict, the next governor."

"Hush! you old devil," she said. She led the horse out and mounted it in one smooth motion. She reached down and pinched the judge on the cheek.

"Why don't ya let it go at that?" the judge said. "You can't climb any higher on the totem pole by convicting a pregnant woman for lying to save the father of her child."

Then she let the horse have its head, the old man standing in the corral, watching after her.

She left Willow in jail for another week, but when she began her labor Dean Miller had called her. About four in the morning.

"The bitch is havin' a fit down here," Miller's strained voice hollered over the phone. "Raisin' hell about havin' her baby in jail. Crying, screaming, cussing, beatin' on the wall. Jesus Christ, she's gonna calve 'bout any minute. What do ya want me ta do?"

He waited for her answer.

"Might not look too good for 'er havin' that kid in jail," he said. "An' we ain't exactly set up fer deliverin' kids here. Somethin' could happen."

It was then that Ava Mueller came to her decision. "Turn her loose, Dean," she said. "I'll draw up the papers for you in the morning."

Miller had driven Willow to the twenty-bed county hospital where within the hour she gave birth to a seven-pound three-ounce boy. Willow named him Henry after the old man as she and Charlie had agreed. Then she moved into Mary's shack until she was able to find a place of her own on the reservation.

Someone had to watch after the old man—she and Charlie had agreed on that as well. He was becoming forgetful. Sometimes he would forget to eat. He never took a bath and his hound was often hungry. Simon Yellow Dog came by on occasion to look in on him, as did some of the other renegades, but their visits were sporadic and sometimes, when the old man did decide to eat, he'd eat nothing but Snickers bars.

Willow had spoken to the old man about moving into a new house, the agency having entered into an agreement with a builder of prefabricated houses who would put a two-bedroom house on the land if the tribal member would sign over a certain portion of his allotment check to the builder until the house plus interest was paid for.

But the old man said he didn't want to live in what he called "them white man's boxes with them slick floors." And he didn't like the noise of the refrigerator. Said it scared the spirits away. "Them spirits don't like comin' to a place with all that racket goin' on." A man who couldn't talk to the spirits was a man who lived alone. He said he didn't want to live alone.

"I'll live with you," Willow said.

"I don' wanna live with no woman. They scare them spirits away, too. My woman, she knew when to be quiet. An' that kid of yers, he squalls all the time."

"He's a very good child. He looks like Charlie, don't you think?"

"Them babies all look alike," he said. Then he took the child from Willow's arms. "So this here is Henry Redtail?"

"Yes," she said. She was very proud. "We named him after you."

"First thing ever named after me," he said, " 'cept a hound I give to Emery Sharp Nose. Emery named that dog after me. Damn good dog." He pinched the fat leg of the child between a bony thumb and forefinger. The dirty hands. "This here boy is gonna be a great man."

"How can you tell?" she asked.

"His name is Henry, ain't it?"

"Yes," she said.

"An' I can tell by the feel of 'im."

"Can you see him?"

"Why sure," he said, squinting. "I can see the little bugger. He is gonna lead his people outta here. Shoulda named him Moses," he said. "Ha. If I had me another kid I'd name 'im Snickers after them white man's candy bars."

Willow had taken a house across the road from the old man's place. She had a good roof put on the one-room shack and to keep the wind out she had the logs rechinked with plaster, straw mixed in it. The floors were dirt like the floors at the old man's place. She visited the old man every day with the child whom, despite the gentle protest of his mother, the old man called Snickers.

And Willow visited Charlie in Rawlins every month. She wrote him long letters on each Sunday. She had not wanted to live when they dragged him off to the penitentiary like a captured beast waiting to be slaughtered. But she knew that for the sake of the child she must live. She wrote in her letters how she remembered when Charlie had told her that geese mated for life. She wrote that she knew how the wild goose felt when the hunters killed her mate, and the hunters laughed and hollered and held the goose up by the neck to show everyone and then threw the limp carcass in the back of a pickup truck. But Charlie was not dead, she wrote, and he would never die, because he was alive where she was alive. When she visited him and could touch him in the visiting room, just touch his hand, she could remember how his touch felt for a whole month.

Charlie was not one for writing. But when she visited he told her that he talked with her every day, that if she listened she could hear him. "Go out into the wind and you will hear me," he said.

"What if the wind isn't blowing?" She was touching his hand.

"If the wind isn't blowing speak to the blue lupine in the springtime and you will hear me."

"And what do I do if it's summer? How do I hear you then?"

"I will speak to you in the thunder. Do you remember how we stood in the rain, and were covered with the spirits, and we were wet like small children who knew nothing but the joy of each other? Do you remember?"

"Yes," she said.

"We have lived many lives to know such joy," he said, "Do you remember how we were with each other at the old man's place?"

"Yes," she said.

"We have lived many lives to know such freedom," he said. "I will speak to you in the rain and in the thunder and you will speak back to me and I will hear you. We are not apart unless we wish to be apart. The prairies are not separate from themselves. The mountains are not separate from themselves. The sky is not separate from the sky. We are of the prairies and the mountains and the sky," he said.

She had brought the child, Henry, to see him. She found herself calling him Snickers and Charlie had laughed. By the time the boy was four it was obvious he would have the stature of his father and already the old man was teaching the child the way of the Indian. Mary had complained of it.

"Look what happened to Charlie," Mary said. That day Willow had found her madly writing letters to all of the congressmen, the paper stacked high on the old kitchen table.

"Yes," Willow said back. "Just see what happened to him. He is so beautiful," and after that Mary said nothing and soon she'd gone out to gather signatures for her petition to save her son's life. Willow saw her, like Lady Gerty, the bag woman she had loved. She could not relieve the merciless pain. She had not tried to stop Mary's futile striving, the compulsion that was intended to succeed or to kill her. One could not save the mother by interfering. One could only love the woman and accept the woman as she bore the endless pain of her fear.

She was grateful for the child who grew strong and happy, and who had become the source of her joy. The child saved her by consuming her. The mother is the mother and she could care for her child, keep him safe, touch him at night in his sleep, fill herself with him in the daytime, with the sound of his laugher in her ears and at night his small, plump body against her.

She washed the child's diapers in the creek, his clothes as well, the smell of fresh wash that had dried on the line sweet in her nose. She planted a small garden irrigated from a ditch she had dug from the creek above, the ditch wandering though the sage, her shovel following the trickle of water as it moved across the prairie. She grew turnips and parsnips and a few potatoes. She grew squash and pumpkins, the sum-mer squash having taken over the garden. She transplanted a dozen tomato plants she had grown in the window from seed and, of course, she grew the easy ones—the lettuce, the spinach and the peas, the beans climbing on old tepee poles she found rotting at the rear of her shack.

Everywhere she went the boy went with her, running, climbing, laughing. Sometimes he laid on the ground very quietly as if to absorb its strength and its wisdom. Often he asked questions she had never thought of.

"Momma, why do bees sting?" he asked.

"It's so if the birds try to eat them they will be stung. It's for their protection," she said.

"Why don't we have stingers?" he asked. "Why doesn't Papa have a stinger so they won't kill Papa?"

She did not know where the child had heard it, the child only with her. She had tried to protect him from the shadow of it, and she did not know how to answer him.

Finally she said, "We shall learn about growing instead of killing," and she showed the boy the small starlike yellow blossoms on the tomato plant. "These are the blooms that will grow the tomato. It is magic," she said. "We will learn about such magic."

The child learned to plant the garden, to weed it, to let the water run down the small ditches by the rows, and he learned many lessons from it. Together they dried the tomatoes and put the root vegetables in sand in a small cellar at the back of the shack. They dried the peas and the beans in the late August sun and when Simon brought her a quarter of elk, she cut it into strips and they made jerky from it as the old man had taught them.

Often she thought of Mary. She thought that if her child became a man and the faceless mob trapped him and the faceless mob meticulously, maliciously planned his death, that she would escape into insanity. Mothers cannot hold on to their minds while they watch the faceless mob kill their child, the mob called "the state."

Once she had gone to Rawlins looking for Mary and had found her worn and lost, her face covered with the dust of the road. Willow had taken her to the New Moon café and bought her a bowl of chili, which was all the woman would eat.

When she looked at Mary her eyes were as empty stars, her hands dirty, the fingernails as well. Willow watched her finish the bowl of chili, watched her eat as if she had not eaten for many days.

Finally Willow said, "Mother, what are we going to do?"

The woman looked up at Willow as if she did not understand.

"We can't go on like this, this torture."

"They aren't gonna kill him," Mary said. She held up her petition. "See, I have all these people askin' the governor not to kill Charlie."

Willow nodded and said nothing.

"I even got the mayor of Greybull to sign it. Look here," she said, turning to a page that had been visited many times. She pointed at the signature. "And I got that big rancher up by Dubois to sign it, too. He let me sleep in his barn that night."

Suddenly Willow said, "We didn't do anything, Mary. But we're the ones who suffer."

"That's what mothers do," Mary said. "Mothers suffer. You never get over bein' a mother. Bein' a mother is a disease that ya never get over."

Willow had wondered at the cruelty of a system that proclaimed justice was to punish the innocent, that punished the mothers, that punished old men like Henry Old Deer, who never spoke of it but who grieved each day for the loss of Charlie Redtail. The old man was innocent and helpless to fight the faceless mob. But he had great power through the spirits and one day his power would manifest itself and, she thought, his power would prevail.

She wondered about a system of justice that destroyed those who fought for justice within the system. Abner Hill had fought for it. He had fought for the innocent the best he knew how and had lost Charlie Redtail. She had seen his suffering. She had wanted to comfort Abner but she could not. Then he lost Mary as well, although neither of them intended to lose the other. His loss of Mary was even the greater loss, for although the woman may sacrifice all for her child, the man will make the final sacrifice for his woman. And he had lost his woman because they had lost the child.

She had wondered about the justice of a system that had left an innocent man smeared as a murderer, an innocent child smeared as the son of a murderer, an innocent mother smeared as the mother of a murderer. That they should kill Charlie Redtail was not punishing the guilty, even if he were guilty. When they killed Charlie Redtail his punishment, even if due, was over. His did not linger on for endless years of torture as would be suffered by the mother and by the old man and by her. And the next innocent generation suffered the poison and the generations following. The expanding injury of it was like the stone she had thrown into the water with Charlie, the rings ever widening until finally the last of them disappeared on the far shore of the lake.

The white man's justice was injustice, barbaric, she thought. The white man claimed to be civilized but he was not civilized. When the Indian wished to punish, the offender was banished from the tribe, but the Indian did not kill one of his own. The Indian did not banish the wrongdoer to be slaughtered by strangers.

In the white man's justice the faceless mob would haul Charlie Redtail into the gas chamber, the father of her child, gasping and dying while the members of the press counted his breaths in his dying. Those who killed him were strangers to the killing, men doing a job for wages—piteous ones at that—a job they did for the faceless mob.

The white man's justice was injustice because it was insane. To punish implied that the punished should learn from the punishment. But what does death teach the man in the gas chamber? How does death punish the dead? Yet it teaches, all right, she thought. It teaches that killing is acceptable, for the mob kills with impunity. It teaches the mother and the child that they must suffer eternally for a crime they did not commit. They must suffer, instead, for a crime the faceless mob committed.

Charlie Redtail would soon die. Then it would be over for him. But the child, already eight, understood. He was the son of a convicted murderer. She had not wanted to taint the system in his eyes, to make him hate the faceless mob, to hate the white man when he was more white than Indian, to hate the power structure when he was born in it, trapped in it by birth. But how could she not injure the child? Must she lie? Or, if she told him the truth, that his father was a hero among his people, that he was murdered by the system, that he was the victim of its greed and its prejudice and its lies, would he not grow up hating the system? Hate would beget hate. And at last would the system not kill him as it had his father and his father before him?

She had spoken often to the old man about this, but his words were not of hate. He spoke of the spirits and of the Mother who would soon take him back. Sometimes she would see the old man leaning heavily on his cane, hobbling slowly across the prairies, the child at his side, and she knew that the boy was safe with him, safe for the moment, and that was as far as her eyes could see.

She had dreaded the day and had gone on from day to day as if the day would never come, like an old man pretends that his last day will never come. She had not wanted to see Charlie. She had not wanted to see this man, not wanting to bear the pain of it. She had tried to keep the pain out, to keep her heart open to the joy of living, to the joy of the child, not the terror of the death of Charlie Redtail.

It was too cruel, she thought, this countdown to death. It was unlawful because it was against the law of nature. Even those with terminal diseases did not know the exact day, the precise minute. One minute after midnight—that was Charlie's time. Only the most vicious sadists could embrace such a horror. The secret of the precise time was the gift of Nature, of the Mother, so that the gift of life was not wasted in counting the days until death.

"Won't you be happy as I am happy?" Charlie had said. "I will soon join the spirits, and your hard waiting will be over. I am glad for that. You will make a new life for you and Snickers." He laughed at the sound of the boy's name.

"A new spring always comes," he said. "It is the way of the Mother."

His eyes were on her, soft and at peace. She was sitting on the small table in the cell leaning back into his arms, her eyes looking up into his.

"I will be happy for you, darling," she said. "It has been too long." She got up. "Let me braid your hair." He turned his back to her and she undid the long braid down his back and then she took a comb from her hair and combed his hair, slowly, her fingers touching his hair, caressing his hair, his back to her so that he did not see the tears falling. And then she began to carefully braid it and when she had tied the small leather tie at the end, she said, "There, you look very handsome."

"I'm ready," he said and she did not know if he was laughing. Then he held her back from him with both hands as if he were speaking to a child. "Don't grieve over me," he said.

She could not speak.

"You must not grieve over me. Your grief would be wasted. I am at peace. I am with the wind and the sage and the small flower in the meadow. I have returned to the Mother and I am free. Your grieving is for yourself. If I have grief, it is for you." He held her to him and they were silent for a long time.

He broke the silence. "Where is Snickers?"

"He is out there with the guard. She's a nice woman. She's reading the Bible to him. I didn't think a few minutes of the Bible would permanently damage him. The poor woman seemed to need to read it to him."

"Let us be together," he said, and he had called the guard who brought the boy to them. Willow had taught him at home, the public schools a cesspool of prejudice and cruelty and hatred, she said. And the old man was teaching the boy the native tongue, which she thought important, because the way of the people is in their language.

When the boy entered the cell he ran to his father and his father took him on his lap, and put his arms around Willow, and pulled her close to him and they were as one. The boy could smell the smell of his father and the father smelled good to the boy. He pushed his head into his father's chest with his nose against the rough cloth of the prison coveralls. After a while Charlie held the boy out from him so as to see into his eyes.

"You have good eyes," he said to the boy. "You will see much with your eyes."

The boy nodded as if he understood.

"I remember, Snickers, when I was a boy your age, and I was with my father. He had eyes like yours that could see many things."

The boy looked into his father's eyes. "I wish I had eyes like you," he said.

Charlie laughed. "If you give eyes the chance they will see many things."

"I saw a red-tail hawk yesterday," the boy said. "The old man couldn't see it," the boy's soprano voice. "He's almost blind, Papa. He's almost deaf, too."

"The old man sees much without eyes," Charlie said.

Then they were silent, the boy on his father's lap and the boy did not wish to break the silence. He looked down at his father's hands and at his own holding onto one large finger. He waited until his father broke the silence.

"You are Arapahoe," he said. The father looked at his son. "You are Arapahoe," the father said once more. And the boy could feel the words take hold of him as if they had great power. And the words changed the boy.

After a while the father asked, "When you saw the hawk, what did you see?"

"I saw that it was free," the boy said.

"You see much already," Charlie said, and he laughed and pulled Willow to him laughing lightly, and he held the woman and the boy close to him so that only the top of Willow's head could be seen.

Then the guard came and opened the door and the guard saw them and he stood there at the door not wanting to be the one who ended it. He saw that the woman was weeping silently, but he could not see the boy except for the small moccasined feet sticking out from under the man's arms.

"It's time," the guard said.

Then Charlie Redtail said to Willow, "There is a word. It is *Yon-ka-tore*. It means 'behind the heart of man.'"

"Behind the heart of man?" Willow asked.

"Yes."

"What is it?"

"It is what I shall have for you until the stars no longer shine," he said. "The word is *Yon-ka-tore*."

The word sounded good to her ears and she said the word back. "*Yon-ka-tore*," she said.

And then the small family began to unfold like the bud of a tulip opening and they moved slowly out from Charlie Redtail like petals expanding, their hands lingering, and their fingers lingering, and their eyes as well, and at last, at the door they turned into the hallway and left the stem like petals falling.

43

The lawyer is always the lawyer.

Abner Hill had grieved over the case, for with its loss he had lost the man he saw as his son. He lost the only woman to whom he had ever said the words. And he lost the last remnant of respect he had held for the justice system. And he lost himself.

As for Mary there had been no blaming, no hysterical scenes, no pointing of anguished fingers. But he knew that Mary no longer respected him, for the man must save the child and he had not saved the child, and he knew that when respect was gone it was like a house with the foundation crumbled.

No need for her blame of him. He blamed himself. Perhaps he should have called Charlie to the stand. Perhaps he hadn't made decisions from the distance that one not so entangled would have made, better decisions bereft of blinding emotion. Perhaps he cared too much.

Maybe Russo could have convinced a Twin Buttes jury with high-flown rhetoric and perjured witnesses. Maybe Russo would have successfully bribed a juror, or the judge, or eliminated the prosecutor in some way, maybe compromised her, maybe more. Hill should have been out of the case. Yes, like the affidavit in the appeals court said, he was incompetent.

He had never thought of competence as being able to corruptly manipulate the system. In that way he was incompetent and he had admitted his incompetence with that in mind when he signed the affidavit the appeals lawyers presented him. But to Abner Hill, being a lawyer had been a sacred trust. He laughed, he, the suborner of perjury sounding like some sweet Jesus boy.

How could a man be a lawyer if there were no soul to the law? But those burdened with souls cannot survive in a soulless world. Respect, he thought: It was about respect, and in the end, respect for the self. But how could there be respect for an incompetent lawyer?

He paced back and forth across the length of his small cabin. He had not slept for days, his hair standing on end, his clothes mussed and dirty, his eyes wild and sleepless. He had not eaten. Sometimes he hollered at the log wall, but the wall did not answer. Maybe if he hadn't put Jordan on the stand, if he had trusted the system, maybe Charlie would be free.

Maybe the jurors possessed what he always believed they possessed— a composite wisdom, something nearly magical, a sense that penetrated the veil. But Mueller had bribed the witnesses. Put that poor lying snitch on the stand. Bribed him with his freedom. Put the lying Miller and the perjuring Jones on the stand. And she had known they were lying.

If he had another chance would he not also bribe a juror? "They were already bribed," he said aloud, the sound of his voice startling him. Bribed by the system. Bribed by prejudice. Bribed by fear. Why not bribe them nice and clean? Bribe them with crisp, new U.S. dollars?

Would he bribe the judge? The judge was already bribed. Ava Mueller bribed him, bribed him by kissing his ass, by chumming with the old fart. The judge was bribed by the system that demanded its vengeance against the Indian, by the system that warned the old devil that if he did not please the system he would be cast out and another bribed judge would take his place. And yes, the judge was bribed by his need for acceptance, for the old boys at Kiwanis to pat him on the back and say, "Well, Henry, you handled that Redtail case just right."

How far would he go, sweet Jesus boy? Would he kill to win the case? They killed. They killed the mother. They killed Willow. They would kill the child and claim it was just one of those miserably unfortunate things. They would look sad, feel nothing, and excuse the system because the system is not perfect.

Mueller put the killer himself on the stand to lie. To convict the innocent. To laugh at the system and to kill again with his lies. Emmett had laughed at him while he struggled within the system to reveal the truth, even if he had to present perjury to present the truth. Yes, he would kill to save Charlie Redtail. Whom would he kill? It would make no difference. He began to sob. Alone. It was all right for a man to cry if there was no one to hear him. But when he was finally done with the weeping, the walls of the cabin were as silent as before, as straight and as strong and he wished he had not wept.

The system had bought Charlie Redtail's life. For Abner Hill that had become the standard liturgy of the case. Charlie's life had been paid for with false testimony. And now that the system owned it, what did they want to do with it? They wanted to let him choke in the gas. They bought his life to gas him. The system must be insane.

Suddenly he jumped up and ran to the nightstand by the bed, pulled open the drawer, and took out the Smith & Wesson .357 Magnum. He sat down on the bed, the gun in his hand. He cocked the gun. The ominous sound of the gun in his hand sobered him. He thought that a man should not kill himself in a frenzy. He should be rational about it. He should give it great thought.

What good was he? What use? He had been convinced he could not win without the perjured testimony. But he could not win with it. Perhaps that was the essence of incompetence. He could never try another case. He was ruined like all murderers are ruined.

Having once put on perjured testimony would he not do it again? Was he not like the killer who had destroyed his soul and could therefore kill again and again, his soul no longer in jeopardy?

He had been the prosecution's weapon from the first day of his practice. He thought of the countless poor who had been convicted, those with pitiful strands of hope still alive, those with a blind faith in the system, those who did not have the resources of mind or money to get justice. Whenever he'd beaten the system he'd beaten it honestly. And he'd beaten the system often enough to convince himself that the system could be made to work. But it had been the magnificent illusion.

He looked at the revolver and saw his face distorted in the reflection on its chrome barrel. Slowly he put the gun to his head. The barrel felt cold, inorganic against the organic temple. Why should he, the incompetent lawyer, now the suborner of perjury, play the game anymore? The law was a rotten game. Life was a rotten game. He had lost in both. The stakes were too high for him and he, the chump who came to the table, had been cleaned out.

Then he thought of the man Emmett Jones who had confessed the murder and who had probably killed the farmer's wife, this paradigm of evil who had probably killed all of his life and was still killing, this man who said he was in tune with the universe with his killing, who laughed at murder, laughed at the ideas of right and wrong, laughed at the system, and laughed at him.

It was the blond man, Emmett, who convicted Charlie Redtail, who murdered him with his cool testimony. And what was in it for him? The sublime joy of the madman, the laughter in the night. He had used the system to kill again. And he was out there someplace killing and laughing at his own psychotic joke. Someone should kill Emmett Jones. It would be a service to mankind. He pulled the gun from his head and examined it. The deformed face on the barrel spoke to him. "What is justice if it is not revenge?"

In the morning he packed a single bag with a change of clothes, put on his old, black leather jacket and his old boots. He wrapped his pistol in a towel and stuffed it into the crack between the seat and the back rest of his pickup and headed out to where he did not know. This trip into nowhere looking for the blond man with the cold, blue eyes.

At first he had followed after Mary, believing that he could help her, and that if fate acted randomly as Emmett insisted, that he could as easily find the man in Rawlins where Mary had recently moved to be near Charlie. He had tried to comfort the woman, to reason with her about her petition, but she said she had to save her boy, that America was a democracy. If enough people signed her petition the governor would have to save him.

"I never know which signature is the one that will be enough. I keep saying to myself, the governor might not save him if it weren't for this one last signature. This is America, Abner. Have you forgotten?" she asked.

He could not dissuade her, and in her panic and her misery there was no room left for him, no room for her comforting voice, no touch of the woman at his hair, her fingers running though it as before. She was gone from him. He had followed her to Colorado when she had gotten lost that time and did not know any longer where she was, and he had brought her back to Rawlins.

Then during the night she had disappeared again and again he had gone out in search of her. But after he had lost track of her he set out on his own, driving from town to town, inquiring as he went.

"You know a guy named Emmett?" he asked the waitresses at the café, the pumpers at the gas stations, the bartenders. "You see a blond guy around here. Probably wears army fatigues? Sometimes drives a Jeep? Stares at you. Kinda weird?"

He had gone from town to town as far north as Calgary and in the winter down into the small towns along the northern borders of New Mexico and Arizona. He had gone as far east as Kansas City, stopping at the small farming towns along the way and posing always the same questions to the people.

He scoured the newspapers for murders of farm women, of random killings, and he had found many. Once in Kearney, Nebraska, he thought for sure he had found the macabre work of Emmett when he read of a farmer's wife who had been murdered and the farmer had been charged with the murder and convicted.

But no one had seen a blond man hanging around Kearney wearing army fatigues. Hill spent a month in the town until finally he had only enough cash to buy gas back to Twin Buttes. Once home he collected ten dollars here and five there from Indians who owed him. He had closed his practice several years before and he'd sold his books to a young kid fresh out of law school who wanted to fight for justice. Then he had gone to the bank and mortgaged his cabin, got enough cash to hold him a year or two, and he'd been off again.

Sometimes he would go to see Charlie, but his visits got further apart, the renewal of his guilt like a relentless inquisitor pointing at him and he had no answer back. Charlie tried to comfort him.

"I coulda been defended by . . . what's that guy's name you were telling me about, that great lawyer?"

"Clarence Darrow," Hill said.

"Yeah, I coulda been defended by that guy and it wouldn't a made any difference. I was in their sights like a deer standing in the meadow with no place to run. Wasn't your fault."

"I shoulda put you on the stand," Hill said.

"Wouldn't a made any difference," Charlie said. "People believe who they want to believe. They didn't want to believe me."

Hill never told him about Jordan. In fact, Jordan had revealed the true killer. But how could he tell Charlie that he had put on the perjury and in so doing had not only violated Charlie's trust, but had put Charlie's soul in jeopardy as well?"

"They believed that blond guy," Charlie said. "They wanted to believe him."

After many months he realized it was futile, this visiting of the living dead, as Hill saw Charlie, this man breathing in the tomb but trapped in the tomb. Nothing came of the visits except the renewal of his pain and although he tried, he could not hide it from Charlie, which in turn pained Charlie.

Charlie seemed at peace—no anger, no panic, no hysterical retching as his appeals were turned down, one after the other. Sometimes in the night he wondered what the man's secret was. Once he had asked him. "Charlie, I remember how you went berserk that time when you were a kid and Mueller had you in for throwin' that other kid through the barroom door. Remember that?"

"Yeah." Charlie laughed.

"How come you haven't lost it this time? You seem so calm about everything—like it's okay."

"I'm finished with my work," Charlie said.

He had gone to see Ava Mueller the day before the execution to plead with her to commute the sentence. Her face lit up when he walked into her office. He shook her hand and took a seat in front of her desk.

He had aged more than the years required. She saw that his hair was gray and his body too thin as if it had not been properly nourished. His smile failed to hide the haunted look that had taken over his features.

"You are looking good, Abner," she said.

He didn't answer. He peered down at his hands. His hands dirty. His shirt, he had worn it for a week.

"You know why I came," he said.

"Glad to see you ," she said.

"I came to ask you to save Charlie's life," he said.

She smiled at him and raised an eyebrow.

"I'm not going to beg you," he said. "What will it take?"

"Still the same Abner," she said and laughed. Then suddenly she seemed very serious. "The system has given him every chance, Abner. He's had the best appellate lawyers money could buy. They've accused me of every unethical act a lawyer could be accused of. They've called you incompetent. The judges find no error in the record. It was a perfect case."

"Don't preach to me like a mother, Ava. He's not guilty and you've always known it."

"How could you say that, Abner?" she said. She seemed shocked.

"How can you deny it, Ava?" he said back. Then he saw that she held the key to Charlie's life and his death and he could not wrest it from her. He should kill her, he thought. He could feel the .357 Magnum under his belt at his belly.

But killing her would do no good. She was not the system. He could kill the lying Miller and the lying Emmett. They were not the system.

The system could not be killed. The system only killed. Killing was the system's prerogative. "Murder seems to be the exclusive privilege of the system, Ava," he said.

"What are you saying, Abner? You always come up with these strange ideas and I have liked you anyway."

"If the system murders, is it not an evil system?"

"You aren't losing it, are you, Abner?" She leaned forward to have a closer look. His eyes seemed covered by a dense fog. "This has been hard on you, I know. You did the best you could."

"That's the ultimate mockery," he said, getting up.

"Let's not part like this, Abner," she said. "Can't we be friends? Just this once, can't we be friends?" She got up from behind her desk and walked around to where he stood. Then she tried to embrace him, but his body was stiff and unresponsive. She backed off from him and laughed at his rejection. "You and I are so much alike," she said.

He stood looking at the woman.

"We both have our principles. We've never let anything stand in their way," she said. "I've been dedicated to bringing justice to the people and although you have resisted me I have respected you. Even the most vicious murderer is entitled to a defense."

He said nothing, standing there.

"And we are alike in another way: The law has been a mate to each of us. The law has been your mistress and my lover. Neither of us have had room for romance, for marriage, for children. We've been utterly devoted to the law."

He said nothing, intent on the woman.

She reached out for his hands. "We should take a little time for ourselves," she said. "It still isn't too late, Abner."

"It is too late, Ava. We are what we have done—or failed to do," he said. Then he turned and left.

He walked down the front steps of the capitol building. Then he saw the man coming up the steps. He felt for his gun. He stopped, letting the man approach. When the blond man reached where Hill was standing, the blond man stopped. He looked at Hill from top to bottom and then laughed.

"Haven't I seen you before?" the man asked.

"I've been looking for you," Hill said.

"And what would you do with me if you found me?"

"I am going to kill you," Hill said.

"How very amusing," the man said. "How entertaining. The lawyer lately turned killer. The lawyer who claims to be against the death penalty who now wishes to inflict it." He laughed again.

At that moment on the capitol steps, the blue, cloudless sky above, the wind in his hair, the blond man standing before him, Abner Hill had experienced no bursting ecstasy, his search over. He saw the sneer, the incontinent mockery on the man's face, the man taunting, jeering at all Hill believed to be good. Hill pulled out the gun.

"Well, well, my good man. Aren't you the little hero? And what a place to die—on the capitol steps of the great State of Wyoming!" He laughed again and then took one step up so that he was looking down on Abner Hill. "Do it!" the blond man hissed. "Go! Revenge will be very sweet to you."

At that moment Hill understood without the words having formed on the edges of his mind. What was revenge but surrendering to the object of one's revenge? If he killed Emmett, Emmett would still be in control.

"Shoot me!" Emmett screamed. "Shoot me, coward! Shoot me!" He was laughing hysterically, looking down at Hill, his outstretched arms beseeching.

Finally Hill said, "I owe you no favors." Then he saw that the man was trembling.

Hill put the gun back under his belt and smiled. "I hope you live forever." Then he turned and walked down the rest of the steps to the street below.

It was then that Abner Hill felt suddenly freed. Punishment is not in death. Punishment is in life. But those who have learned to live are not punished. And those who have learned to die are also not punished.

He had dreaded this pernicious moment when he would see the eyes alive, the flesh alive, and know that the eyes would stare endlessly after the flesh had rotted away because he had failed. He would not have the strength to bear it, nor the will. The pain of his failure had returned every day for eight years. Often at night he awoke with it throbbing out of his dreams, and awake he would see Charlie Redtail struggling in the gas. At last he must face it, the time upon him.

The guard led him to the small cell. Charlie was still gazing out the window when he entered. Charlie turned to meet him.

"Well, what brings you here, Abner?" He laughed.

"In the neighborhood. Thought I'd drop by," Hill said. "How ya doin'?"

"Doin' good." He seemed as light and happy as Abner had ever seen him.

"Anything I can do for you?"

"Yes," he said. "One thing. Did you ever stand in front of the court naked?" Charlie asked.

"What a strange question."

"Would you walk in front of the judge and jury naked?"

"Of course not." Hill tried to laugh. "Although I've often thought that if everyone in court were naked we would be more likely to tell the truth."

"Well, then you might understand why I don't wish to die while the people gawk. Death is my private experience."

"They think it's theirs, Charlie."

"This wrestling with death, is it not like when one makes love?"

"Never thought of it like that," Hill said.

"One does not make love in public."

"No."

"But they wish to watch?"

"Yes," Hill said. "I'll tell them you don't want witnesses, but I can only tell them," Hill said. "The law provides for witnesses."

"They wish to deprive me of life. And they wish to deprive me of the experience of death. These voyeurs. How strange they are." He laughed his high, soft laugh, no anger in it. "Will you tell my mother and Willow not to come?"

"I will."

"And you as well, Abner."

"You wish to die alone?"

"I will not die alone. Most men die alone. My father Joseph will guide me through it. You will be happy for me?"

"Yes, for you. What do want me to do?"

"You have done enough. My son, Snickers, he is with Willow and the old man. My son is Arapahoe. It is all good."

"Nothing more?"

"Tell the old man I have learned the word and it is very good."

"Yes? What is the word?" Hill asked.

"The word is *yon-ka-tore.* It means 'behind the heart of man.' "

"What is it?"

"It is as I see it in your eyes," Charlie said.

"And I in yours," Hill said.

Then they were silent for that time, which was not long but in the silence covers many lives. And when the guard came, Hill embraced the man and the man held Hill to him as the father holds the child.

Charlie was smiling as he let Hill go. Hill did not wish to leave, but he smiled back.

"*Yon-ka-tore*," Charlie said.

Then Abner turned and left the small cell and he heard the sounds from his own lips: "*Yon-ka-tore*."

44

The mother is the mother.

She had started a petition and got 5,424 signatures. The petition was simply written in the careful hand of Mary Hamilton. It read: "*To the Honorable Governor of the State of Wyoming: Please save the life of Charlie Redtail. Thank you.*"

The writing was followed on the page by hand-drawn lines for the signatures. She stopped people on the streets and in the stores and told them that her son was not guilty. When she presented the petition most people looked at her with pity, and most said, "Sure, lady," and signed the paper, the front page tattered and dirty, the front page with coffee stains on it and the bottom corners bent up.

She had lost her job on account of the petition. Faye Bosworth said he didn't want his customers bothered with it, Mary going up to them with the petition along with the menu, the petition along with the coffeepot, the petition along with the customer's check. Bosworth had warned her, but she said it was her work and she had to do her work, so he said she would have to do her work elsewhere and that he was sorry.

She had called the governor and he had been most gracious to her, himself a small-town lawyer from Buffalo, Wyoming, who looked a lot like Abraham Lincoln but whose name was George Ruettenberg, a man who drank a lot of whiskey and answered his own phone at the governor's mansion. That was before Ava Mueller. She had taken the bus to Cheyenne to see him and he had actually listened to her, it being Wyoming, and, as Ruettenberg saw it, everyone in that small state was entitled to an audience with the governor.

"Wasn't a fair trial," she said. "They put on lies against my boy."

"I know old Judge Hankins," Governor Ruettenberg had said. "Known him for thirty years. He's as honest a judge as ever took the bench." Behind his desk and on the right the American flag stood at attention and the Wyoming flag at attention on the left, its white buffalo in the center of a blue field. The governor saw the woman looking very small, huddled in the chair in front of him, wearing her black waitress shoes. What do you say to a mother?

"But to kill him," she said, staring at the governor, searching the eyes of the man who looked like Abraham Lincoln, "to kill him for somethin' he never did, doesn't that seem wrong to you?" she asked.

"Well, yes, that would be wrong," he said.

"Then you are the governor and you can make 'em stop it." She had taken the last of the money from her grocery can to make the trip. "You can make 'em stop it and I am here askin' you to do it."

"I'll look into it," he said. "I surely will." He gave her a kind smile and he got up and then there was nothing for her to do but to get up, too. The secretary was polite when she came for her and escorted her to the door. After that she had waited for six months for the governor to give her his decision. She had not wanted to pester him, him a busy man and all. He might get upset with her and turn her down if she pestered because men do not like women who pester them.

That the governor had not answered her gave her hope at first. Maybe he was looking into the case, investigating, and investigations take time. She watched the papers every day. But when she had heard nothing after six months she called the governor's secretary and the secretary said she remembered her. She said she would inquire of the governor, although he was at a governor's conference in Baltimore. Two months later Mary called again, but there was a new secretary. She was a kind-sounding woman and said she would try to find out what the governor had done in her case and would let her know as soon as possible and that was the last she had heard from the governor.

Abner Hill had tried to comfort her, but he was unable to reach where the pain resided in the woman. And, because of her own pain, and although she had tried, she had been unable to console him. It was as if the injured were called to tend to the injured. Hill had seen it before— parents who had lost a child unable to stay the course in the marriage because both were devastated and neither could administer to the deep wounds of the other. In her heart the woman looked to the man to protect her child. He had failed, and in certain places she had tried to blame Hill, although the best part of her believed he had done all he could do. Yet she was unable to comfort him.

And he had needed to tell her how the verdict had wounded him. It was as if he had been stabbed and was bleeding slowly to death. He felt the life draining out of him, but he could not expect her to understand his pain, bleeding as she was from her own wounds. In the end, he could not rescue her from the knife because the knife was in him.

He sat at the table across from her and she poured the coffee as usual, and he stirred and stared and saw nothing. He spoke of the appeals and he tried to be enthusiastic about them, even optimistic, but he knew that none of the appeals would be granted. Then she said one night, "They claim you were incompetent, Abner. That's what the paper said that the lawyers filed in the court."

"That's what they say in a lot of cases like this, Mary. Maybe if they can convince the court that I didn't do right the court will give Charlie a new trial."

He didn't say he'd done his best. He thought he hadn't. He thought he ruined his karma by putting on Jordan's testimony. The crime of it was rotting in his heart.

"I know," she said. "But were you what they said? Incompetent?"

"Yes," he said. "I suppose so." What else could he have said, his incompetence her hope and her charge against him. He was incompetent and they were going to kill her son.

She blamed herself. She had done the best she could when he called her to testify. Maybe if she had understood the questions better the jury would have believed her. Maybe she was incompetent like Abner, she thought.

The cost of bus fare to Rawlins to see Charlie had become a great burden for her, the meals out, often only a bowl of soup and sometimes a plate of chop suey at the Chinese café on Main Street. William Hamilton had offered many times to help and at last she had taken his help with the understanding that someday she would pay him back. He rented a small apartment for her above the drugstore and she wandered the streets of the town with her petition. Sometimes she would take the bus to Rock Springs, a hundred twenty miles to the west, and there she would spend all day gathering signatures on her petition and then take the eastbound bus back to Rawlins that same night.

In the latter days she got to wandering so that Abner Hill could not keep track of her and Hamilton could not find her. She would be gone from her apartment for days. How she survived and where she slept they did not know. Once Hamilton sent out a private detective to find her and the detective found her wandering in the streets of Ft. Collins,

Colorado, her petition clutched in a dirty hand, the dirt under the fingernails, and her without a penny.

At first she had gone to see Charlie on every visitor's day, which was Thursday. But Charlie insisted that the visits only hurt her worse. He said, "Mother, I want you to think of me when I was free. See me wandering through the forest and up Spirit Mountain in the springtime and the lupine are blooming and blue and I am happy. You can go there if you wish. I go there often. I am there most of the time. One can be where one chooses. I do not choose to be here, Mother, and I am not here. They cannot imprison me where I do not wish to be."

He had tried many times to encourage her to accept his fate. "It's no one's fault. Some are picked to suffer. Some are picked to be rich and some powerful. The picking is random. We do not control. The universe does not even control itself," he had tried to tell her.

But she had never understood that. Instead she showed him her petition and said she was going to get him out, no matter what, or she would die trying. Better to die trying than to live without trying.

Finally Charlie asked the warden to stop the weekly visits, to tell his mother that she could come once a month—new rules by the administration concerning death row prisoners—and the warden had done him that favor.

In the last week Mary Hamilton took the bus to Cheyenne to see Ava Mueller. Mueller had defeated George Ruettenberg in the Republican primaries. She had garnered statewide attention in the Redtail case and had been widely acclaimed as the fearless female prosecutor of Fetterman County who would not be intimidated by white man or red. The people of Fetterman County saw her as a politician who made good on her promises. She had promised to uphold the law, to bring law and order to the county, and she had done it. The county, being the third largest in the state, exercised a major influence on the Republican Party and, as a native daughter with a promise to the people to replace a do-nothing administration with one dedicated to growth and prosperity, she had been able to gather considerable support from across the state.

The secretary in Governor Mueller's office had seen the woman waiting at the door when the secretary had come to open up at eight sharp in the morning. The woman looked pale. She wore a soiled once white scarf over her head. Her black cotton coat was frayed at the sleeves and revealed stains of various origins across its front. She carried a shopping bag in which was carefully wrapped in newspapers her petition containing 5,423 signatures of persons asking the governor of the state of Wyoming to save the life of Charlie Redtail. "May I help you?" the secretary asked as she put her key into the waiting-room door.

"Yes, ma'am," Mary said. "I came to see the governor."

"And what is your business?" the woman asked, still standing in the doorway.

"I was wantin' to talk to the governor 'bout my boy, Charlie Redtail."

"You are Mrs. Redtail?"

"No, ma'am, I'm his mother," she said. The woman saw that her eyes were tired.

"Well, the governor won't be in today," the woman said.

"I will wait here then 'til tomorrow," Mary said. "They are gonna kill him on Friday." She said it as if she were reciting a doctor's appointment.

"I will see what I can do," the woman said. "If you will wait here." Mary followed her into the large waiting room that was decorated with the photographs of the preceding governors of the state, the straight, severe oak chairs against the walls, the floors covered with thin, gray carpet. When she returned, the secretary helped her up from her chair and said in all kindness, "The governor will see you tomorrow morning at this same time. Do you have a place to stay?" Mary did not answer at first. Then she said that yes, she had a place to stay.

That night she slept in the Greyhound bus depot. "Hope the governor helps ya," the janitor said. He was black. "She don't help many folks. Just them big companies. How's your boy?" He was sweeping behind the ticket counter and emptying the waste basket into a plastic bag. He saw that she was weary. "You can lay down over there if ya want."

"Thanks," she said. "I got me some work ta do." She approached a man who looked like a bum. "Could I get ya to sign my petition?" she asked. "They are gonna kill my boy on Friday. You heard of him? His name is Charlie Redtail and he never killed anybody."

"Sure, lady," the bum said. He signed the petition and offered her a dollar, which made 5,424 signatures.

In the morning she was ushered into the office of Governor Ava Mueller. When Mary came into the room the governor rose up from her desk and rushed forward to help her into her chair. Then she pulled up a chair beside Mary and leaned over to her and grabbed both of her hands.

"You are looking good," Mueller said.

"No, I don't look so good," Mary said. She lifted her eyes up to the governor, the small early cracks appearing in the porcelain of Ava Mueller's face. But in most ways Mueller looked like she had looked in the courtroom in her gray business suit, the white collar buttoned up to the neck. She wore a string of pearls.

"I'll bet those are real pearls," Mary said, not knowing how else to start. Then before the governor could answer she said, "I got this petition for ya." She opened up her shopping bag and withdrew the clipboard carefully wrapped in the newspapers. She folded the newspapers and put them back into the paper shopping bag. Then she handed the clipboard with the petition to Ava Mueller. "I won't be needin' this anymore. This is for you. I got five thousand four hundred and twenty-four signatures on it. They are all people in the state, 'cept twenty-two in Colorado," she said. "They are askin' and I am askin' that you spare Charlie's life."

"I see," Mueller said, taking the petition. She thumbed through the pages two inches thick. "You've worked very hard. Did you gather all of these yourself?"

"Yes, ma'am, I did," Mary said. "Took me eight years."

"It has been a long time, Mary." Ava Mueller looked at the woman, and although she saw the woman's pain and tried to shut it out, yet some of it sifted in, like the cold of the blizzard through the cracks of a cabin, and the governor had wanted to hold the woman, old beyond her years. In Mueller's mind she could feel the woman's bones against her body, the woman's body retching as she wept and begged. But Mary did not weep. And she had not begged.

"They are gonna kill him on Friday," Mary said.

"I know," Mueller said. "Does Billy know you're here?"

"He tries. But he can't keep track of me."

"I've been monitoring the case," Mueller said.

"What do you mean?" Mary asked.

"I've been watching the appeals and all the rest."

Over and over Mary had played through this moment in her mind. She knew she could not accuse Mueller of having convicted an innocent man. Instead Mary said, "You never were a mother, were you?"

"No," Mueller said. "I've always envied any mother."

"I was thinkin' how I could talk to you, you being the one that convicted my son and all. I figgered I wouldn't know what to say to you."

"I didn't know what I was going to be able to say to you, either, Mary," Mueller said. "I thought about it all night."

"I slept at the depot and I was talkin' to the man down there that's my friend, an' he said I should jus' talk to you woman to woman."

"I think he's right," Mueller said.

"It won't do any good to kill Charlie," she said. "You could pick up the phone there and save him."

"I have given it a lot of thought," Mueller said. "It has laid heavy on me, Mary." The governor was still holding her hands as they sat across from each other.

"A mother can't stand to have her son killed," Mary said. She was without tears.

"I know," Mueller said. "I've known Charlie since he was a boy."

"He never was a bad boy," Mary said. "He never hurt nothin' or nobody in his life."

"Mothers are mothers," Mueller said.

"He's a good boy still. He tol' me to give you his best wishes."

Mueller nodded without saying anything. Then she said again, "Mary, this has laid heavy on me. I will give your petition a lot of thought. I haven't made up my mind yet as to what I should do. I have a lot of things to consider. It is not easy being a governor."

"I wished I could help ya," Mary said. "It isn't easy bein' a mother either."

It was ten o'clock in the morning when Mary had walked into the cell and sat down across from her son. Then she got up and she did not say anything. She walked over to Charlie and curled up in his lap like a small animal and she held on to his arm, and in her mind she was holding the baby. They were in the old trailer that she and Joseph had lived in down by the river. She was alone. And she held the baby and rocked the baby in her arms.

He held his mother in his lap, this small child, and he knew that no one could comfort her. One cannot be nurtured unless one accepts the nurturing. She could not heal until he was dead. The old man said death brings on new life. He held her close to him and he rocked his mother.

When the guard came he let her go, but still she held on. At last the guard gently pulled her from her son and lifted her to her feet.

45

The brother is the brother.

It would be his turn to see Charlie when his mother got back from the small room at the end of the hall. What could he say to his brother?

He could never tell him of his involvement in Spirit Mountain nor that he had hired the witness, Jordan. How could he be a brother with all of the dark secrets? But he couldn't lay the ugly on Charlie, not in his last hours. The time had passed for confessions. Best that dark secrets never see the light.

He had wanted to go back to the time when they were boys together on the basketball court. They were one then. Now they were separated by the secrets. And by more. Often he had wondered: Would he have become as Charlie had he gone with his father? What if he had walked with his father to Spirit Mountain on that day and after that had watched in horror as his father was kicked to death? What if Miss Melbourne had gotten the Harvard scholarship for Charlie and he instead of Charlie had spent his life with the old man? Was he not the same as Charlie, the egg split in identical halves?

He had believed he had been in control of his life, but he was not in control. Never had been in control. Made the money, believed he was successful, that he had earned it. But he was like a log floating in the stream. He had not chosen the stream, nor set its course. And what forces had place him there he did not understand.

Sometimes he thought it was God. God had been good to him, he thought. But why him? And why not Charlie? Charlie had always been a better person, he thought. No greed in the man. No brazen acquisitive forces. No hatred. And the peace. He had peace.

Sometimes he thought they were fickle forces, not fair, not fair to him, not to Charlie. The forces had deprived him of peace. He had power. But no power. He had wealth. But no wealth. Charlie was rich, he thought. He had a woman. He was loved, at least by those who were hated, by the renegades. Hamilton was hated by all who were not fed by his dollars and loved for only his dollars. Charlie was attached to something. Billy had struck at it, like a jealous child strikes at his playmate. Still he thought the Indians were dumb, drunk, indecent. Their ignorant attachment to the valueless had disgusted, then wearied him. Their intransigent connection to Spirit Mountain was the passive-aggressive reaction of the weak who had no courage, the lazy who would rather slobber in the bars than work.

But black secrets between brothers were like a shroud over the dead—the shroud between them. That was the evil of dark secrets. Charlie had a right to go in peace.

And while Charlie was still alive he had wept more than once over the death of his brother. "I killed him," he heard his words, sometimes aloud in the night. Still he had faith. Mueller would commute. Everyone has a price and Mueller had hers. What was wrong with the bitch? Why hadn't she called? She could get a lot more mileage out of a camp for the Girl Scouts than by killing Charlie Redtail, for Christ's sake.

Then he looked up and saw his mother trudging down the long hall back from Charlie's cell. As she passed cell eight the prisoner there reached out to touch her and said, "God bless ya, ma'am." She wasn't crying when she walked past Billy. She walked, as if blind, stumbling every step or two until she came to the end of the hall where a guard was waiting.

"You're next," a guard said to Hamilton.

He had reached out for his mother, but she walked on as if she couldn't see him. He turned to go after her, but the guard stopped him. "You comin'? You're next."

Then Hamilton followed the guard down the hall to the room and when the door was opened, he saw Charlie standing at the window gazing out. Hamilton stood at the doorway, his brother in front of him, his brother alive. He wanted to remember him that way. He saw the man breathing, the brother in the sunlight without concern for the shadow.

"Isn't it magnificent?" Charlie asked without taking his eyes from the window, the great mountains gray in the distance, his face like a child seeing the first purple shooting star on the prairies in the spring.

"Right," Hamilton said. He struggled to find the words. He sat down across from Charlie, Charlie still staring at the sky.

The small room in the prison was like the small closet of a bedroom they shared in the shack of their childhood. The room in the shack, the spirits descending, the transmogrification like a screen on the stage descending. Billy looked out the dirty little window on the north, the curtain pulled aside, the gray, blistered walls of the shack, Charlie standing at the window. He could smell the oatmeal boiling on the stove, the sound of his mother in the kitchen hurrying with their breakfast.

"It is very beautiful," Charlie said.

"You seein' things again?" The boy's laugh. "I'm gonna tell Mom you're seeing things again."

"The sky sees," Charlie said. "The sky is the eye of the Great Spirit."

"That's dumb," Billy said. "You been talkin' to the old man. I'm gonna tell Mom you gone nuts again. Where'd ya get them orange coveralls?"

Charlie turned to see his brother, the small table between them. The man's eyes distant. "Do you know what the sky sees, Billy?"

"You goin' nuts again. That's what you're doin'," Billy said.

"Something you want to tell me, Billy?" Charlie took a hand of his brother lightly in his hands and sat down across from him.

Hamilton looked at this brother and then as if he had escaped from his delusion he said, "I killed the son of a bitch, Charlie."

Charlie said nothing, watching, his eyes kind.

"The Spirit Mountain Project—I owned it," Hamilton said.

"I know," Charlie said.

"How did you know?"

"It was of your spirit," he said.

Hamilton stared. Then Hamilton said, "If they kill you they kill me. We're one, Charlie. That's how we've always been."

"Are you ready to die, my brother?"

"They're not going to kill you, Charlie. I bought off the fucking the governor."

"Why would you do that to me?" Charlie asked.

Billy looked at his brother for a long time. Finally he said, "It was my fault. If I hadn't fucked with Spirit Mountain you wouldn't have had to kill Cotler."

Charlie said, "It is not so. I did not kill the man."

"Then who?" Hamilton asked.

"It does not matter. If we knew who killed the man it would change nothing."

"The spirits got back at me," Billy said. "I never believed in the spirits. But they got back at me."

The guard came. They heard the turning of the lock on the door.

"It's time," the guard said.

Hamilton got to his feet, reached in his pocket, and handed the guard a hundred-dollar bill. "Can't you see? My brother and I are talking."

"I see," the guard said. He stuck the bill in his pocket. "The hundred will buy you another minute." He laughed and closed the door behind him.

"This is not going to happen," Billy said. "Don't worry. I'll take care of it."

"I'll see you on the mountain," Charlie said and then, as the door closed behind his brother, Charlie Redtail escaped into the view from his small prison widow, into the distant mountains where the spirits of his ancestors were dancing.

46

At Rawlins, Wyoming, the same half-moon shown down on the twin towers of the state penitentiary, the pale light lingering on steel bars. But for the bars one might have thought it a replica of an old stone castle or a poorly conceived cathedral. The bars extended up from the front door through the second story of the structure. The front door itself was guarded with steel bars and the sparse windows on the front were all similarly protected. The light of the half-moon made waves on stone and steel as dark clouds moved across the moon in the wind and the old cottonwood trees that lined the driveway to the front door of the penitentiary were bent in the wind, the young leaves on the trees clinging to the branches like children to their mothers.

Outside a small crowd had gathered. Members of Amnesty International had come to protest the execution. One man had flown in from England, another from Germany. There were representatives from several other countries. The killing of men for punishment was barbaric, they argued. The United States was the only western nation still to embrace the death penalty, all of Western Europe having long ago abolished it. The people on that side, most dressed in black, stood quietly holding hands. They displayed signs, one reading: WHEN THE STATE KILLS IT MAKES KILLERS OF US ALL. Some of the people were singing hymns, their voices unblending.

Across from them was gathered a larger crowd of ordinary-looking people, some children, one man hollering back that killers ought to be killed. Another on a loudspeaker with the voice of a Baptist preacher was chanting, "There is mercy in this killing, friends. Be thankful unto God. God is mercy. God is love."

The smell of flesh burning, the pungent smell of hamburgers broiling on portable barbecues. Some played loud country music, their car doors open, the people laughing. They jeered at the protestors. The man on the loudspeaker was at it again: "Those who are against justice are the friends of the devil. The devil loves murderers. Praise God."

By 11:30 the wind was blowing even harder, nothing to stop it across the long prairies, the wind running like wild horses on the Red Desert. But the people stood in the wind, braced against it, and watched their watches. Some of the mothers were resting in their cars, the children asleep in the backseats. But some of the men were still standing, some drinking, laughing loudly.

The sheriff's deputies from Carbon County were in obvious attendance. They milled through the crowd with their hands on the butts of their nightsticks. They nodded in a friendly way to the people and some stopped to talk, but they made no attempt to put a stop to either the protestors or those who protested the protestors. This was America. They could say and do what they wanted so long as they didn't get out of hand.

Inside, the preparations for the execution having been completed weeks earlier, there had been no last-minute scrambling, the warden, J. D. Beechem, taking pride in the fact that his administration could be counted on to perform the tasks specified by the law in a timely fashion. At 11:45 P.M. the press was in force, occupying their assigned seats opposite the chamber, its members now talking in low voices among themselves.

"Ever been to one of these before?" Bill Morey from the *Cheyenne Tribune* asked Robert Stewart from the *Casper Star*.

"Never have."

"Wonder how long it takes 'im to die?"

"Not long, I suppose."

"I hear his family isn't coming."

"Yeah. I tried to interview his mother but she wouldn't talk to me. Then I tried the girlfriend. Had a kid by him, ya know. She wouldn't talk either."

"Oh, yeah? Where are they?"

"Saw 'em in town at the café. Lawyer with 'em, the one that lost the case. Little kid there, too. Cute little cus, braid and all."

It was 11:58 P.M. by the clock on the wall above the gas chamber, the clock correct by Greenwich time. The warden sat in the officials' booth, the red phone by his hand. The people were silent.

At 11:59 the doctor nodded that the long stethoscope affixed by a strap to the condemned's chest was operating so that the doctor, seated on a steel folding chair outside of the chamber, could monitor the heartbeat and pronounce death. The doctor was a youngish man, a general practitioner from the town who delivered babies and prescribed the latest antibiotic for colds. He wore a pale, gray face and a dark business suit.

At midnight, the clock in the church began its chiming followed by twelve slow strokes. The midnight *Zephyr* on the Union Pacific came roaring though on time, its bells dinging in between the long blasts of the whistle. Those protesting the protestors began a loud count that could be heard inside the prison: "Fifty-five, fifty-six, fifty-seven, fifty-eight, fifty-nine, now!"

Inside, those gathered could hear the cheering. The warden cleared his throat, but otherwise the people were silent, as if listening to hear death knock at the door, as if gathered to see death march in, to see death snatch up the soul of the condemned and to flee. The people gathered held their breaths, as if by breathing they would die with the condemned. The people counted the seconds to themselves. They watched the man in the chamber, saw that he was breathing, and when the clock read 12:01 the warden nodded.

In the morning the *Casper Star* carried an account of the execution under the byline of its staff reporter, Robert Stewart:

> There were some who believed that the governor might stay the execution since rumors persisted that new evidence had been discovered.
>
> "Such rumors always spoil an execution," Warden J. D. Beechem said. "People without respect for the massive effort the law expends to see that the accused has received due process, and more, nearly always spread such rumors to forward their own agendas. None of us take any joy in this. But we do our duty as it is outlined in the law. The people make the law. We merely carry it out."
>
> The convicted murderer, Charlie Redtail, was led to the gas chamber, his hands in cuffs, his legs in shackles. He walked in orange prison coveralls very slowly and very straight. He wore a long braid down his back and his face was without expression. He was barefooted, the warden reporting this was a harmless request on the part of the prisoner since after the execution any shoes and all clothing would have to be removed for the safety of the prison personnel.
>
> The prisoner did not resist the guards. Indeed, he assisted them as they strapped his arms, legs, and upper torso to the chair in the center of the chamber, a five-sided steel affair approximately eight feet in diame-

ter which the warden assured had been tested many times for any possible leaks.

Warden Beechem previously warned the press that no one representing the clergy was present to administer last rites, this was according to the wishes of the condemned, Charlie Redtail, who had requested that none appear. Redtail told the warden he was with the spirits and that the warden need not worry.

Then the warden, from the officials' booth, asked the condemned man by phone if he had any last words, the warden's voice being projected into the gas chamber by a loud speaker. The condemned man said that he did.

"What are they?" the warden asked.

"*Yon-ka-tore,*" the condemned man said.

Then the chamber door was closed and the locking wheel turned until the door was tightly sealed against the rubber gaskets. The condemned man looked straight ahead. The red telephone by the warden's hand did not ring.

When, at 12:01, the warden gave the sign, the condemned man saw the cyanide wrapped in cheesecloth drop into the acid pan, the executioner in a separate room at the warden's signal, having operated a lever that released the cyanide into the liquid. This, we were told, caused a chemical reaction that created hydrogen cyanide gas that immediately seeped up through the holes in the steel chair and soon filled the small room.

Beechem said he had advised Redtail to take deep breaths after the gas was released as that would considerably lessen his suffering, such advice much easier for the warden to say, one supposes, than for the prisoner to intentionally inhale the deadly fumes designed to kill him.

In medical terms, victims of cyanide gas die from hypoxia, the cutting-off of oxygen to the brain. The initial result of hypoxia is spasms, as in an epileptic seizure. Because of the straps, however, involuntary body movements are somewhat restrained. At our briefing we were told that seconds after the prisoner first inhales, he would feel himself unable to breathe, but would not lose consciousness.

We watched the fumes begin to rise from the sulfuric acid. The prisoner, of course, was expected to contribute to his own death by actively inhaling the lethal fumes. When the fumes enveloped Charlie Redtail's head he took a quick breath. His face became red and contorted as if he were attempting to fight through tremendous pain.

His mouth was pursed shut and his jaw was clenched tight. Redtail then took several more quick gulps of the fumes. At this point his body started convulsing violently. His face turned a deep red and the veins in his temple and neck began to bulge until this reporter thought they might explode.

After about a minute Redtail's head leaned partially forward, but he was still conscious. Every few seconds he continued to gulp in. He was shuddering uncontrollably and his body was racked with spasms. His head continued to snap back. His hands were clenched.

After several more minutes, the most violent of the convulsions subsided. At that time the muscles along Redtail's left arm and shoulder began twitching in a wavelike motion under his skin. He did not stop moving for approximately eight minutes and after that he continued to twitch and jerk for another minute. Approximately two minutes after that the doctor nodded, and we were told that the execution was complete. Charlie Redtail took ten minutes and thirty-one seconds to die.

An exhaust fan then sucked the poison air out of the chamber up through a thirty-foot exhaust stack. A half hour later orderlies entered the chamber wearing gas masks and rubber gloves. They unstrapped the corpse from the chair and before it was removed from the chamber sprayed it with ammonia, front and back, which is said to neutralize all traces of the cyanide that might remain, thus rendering the living safe from the dead. The training manual advised prison workers to ruffle the victim's hair to release all trapped cyanide gas before removing the body, but Redtail's hair was in the one long braid which made this operation impracticable.

Dr. Richard Traystman of John Hopkins University, commenting on the procedure, said, "The pain begins immediately and is felt in the arms, shoulders, back, and chest. The sensation is similar to the pain felt by a person during a severe heart attack, where essentially the heart is being deprived of oxygen."

Traystman added: "We would not use asphyxiation by cyanide gas or by any other substance in our laboratory to kill animals that have been used in experiments."

None of those in attendance were able to discover the meaning of Redtail's last word *Yon-ka-tore*. He will be buried in the Hiram Falls Arapahoe Cemetery next to his father, Joseph Redtail, who preceded him in death.

*   *   *

That night Abner Hill had finally found Mary. She was wandering the streets of Rawlins asking people to sign her new petition. From inside the café Abner Hill had seen her standing on the corner in the blue light of the café's flashing neon sign, the light flashing on and off her face, and in the night her face appeared strange and foreboding. Hill stepped out onto the sidewalk in front of her. She saw the man approaching.

"They are gonna kill my boy tonight. Could you sign my petition?" she asked, and Abner had taken her in his arms and had held her there. At first she tried to pull away. Perhaps it was the familiar smell of the man or the way he held her that told her who he was. At last she said, "They are going to kill him tonight, Abner. One minute after midnight. Can't you stop the clock?"

"No," he said.

"Can you get a court order or somethin'? You always could get a court order."

"No, Mary," he said. "I can't get a court order. How long has it been since you've eaten?"

She looked at him as if she didn't hear him.

"I've been looking for you everywhere," Hill said. Then he took her by the arm and led her into the café. "We have to eat something. Willow and the boy are inside."

They were sitting in the back booth and Hill had told the people from the press that none of them wished to make a statement.

"We need to be together," he had finally said to Mary. "We are the family." The child was silent, his head leaning against his mother's side, the boy's face gaunt and weary, Willow slowly patting him where she had her arm around him, the boy gazing off into space.

"Where's Billy?" Mary asked.

They shrugged their shoulders. Finally Willow said, "Maybe he's gone to talk to the governor."

"We should take Snickers home," Abner said.

"I have to be here," Willow said.

"Charlie said he didn't want us to be there," Hill said. "Asked me to tell you."

"How could he say that?" Mary said. "I'm the mother."

Willow said, "He can't go with no one but strangers watching."

"It was his last wish," Hill said.

They were silent, but the noise in the café filled in, the slamming of the plates, the laughter of the people, the waitress hollering in the orders.

The cigarette smoke and smoke from the grill fogged the room. Suddenly Mary attacked the bowl of chili in front of her. She ate like a hungry animal, like an animal that had not eaten in a month. She stopped only to break some soda crackers into the chili. She ate like someone freed of a demon, as if acceptance, the sudden gift, were at the bottom of the bowl. She did not look up at Abner as she ate. She ate furiously and by the time she was at the bottom of the bowl she was breathing hard. Then she looked up at Abner.

"Take me home, Abner," she said.

And he took her home that night, Willow and the child as well, all crowded into the pickup.

They drove into the empty night, the moon behind the heavy clouds, Mary next to Abner, her head on his shoulder, Willow by the door, the child at last sleeping in her arms, his feet on Mary's lap. The cottontails scurried out on the road in the headlights and from time to time one froze and stayed in the path of the pickup and Hill braked and swerved to miss it. The people in the pickup did not speak. Hill glanced at his watch.

No one asked him the time.

47

The old man was nearly a hundred, some thought a hundred at least, no one knowing for sure, the old man not speaking of it. He said, "The moons come and the moons go. The stars empty themselves and fill once more. The coyote has her pups in the spring and old men become children again and return as the child to the womb of the Mother. Time is for white men. Time is their devil. The Arapahoe knows no such devil."

On that June morning following the execution, the spring still on the earth and in the air, the buds still soft and the tiny, gray puffs the blooms of the willows, the old men on the Twin Buttes Reservation walked with their memories, the old men walking silently, alone with themselves in that place where the birds were at war and attacked with their songs.

The old men trudged slowly up Spirit Mountain as if following the spokes of a great wheel toward the hub where the spokes came together. They walked from different beginnings to the top where the spirits of their ancestors met, and in the early morning it was hard to tell the old men from one another, their faces afire from the spirits and in the sun. Among them for the last walk up was the old man, Henry Old Deer. His bones understood this, his heaving chest agreeing.

He had begun the long trek at one minute past midnight. He had walked alone, each step painful. He stopped often, often after each step, and was panting like a dog in the August heat when he took his last step at the top. By then the sun had already shown itself, the darkness having fallen away to the new bright day.

The Old Man of Much Medicine looked around him. The others were already there, the old men singing, but the old men as children to him, their voices not in unison. Some softly sang the coyote song to themselves, and some chanted the buffalo song. If one listened carefully the sounds were the sounds of the coyote and also the wailing of the loon and the cry of the wild goose. They were the sounds of old warriors and old shamans, of the spirits, and the high ecstatic cry of old men happy in the sun of spring. And they were the cries of the child freshly released from the womb who still spoke the language of the universe. And in the sounds the old man heard the voice of Charlie Redtail.

Some of the old men said nothing and stood alone, stood gazing out over the long prairies and at the distant Twin Buttes range, the tall, white peaks, the snow of winter still on them. In their old, hot lungs, the crisp air gave new life and their lungs drew in the spirits and they could feel the spirits enter their bodies.

All of the old men having arrived, Henry Old Deer sat down and from the pouch around his waist he withdrew the flint and steel and began to strike the steel against the flint for the sparks. When one caught on the charred cloth, he raised it gently in his shaking hands, like life in the nest, like the heat from the womb of the Great Mother. His hands raised to the clear spring sky were in worship of the Mother, and he blew on the spark and the tinder burst into flames. Then he made the fire of sagebrush, for bad spirits do not like the smell of fresh sagebrush burning.

Then the singers gathered around the fire, the singers who were also the drummers, the ones with the old, wild throats. They gathered around Henry Old Deer and they pulled out their drumming sticks from under their belts and seven drummers, some with their backs to the fire, some with their faces to the sun, all warmed, all with their old eyes squinted like cracks, began to sing. They sang to their ancestors who like the coyote and the wild goose could understand the sounds that were the sounds of the Mother.

The seven old men not always in unison joined in the beating of the drums and in the high cries the sounds of joy and pain were often the same, like the ripples in the high mountain streams are of both joy and of pain, the sound the same. Henry Old Deer hit the last note, and all of the drummers hit it with him, and on the last note they were in unison and in the silence.

"When I was a child I remember the men in their tepees and the women tended the children. Then some could still speak the language of their ancestors," Henry said.

"It was good then," an old man said.

"When I was a child I remember the old men who had fought the white man in many battles and they were proud men. I remember the old women who made the pemmican from buffalo and chokecherry."

"It was good then," an old man said.

"When I was a child the men hunted. And the people were a people."

"It was good then," an old man said.

"So shall it be again," Henry Old Deer said. "I have spoken."

Then Henry Old Deer looked across the long prairies, past the red-tail hawks, two soaring, soaring in slow joy. He looked past the dots below that the old men knew were their shacks, which were dark scabs on the Mother's hide. Some of the old men saw the hawks, some their eyes clouded.

"You see the red-tail hawks, Henry?" an old man said.

"Of course," Henry Old Deer said in disgust. But he was looking in the wrong direction, off to the Thunder Mountains to the north, which he could not see.

Then the men sang the songs that called in the summer. May there be much rain on the dry prairies. May the small animals be happy once more. May Coyote escape the traps. May Antelope have twins. May our ancestors bless us on this mountain, this holy mountain where the Mother sees all and from this mountain where one can see the Mother.

Then Herman Little Shield said, "May the Great Spirit bless Billy Redtail for giving back to us what belonged to us from the beginning."

The old men began to call out the names of their ancestors: "Little Owl. He is with us. And the great warrior named Friday who was taken as a boy and schooled by the whites but who came back to his people, he is with us. And also Sharp Nose and Black Coal. And Joseph Redtail is with us."

"You shall be the first to speak his name," Herman Goes in Lodge said to Henry Old Deer.

"Charlie Redtail is with us," the old man said. They were silent for a long time and when they heard the trill of the meadowlark, Henry Old Deer spoke again. "Charlie Redtail was my son. He lived a long time and was very wise."

After that the old men sang many songs to the spirits, and there was a joining of man with the mountains, man with man, man with the spirits of men, man with the bursting springtime that could not be held back and man with the song of the meadowlarks that could not be held back. Then the old men walked down the mountain.

It was then as Henry Old Deer was slowly descending that the boy saw the old man and it was then that the boy began to run to him. The old man saw the boy was running and that sometimes he stumbled as if he were injured, like a fawn struck in the belly by the hunter's bullet. The old man stopped and squinted his eyes. The old man knew the boy. And the old man had known that in the spring when the meadowlark was mad in song that the child would come.

"That there is that Redtail kid," Arthur Antelope said. He was an old man with better eyes.

"I know who he is," Henry Old Deer said.

"That there is Charlie's boy, that kid named after you, Henry."

"I know who he is," Henry Old Deer had said, and the Old Man of Much Medicine had gone down, in the hard way of old men going down, to meet the child running up. And when they reached each other the boy grabbed hold of the old man and held on to him and would not let him go.

Acknowledgments

I am often dismayed at the astounding transformation a single turn in the road, a passing remark, a serendipitous encounter may have upon our lives. I met Lisa Drew one morning in 1981 in her small office in New York. She was then at Doubleday and later became the editor of my first book, *Gunning for Justice,* and two other books that followed.

I remember how anxious I was about letting the manuscript go and how, like a jittery, expectant father, I waited for Lisa's response. One day I couldn't stand it any longer. I called her. All I could think to say was, "How's my baby, the one I sent you in the mail?" I shall never forget her euphoric reply. "Your baby is pretty damn good," she said. Those and her subsequent words of approval hurled me into this wondrous pilgrimage as a writer. Others might not have uttered such encourangement to one as diffident as I in my work, to what less fortunate end I can only wonder.

Time, other houses, and other books and circumstances separated us for many years. Lisa moved to Scribner with her own imprint. When *Half-Moon and Empty Stars* was at last completed I again sought out Lisa Drew. The reason was simple. This was my first tentative, fearful foray into this novel-writing business. I needed Lisa Drew.

The book was large, perhaps bloated and begged for editing. I doubt there are many busy, sane editors who could or would have taken the trouble. She did. And she did it out of friendship first, the business of it be damned, a vestige of better times in publishing. She did it out of caring for what she saw in the book, for her belief that, yes, this baby was born and that it would be allright. If I should ever become a novelist, if, indeed, I have ever become a writer, I owe it, in large part, to Lisa Drew.

I thank my great agent and friend, Peter Lampack, whose contributions to a first novelist went miles beyond the duties of an agent. I don't know how many times he read parts or all of the book and many of his suggestions are reflected in how this book was crafted. He did so, again, out of a benevolent heart and a belief that something worthwhile might eventually come of his effort.

I remember how this novel was begun. Spencer Aronfeld, a young lawyer, a student of mine and friend, was assiting me on a book tour for a previous publication. I shared with him my long, enduring ambition to write a novel. Between those frantic stops and while in the air, I wrote passages, sketches, scenes, and shared them with him. We talked of the storytelling skills that mark both the successful trial lawyer and novelist and from this early pollination the first version of this novel began to take its primitive form. Thanks also to Sarah Argyropoulos and Carolee Krieger for their thoughtful perusal of the manuscript and their useful comments.

I am grateful always to my darling Imaging, who read these words many times and offered her sound, loving advice, her comfort, and her eternally available ear. Without this woman this man could never create.

GERRY SPENCE
Jackson, Wyoming
www.gerryspence.com